My Father's Lands

Ger Burke

WORDSONTHESTREET

First published in hardback 2009 by
Wordsonthestreet
Six San Antonio Park,
Salthill,
Galway, Ireland.
web: www.wordsonthestreet.com
email: publisher@wordsonthestreet.com

This paperback edition published 2010 by
Wordsonthestreet

ISBN   978-1-907017-01-8

Cover design, layout and typesetting: Wordsonthestreet
Printed and bound in the UK

My Father's Lands

ABOUT THE AUTHOR

Ger Burke spent the years of early childhood on a farm in Co Galway. Having lived in London and later Boston Ger returned to live in Co. Mayo.

My Father's Lands was started in Holyoke College, Massachusetts and finished on the shores of Galway Bay.

A former teacher of English and History, Burke has had many literary successes both in print and radio since becoming a full-time writer.

My Father's Lands is a first novel.

See also www.myfatherslands.net

To

Mel, Judith and Ailbhe

who are always there

Acknowledgements

In researching the period in which *My Father's Lands* is set, I consulted many books and articles. I drew particular inspiration from the insights in *The Great O'Neill* by Sean O'Faoláin. I must also acknowledge my debt to the following:

Brady, Ciaran, O'Dowd, Mary and Walker, Brian, Foreword Beckett, J C *Ulster An Illustrated History*. Chambers, Anne *Granuaile*. Collins, M E *Ireland 1478 – 1610*. Evans, E Estyn *Irish Folk Ways*. Falkiner, C Litton *Illustrations of Irish History and Topography*. Foster, R F *Modern Ireland 1600-1972*. Green, Alice Stopford *The Making Of Ireland and Its Undoing 1200 – 1600*. Howarth, David *The Voyage of the Armada*. Hughes, Kathleen *Early Christian Ireland: Introduction to the Sources*. Kavanagh, Peter *Irish Mythology: A Dictionary*. Nicholls, K W *Land Law and Society in 16th century Ireland*. Green, V H H *Renaissance and Reformation*. Hayes-McCoy, Gerard Anthony, *Irish battles*.

My gratitude and affection to my editor, Tony O'Dwyer, who made my novel shorter and better! His encouragement and constancy are cherished.

For their valuable input and support my thanks to: Patricia Burke Brogan, Sandra Bunting, Ronan Bennett, Michael Collins, Sean Donegan, Kevin Donnelly, Gerry Dukes, Margaret Faherty, Jarlath Fahy, Maureen Gallagher, Judith Gannon, Catherine Heaney, Mary O'Rourke, John Sherlock, Breid Sibley, Ingrid Wall.

Thanks to my sisters Alice and Patricia, my brothers Dermot, Gerald and Noel and their spouses for their constant love and encouragement.

Finally thanks to the close friends who helped along the way. They know who they are.

HISTORICAL NOTE

By 1540 King Henry VIII was finding it expensive to maintain an army in Ireland. Also he wanted to reduce religious opposition to his split with Rome. Therefore he needed to seek a peaceful solution to his Irish problems. To this end a conciliatory treaty was drawn up with the Irish lords called *Surrender and re-grant*.

The core of this treaty was that, instead of being treated as enemies, the Irish were now to be accepted as royal subjects under English law. However, to qualify for this new status the chieftains had to surrender their lands to England and be re-granted them under English law, together with an English title, such as Baron or Earl.

Under the old Irish system the lands of a ruled territory belonged to the entire clan. Succession was governed by the law of *Deirbhfhine* and was elective, with the rights of election confined to male members of the sept whose great-grandfathers, grand-fathers or fathers, had previously been chieftains.

Under *Surrender and re-grant*, however, the chief was made sole owner of the lands with power to bequeath them to his heirs.

Surrender and re-grant made *Primogeniture* a legal substitute for *Deirbhfhine* so that now the eldest surviving son was entitled to succeed a dead or deposed father.

The clash between the Irish law of *Deirbhfhine* and the English law of *Primogeniture* led to bitter disputes among the Gaelic clans, resulting in civil wars within many surrendered and re-granted territories.

Surrender and re-grant also left the Irish exposed to the horrors of plantations which the treaty brought in its wake.

CONTENTS

PART I

1582-1584

I perceive them to be men of such nature that they will sooner be brought to honest conformity by small gifts, honest persuasions and nothing taken of them than by great rigour.

- St. Leger, King's Lieutenant 1540-1547
(advice to Henry VIII on the Irish chieftains.)

Chapter One

"Glenone belongs to my father, not to him," Rory Maguire shouted. In the murky light, he eyed his brother Matthew and the assembled clansmen for a reaction. Their attention was fixed on his twenty-two year old uncle Eoin marching, flanked by his troop of *Gallóglaigh,* towards the square-hewn coronation stone to be proclaimed The Maguire. "That's why he waged the war, to steal my father's land," he shouted louder this time.

"Hush Rory," Matthew pleaded, "or he might kill us too. Under Gaelic law Eoin *has* the right to succeed."

Rory's stomach churned as he watched his uncle sit on his 'throne', pull his mantle around him as if it were a purple robe, and examine the crowd. Rory felt his uncle's sharp eyes rest on him and though his heart hammered against his ribs, he did not lower his gaze.

The air of expectancy in the valley heightened. Under the misty clouds the crowd huddled, waiting. Rory picked up a stone and threw it aimlessly. It was hard to believe that the clan war was over.

He had come to dread the unexpected sound of horsemen galloping in the direction of his home, the times they had fled to the woods fearful that uncle Eoin had come for them, and freezing nights spent shivering on frosty grounds. But the aftermath, he knew, could be even worse. His father was dead, killed by his own brother. There was nobody to challenge his uncle's claim to Glenone except Matthew, and he was only a year older than Rory himself.

At last the ceremony began and the most elderly man in the clan struggled forward. Holding, as was custom, a white staff in his left hand and a golden slipper in his right, he stopped three feet from Eoin and blinked. "Bad for the bones this mist is".

His uncle eyed the crowd warily as he accepted the symbol of sovereignty.

Rory was surprised by the steadiness of the old man's hand as he held the ancient slipper aloft and with a flourish threw it over Eoin's head. When the bishop shook holy water, he instinctively made the sign of the cross with the others. He was glad that when *uirrithe* of Eoin shouted a war cry, the response was only half-hearted; many had died in the war between his father and uncle. But his smile faded when Eoin rose from his seat, stood to his full height and, brandishing the staff above his head, generated the best cheer yet, "Maguire *abú.*"

As Eoin wove his way through the multitude, noblemen dressed in coloured cloaks in the English style inclined their heads towards him while the mantle clad natives bowed. It was only when the crowd around him scattered that Rory realised he was swaggering in his direction.

He felt like running away, it was easy to be brave when his uncle was at a distance, but before he could act, Eoin whispered to a *Gallóglach,* nodded in Rory's direction, and then changed course.

The young fighting man approached and addressed him and Matthew. "You wains are ta be a' the feast this evening. The chief expects you ta celebrate his victory."

Now that the ordeal was over for him, Rory made his way from the investiture field back to the encampment.

Matthew blew the chill from his hands. "We didn't get a chance to show off our new apparel."

Rory felt appalled at his lack of understanding of the danger they faced. "You'll get another chance at the feast this evening". He kept his tone neutral. There was nothing to be gained from frightening his brother.

As they made their way through the undulating drumlin countryside, a fluid sun saturated the ground with light. "It's good the mist is clearing," Matthew said. "I can see in the distance that there's a shelter built. See there!"

Following the direction of Matthew's finger, Rory spotted a clearing at the entrance to the forest. He had forgotten they were so near the camp until he saw his fosterers Cormac and Maeve running forward to meet them.

"Thank God you're back safely." Cormac gestured towards a lively fire. "It's time you got out of those damp clothes and got heated up. You look frozen." Rory doffed his mantle and threw it on the ground. Maeve handed him his dun trews and he pulled them up under the blue tunic she had left to warm on a makeshift bench beside the fire. He flexed his arms as he revelled in the comfort of his everyday garments.

"Remember to fold your new apparel Rory." Matthew, still in his 'inauguration' clothes, stood warming his hands by the blaze.

"You'll need them for the feast this evening".

"I will. Don't fret." The churning in his stomach he'd had since uncle Eoin was installed as chief of Glenone, worsened.

Cormac looked at him fondly and then pointed towards the path to the river. "That daughter of mine is at the stream. They're hauling water."

He ran down the track. Soon he could hear Finola's voice. "Here, this one is ready to go," she was saying to a servant. Her sleeves were rolled up as she filled her pail and emptied it into a larger vessel. When she saw him, she waved and stopped working. "You look glum Rors. Want to tell me?"

"We have to go to uncle Eoin's feast this evening."

"Oh!" Finola ordered a servant to take over and they both ambled towards the river and walked along the bank. "There will be a lot of sweet meats," she said sounding uncertain. "There's nothing nice to eat at the camp." She tugged at her hair.

"I wish I could find a way out of going," was all he could say.

When they got back, Rory took an oatmeal biscuit from the top of a flat stone, left on the ferns, but, after the first bite, lost his appetite. Matthew was sprawled on the grass nibbling at one too. When he saw his brother's morose expression, Rory suggested they play a game.

When he grew tired of fooling with Matthew and Finola, he slumped against a tree.

"They should stay away," he overheard Maeve insist from somewhere nearby.

He assumed they were referring to the feast when Cormac replied, "We've little choice but to let them off."

Though Maeve had always warned him against eavesdropping, he continued to listen.

"You had good relations with Eoin before the war. You could go with them."

"It would only arouse his ire Maeve. If anything went wrong, I'm in no position to fight Eoin Maguire. My first loyalty must be to them."

"Will they be safe?"

"Remember Eoin's servant Padraic? I've engaged him to see that ... I'll tell you about it later. Rory could be anywhere. That lad has the ears of a bat."

Rory roused himself from his brooding when Ultan MacGrath, the family *file*, came out of his bothy and called to him to sit on the bench beside him. Usually he was frightened by this poet who could *rhyme a man to death*, but today he radiated kindness. He beckoned to Finola and Matthew to join them. Then he taught them how to compose a poem. It ended with:

"Matthew and Rory like a fairy host,
invisible on the whirlwind
set off for the feast,
and supped the most."

Maeve came to stand at his shoulder. Turning to her, he said, "The muse will think I'm crazed."

"I know. Strange to see you writing about two *garsúns* going to a banquet. A change from cattle raids or, *invaders who subdue Ulster while Gaelic chieftains kill each other,* she said quoting his latest poem.

Cormac came towards them. "Speaking of Gaelic chieftains, it's time to get ready for Eoin's festivities."

Matthew's bottom lip protruded. "I don't want to go."

"You have no choice." Cormac was adamant.

While they were changing back into this morning's clothes, Matthew continued to insist that he was staying at the encampment.

Rory said nothing. He knew his brother. In the end, he would go.

Chapter Two

As uncle Eoin's stronghold came into view, Rory tugged at Matthew's sleeve and pointed to a pall of smoke. "That's a good sign. It means the food will be hot." He tried to make his tone light-hearted. "I wager it'll be pork. I think I heard the pig squealing!" This talk of food had brightened the dark mood that had hung heavily since they parted from Cormac.

"The smell is making me hungry." Matthew bolted down the slope. "Last one there is a snake," he called.

Rory started after him. Better *wriggle* along then, he thought to himself. Though he was younger, his legs were longer than Matthew's so he would be able to pass him easily. But when he was close on his heels he decided to slow down and let him win.

A satisfied look appeared on Matthew's face when he arrived first at the castle. "You'll have to shake yourself a bit more if you want to outstrip me," he boasted.

Rory smiled to himself.

Uncle Eoin's castle stood five storeys high and sulked like an inhospitable giant in the midst of Glenone. Its narrow windows failed to relieve the forbidding appearance of its dark stone. On the ferns, in its grim shadow, the guests sat on cushions and balanced platters, heaped with food, on their knees.

As Rory and Matthew arrived, minions dragged out more trestle tables and the guests, abandoning the cushions, surged towards the tables. Next servants came out from the kitchen with wooden platters, piled with slices of pork and beef. A comely maidservant moved between the tables replenishing tankards of ale.

Rory spotted two empty spaces on a bench and he and Matthew grabbed them. Their table was already smeared with butter and honey and *uisce beatha* splashed from overfilled goblets. His uncle's *uirrithe* would have been drinking whisky since the investiture so there was bound to be a fight, Rory realised with a certain glee. As if he'd read his thoughts, a man near him whacked his neighbour across the head with a platter. Soon others joined in.

"My biggest chestnut on the fat one with the red face being next," he said to Matthew laughing. "Oh! Wait. I'm wrong. The harpist is getting ready. The fighting will have to stop. The *uirrithe* will calm and listen to the *reacaire* list uncle Eoin's praises."

"Pity." Matthew's face fell.

"Before he starts, I'll get the food." Rory sprang to his feet.

An abundance of victuals adorned the trenchers on the side tables. He cut enough meat for both of them and heaped it on a platter. As he crossed the field to rejoin his brother, a wolfhound, belonging to his uncle Eoin, loped across his path and upset his balance. Wild garlic and sweetmeats slipped to the ground. Conscious of his uncle's scrutiny, from the victor's table, he felt infantile and clumsy.

By the time he sat down, laughter and slurred voices were drowning out the music of the harp. Uncle Eoin glared at the crowd, quietening them and the narration began. Rory concentrated on his beef, tearing the meat apart. There was no Maeve to correct his table manners, so he stuffed his mouth to bursting.

A hireling approached them, his lips shaded by a *crommeal* and his eyes by a *glib*. Rory couldn't see his face at all. He knew that the English hated the *glib*, blaming the fringe of hair for disguising outlaws. The hireling leaned, first over Matthew's shoulder and then over his and poured mead into their goblets.

The light was beginning to go from the sky and dark clouds gathered.

"It's going to rain," Rory said.

"It'll only be a shower. Nobody is moving." Matthew took three fast gulps of his mead.

"Drink more slowly," Rory cautioned. "Your face is glowing like a Dundalk beacon."

The *reacaire* continued to extol Eoin's virtues. The first heavy drops began to fall.

"Let's get out of here Matt," Rory said.

Matthew plucked at the neck of his tunic. His normally freckled face was now a rosy pallor. "Rory," he said. "The mead tastes odd. I feel ..."

"For God's sake, leave the rest," Rory said taking the goblet from him.

Suddenly Matthew keeled over, burying his face in his trencher of food.

The maidservant approached and lifted Matthew's head now

18

plastered with grease and bits of gristle. She put a chapped hand on his forehead and said, with a puzzled expression, "'Tis roastin' he is. Sure, 'tis only a dropeen he had. Still, this should do the trick. From a holy well 'tis." She threw the contents of her pitcher of water over Matthew's head.

Rory leapt sideways to avoid the splash, accidentally knocking his own goblet of untouched mead sideways. It flowed along the table onto the ground.

"'Tis inside we should take him." The maidservant clicked her tongue against her teeth. "'Tis from a boghole that blessed water came, I'm thinkin'."

Uncle Eoin continued to listen to the harpist and the *reacaire.* Some guests rose from their tables to help Matthew but, seeing The Maguire acting as if nothing had happened, they sat down again. Two male servants carried him into the castle.

Rory clutched Matthew's mantle to his chest and hurried after them.

He failed to see the wolfhound, who had tripped him earlier, lick the grass clean of the mead he had spilled, and convulse in a corner.

The early autumn rain bucketed down and beat on the roof. The deluge lashing against the straw was a contrast to quiet breathing. Matthew had been too poorly to lug himself up the winding stairs to the sleeping chambers so uncle Eoin had ordered the servants to leave him on a pallet on the dining hall's earthen floor.

The trestle tables and forms had been hauled out to the field for the banquet and now the chamber had an empty look. The lack of furnishings made Matthew look smaller.

A servant, his wet hair plastered into his scalp, opened the door and two others, equally wet, painstakingly manoeuvred a trestle table into the hall, pushed it against the far wall and left without a word.

Rory paced about in the faltering light given off by the tallow candle. He was in the fortress of an uncle he was unable to trust, surrounded by enemies and felt like a chicken in a fox's den. Picking up a besom, he swept the rushes. Dust rose making him sneeze. The smell of soiled bedclothes, mixed with sweat and garlic, nauseated him. A servant entered. "Did you tell Cormac what happened to Matthew?"

"I did to be sure Master Rory. He went back to tell the family. In the wink of an eye "'tis here he'll be." He looked at him from under grey eyebrows. "'Tis not you should be sweeping the rushes."

"I'd be gone with the fairies if I just sat and looked at him."

"Stop distressing yourself," the servant said. "With the blessings of God, 'tis better he'll be in no time."

The door opened again and a blast of cold air passed through the chamber. Seeing Cormac enter, he flung the besom into a corner and rushed to embrace him.

"Rory," Cormac said, "Where is Matthew?"

In the dim light Rory pointed towards the pallet where his brother lay.

Cormac walked over to him. "He's chilled. You can doff his garments if he gets too warm but now he needs heat," he said to the servant.

"To be sure sire, we didn't know what to do. There was only himself interested." The servant gestured towards Rory. "He's too young to be knowing anything."

"He must have warmth," Cormac repeated.

"Maybe 'tis right you are sire. 'Tis not for me to be sayin'."

Rory and Cormac sat with Matthew in front of the fire the servant had prepared before going to his pallet.

Matthew rolled his eyes and muttered incoherently.

"He's sweating like a hog," Cormac said. "We'll let the fire die."

Hours later Rory was still sitting on the ground, his legs stretched in front of him. Cormac sometimes strode up and down or sat on a stool beside Matthew's pallet.

The rain stopped. In the awful silence Cormac lit a fresh candle from the stump of a dying one.

When Matthew shivered, Cormac wrapped his mantle around him. "We should get this fire rekindled," he said. Kneeling in front of the embers, he rearranged the peat with an iron tongs. His movements were slow. The splits of wood refused to catch hold so he worked the bellows. Under the gusts of air, they caught fire and sputtered to a healthy blaze.

Stretching his toes, Rory began to doze to the sound of the crackling wood. In a half sleep he felt Cormac put his mantle over him and tuck it beneath his chin. Before he slept he pictured the face of a lady, caring and luminous, looking down on Matthew.

Dawn light was spilling into the room when the servant came back. "He's like a bilin' pot," he said as he replenished the wood. "'Tisn't needing this he'll be."

At first Rory thought he was at home in Mulahinsa and that all was well, but then he remembered his plight. He stifled a sob. It was difficult to believe that only yesterday morning Matthew and himself had watched uncle Eoin being crowned Chief of Glenone.

He spent all that day by Matthew's pallet too worried to eat and only realised that many hours had passed when darkness fell and servants appeared to light the candles.

A physician arrived, sent by uncle Eoin, to examine Matthew. He wrinkled his nose at the foul smell in the room. "A severe dose of ague," he said as he took a container with a greeny blue concoction from his bag.

"I want him to sit up and take this." He turned to Rory. "You're his brother. You'll be able to administer to him better than me."

Rory slid his arms around Matthew and lifted him.

"If you could get him to partake, it would cure him," said the physician protecting the compound from Matthew's lolling head, cursing when a drop spilled on his frieze.

"Taste it Matthew. You need to get better." Rory tried to sound reassuring. He knew from Cormac that this man was a barber, a mountebank who didn't belong to a medical family and unlike uncle Eoin's personal physician, had never attended medical school.

Matthew was too weak to sip from the vessel.

"He's too frail to bleed," the physician said finally and slunk from the chamber.

"Upstart," Cormac mumbled at his retreating figure. "All he can do is put together a cordial to cure Eoin Maguire's belly after a feed of *uisce beatha.*"

"But he said it was the ague, Cormac. You heard him. Matthew will get better. He had a fever before and he got better ..."

When Cormac remained silent, Rory's lips quivered. "Will he d ...?" He failed to articulate the dreaded question.

Cormac folded his arms. "We have to wait and hope."

21

By noon Matthew was sleeping peacefully.

Rory drank a goblet of whey and chewed two oatmeal biscuits, his first nourishment since the feast.

Later the food rumbled in his stomach as he lay on his back and stared at the domed roof.

About an hour later he heard Matthew mumble to Cormac, "Please take me home. Not to the camp but home, home to Mulahinsa."

"I'll take you out of here soon, I promise," Cormac answered.

In the days that followed Rory left Matthew's side, only occasionally, to visit uncle Eoin's private chapel. In the quietness of the half-darkness, in what was less a church and more a shrine to Our Lady, he felt less anxious. His mother had died of dysentery when he was four. His memory of her was vague, but the statue of the Madonna comforted him, made him feel he had another mother who looked out for him. She would keep Matthew alive.

"Will you be here when I'm gone?" Rory asked, before he set out for the camp.

"I will," Cormac said. "I'll take care of Matthew. Finola is expecting you to join her. She'll be coming back if you delay any longer." Cormac shooed him out.

He felt the wind at his back as he ran across the fields and over streams and finally laboured up the hill to the wood's edge.

When he arrived, Brigid was outside a bothy squeezing trews from a tub. After enquiring about Matthew, she said, "Finola is gone this two hours looking for *dearógs*. She expects you to folle her. 'Tis stepping it out you should be."

As he picked his way through the fern, he stopped when he came to a tree with his and Finola's initials. He imagined he heard her voice as it had sounded then. "Rors put my name with yours."

"It would take too long," he had said.

"Just carve *F* and *R*."

Looking at the bark now, he was glad their names were linked. When he was older, he intended to marry her.

He spied a lone figure in the distance and knew it was Finola. She looked a lot younger than eleven as she sauntered among the oaks and elms. Running to take a vessel of d*earógs* from her he said, "Ill carry that."

"I told you before. My backbone is short not weak."

"Why are you leaving so early?" he asked, tweaking her plait.

"I'm here since morning." She raised the vessel of fish for his inspection. "I want to keep them for Matthew."

"He's getting better. He waved at me before I left this morning," Rory reassured her.

Finola's smile disappeared when she spotted Brigid coming towards them and she said with a sigh, "She'll have food ready for me. She thinks I need feeding."

Rory agreed that Finola was too thin, but he had more sense than to tell her. "Won't it be grand when we're all back in Mulahisna?"

When Brigid reached them, she looked first at Finola then at him. "'Tis a message Cormac sent, Rory. You must go back to your uncle Eoin's."

"Why?"

"Surely be to God 'tisn't foolish questions you're asking. Wastin' time." Her tone softened. "The sooner you get there, the sooner you'll know what's happening. 'Tis naught serious I'm hoping.' Little Matthew pining for ye that'll be all."

"I'll tell Maeve," Finola called after him as he ran back again towards Eoin's stronghold.

Matthew was dying; Matthew was dead; he was alone. His thoughts tormented him as he plunged down the incline to Glenone. When he reached the castle, he fell against the chamber door, using his weight to push it open.

The hall was bright, lit by many candles, a sign of impending death. Cold ashes were heaped in the middle of the room. A garlic smell lingered in the air.

"Is he dead?" he shouted at Cormac.

"He became feverish a while back. He's been calling for you."

Matthew was turning his head from side to side digging his nails into the mantle covering him. He mumbled towards the ceiling, "Help me. Where is Rory? I'm frightened. Help me."

Rory tiptoed over to him, "Matthew, I'm back." He wiped Matthew's face. "Talk to me. It's Rory."

Cormac said, "Easy lad. Let him go in peace. He knows you're here."

At that moment Matthew's damp hand moved in his and he felt what Cormac said was true.

Soon the hall began to fill with women and men swaying at the bottom of the pallet, their hands joined, their eyes shut, their voices rising and falling in rhythm. "Stay with us. Don't leave your brother alone with a broken heart," they chanted. Rory swung from side to side, too, soothed by the cadence.

Matthew's rambling stopped. The blessed candle fell out of his hand and the crowd fell silent. A servant opened the door to let his spirit leave.

Rory kissed his cold lips and gripped his hand.

Cormac came towards him and gently separated him from Matthew. They walked towards the door together, staying close to each other.

He turned to look one last time at his brother on the pallet, his fair hair framing his face.

Chapter Three

It was early evening when Cormac walked away from the woodland camp where he had left Rory with Finola and Maeve. He had told them that he was going to Glenone, which was partially true; he intended to go there later.

When he reached the small lake where he had arranged to meet Padraic, he was already waiting. Cormac looked around to confirm that he had come alone. Then he made a noise to signal his arrival and to reassure him that he had no intention of attacking him from behind. His purpose was to talk. "Padraic." His tone was neutral. "Good you could meet me."

Padraic tugged at his glib. "'Twas at twilight we arranged to meet. I keep my word."

"I thought," Cormac said, "that because of Matthew's death it would be difficult to get away."

"'Twasn't."

"That maybe with all the commotion at Eoin's preparing for the wake ... you're a great man to have come."

"'Twas to promise to meet you I did. I never break a promise."

"That's a favourite boast of yours." Cormac's tone chilled.

"'Tis to be sure."

"You were here on time. You kept that pledge."

Padraic looked less certain as he noted the emphasis on Cormac's last words.

"I must admit I sometimes fail to do what I promise. Events or people stop me ..." Cormac's expression mirrored the gathering dusk.

"Sure the same thing happens to me. Sometimes ..."

"I wanted to make sure nothing happened to Matthew or Rory by hiring you." Cormac paused. "You promised to protect them." A nerve twitched on the side of his jaw. "And of course you never break a promise."

"'Twas to watch every morsel that passed Rory's lips I did your honour." Padraic pushed the glib back from his eyes. "Not a bite did Matthew touch. Sure 'twas to him you told me to pay special heed."

"He drank," Cormac said. "You gave the drink to him."

"Padraic smirked. "'Twas the food you said to watch, Sire."

"You're correct."

"So I thought it safe to give him mead."

"You would." Cormac's tone was icy now.

"Surely be to God drink and food are different. Eoin Maguire said that 'twas sickly Matthew was when he came to the feast. That he was a delicate wee lad."

At the mention of Eoin Maguire, Cormac's colour rose. He drew a dagger from the belt of his tunic.

Padraic's back was to the lake, his escape hampered on all sides by brambles and scrub. "'Twasn't anything I did. Sure as God is my judge."

With one swift movement, Cormac embedded the blade in the flesh of Padraic's neck. He fell backwards into the watery slime and lay there, clearly visible. Cormac crossed Padraic's hands on his chest and dragged the corpse into deeper water where it sank slowly. A spurt of blood spilled onto his shoulder.

He cleaned his hands on the grass before going on to Eoin Maguire's domain to check that they were showing proper respect to Matthew's dead body.

Back in the camp Rory was sitting beside Finola on a tree trunk. He kept up a flow of talk in an attempt to banish the images of Matthew squirming on his pallet, dripping sweat, shouting at the ceiling, unable to recognise him. Earlier Maeve, fatigued, had gone to lie down. When Cormac returned, he stayed up with them for a while and told them stories. Then, grey with exhaustion, he had gone to join Maeve.

When Finola's eyes began to close, Rory suggested that they too go to their pallets.

Trying to sleep, he remembered praying in uncle Eoin's oratory for Matthew to get better. How foolish he had been to trust The Madonna. He had no mother in heaven; a shiny statue had fooled him into imagining her. The Madonna never appeared in his dreams again.

It was barely light when he heard Finola's voice from outside the shelter and dragged himself to a standing position.

"They're ready to leave. We decided to let you sleep." She looked away from him towards the distance. "The funeral will soon be over. I'll be waiting when you come back to Mulahinsa."

Rory was sorry Maeve had insisted that Finola and the retainers break camp that morning, that they would be absent from Matthew's funeral. Though Brigid and Dara had been permitted to come, they were servants not family.

Because it was tradition it was thought necessary to bring Matthew by the longest route to the burial ground. When the *cortège* made a sunrise circle beside a lone thorn bush to confuse Matthew's spirit, lest it wanted to return from the spirit world, Rory said to Dara, "I'm the only one of his blood family alive. He will stay where he is."

Dara said quietly to Brigid, "'Tis true what the poor lad is sayin'. Matthew is better to be 'mid bones and skulls than living in fear of Eoin Maguire."

Standing at the hole dug for Matthew's body, Rory pressed his hand against his cheek, willing himself not to cry. Lords and ladies stood around talking indifferently. Wind blew the wisps of hair that covered Bishop MacCavell's skull.

Cormac instructed hirelings to take the coffin from the slide car and manoeuvre it gently onto the grass. He then signalled to Rory and nodded towards the grave. Rory picked up a fistful of earth and scattered it on the coffin; he flinched at the deep, hollow sound it made on the wood.

Dara and Cormac lowered the coffin into the maw. The bishop sprinkled holy water on it and the *mná caointe* began the mourning prayers.

When it was all over, Fineen Quin stepped over to Rory and said, "Do you think I'll ever give the staff to you m'lad or will you go with the English ways like your father?" He felt a fat spit from Fineen Quin's mouth near his sandal. "Sure I suppose 'twill be what suits, like the rest of them."

The old man's outburst had reminded him of his precarious position, as the only remaining threat to his uncle's power, and triggered his hidden fears. Now that his father and brother were dead, *he* was entitled, under English law, to inherit the domains over which uncle Eoin was chief.

Whispers of treachery about Matthew's death came back to him, rumours about a poisoned wolfhound. His head ached. All he wanted was to go home to Cormac's castle, drink ballyclabber and sleep. While Brigid was talking to a servant of uncle Eoin's, he saw his chance. He sneaked behind her back and ran towards Mulahinsa ...

A brave autumn sun pierced though rain clouds casting weak shadows on the ground. Rory pretended to himself the silhouette in front of him was Matthew. This thought relaxed him somewhat; the pounding in his heart lessened and his thoughts became less jumbled. He stopped in the shade of a copse to rest but here the shadow disappeared and he felt very alone once again.

The calm he had felt before disappeared. He longed for the touch of Finola's hand and the sound of her voice. But she had gone back to Mulahinsa. And now there was a sharp pain in the sole of his foot.

Hunkering down beside a boulder, he took off his sandal and examined where a shard of rock had perforated it.

The sky had become greyer. When he lay back against the stone, he felt his head droop and he slept.

He began to dream that he was at Mulahinsa and that he had fallen asleep, as he sometimes did, lying against the *bawn* wall. Matthew, Finola, Cormac, Maeve, Brian, and Shane, his family, were there too and he could hear them talking to each other. The voices came closer and in a half-sleep he realised they were nearby, coming in his direction. When he realised where he was, he quickly slid on his belly to the other side of the rock out of sight.

"In my humble opinion someone was lying here."

It was Cormac. His opinion was always *humble.*

Cormac's face appeared above the boulder. "You foolish lad, why did you run off?"

"I didn't know what to do." Rory was close to tears.

"I should have known how upset you'd be and kept a closer watch on you." Cormac wiped his face. "Brigid told us you had disappeared. She looked everywhere for you." His breathing slowed. "Thank God you're unharmed."

But Rory, exhausted, only craved more sleep and to dream again that Matthew was still alive.

Chapter Four

Rory was pleased to be back in the chaos of the stone kitchen at Mulahinsa. Even so, the smell from the rack of lamb roasting on the *bir* was failing to make him feel hungry.

While he was away, he noticed they had added two more flitches of bacon to the three which were hanging from hooks on the ceiling. Teresa, the maidservant, had her hands in a tub washing copper pots and pans for the evening meal. Her sister Caitlín, sweat streaking down her face, was turning the *bir* over the fire.

Rory found it difficult to decide which of the twins looked worse. Caitlín with her face and hands covered in burns from flying sparks, or Teresa with her shoulders hunched from bending.

He liked them both. Matthew had trusted them to feed Ferdia his wolfhound and though they occasionally forgot to feed the other dogs, they never forgot his. The dog was in the kitchen now gnawing at a bone. After picking it bare, he came and sniffed around Rory's ankles but soon walked away whimpering. Though Rory knew it was because his scent was different from Matthew's, he still felt hurt.

When he took the lid off a vessel of pottage full of chicken brawn, which was left on the flagstones beside the fire, the soup looked thick and appetising. But since Matthew's death he had lost his desire to eat.

The door opened and Finola walked in.

"I've been searching for you Rory. Mother asked me to get you food." She paused. "She said you've been eating very little of late."

"I'd offer anything for a platter of oatmeal biscuits and a vessel of sweet milk," he lied, wanting to set her mind at rest.

"Anything?" Finola made her eyes small. "You'd let me do your hair?"

She placed the biscuits on a platter and poured milk from a pewter ewer into a goblet. "There!" She lowered her tone to prevent Caitlín and Teresa hearing. "You should eat in the hall. Mother will murder you if she catches you eating here. She regards the kitchen as a place to cook. *And* the space on the table is limited." She pushed a kneading trough from under her elbow.

"I'll risk it," Rory answered.

Brian, Finola's brother, then came into the kitchen.

"What are you doing here?" Finola asked. "Dinner will be sometime yet."

"I wanted time to myself. It's the only place I could think of."

"We're going to eat here, but we'll be quiet. I'll be doing Rory's hair and he'll be devouring this." She indicated the food.

Finola bunched the back of Rory's hair into a ponytail, causing the watching Brian to cringe. But, when a few minutes later, she pulled the short hairs at the nape of his neck and he yelled like a stuck pig, Brian's wince changed to laughter. This surprised Rory. Brian was usually very earnest as befitted an elder son in line to succeed his father as chief of Mulahinsa.

He was an heir now, too, Rory realised. To Glenone. Matthew's death had made him the elder son, the only son.

Peering sideways from under Finola's grasp, at Brian, he said, "Does Shane mind that you are *Tánaiste?* I know he would love to be the next chief."

Brian coloured then said, "I'll succeed as chief because my grandfather, like yours, accepted the English *Surrender and re-grant* treaty." He rubbed his face with his palms.

"Do you think ye'll fight like Father and Uncle Eoin?" Rory felt himself pale at the mention of the war that had killed his father and caused Matthew's death.

"I hope not. Succession squabbles only help the English to *divide and conquer.*"

"*Divide and conquer,*" that's what they did to my father and uncle Eoin, isn't it Brian?"

"Yes it is. It's such a simple idea; it succeeds all the time." Brian's tone lightened. "If you like, I'll give you a practical demonstration. And provide you with an excuse to escape Finola's ministrations. Come on outside."

Delighted, Rory slipped from his seat and followed Brian out into the air.

Brian grabbed several sticks, used for driving cattle, which were leaning against a wall. Then he took a rope from his tunic pocket and tied them in a bundle. "Here Rory, try to break them."

Rory laid them over his knee and leaned on them. "I can't."

His face reddened with effort.

"Give them back to me." Brian undid the string. Taking one stick, he broke it in two. The second one was as easy to break. He handed three others to Rory. "See can you break these now."

Rory put one against his bent knee and split it. He broke the others easily with his hands. "*Divide and conquer.* The English have a winner," he said.

On a balmy Wednesday morning of the succeeding week, Finola and Rory carried two rod baskets stuffed with left over silks, satins, and wools. Finola's mother had given her a conglomeration of sombre browns, blacks, beiges, and duns, leftovers she intended to dye bright colours and hang on her wall. Rory loved the mess the dye made and the way it turned Finola's fingers into rainbows. For weeks after dyeing, she had circles of blue, green or pink under her nails.

He saw Finola's father before he could see them. Cormac was clearly in his view as he leaned towards Joan O'Rourke and kissed her. His complexion was flushed.

"I expected to have a free rein at the colouring but now my mother will be in the Dye and Weaving house before us; it's where she goes when she's distressed," Finola said, as she stood listening outside the door to the noise of the looms.

Rory opened the door a crack and stuck his head around it. Women from the huts were spinning, weaving and throwing the shuttle. One of them looked up and, assuming he was looking for Maeve, gestured towards the dyeing section at the other end of the chamber.

They found her elbow deep in a barrel of colour.

"On my way in, I saw Joan O'Rourke," Finola blurted out.

"I hope you greeted her properly." Maeve's voice was cool. "She is your father's friend."

"I thought I'd have fun with these," Finola held up her remnants. "But the humour has left me."

"Anyway," her mother continued, "Niall wants to revise some Latin nouns with you both. Go and see him now." Her tone was sharp.

"I expected to be doing something pleasing - like dyeing," Finola said. "Instead I'll end up in the school-room."

"You should be grateful your father gives you the chance to

31

learn Latin and Greek. Few chieftains educate their daughters," Maeve retorted.

On the way to the schoolroom Finola said, "My mother will soon be like the other lords' wives sharing their homes with their husbands' mistresses. What's wrong with her? Brehon law says she can get a divorce. Why doesn't she?"

Rory remained silent. He knew Finola had her father's strong will, even a little of his quick temper. Resignation was her mother's *forte*. She would abhor the notion of divorce.

They entered the rectangular chamber of the schoolroom, walked past the stone sculpture of Cuchulainn and lingered a moment by the whitewashed wall where a tapestry hung. It depicted a translation from Latin of a description of Ireland in the ninth century, during the golden age, before the Viking invasion.

Long before Queen Elizabeth's reign, Rory often thought wistfully.

Niall sat on his three-legged stool; Finola left her basket on the floor and she and Rory went to their usual desks.

As if continuing immediately from a previous lesson Niall began, "Now for Latin. Some nouns to decline. You first Finola."

"What a dull assignment for a beautiful day!" she said. "The sun is shining. Shane isn't doing any work."

"You shouldn't be envious, Finola. Your mother has given permission to Shane to be absent," said Niall rubbing a thin hand across his brow. He opened the door. "That'll cool the air." His steps were quiet as he returned to his table and sat. He said, "We have already learned that Latin declensions are ...

"Oh God ... dd." It was Finola.

Rory looked at Finola lying on the floor, legs askew on the stone flags. Instinctively he knew she was pretending. He felt like saying "Finola, Niall is not that much of a fool Get up!" But he remained silent.

Niall calmly rose from his chair, walked to where Finola had thrown herself and stared at her long and hard.

He scrunched up his eyes, thoughtfully. Then he took a pitcher of spring water from the table and poured its contents on top of Finola's head.

She jumped to her feet. Her hair clung to her head like a second scalp. Drips lodged, for a second, on her eyelashes before running down her face and neck and inside the collar of her frock. A puddle lay where her head rested.

"Don't resort to deceit to get what you want," Niall said. "I'm sure Rory knew you were pretending too." He glared in his direction. "If you feel so strongly about Shane being free, go out and join him. It'd be better than play-acting."

"I don't want to go now," she said and stayed at her desk until they both could recite the declensions flawlessly.

"Bring your pannier," Niall reminded her before she left.

She snapped the basket from the ground and marched out with Rory following.

When they were away from the schoolroom, on their way to find Shane, Finola began to scratch. "Rory," she said, "I think *Oireach* has started on my legs."

"That's impossible. A rash like that would take ages to start and anyway it was your head that got drenched."

"Do you think?" Stopping, she tugged up her frock and curved herself into a half squat on the ground. Pulling at the flesh on her inner thigh she examined the inflammation. "There. See the red marks."

"It's most likely a midge bite," Rory said, being deliberately dismissive; a heated sensation had engulfed him. "What you did was foolhardy." It was the most stern he had ever been with Finola. But he was perturbed by what was happening to his body, and he sensed she was the cause.

Chapter Five

Light shone through the narrow windows in the sidewalls of the great dining hall and beamed on the bubbles in Cormac's wine goblet. He disliked using a platform, preferring instead to sit at the top of the chamber at a table beside Maeve. His trestle stood on rammed earth, with rushes and straw cushioning his feet, like the rest of the household. But to ensure that Cormac avoided having to wipe his sandals on dogshit, the wolfhounds were not allowed near and were only permitted to beg scraps from the tables in the body of the hall.

The dining hall was bigger and brighter than the one at Glenone where Matthew had died. The kitchen, built from stone instead of the usual combination of clay and mud, was separate to the main building but was joined by an enclosed passage and ran parallel to it.

Cormac was twirling his goblet waiting to hand it to Brigid for a refill.

When she came from the kitchen she stacked the three platters that Rory, Finola and Shane had used and put the leftover butter and cheese aside for Lizzie, the cat. Cormac handed her the goblet and she left down the dishes and walked back with it to the kitchen for the third time that evening.

"I thought she'd never finish." Cormac turned to Maeve. "I want to talk to you."

Maeve sat still. She whispered, "If it's about Finola seeing you with Joan O'Rourke, I ..." Her lips were a thin white line.

"It's about Eochy O'More."

Her brow unfurled.

Rory said, "I remember him from uncle Eoin's feast. Someone hit him over the head with a platter." His voice began to tremble. "Matthew and I had a wager about who'd win." At the mention of Matthew, Finola and Shane shifted on their form.

Cormac turned to them. "I can see you're longing to leave."

Rory nodded in unison with the others.

Cormac motioned with his head towards the door giving them tacit permission to exit. When they were gone, he said to Maeve, "I wanted to discuss Rory as well but was reluctant to do so in his presence."

"What did you want to say?" Her voice was even.

"Because of his youth he's less a threat to Eoin Maguire now, but in the future he'll be his chief rival."

"I agree." Sipping her buttermilk, Maeve looked at Cormac from over the rim of her tankard. "The English will support him when he comes to his majority. It's the intervening years we have to worry about."

Cormac nodded. "His mentioning of Matthew has increased my apprehension about the silence from Glenone. I'd like to find out what's going on in the head of Eoin Maguire." He paused. "Eochy O'More, we mustn't forget, is married to his wife's sister."

"Yes," Maeve answered. "I know."

"Eochy O'More is giving me trouble. He accepts that he has to pay cattle as rent, but resents the other charges. I'll pay him a visit and at the same time discover what plans, if any, are being hatched for Rory."

Brigid returned and dipped the clean goblet into the wine vessel that stood in a tub of cooling water and handed it to Cormac.

"He hates our right to *cuid oidhche*. It kills him to have to supply a night's food and lodgings for us." Cormac licked the wine from his drooping *crommeal*. "It'll be interesting to see how he behaves tonight when I arrive with the whole retinue."

"Tonight?"

"Yes, I've sent a messenger announcing our arrival."

Maeve fiddled with the brooch fastened to the neck of her frock. "Drink less of the grape Cormac. Your face is scarlet." Cormac gulped the rest of his wine.

Maeve looked at him carefully. "Let that be your last. You'll need all your wits if you intend to lead a successful expedition against Eochy O'More."

Cormac looked at him in dismay as, continuing to frown, Ultan MacGrath held his hands towards the heat of the fire banked in the middle of the room. Sitting on a stool to the left of the flames, his hands slid up and down the blackthorn stick between his legs.

"I've the rhyming dryness I tell you. No. 'Tis me own bed for me tonight, not rambling off to Eochy O'More's domain I'll be. Freezing with the cold I am." He made a grumbling noise deep in his throat. "'Tisn't two words I'd be able to sling together." His eyes became foxlike. "Expectin' you tonight he is, so froth at the mouth if you want but don't touch a weapon. If need be, you can take him by surprise tomorrow." He coaxed, "'Tis a great piece entirely I'll pen for you when you teach Eochy O'More a lesson. Another praise poem about the chief of Mulahinsa is due."

On the evening of his visit to Eochy O'More Cormac did not want to hear his poet refuse to accompany him but, like any sensible chieftain, he was afraid to draw his wrath upon him. A satire would challenge his power even more than Eochy O'More was doing. He had no choice but to go without him.

Mooreland stretched across the five isolated miles to Eochy O'More's dwelling. A string of hillocks, a few rowans and two still lakes softened the harshness.

The soldiers' steps were light as they marched three abreast, the outer row on the margin of the trail. They knew they were on their way to being nourished, wined and entertained. Wind caught at the kernes' cloaks and mantles and puffed them up. Their long hair snarled in the wind. Some complained about Ultan MacGrath's absence, but men close to Cormac quietened them.

Near the end of their journey, the sky blackened and all they could see now was the glimmer of water and the dark skeleton of the knolls and castle looming. The guard on the battlement lifted his hand and circled his mouth, as they approached, shouting back to somebody behind him.

A few minutes later, Eochy O'More stood framed in the door rubbing his paunch. Though his skull was without a rib of hair, his eyebrows were bushy enough to cushion a *scaltán*. His chin rose, he straightened his shoulders and planted his feet firmly on the ground.

"Is there no lady of the house to give me a welcoming kiss?" Cormac smiled a little too brightly.

Eochy O'More outstared Cormac. His face could have been carved out of the same stone as the walls around him. "No." Then after a pause he said, "The servants have laid the table in the hall. They will seat you. All at the same one remember," he cautioned the attendants.

The servants, with barely concealed smirks, did Eochy O' More's bidding.

Cormac and his men sat at a long table while ragged servants laid out platters, bent and cracked. The deal table they were seated at was pitted and split, and smeared with what appeared to be rancid butter. Cormac rested his elbows by his side.

The O'More *file*, his eyes glinting when he saw Cormac was without a rhymer, was ensconced on a podium ready to eulogise on the greatness of the O'More family.

Cormac tore at his horsemeat and spat gristle on top of the pieces of hare and magpie on the ground.

The faces of the swordsmen, horsemen and kerne were glum as they nibbled at their food. Their spirits revived briefly when the servants approached with wine.

"The bloody stuff is as sour as a crab apple," a brawny man beside Cormac shouted, his hand reaching for his pike.

Cormac dug his fingers into the man's arm. "Easy." He gave the soldier a cautionary glance. "We'll bed down early and be fresh in the morning." He beckoned to a maid carrying a vessel of wine. As she leaned over to pour, Cormac looked down the v between her breasts and fondled her backside making her frock crumble between her legs.

"'Tis terrible you are Sire, and me only a serving girl."

"In my humble opinion, you're a comely lady fit to be a queen." He glanced at the hovering Eochy O'More. "I think your lord agrees with me."

Blushing, the maid cast an eye in the direction of her master and jiggled her breasts.

At the end of the meal when the servants returned to remove the dishes, Cormac overheard their gossip. "Molly is whoring again. The master will throw her out if he catches her."

Molly tossed her head and let her hair braid slip to her shoulders. Her breasts rose and fell quickly as she tilted them towards Cormac's face; her moist tongue circled her lips. "I'll be showing you to your sleeping quarters Sire."

Cormac, his face florid, his eyes full of anticipation, followed her.

When Cormac arrived back at Mulahinsa the next morning, he told Maeve, "Eochy O'More's retinue insulted us any way they knew how." Then, avoiding her gaze as he mentioned Molly, he said, "I discovered from a talkative servant that Eoin Maguire is plotting to rid himself of his nephew. We'll have to be extra careful with Rory."

"It's better to know which way the wind blows. I'll tell the others to stay with him as much as possible."

"Yes that'll be a start. For now, I have enough to do to teach Eochy O'More a lesson. He challenged my power with his lack of hospitality. If he gets away with it, the word will spread and, like a pack of wolfhounds scenting blood, my *uirrithe* will gather for the kill. I'll have to defeat him."

"When?" Maeve asked.

. "It has to be today," said Cormac. "As Ultan MacGrath, my indolent *file,* rightly said better to take him by surprise. If we go now, he will be unprepared for our return."

Cormac left to prepare for a second journey to Eochy O'More in twenty-four hours.

As they neared the O'More's castle the horsemen behind the infantry looked at the sky with troubled faces. "'Twill be a divil if there's a shower. Angry that sky looks," said one.

Cormac gave the order, "Have torches ready. We need to get this over before the rain."

The swordsman next to Cormac relayed the order to the men behind. The word *torches* rippled through the rows. Men on the left of each line raised their twisted tufts of straw, tied at the base, and waited for the order to set them alight.

The air shivered with passion.

"There's our gold." Cormac's eyes flashed with glee as he pointed to the small black cattle milling in the outfields. "Drive them off," he instructed the main body of soldiers. "A few of you can flame the thatch."

"There's nobody around. 'Tis as easy as robbing a corpse on the battlefield," a horseman shouted as he drove the cattle towards Mulahinsa.

Kernes, their brands aglow, scaled the wall and fired the thatch. The breeze fanned the flying sparks and soon flames licked their way to the body of the castle. The stones blackened but stood firm.

From within the castle walls a chorus of *yoo hoos* followed by the curse "May you grow the underbelly of a sow and die roarin'.

God blast you to hell and garnish you with horns." And a troop of whisky nosed retainers tottered out.

"Tell your lord," Cormac said, "that he'd better pay his dues. Next time we'll take hostages as well as cattle." Cormac shook his head so vehemently that his cap slipped to the ground. He took the cone from the horse-boy running beside him. "Good lad." Plonking it back in place he said, "When the hat is on, the house is thatched."

Amidst the laughter following his quip, Cormac failed to notice the servant Molly slink from the castle, slipping and sliding in the muck ploughed by the cattle's hooves, a torn sack on her back.

Chapter Six

"I wish I could be on my own. Since Cormac came back from defeating Eochy O'More, there is always somebody with me. When I think I'm alone, I feel Brian or Niall's eyes on me. Or you." Rory looked accusingly at Finola. "You often spring from nowhere, too."

Finola, pretending not to hear, knelt on the ground and touched a plant with yellow flowers. "Look Rory. It's so brave. It's the only one."

In the glow of her excitement, his resentment faded. "Spring. It'll soon be time to move to the booley."

"I know. This is the best time of year. I love driving the cattle through the hills and bogs to the mountains," Finola said. "But I don't like the cleaning that goes with it."

"Me neither," Rory agreed. "I'll get out my 'kerchief. There will be dust everywhere. It's as well it only happens once a year."

When he entered the castle, Caitlín was stripping the pallets and collecting clothes for the wash, pounding them pitilessly with her wooden bat. Teresa brushed the house, washed the floors and tubbed fat for the candle maker. The new servant Molly, her expression like thunder at the indignity of the task, plucked feathers from the hens to cure for bolsters and pillows. Brigid stayed in the kitchen preparing to make butter and cheese and bake bread to eat on the way.

Some days later the booley was ready to move. There was an air of excitement as the women, children and herdsmen took their leave of the men who were left to sow the crops.

The black herds were full of suppressed energy as if they, too, felt a touch of summer lunacy. The herdsmen driving them joked with each other and raised their sticks in exultation of a summer of freedom. Maeve sat in a slide car, a wheelless vehicle, pulled by horses, sometimes favoured by her if the journey was going to be long. The women and children walked side by side. Babies were cradled in their mother's arms. Rory and other boys of his age walked beside their mounts. When a layer of dust rose behind them, Rory looked at his newly washed clothes and suppressed a smile. Despite all the washing that had been done to them in the castle, they were already grubby.

Then, when without warning, a dirty cloud opened and rain

washed the countryside, he squelched through mud that moments before, had been dry dust.

"Don't let a bit of water dampen our spirits." Finola began to sing in a melodious tone, her voice soaring.

Rory wondered how such small lungs could reach such a pitch. As they put words to the tunes, the air became alive with sounds.

"Diarmaid, *you* can easily think of words that rhyme," Rory turned to the boy leading the horse beside him.

Finola agreed. "Ultan MacGrath would disown you as his grandchild if he thought you reneged."

At the reference to his august ancestry, Diarmaid swelled with pride.

"We always have a new song after the booley so this year can't be different," Rory said.

"I'll ask grandfather to *snas* it up. He might put it in the *Duanaire* under *Booley songs*," said Diarmaid.

Rory loved it when they all shared in the excitement of the compositions. Last year, a few months after the booley, he had been delighted when he had opened the big book and recognised one of his phrases.

When they heard the sound of a plunging stream, which flowed along the northern side of the hollow, they knew it was time to choose their site and stopped singing.

If it had been wild instead of showery, the herdsman in charge would have thrown his hat into the wind to see where it would land, but now he had to mark out a site with a row of stones. The fairies were the final arbiter of where they would set up the booley. If they failed to touch the stones during the night, they were giving their permission to use the space for three months.

Later as Rory lay on straw, the darkness a shroud around him, rain pouring down, he rubbed his dripping face with the back of his sleeve and wished that Dara had ignored the possibility that the site was a fairy pad and allowed them to start building their booley huts. Leaning over, he whispered the thought to Finola.

"Sometimes you're a bit daft Rory Maguire," she said. He heard her draw her breath. "Do you want to invite more bad luck?"

A sparrow hawk flew in circles above a wood near to the site they had chosen the previous night. As he came close to his nesting place, his lacklustre notes broke the silence. Rory and Finola sat on the ground and listened to a yellowhammer take up a tune from the hedgerows.

"A little bit of whey," Finola warbled along with the string of sounds. "No ballyclabbeeer," she finished in rhythm with the bird's prolonged note. When she heard the thin buzzing of a long tailed tit, she said, "They have all turned out to greet us. Let's sit back and listen." The birds chanted in the grasses, hedges absorbed the sunlight. They linked arms.

After ten minutes of easy silence, Finola spoke again, "I bet I'm green." Jumping to her feet she pulled her dress forward from around her backside. "I knew. A grass stain."

Rory looked at a blob of honey on his tunic. "There's nobody to see it in the hills and bogs."

"No English to call us savages you mean," Finola said.

"They think we're the wild Irish because we even go on the booley so it doesn't matter whether they can see us or not."

Finola bobbed her head. "In Europe it's called transhumance." Her tone was sardonic. "The English consider it uncivilised because they don't practice it themselves."

"And barbaric," Rory added.

"It's time we started working." She looked at the other families starting to build the booley huts. "We must do as much as everybody else. It was our choice to come."

Rory knew she spoke the truth. Usually the chieftain's wife and family remained at home while the booley took place.

Finola's narrow feet fitted easily into the spaces between the branches as she helped build the huts. She even managed to get to the top and put on the thatch. Each time she had got stuck the previous year, Shane had been there to help her. On this occasion he had slept late and by the time he had surfaced, Finola and Rory were already back with four trees. He had sulked since.

Three months later, and their last day at the booley, Shane's bad temper had become a pattern. As Rory mixed sorrel leaves into the cows' blood on his platter, he smacked his lips and thought of Shane's maltreatment of Finola. There was the time when he insisted that she had robbed a bird's nest when he was the one who had deliberately smashed the eggs. Or when he had stolen his mother's head dress, thrown it in the river and blamed Finola. Or .... He had told his mother that Finola had kissed him. That she had stuck her tongue into his mouth until he, afraid he would choke, had started to cry. What had most distressed Rory about the lie was that he would be babyish enough to weep if something as wonderful as that had truly happened.

A year passed. May came and the foray of pre-booley cleaning started again. Maeve walked around like a queen bee looking for drones, reprimanding any servant who paused in her work.

"A good beginning makes a good ending," Shane said in an imitative tone, low enough that his mother was unable to hear. But in this situation it *will* be a good ending. This slavery means we'll be leaving for the mountains."

What has he to complain about, thought Rory. He had done little to help since the manoeuvre began. It was he and Finola who had lugged Shane's straw filled mattress when he complained of a sore wrist. It was they who ... There was no benefit dwelling on it; he was lucky to have escaped schoolwork for a short while, and he would ruin it if he wasted the time agonising about Shane.

He lay on his belly on the grass beside a mound of clay, his elbow supporting his head, chewing absently on a blade of grass, secure in the knowledge that a passer-by would be incapable of seeing him. Leaning down, he used his free hand to turn a stone covering maggots and snails. Finding them uninteresting he turned instead to look at a horde of ants that were working as hard as the household preparing for the booley.

When Cormac's voice, warm and deep, and Brian's expressionless tones interrupted his thoughts, he raised his hand to attract their attention but noticing their heads so close together and their expressions so troubled, he became loathe to interrupt and lowered it again. Aware of a vague feeling of guilt, he pricked his ears to listen.

"We are unable to look after him forever," Brian was adamant. "It's well over a year since Matthew died, and we still have to be as careful."

"In my humble opinion, they will leave him alone while he is at Mulahinsa. They know we're protecting him."

"When Rory is in the hills and many of the men are here, Eoin Maguire would have a good opportunity to do him harm," Brian said.

"Perhaps the herdsmen could look after him like they did last year." Cormac sounded doubtful.

"It would have been too soon to try anything at last year's booley," said Brian.

"We could keep him here with us." After a moment's thought, Cormac added, "No, that would be impossible. It would require someone to protect him all the time. You're correct. Last year would have been too soon. Many have forgotten Matthew's death by now. Eoin Maguire will soon try to get rid of him."

Rory felt ill. He was a Maguire not an O'Hanlon. The blood that ran through his veins differed from Finola and Shane's. As he tramped back to the castle, his feet felt as if a hundredweight of stones was dragging them down.

He met Finola who, before he had uttered a word, sensed something was wrong and asked him what was troubling him. When he had finished spilling the contents of the overheard conversation to her, she said, "Rors. Stop worrying. Father will see that you remain unharmed. I'll keep an eye on you, too."

She gripped his hand and he felt safe.

Chapter Seven

One day after weeks of rain, the skies suddenly brightened to a much welcomed blue. Rory, not trusting that this good weather would last even until noon, seized the opportunity to go outdoors. Restive for days, he had paced the rooms of the castle and was now in the mood for adventure. As he came outside he discovered that Shane had been of like mind and was already outside sitting by the wall of the castle.

He had been uneasy with Shane ever since they had come back from last summer's booley. They were growing apart, Rory becoming more mature than Shane. Since the booley, such childish pursuits as climbing trees or playing leapfrog lacked appeal. Though he still liked to snare rabbits or practise with his bow and arrows. However, when Shane suggested that they go skimming stones on the Swift River, Rory readily agreed. Cormac had ordered him to stay within sight of the castle and the prospect of a day's freedom from restrictions made it all the more exciting.

The spate of rain had churned the tracks into marsh but, despite the slippery surface and the potholes brimming with water, they ran exulting all the way to the river, slowing only to sidestep the odd boulder and occasional tree stump. Soon they heard the gurgle of river-water and they made their way towards a secluded part of the riverbank bordered by low bushes and a few scattered trees. They stopped when they saw the familiar sweep of woodland ahead. The real forbidden territory was the forest where the river had its source.

Shane's chest rose and fell rapidly. "I'm going to sit for awhile." He stopped beside a felled tree. "This is like the form at home."

Rory leaned over and scooped a handful of water from the flow.

"I'm going to win this contest," Shane said.

Noticing watercress growing in the stream he got off the tree trunk, and bent full over to pluck some leaves. Then, his mouth full, he called to Rory in an indistinct lilting voice, "Somebody coming."

"What did you say?" Rory asked.

"I said somebody's coming."

Rory looked along the goat track and saw a strange man

whose *glib* hid his forehead and a *crommeal* covered his upper lip. He carried a pack under his arm. An image flashed through his mind of the servant named Padraic, who had served Matthew the mead. He had the same hairy concealment.

When he reached for his quiver, he felt the arrows, but when he put his hand on his chest to pull down his bow, there was nothing there but his tunic. He had expected to get round to target practice during some part of the day, so he was certain he had put it on when he left the castle. He stared in disbelief at his chest. There was the remnant of the string that had secured it to his shoulders. It must have snapped. Shane, of course, never bothered to carry one.

Snippets of an overheard exchange between Cormac and Brian came back to him. "Eoin Maguire will be plotting mischief." Were those the exact words? There was sunlight on the river, but the trees along the bank cast shadows on the ground.

A buzzing started in his head. The man was coming closer, an arquebus visible under his arm. Shane, unconcerned, was busily looking for good flat skimming stones. If he were alone, he would already have fled. He grabbed Shane by the shoulder, his nails digging into him and propelled him in the direction of the wood.

"We can't go into the forest," Shane protested. "We're not allowed. It's dangerous."

Putting any thoughts of wolves from his mind, he stayed close to the riverbank and dragged Shane upstream. He entered the forest at a place where the trees were low and sparse and picked his steps carefully until they were walking through thick undergrowth and the trees grew tall and close together. They came to a path of flattened brushwood used by hunters. Cormac told him once, he remembered, that someone following a trail would go downhill since that was less dangerous and quicker. "We'll go this way," he said, climbing upwards.

"Where are we going?" A mean expression had slipped onto Shane's face. "If father finds out, I'll have to tell him this was your idea."

Rory knew that even if Cormac failed to find out, Shane would tell him anyway. He began to wonder had he been hasty to run into the forest just because of a stranger walking the river bank.

And anyway the stranger didn't seem to be following them.

"We'll go home," he said to Shane. "Nobody will have missed us if we go now."

But Shane had begun to delight in the adventure. "I'm not going home without having some fun," he said. "Let's play leapfrog here." They had come to a small clearing. "There's just about enough room." He had donned a stubborn expression. "I'll go first. Be sure to stoop low. I want to be able to jump over you."

Better play for a few minutes to satisfy him, Rory reasoned, as he held himself as low to the ground as his long legs would allow and let Shane glide over his back.

"Now you be the frog," Shane said, as he bent himself in two.

When he was half way over his shoulders, Shane, with a hint of glee, rose slightly and Rory fell awkwardly onto the damp leaves. He tried to rise but a stab of pain darted through his foot. Easing himself into a sitting position, he gingerly felt his ankle. The frieze of his trews irritated his skin. He fought off a feeling of faintness. "Shane, I've hurt my foot," he said weakly.

Shane ignored him.

As he made another effort to stand, a ripple of pain shot through his lower leg and ankle. Grabbing at the notches of a tree he managed to struggle to his feet. Leaves and twigs stuck to his clothes. His body tensed in spasms when he put his weight on his foot. The only way he could alleviate the pain was to rest against a tree and hold his injured foot clear of the ground.

"You're in the right position for a tickle." Shane started towards him but stopped when he saw Rory's pained expression.

"Will you look for a branch to help me walk?" Rory asked. His neck ached and he began to panic when he recalled the stranger in the trees looking for him.

Shane sprung to his feet and searched among the branches and slivers of bark around him. "Won't I be a hero when we get back," he said.

Eventually he chose a branch long enough and reasonably straight. He looked like a man who had picked a winner at a cockfight. "Here this will support you."

Rory, feeling more secure now that he had a branch to lean on, considered that perhaps he'd be able to go back some of the way with Shane. He was about to make the suggestion when a rustling in the trees stopped him. "Shane. Get help, run and get help," he tried to gasp but the words lodged in his throat before being spoken; his stomach churned.

The noise became closer, louder and more insistent. It sounded inhuman. He touched his quiver. He had his arrows, he knew, but he hoped somehow a bow would miraculously appear. As if it were an incantation against evil, he found himself murmuring Matthew's name. He balanced himself on his makeshift support.

The rustling stopped for a moment. In the sudden silence he could hear his own breathing. There was a lurching sound and he found himself staring into the wild eyes of a grey wolf, a ribbon of blood streaming from his rump where he had been wounded. An animal stench mingled with the smell of blood.

For once Shane stood still.

Rory had to do something. If the wolf came near enough, he could maybe stick an arrow in his eye and blind him. A hard ball developed in his throat and for a moment he had difficulty swallowing. His head throbbed and, momentarily, he forgot about the pain in his leg.

The wolf, demented by his injury, arched his body. Lowering his head for a charge, he was within inches of Rory. His hot breath reeked. Rory aimed directly for his eye. As the beast backed off gasping, a whitish ooze ran down his snout. He reeled, howling with pain.

Shane frantically scurried through the brush. Snarling, the wolf sprang again, this time in the direction of the noise. Hindered by his impaired sight and the open wound on his hindquarters, he clawed at the air. Shane floundered in the scrub. The wolf bared his teeth and attacked again, this time ripping at Shane's jugular.

Rory threw his remaining arrows at him but it was like throwing needles at a rhinoceros. He even threw his makeshift crutch at him but to no avail.

A shot sundered the air. Skin bedecked claws fell from Shane's throat. The wolf rolled on the ground, fresh blood dripping from him, his own and Shane's. His eyes were open, staring. Shane collapsed; his fair curls looked like strings of gold on the damp leaves.

A man ran to where he lay. He pulled off his shaggy mantle and wrapped it around him, picked him up as if he were a baby and held him to his chest. Shane's legs hung limply.

"He must live. He can't leave me, too," Rory whispered to himself as he sat helpless on the ground trying to stop shaking. The soft breeze blowing through the trees was unable to comfort him and the eerie atmosphere of the forest added to his nervousness. He shivered again at the image of the stranger carrying Shane away, while he lay helpless in the dirt. He wondered who he was. If he had been a hunter looking for bounty, he would have claimed the wolf.

The sweat, which earlier had covered his body, now chilled him. His mouth tasted of chalk. Groping about for wet leaves, he licked the meagre moisture from them and rubbed some over his face and neck.

He retrieved the branch he had thrown at the wolf and hoisted himself to a standing position. The image of Shane as he last saw him began to haunt him, his eyes glazed, his flawless skin a buttermilk yellow, a finger of his limp hand slung over the rescuer's shoulder, pointing at him.

If he had kept Shane out of the woods, if he had stayed calm, they would now be skimming stones on the Swift River and counting the ripples. He made the sign of the cross and though the familiar act of blessing himself had a calming effect, he was unable to pray.

As he began his slow journey back to Mulahinsa, his foot dragged and he stumbled over uneven ground and rain-filled ruts. Each time he fell, his clothes became more and more soaked and covered in dirt and slime and sodden leaves. The swelling foot stretched the strap of his sandal. It bit into his bare skin until he could stand it no longer. He pulled it off and then, realising he would balance better without any, he threw both of them away.

Thinking he heard voices coming towards him, he felt a mixture of emotions, elation that it would be Cormac, fear that the stranger had returned, grief that Shane was dead. But no-one came through the brush. The voices were in his head.

A purple cloud obscured the sun and darkened the woods. More rain fell and mixed with the tears running down his cheeks. He thought he heard the voices again. Then they faded. Hunger pangs gnawed at him. His skin crawled beneath the filth. The rain stopped and the sun emerged. He leaned his head to one side. The voices were back.

Suddenly, Cormac, Brian and a tear stained Finola stood in front of him, along with the mysterious stranger.

Cormac's eyes narrowed. Rory felt a stab of renewed fear.

"I had to come," Finola said, squeezing his hand. Her eyes, anxious and bewildered, riveted on his face. "They wanted me to stay at home but ..."

"Enough, daughter." Cormac's fists were white at the knuckles.

With one quick movement he stood in front of Rory and slapped him on each cheek.

"Father, stop. He's only eleven. Leave him alone. He has suffered enough for one day." It was Brian, his voice full of reproach, running towards his father.

A muscle in Cormac's cheek twitched. His face infused with colour.

"Shane," was all he said, and turned away.

Brian and the stranger fashioned a bed of interwoven branches and tied it between two stalwart sticks. It was a bumpy ride as Cormac and Brian carried Rory back. Finola walked beside them. "Is your leg paining you?" Her face was the colour of cinders, her spattering of freckles like specks of ashes, as she braved her father's glare to ask the question.

"Is Shane dead? Did the wolf kill him? Tell me the truth Finola," he said from the stretcher.

"No." Cormac answered for her.

"Is he going to die?"

"He will live."

Sensing there was something else wrong, Rory repeated, "At least he's going to live."

He caught Finola's eye and nodded towards Shane's rescuer, the mysterious stranger.

She looked confused for a moment but then said, "It's Tadhg Macmahon, Nollag Macmahon's nephew. You remember Nollag. He used to come through our lands to buy our wool and hides." She bent low and continued in a whisper. "You should remember. We used to make fun of his pointed ears. We always said they looked like a fawn's."

What a half-wit he was. Nollag was a grey merchant who paid the family for the right to ply his trade unmolested in their territory and this was his nephew.

Shifting on the branches of the stretcher, Rory reached his hand along his leg to soothe the spasms of pain. He found it difficult to understand why, despite his being Nollag's nephew, he still felt distrustful of the way Tadhg was glaring at him.

Brian and Cormac left Rory's bed on the flagstones outside the door because it was too broad to haul inside. "You'll have to get some help," Cormac said. "Our first duty is to attend to Shane." And he hurried away.

"Finola, get two servants to aid you," Brian shouted over his shoulder. "I'll be back as soon as I can."

She bent down to Rory. "I'd better do as Brian suggested," she said and rushed off.

Time crawled. The pain in his leg worsened. Why had Cormac and Brian left him? He closed his eyes and dozed lightly.

"Sorry I was so long, Rory." Finola was standing over him again, her budding breasts rising and falling as her breathing quickened from exertion. "I could only find one person who was free. They're all looking after Shane. He seems everybody's favourite."

The stocky minion who had come with her joined in. "Favourite, 'tis never a truer word you were sayin' miss. Sure the saints in heaven mustn't have known what was happening. The divil of a story it is. Dragging an innicent boy into the forest like that. Madness." As he talked, he tied Rory to his bed with stout ropes.

"Why are you doing that? Help him off and support him in." Finola's face reddened angrily.

"'Twould take too long. I have to get back inside. Her ladyship's orders." The servant's thick muscles swelled as he turned the bed on its side and heaved it through the doorway.

Rory's weight strained the thick cords and they bit into his wrists and ankles. He clamped his teeth to ease the pain. The servant dumped the stretcher among a pile of crates, half mended ploughs and old worn clay vessels.

Finola came down the stairway a knife clasped in her hand.

She got on her knees beside him and cut the ropes. "Give me your hand. I'll help you up." Her slim body inclined towards him.

"I can't. You're dragging me down," he said irritably.

Brian emerged through the shadows and took Rory's other hand. "Put your arms around us Rory," he said.

Together, they pulled him to his feet.

"That's it. Hop on one foot. We'll take you round the back to the kitchen."

He was able to settle his arm comfortably round Finola's neck but he had to stretch to reach Brian's. Neither of them had thought of replacing the sandals he had thrown away and he became conscious of the thistles stuck to his soles and pricking his feet.

Brigid waited for them in the kitchen beside the most comfortable chair in the castle, which she had carried down from the parlour.

Maeve stood by with a heartbroken expression. But when she spoke her voice was cold. "Prepare Rory some vittles Brigid." She evaded Rory's eyes. He could have been Matthew's wolfhound in search of scraps.

"No need. 'Tis ready I have some," said Brigid.

Maeve's lips curled. "You're taking the law into your own hands a lot tonight Brigid."

Though her pallor whitened, Brigid's step was firm as she walked towards Rory and placed three oatmeal biscuits into one of his hands, a vessel of sweet milk into the other, and six hazel nuts on his knee. "I know how you do be lovin' the nuts."

"Is Shane dead?" he asked for the second time that day.

Brigid turned away not answering.

Finola tugged at her plaits. "He's not … dead."

She's lying, he thought. Her brown eyes were darker than usual, a giveaway.

"I want to see him. Please, I want to see him."

Maeve interjected. "He's not fit for visitors. He will not be able to …" Her voice sharpened. "You know yourself the bed-chambers are on another level. You've caused enough trouble without expecting people to lug you up to him. Drink your milk and go to sleep. Brigid will move your bed down."

After what had happened, Rory no longer felt welcome in this house. After all, this was Shane's home not his and to add to his disquiet he felt they were hiding something from him.

Chapter Eight

The castle bed-chamber was dim in the afternoon light as if the place had been mourning Cormac's absences and the good times that were gone. It was his first visit to the room for days. His head was bowed in thought.

Maeve entered and closed the door behind her.

Cormac turned to her and said, "I asked you to meet me here because I would prefer not to be interrupted."

She eyed the wide mattress, but when Cormac coughed self-consciously, the bright look left her face.

He put his hand on her arm impersonally and guided her to a stool opposite his own. "Maeve, we have to let Rory go," he began.

She stiffened as she realised that this was definitely not an attempted seduction.

"Shane is healthy again," Cormac continued, "as healthy as he'll ever be, bar a cure. He'll be able to go with the others to the booley but we'll have to make alternative arrangements for Rory."

"You're very hard on him. I know we were all shocked after the accident." Maeve's voice faltered. "I reacted badly at the time as well, but I now understand that he didn't mean to lead Shane into danger. We should let bygones be bygones."

"I try to be kind to him. God knows he has suffered enough," said Cormac. "But when I think of Shane never to talk again, I find it difficult. It takes all my determination to keep my temper."

"You worry about his safety. Anxiety makes us all cross."

"Poor Finola. She's the only one who looks after him." Cormac's eyes glistened. "Courageous little one that she is. I have made it hard for her." He shook his head. "I hate to see her entertaining him instead of Shane."

"Your daughter has circles under her eyes from trying to look after both of them," Maeve said. "And Niall is complaining about her absences from the schoolroom."

"It would be better for everybody if we accept Sir Walter Carew's offer," Cormac said.

"I still think it strange that he wants to bring the lad with him to England."

"It *is* strange." Cormac fingered his *crommeal.* "Though he has

53

been here, periodically since he was seventeen, he has never changed his attitude towards us. In my humble opinion, he is like the other captains who become generals still thinking we're wild beasts. What makes it even more puzzling is that he hated Con Maguire, Rory's grandfather."

"Yet he had a strong affection for Phelim, Rory's father." Maeve's voice held a question.

"Cold divil that he is, I find it hard to imagine him having affection for anybody, though rumour has it that there was a time when he was not so disciplined. Hard to believe he used to be nicknamed the seducer."

Maeve's face coloured at this mention of fornication as if it reminded her of Cormac's infidelities. "I saw him at Glenone when Phelim died. He was pretending to be unaffected by the death, but I could see he was distressed. Initially I thought it was the effects of whisky or wine until I noticed that he was refusing any drink, even sweet milk."

"He would have quoted scripture if you asked him," Cormac retorted. "Follower of that Knox fellow he is ... very puritanical. He is making reparation for past sins. It'll be a terrible change for Rory living with such a man, but I can't see any other course."

"A taste of Puritan abstinence will do him good," Maeve looked directly at Cormac. "I'd prefer if he differed from his grandfather."

"Or me."

She ignored his interruption. "It's certain death if he stays in Ulster. Connaught or Munster would be no better."

"He'd be safer in England than in the Pale."

"I agree," Maeve said. "There he'd learn how the English think, how they live, why they show such interest in Ireland. He'd learn to speak English like a native and be able to anticipate their treachery."

"We were tricked by *Surrender and re-grant*. I understand why my father accepted it, but I hate the clan wars it has caused," Cormac answered.

"Next time your *uirrithe* refuse to pay their levies will you refuse to go into battle against them?"

"It's hard to go against custom."

"Custom without reason is but ancient error," Maeve said.

"We have fallen into England's trap."

In the dining hall Rory was dividing a piece of venison and casually feeding it to two wolfhounds at his side.

"Rory, clean your hands," Finola sitting at the table with him ordered when he continued with his meal.

But he was preoccupied. "Cormac intends to send me away," he said.

"If those dogs stay, he definitely will. You know how Mother hates animals near the top trestle."

At the other end of the table Brian had finished his meal. He beckoned to Finola who went and sat by him.

As the two talked rapidly, Rory fidgeted on the form. Brian was explaining something to Finola and from her stance he knew she disliked what she was hearing. He tried not to listen but he still picked up words like *father's friend* and *England.*

"What were you muttering about to Brian?" he asked when she resumed her seat beside him. His eyes watered. "You know where I'm going, don't you."

"You know where I'm going," Finola mimicked playfully.

"Please Finola. I want to know. Where am I going?"

"Father will tell you himself. Brian said he wants to see you when you've finished your meal." She led him to the door. "Go on," she said. "It's worse being in the dark about it."

Outside a faint sun was attempting to warm the day. When Rory approached, Cormac tried to be light-hearted. "Rory, is your leg well enough to take a short walk?" he asked. "It's a lovely summer's day. You'd enjoy the fresh air." But his eyes were apologetic.

Rory's felt his heart hammer and a sour taste seep into his mouth.

"For a boy of eleven you have endured a lot," Cormac was saying.

He had a feeling his life was about to be upturned again and that it was Cormac who would decide its direction.

As they strolled down the path, he felt the touch of the light breeze on his face and the familiar odour of manure in the air. He did his utmost to hide his apprehension. As he looked back at the castle, the centre of his existence for seven years, he knew he would be leaving his home again.

"I know you're curious," Cormac continued. "There is no correct way to say this. A friend of your father's, Sir Walter Carew, contacted me. He sided with Phelim in the civil war. He has asked our permission to take you to England with him."

"To England?"

"He has a house at Margate in Kent, and one in the City of London. His son George is a few years older than you, and he has a younger daughter. The three of you should become good friends."

Rory felt a drum beat in his head. "I remember a Sir Walter Carew. I met him in Glenone, but I didn't like him. He referred to us as savages and was always telling me to walk straight with my head high."

"Lady Carew is a kind and cultured woman. When you get to England, you'll change your mind."

"I don't want to go. I don't want to leave you. I want to stay here. I'm sick of people shunting me about." Rory half lifted his foot to stamp it, but pain stopped him.

"Don't be childish Rory. Edward Tudor was your age when he took over the throne of England. He didn't pound his foot on the ground when affairs of state went against him."

"Niall told us that Edward VI never ruled himself ... that the Duke of Somerset and the Duke of Northumberland ruled for him."

"Yes, I know all that," Cormac said. "Rory, you're an intelligent boy. This is a chance for you to learn many new lessons. Someday, you'll take your place in Ulster with other powerful chieftains."

Cormac draped an arm across Rory's shoulders. "Relationships have been bad between us in the last while, lad. The accident with Shane distressed us all. I regret being hard on you. You're like my son ..."

"Oh! Cormac, it's all right as long as you forgive me. I'm sorry I led Shane into danger."

"I know you are. Embrace me. When you come back, you'll be too tall for me to reach."

On the way back to the castle with Cormac, Rory drank in the sight of the fields, hedges and streams as if for the last time and listened for the faint gurgle of the river Swift as it wound its way out of the forest. His days of skimming stones were over. Shane would never again shout that he was the winner unless, as the physician predicted, his voice returned unexpectedly following a shock. Although the wound on his throat had healed, he was unable to utter a syllable.

"Who will be my friend in England?" Rory asked Cormac. "Hardly anybody in Ulster likes Englishmen." He tried to stop his voice rising. "Their own country must be awful. If it were an agreeable place, Sir Walter Carew would have stayed there and left us alone."

He looked at Cormac expecting a response but he turned his head away without answering.

Feeling alone ... very alone, he opened his mouth and then closed it, overcome. What, after all, was there to say?

Chapter Nine

Sir Walter Carew sat at his desk in English headquarters in Newry. The candle by his side flickered a moment and went out. Putting his hand in the left hand corner of the third drawer on his right without haste, he took out another one and lit it. Its pale light spread itself over the manuscript he was reading. He began to ponder his monarch.

When he was nineteen, Elizabeth had succeeded to the throne, her step-sister Mary Tudor having died childless. Elizabeth was twenty-five, tall, beautiful and spirited. When he first joined in her service, Sir Walter had been doubtful about her ability to rule, he now felt that she was as good as any king.

But reflecting on his queen's prowess would not solve his problem. He took the manuscript in his hand and reread it from the point where Her Majesty had told him that she particularly wished:

Rory Maguire son of Phelim reared far from the barbarous influence of his Irish foster parents where he will taste of the refinements of civility.

He studied the scroll that had been in his possession for several weeks a few moments longer, then rolled it and put it in chronological order with the other dispatches. Sitting upright, both feet firmly on the ground, he reviewed the queen's suggestion that he bring Rory Maguire to live with him in Chalk Hall. As he studied his reply, he decided that he could always change his mind and add a postscript to the political dispatch he had prepared.

Recalling the history of the Maguire family, he felt a wave of disapproval as he considered the Gaelic custom of *naming* a father. It allowed a mother to claim paternity rights for her child until he was fourteen and was still practised by the Irish. He was convinced that women used it as a chance to claim impregnation by noblemen to enrich themselves.

Rory Maguire's father Phelim had been five when his mother Catherine Reilley, a wheelwright's widow, bound him to Con Maguire. Con had acknowledged Phelim as his son, accepting Catherine Reilley's charge. He must have had carnal knowledge of her or else he would have refused to rear the boy Phelim, or accept Rory as his grandson.

Sir Walter had never liked Con Maguire. His behaviour was barbarous, just another reason why the English should force the natives to change their heathenish ways. He felt the same about Con Maguire's younger son Eoin Maguire.

When Con Maguire died, Eoin Maguire had insisted that he was *Tánaiste* instead of Phelim for two reasons. Con Maguire had no right to accept *Surrender and re-grant*. The land belonged to the clan not to him. Under Gaelic law, the clan had elected Eoin Maguire as next in line to be chief.

He reviewed the first argument. Born in 1540, Sir Walter had been two when the Irish chiefs signed *Surrender and re-grant*. His conscience was clear.

The second reason Eoin Maguire had given was that Rory's father was illegitimate, not the true son of Con Maguire. It could well be, but Con Maguire had accepted Phelim as his son. Eoin did not have the right to dispute his father's decision.

Though it was unfortunate that in the ensuing war between the two brothers he had been on the side of the vanquished, he stood by his recommendation that the English remain an ally of Rory's father and that they should send forces to help him. Now, as victor in that civil war and with his wealth of cattle, Eoin Maguire was among the forceful independent chiefs in Ulster that England must defeat.

He had last seen Eoin Maguire at Phelim's wake; he had gone to see the corpse to convince himself that Phelim was really dead. Even now, he felt a stab of pain; the burying of his child is the hardest trial a man can endure.

Phelim's remains had been overboard in a chamber crowded by men and women drinking copious amounts of the *uisce beatha*. He recalled their lewd contortions as they played a game called the *Bull and the Cow*. From what he had seen before averting his eyes, he was sure of the game's pagan origin.

The size of the attendance had surprised him, but he should have understood that the son of Con Maguire would have lots of allies and many enemies. The Irish had a talent for glorifying death at wakes and funerals.

Often he wondered if the reason he had come to Ireland was to make reparation for the sins of his parents. When his father laid the cat o'nine tails on his back as a punishment for wrongdoing, he had borne it stoically, believing him to be a moral man and a committed Protestant. Roman Catholicism had been a dirty word in their household, although this was not acknowledged openly. Henry VIII had, after all, remained Catholic albeit without the pope.

When Henry VIII died, his only son Edward was nine. Sir Walter's father had been delighted that the regents who ruled in his name were both Protestant. He could practise his religion without fear of persecution. When Edward died of tuberculosis at fifteen, his Catholic stepsister Mary succeeded him. His esteemed father, to win royal favour and church property, had changed his religion and was responsible for hundreds of his co-religionists burning at the stake.

As if it had happened yesterday instead of twenty-eight years ago, he remembered his father's reaction when he challenged him about his betrayal.

"How dare you speak to me like that," he had said in his authoritarian tone. "You know Protestant teaching on respect." He had slapped him over the head.

Sir Walter's forty-four-year-old head reeled. He was that sixteen-year-old youth again instead of a titled peer of the realm.

He remembered his father saying, "I will have you sent to Ireland. The barbarians there will cool your ardour." When he had returned, his father had become a Lord and a wealthy landowner. Sir Walter swallowed noisily.

Thinking about the past, he knew, did not solve the problems of the present. Neither would a Maguire in his household. He would write and tell *Her Majesty* that he had changed his mind. That what she suggested was impossible. The responsibility would be too great. It was unfair to ask Anne to receive the boy into Chalk Hall. To ask his children to welcome a native Irish boy into their cultivated world.

Sir Walter rubbed his red-rimmed eyes. Queen Elizabeth disliked when somebody thwarted her plans. He had already informed her of his willingness to serve; it would damage his reputation. Rising, he quenched the candle. His night prayers would include his dilemma. When he knelt, he welcomed the penance of the cold flagstones against his knees.

Early next morning he took a page from the bottom middle drawer of his desk and added an appendix to it. He wrote:

I will refer to my previous dispatch briefly. As Your Majesty's servant, I want to reiterate that it shall please me to give the boy Rory Maguire shelter.

Again, I wish to tell you that I shall take special care of his upbringing. When he returns to Ulster, he will be a loyal Englishman.

Feeling pleased, he signed the missive and applied the seal. He was now ready for his trip to Munster.

Sir Walter was enthused by the expedition to the south to meet with the lord deputy Sir Samuel Fenton. England was on the eve of planting Munster. He looked forward to a chance to correct blunders they had made in the Plantation of Laois and Offaly under Queen Mary.

He knew that eventual success depended not so much on him, or the other officials who carried it out, but on the ability of Munster men to resist a plantation. The English army had destroyed large quantities of cattle and crops in the rebel areas following the Desmond Rebellion. There was widespread famine and the population had been much weakened.

When he rested in Dublin, he talked to his colleagues in The Castle before setting out on the last part of his expedition, riding with his retinue through the pastoral lands of the midlands.

After almost a week on the road, the men were tired. Sir Walter slept badly unaccustomed to the fleas and dirt. As the horses plodded their way over the pathways and bogs, he felt tired of the featureless landscape. The fields were not enclosed with hedges, as in England. Instead makeshift fences of brushwood divided the areas into strips. However, many of them disappeared into home fires in winter.

Beneath the yellow clouds, the bogs were dark and damp. Fog masked the shades of green and added to the monotony. Suddenly, a horse at his rear stumbled, unseating its rider, its hoof getting stuck in the yielding bog land. Sir Walter's expression grew as black as the surrounding forests as he reined in and addressed the soldier on the ground.

"Riding in the Irish countryside is no place for a nap. Due to your carelessness, that horse could have broken his leg. Remount and concentrate."

The quality of fighting men was getting worse. Officials sent the dregs to Ireland. He turned to his lieutenant. "Thank God, we are nearly there."

Sir Samuel Fenton's tents, well erected and containing plentiful room to stand, were visible in the distance. Sir Walter disliked sumptuousness but he felt it was fitting that, even in the wilderness, the lord deputy's quarters mirror the grandeur of Queen Elizabeth whom he represented.

Inside the tent Sir Samuel was patiently listening to the pleas of the Irish lord kneeling before him. He raised a hand to acknowledge Sir Walter's arrival. Sir Samuel Fenton's eyes reminded Sir Walter of the portrait of Henry VIII by Hans Holbein the Younger that hung in the gallery in his London house. Everybody knew that the king had sired Sir Samuel Fenton's father on the dishonourable side of the sheets. It had been the reason for King Henry's special affection for him and the explanation for the peerage now enjoyed by his grandson.

"I've only a paltry amount to bestow as a gift on your lordship," the Irish lord was saying. "Shamefully small for a MacCarthy to give, but with the war and all. If only I could, I'd make it ten thousand to please your worship."

"Yes, yes, yes," Sir Samuel Fenton said, "I'm sure you would." He clicked his fingers, the order to a soldier to relieve him. "See that he leaves all the cattle he possesses." He pulled his ample body off the stool and hitched up his hose, revealing wrinkles of fat. His eyes were flint-like as he addressed Sir Walter. "The natives will re-establish themselves if we delay making this damned plantation." His breathing had quickened from the meagre exertion. "They are beginning to get their confidence back."

"*He* is submissive." Sir Walter nodded towards the lord, still on his knees.

"In appearance only. That is why I agreed with Her Majesty that we require your presence." Sir Samuel rubbed his hands together. "Your task is to oversee the land commission who are mapping for confiscation. Keep Burghley informed, either by letter or direct report, how events progress."

"Within the next month I have to return to England in the Queen's service," Sir Walter replied. He thought of Rory Maguire. "I will do it then. In person."

The next morning Sir Walter woke to the sound of Sir Samuel bellowing from the main tent. He pulled on his hose and rushed out to find the cause of the commotion.

Sir Samuel's complexion was purple.

"King Henry's temper," Sir Walter muttered. Then in a quiet tone he said, "Something wrong?" He hoped his calm would restore the other man's equilibrium. He hated volatile people.

"Vanished, they have all vanished. In the middle of the night MacCarthy stole back the cattle he gave us." Spittle dribbled down Sir Samuel's chin. He stared at Sir Walter. "I'm relying on you to get the information that will tell us how much land we can take from these Gaels."

In spite of his dislike for him, Sir Water found himself agreeing with Sir Samuel Fenton that it was time to cripple these heathens.

Chapter Ten

Dark clouds had gathered and raindrops, big as beads, quickly drenched Rory even as he ran to escape the deluge. He squatted low on his haunches against the *bawn* wall. Around him the cows had gathered too, their backs to the mass of stone attempting to escape the effects of the sudden downpour. There was a smell of cow dung in the air but summer was beginning and the cattle would soon be roaming the hills.

This time when the booley moved to the mountains and the young people composed their yearly ditty on the way, he would be in England. Brian too was gone to visit his cousin MacCarthy in Munster. Tired of hearing about conflict in the south, he had decided to go down there to see for himself.

"Rors. Rory, where are you?" Finola was shouting from the door of the castle.

"Here," he shouted back. "I'm sheltering under the bawn wall."

Rain sparkled on her hair as she raced out and hunched in beside him. Her face was pale. "I was looking inside for you."

"I wanted to be alone. It began to rain, so I took shelter here." He sounded peevish.

The animals stomped and milled around them in the enclosed space. "We'll miss you Rors," Finola said almost in a whisper.

His fear must have shown on his face because she added, "Father will send you somewhere safe." Then fingering her hair, she said slowly, "When you come back you will be older ... and ... and ... I will marry you."

Rory was taken aback by this sudden declaration. He felt his heart jump. At a loss how to answer he said, "Shane will recover his voice. I'll get Glenone back. We'll be as happy as we used to be."

As if to underline the absurdity of his response, a black cow nearby raised her tail and deposited *cac bó* on the ground at his feet.

"She wanted to give you a present before you went," Finola laughed. Her face went serious and she leaned closer to him. "I do, too," she said and kissed him on the mouth.

Feeling the softness of her lips, he went red with pleasure. Finola had kissed him before, but he never remembered feeling like this ... that he wanted to pull her to him and kiss and kiss her ... and do as Shane had lied she had done to him at the booley, feel the silkiness of her mouth with his tongue.

The air around him stank of cow dung and his stomach was growling from hunger, but he had to avail of the opportunity to do what he had planned since he first heard he would be leaving Mulahinsa. He was parting with his most precious possession, but his present seemed a bit childish now in comparison to hers.

Finola stood on tiptoe, her eyes smouldering as she leaned slightly towards him.

"You can have the first bow Cormac made for me and the first arrow I ever shot." He looked anxiously at her for a reaction and felt elated when, smiling, she accepted the weapon from him and was still cradling it as they walked through the rain towards the castle door.

At the fortress in Munster Sir Walter reined in his horse and dismounted, passing the bridle to the groom. He untangled the sack containing his reports and climbed the steps to the stone fortress the English had commandeered after the rebellion.

Though he found it difficult to get used to the bare stones and the absence of tapestries in Irish dwellings, he thanked God that he would not have to endure another night among the trees, where midges crawled up his nostrils and straw stuck to his back. Here he would have spring water to wash himself and at least nothing worse than feathers in his bed. Neither would he have to listen to the ramblings of the Irish lords.

The trestle was partially set for the evening meal in the great hall, but he was disappointed there was as yet no food. He heard somebody call his name and turned. "Sir Walter Carew?" The voice split the silence again. The last of daylight poked through the slits of windows and he barely made out the figure of a man of medium height, in his twenties standing behind him.

"Who are you?" Sir Walter partially closed his eyes. He found this effective when he wished to diminish someone.

"My name is not important," the young man said.

"Perhaps, but I like to know on whom I'm wasting my time."

"Brian O'Hanlon." The man's frown attested to how much he hated petitioning an Englishman. "I've come to plead for my kinsman MacCarthy. Lord Deputy Fenton hounded him from his lands and has determined that he shall die."

"I am unfamiliar with the person to whom you refer. But if Sir Samuel Fenton thinks your kinsman worthy of such treatment, I'm sure he deserves it," Sir Walter answered.

"For reclaiming his own cattle he deserves to be hunted like an outlaw? A man who took no part in the rebellion."

So MacCarthy had been the kneeling man's name, Sir Walter thought. Any man who could make Sir Samuel Fenton dance with anger deserved a medal not a rope. But he said, "It is not within my power to interfere with justice in Munster." He made his voice sound forbidding. "Good evening."

"The blessings of God on you, too," Brian said sarcastically before the servant led him out.

O' Hanlon ... the name of Rory Maguire's foster-father. Chance? He thought not. The way the natives bred they were scattered from tip to toe of the country. Perhaps he would intercede for him after all. A minor chieftain left alive for a while longer would not pose a threat.

Next day, before embarking on his trip northward to claim Rory, he put it to Sir Samuel, "An important member of the Pale gentry asked me to intercede for MacCarthy" he said. "We should not irritate that class needlessly, especially with this parliament imminent."

"Be wary of your petitioner Sir Walter. A rebel no doubt." Sir Samuel Fenton waved an admonishing finger and puffed out his cushioned chest. "We have already hanged the knave. I checked among his enemies and discovered that this MacCarthy was a powerful force behind the natives during the war."

Sir Walter hated to appear a fool. His father had always said he was too credulous. He would remember the scoundrel who had put him in such a humiliating position.

When he had ridden three miles from the Lord Deputy's sight, he stopped. Still sitting on his horse, he reached into his sack and took out some vellum. He placed it against his thigh and in bold letters inscribed the name Brian O'Hanlon.

Clouds raced across the morning sun dimming the castle at Mulahinsa where the O'Hanlon clan had gathered. Already, the day was filled with an oppressive heat that augured a storm. Sir Walter was glad that Cormac O'Hanlon had followed the instructions in his *communiqué* to him and had minimised the nonsense of long goodbyes by having the handing over outdoors. He was too well aware of the Gael's love of drama.

He wiped his face with his handkerchief. This heat made him ill-tempered.

Women, bareheaded and barelegged, winked and nudged each other as they weighed up his soldiers. His white stallion moved skittishly on the dust. A girl ran forward to rescue a speckled hen that had run under its hooves.

A young boy said, "Is this the gentleman come to take master Rory to England?" And a woman playfully replied, "'Tis surely, Murrough O'Toole, and 'twill be with him you'll be going if you don't do what you're told."

These people were so dim-witted, Sir Walter thought. They knew only rough paths, were at home in the forests and had never seen anything larger than a castle. If they avoided famine, raised enough oats, and had enough to drink, they were happy. Chieftains, bishops, and a queen held their fates in their hands yet they were content. He felt sure they had no notion of the duty to civilise that motivated him. His grip tightened on the reins. Sometimes he wondered whether God had placed too much of a burden on Englishmen.

Dismounting, he threw the reins to his groom and signalled to the mounted soldiers at his rear to remain on their horses. Then he walked through the crowd of onlookers towards a man, who, from the deliberation of his stance, he presumed to be Cormac O'Hanlon. As he looked at the boy standing by Cormac's side, he said, "This is my ward?"

"Yes, this is Rory Maguire." Cormac nodded.

As Sir Walter rested his hand on Rory's shoulder, he felt a faint tinge of excitement, which he quickly stifled. "Is the boy ready?" he asked.

Cormac was equally abrupt. "As prepared as we can make him," he said.

Sir Walter gestured to a soldier who dismounted and heaved Rory's heavily corded chest onto a packhorse.

A groom led a pony, chestnut brown like his own but yet not his, to where Rory stood. He felt like running into the *bawn* and hiding among the cows, but he knew he must be brave. Cormac bent and lifted him off his feet, holding him briefly. Maeve took his hand and squeezed it. Finola, brandishing his bow and an arrow, could manage only a weak smile.

Already he had bidden good-bye to Shane lying on his pallet, but now to his surprise he was standing at the door looking out weakly. His eyes were clouded; his skin was the colour of whey; his bony arms hung by his sides, a parody of their former plumpness. But he mustn't think about Shane now. He needed to harness his courage and leave with dignity.

He had been taken from his home once before to be fostered by Cormac and had survived, had grown to love his foster family deeply. Cormac expected him to be brave so, though he felt like crying out, he dutifully complied when Sir Walter gestured to him to mount. But before he threw his leg over the pony, he unbuckled the stirrups and removed them. "Gaels don't use these," he said with vehemence and flung them to the ground.

Sir Walter remained silent throughout and for that Rory was grateful. He would have found it hard to bear if he had tried to camouflage what this was, a man fulfilling orders from his queen to take him into his household to, he remembered the words Cormac had used, *proselytise and anglicise* him.

Rory felt the reins damp in his hands as, following behind Sir Walter, he coaxed his horse into a canter. When he reached the brow of the hill, he stopped a moment and strained to look back, the glaring sun dazzling his eyes.

Sir Walter continued to look ahead. His retinue concentrated on guiding their horses over the marshy ground.

As they passed the wood beside the river Swift, the horses behind Rory whinnied. His memories of skimming stones and *dearóg* fishing in this place had been tainted by Shane's tragedy. The trees beside the river appeared dark and threatening to him now.

He silently bade goodbye to the mills, where *na síoga* came to grind their corn, and to the stones where the little people rested before they carried their grain sacks away on their backs. He used to sit with Matthew by the trickle of water that rose here through the fern and heather from the *síog* spring, spilled onto the stones, and disappeared.

When he passed the forest near Glenone, he thought of the tree carving of F & R. His initials stood beside Finola's. They would be there when he came back.

As he rode further into his uncle Eoin's domain, he imagined he heard Matthew and his father talk to him. They told him that he must return here and reclaim this land. Their blood, Rory's blood, not the blood of an uncle or cousin must run in the veins of the chieftain of Glenone.

Sometime before they reached Dundalk they passed by a stone built castle with its surrounding cluster of huts. Farmers were ploughing in the infields. These were the first people he had seen since leaving Mulahinsa. Before that he had been surrounded only by mountains, lakes and bogs.

This was what Sir Walter must have meant when he had said to his father that Ireland was to him 'one unexplored fastness after another'. He remembered the exact words because he had asked his father what they meant. "Sir Walter misses the reassuring landmarks of England," his father had answered. Sir Walter had expounded a lot on Ireland. Another phrase Rory remembered him using, because he had voiced it so often, was 'Godforsaken wilderness.'

For most of the way he rode alongside Sir Walter. Sometimes, they changed to single file to manoeuvre the mountain passes but now on a wider path they were together again. He examined the silent man beside him; he was tall in stature, without an inch of surplus weight. Not rugged exactly but solid. His slate grey hair was cropped closely, his beard neatly clipped. His cloak draped about him in flawless folds. When he told his men to dismount at a ravine to water the horses, his voice was soft but stern. Everything about Sir Walter Carew was stern and all seeing. His penetrating eyes measured and understood. All-seeing, Rory thought. Like God.

Sir Walter had remained silent during the journey and Rory felt grateful for that; it would have been difficult to respond without showing his animosity. He had disliked Sir Walter when he had first met him in his father's house. He disliked him now.

PART II

1584-1592

In time the savage bull sustains the yoke,
In time all haggard hawks will stoop to lure,
In time small wedges cleave the hardest oak,
In time the flint is pierced with softest shower.

-Thomas Kyd, 1558-1594.

Chapter One

It was early evening. The air held a refreshing tang. The stickiness had gone out of the day and a soft drizzle had begun to fall. The journey by horseback from Mulahinsa to Dundalk was over and they had reached the coast. Though Rory was leaving Ulster to sail for England and had many misgivings about his enforced departure, he found his interest in these new surroundings quicken.

Sir Walter Carew wore a sombre expression as he swept aboard the caravel that would bring them across the Irish Sea. "Take this chest and put it in the hold. That sack, too. Be careful," he ordered a sailor.

Soon they were under sail and the coastline of Ireland was vanishing into the mist. Rory felt the gentle swaying of the ship begin to soothe his body and mind. When he looked into the water, he fancied that if he had a long stick, he could make waves all the way to England. As he looked at the mountains receding into the distance, he thought of Mulahinsa and of Finola and wondered what she would be doing at this moment.

Sir Walter walked to his side. "Hold on to the ropes Rory," he told him. "It is starting to get rough." As if to confirm his words, a gust tore at the lateen and sea gulls squawked and pivoted above the water. There was no need for a stick to make breakers anymore. The up and down motion churned Rory's insides. The white froth on the tops of the waves reminded him of Brigid whipping milk in Mulahinsa.

A sailor swayed in the wind near them as he adjusted the riggings.

"If they don't hold, we're in trouble." Sir Walter's words were more to himself than to Rory. He looked questioningly towards his ward. "We'd better go below. I have arranged a hammock for you on the berth deck. Your name will be on it."

When Rory failed to respond, he said, "I hope I am correct in assuming you are able to read. If there is any difficulty, mention my name. My cabin is at the rear, level with the gun deck. The berth deck, where you will sleep, is one down."

When they reached the gun deck together, Sir Walter suddenly put his hand to his mouth and bolted towards his cabin.

Rory was alone now. For a moment he experienced a feeling

of acute loneliness, an ache deep inside. Reluctant to go to his cabin just yet, he retraced his steps back up on deck. The wind whipped against his face. The whiff of salt air was so much better than the fetid air below, but his head still felt muzzy. The feeling of loneliness returned. His future yawned in front of him, empty. He saw black spots before his eyes. A vision of Finola came to him. She was clinging to the rigging, her cloak blowing about, her black hair streaming down her back, confronting the wind and laughing as it tore through her. Her recklessness found an answering response in him. His arms reached for her and lifted her as if she were thistledown. She soared in his arms and where the music in his head began, hers continued. They danced under the spray and frolicked on the heaving ship together. He looked at her upturned face in the circle of his arms, "My sea sprite. My síog," he cried.

But then the vision died and he heard again the creaking of the ship as it heaved its way through the rough seas. There was no Finola. The deck was empty. He felt he was going mad. It was dangerous to be up here.

As he made his way below, he met a sailor. "Glory be to God, his lordship is as sick as his soldiers." He pulled at his nose. "I didn't know people like him could vomit." Rory, still shaken from his hallucination, remained silent.

The berth deck air smelt of sweat and dirty apparel. Soldiers lay on hammocks, some still open-eyed. Two others were hunched over a vessel eating slowly. Rory found an empty hammock with a scrawled message clipped to it. As he tried to make out the words, the boat tilted and he was thrown onto the canvas. Pulling himself up, he tried again and read in Sir Walter's neat handwriting, *Rory Maguire (Carew.)*. He lay down.

When the wind waned, the ship's tossing steadied. The swinging lanterns overhead stilled. Rory recalled his delusion; he had been so convinced that Finola was real. He looked at his spray sodden tunic and trousers; he could still feel her breath on his face. *Imaginative people create their own hell when they conjure misfortunes*, Niall once had said to him. They could make their own heaven, too, he thought. He would take Finola with him. His resolve strengthened; his tension eased and his loneliness lessened. He would survive Sir Walter Carew's house and return to Mulahinsa.

Suddenly he remembered that Sir Walter was ill. He knew what would help. He put his hand under his tunic and felt for the bag Maeve had sewed for him from left over frieze. Cormac had persuaded her to make it and she had designed it solely to transport what Rory now extricated from it. With this, he could help Sir Walter.

Because his hammock was rank with disgorged food, Sir Walter was now lying on the bare boards of the cabin floor. His face was ashen and his head throbbed. There was nothing left in his stomach to make him sick. He drifted in and out of sleep. The folded mantle under his head felt comfortable. He wondered who had put it there.

When he opened his eyes, he was surprised to see Rory, on his knees beside him, dipping a cloth into a vessel. Squeezing the excess water from it, he leaned over him and wiped his face. Sir Walter disliked being in this position. He was Sir Walter Carew and Rory was his charge.

"Would you like a drink?" Rory asked.

Despite his humiliation, he felt too thirsty to refuse. He sat up slightly as Rory held a flask to his lips. Feeling the strange liquid touch his tongue, he spluttered. "That is not water. That is ...that is...alcohol."

"Uisce beatha," said Rory. "Cormac said that, in his humble opinion, there is no medicine to beat it. Even if it fails to work you'll feel better."

"Leave and take your cures with you." Sir Walter tried to shout. "I managed before you came to help. I can manage now." He tried to sit up but felt too weak.

Rory put his arm around him. "That's it, I'm feared if you refuse to take another sup."

The boy's confidence and refusal to be intimidated surprised Sir Walter. His own children, back in England, were not so competent.

"I'll be back," Rory said and left the cabin.

He went down the stairway to the berth deck and made his way to the galley.

The cook, a scrawny man, was sitting bent over a sandbox where a fire blazed under a large cauldron.

"You look as if you could eat something," he said when he

spotted Rory. He stirred the contents of the cauldron with a big spoon and was about to ladle out some pottage.

Rory took a few mouthfuls. "I prefer milk," he said.

"Well, well, a foin little Irishman we have." Cook appraised him. "I have some, but it has gone sour."

"Can I bring a drop with me?" Rory asked.

He walked back to Sir Walter's cabin careful not to spill any. "I brought you ballyclabber," he said, "as you won't touch the *aqua vitae.*" He held out the goblet. Sir Walter's nose twitched at the vile smell. "You expect me to drink that. I hate your Irish milk and I don't want any more of your remedies. Understood? Now leave me."

As Rory retreated, Sir Walter felt his stomach dry retch again. He felt ashamed, an emotion he had been unfamiliar with for a long time. And that past shame, he recalled, had also involved a Maguire.

After two days of nothing but the span of the sea on all sides, the coast of England appeared on the horizon. Slowly it grew to a landmass with cliffs and bays. The crew and the soldiers began to busy themselves with carrying goods from the hold. Rory was the only one who had hastened up on deck to look at Bristol's port. He was relieved that he would have land beneath his feet again. As the ship pulled into the quay, he told himself there was too much to see to waste time being fearful of the future. That no matter what happened he would live through it.

Caravels lay anchored in the harbour with their cargoes of Mediterranean wine and Turkish spices. As Rory watched the exotic sailors, he thought how differently they looked to the one-eyed pirates with cutlasses and wicked smiles in Cormac's stories.

But he became more interested in a group of men standing among the chaos of the dockside. They were dressed in trunk hose and long-waisted doublets under short capes topped by a muslin ruff and on their heads wore tall feathered hats. One of them waved in his direction.

Suddenly Sir Walter was at his side. "Come with me. We are disembarking." He beckoned imperiously to the deck hand staggering under Rory's trunk and they went down the gangplank. When they reached the bottom, the workers he had watched from deck, recognising the livery of the queen, left down their crates and stood to one side. The man who had waved to them approached. Rory noticed his shoes, each adorned with a large rose. He bowed to Sir Walter. Though his voice was low, Rory heard him repeat the words Her Majesty several times.

Now that the time had come and he was going to Sir Walter's mansion at Margate, he felt frightened again. He missed home. The final parting had been silent; Sir Walter's disposition had affected everyone and rendered them as speechless as Shane. If Sir Walter had that kind of power over Cormac, as well as his soldiers, what power would he exert over him?

His surroundings were stranger now than when he had gazed at them from the deck. A babble of curious accents and languages floated around him. Anticipating a long walk to Margate, he was surprised when the driver of a four-wheeled carriage climbed down, opened the door and, grabbing him under the arms, deposited him on a plush seat. He then sat in beside him. Rory found his presence oddly comforting.

When Sir Walter appeared, the man got out, tipping his hat. "Took a liberty I know Sir, but I thought the little tyke looked a bit lost."

"Quite." Sir Walter sat into the carriage. Prior to closing the door, he said, "Spence."

"Yessir."

"I hope you do the job I hired you to do as effectively."

"Yessir."

Rory heard the noise of the wheels on the cobbled streets and with a sudden movement that threw him to the other side of the seat, they were on their way.

They journeyed through parts of Gloucester and all of Wiltshire on the first day. Soldiers changed the horses every thirty miles. Sir Walter only spoke to impart information.

They stopped for the first night at an inn where Rory was fed on roast duck and slept on a bed in a small chamber. The next morning after a breakfast of an unfamiliar fish, which he left uneaten, they were back on the road. They travelled all that day through Berkshire and Surrey.

Despite his determination to take in all of the countryside and to be able to relate everything in his first letter to Finola, he felt his eyes close. At intervals Sir Walter woke him, and he had to leave the carriage so the horses could be changed. After they had spent the night at their second inn, he felt less tired. They would be starting what Sir Walter had told him at supper, was to be their last day's journey. "We will start early in the morning. We should be at Chalk Hall by evening," he said before retiring.

The following day they crossed the border into Kent and Rory began to feel better, more refreshed and able to take more interest in his surroundings.

The rest had agreed with Sir Walter too. His manner had lost its earlier irritation. Perhaps he had been feeling the effects of his seasickness. He talked to Rory about the countryside.

"As you see Rory, unlike Ireland, trees are thin on the ground here. This is because the forests of the Weald have provided iron furnaces with charcoal for thousands of years." Sir Walter pointed to a plant with green, cone like flowers clinging in clusters to sticks placed in the ground. "Those are hops," he said. "The bigger flowers are the females. Ale, Kent's latest agricultural industry is made from them." Sir Walter's tone sounded disapproving. "The poles are needed for support while it climbs. Charcoal is burned in the oast houses. Timber is required for both. That, together with the swell in the demand for iron, has caused the disappearance of our bowers."

Then, almost in mid sentence, Sir Walter stopped talking and fell asleep.

Rory continued to look from the carriage window at the surrounding countryside. Occasionally they passed through villages with paved streets, a new sight for him. The buildings were grouped neatly around a patch of grass in the shape of a diamond. Unlike Mulahinsa where the tenants built their huts at random round the castle.

Sir Walter stirred suddenly and looked out the window as if he had been waiting for this exact point. He ordered the driver to stop the coach. "Ride ahead and tell Lady Carew of our arrival," he ordered a horseman. Then they travelled on in silence until the coach wheels rattled noisily over a cobbled courtyard and pulled up in front of a redbrick mansion. Sir Walter began to expound again.

"This house is built in the shape of the letter H," he told Rory. "My father commissioned it during the reign of Henry VIII. The houses that are built now are in the shape of an E for Queen Elizabeth."

It was indeed different to Cormac's castle built for defence not luxury, where Rory had spent most of his life. This house had matching windows and wings and, as Niall would have said, a symmetrical appearance. The structure standing upright on the roof was, he presumed, a chimney. "It's nice-looking," he said trying to conceal his real awe from Sir Walter.

"This house is plain, Sir Walter said. "My father worked closely with the master mason and stifled suggestions of weather vanes or heraldic beasts or any other such frippery."

As they alighted from the carriage, a figure came out of the house and walked to meet them. It had to be Anne, Sir Walter's wife. Rory studied the ground.

"You're back." She kissed her husband warmly and put her arms loosely around his waist. "Welcome."

Sir Walter proffered his cheek to receive the contact and released her quickly.

Rory liked her lively and interesting voice. Her hand on his shoulder felt soft and firm. Without giving any inclination that she had just now discovered his existence, Anne tilted his face. "You must feel tired," she said huskily.

Forced to look at her, Rory's first thought was that she was younger than Sir Walter and not as beautiful as Maeve or Finola.

He felt himself stiffen as she moved her hand to the small of his back and pulled him to her. She smelled of roses. Feeling the silk of her gown on his cheek, he relaxed somewhat.

"We will look after you," she whispered. "You'll be my second son."

That night he found the canvas mesh underneath him uncomfortable; he missed his pallet. Fatigue had made him listless in the inns where he had stayed during the journey, so he had been unaware of the bedding. It was as if he were experiencing everything for the first time.

Sniffing the clean air, he yearned for the smell of wax from the Mulahinsa candles. There was no need to wrap himself in his mantle here; the warm chamber was draught free. A tapestry depicting the royal arms divided his room from a servant's. The E R for *Elizabeth Regina* suddenly reminded him of Lizzie, the cat, back home and of Finola. He felt upset, but he stopped himself from crying. Hunching his shoulders, he made a fist and pressed it to his lips; tears were for broken arrows, stomach aches and childhood … things past.

"Are you awake?"

Rory made out the figure of a boy standing near his bed.

"Don't be afraid. It's only me. George … George Carew." He came and sat on the bed.

"I thought you'd be lonely and might like some company; I wasn't sure whether I should come or not."

Rory sat up in bed adjusting his eyes to the blackness. Two anxious orbs peered back at him. George was fumbling with a robe the like of which Rory had never seen. When he noticed Rory's glances he said, "My mother made it for me. It keeps me warm when I go to the water closet." He rubbed the velvet with the back of his hand. "You can feel it if you want. It's very soft."

Going into ecstasies over a long piece of material that made him look like a girl was asinine, but Rory reckoned he'd have to get used to it. This was England. He put his palm on the pile and took it away again quickly.

"Isn't it lovely?" George dangled his thin legs over the side of the bed.

How did they hold him up? Rory thought. He would beat him easily if they ever got into a fight.

"You will be joining us in the classroom tomorrow."

"I thought I'd be going outside to learn." Rory felt suddenly downcast. He'd been hoping to leave Chalk Hall every day.

"No. A resident tutor teaches us at home. I went to school for a short while but father said it was not strong enough in its religious teaching."

"Oh!"

"A man who is waiting for a call to the ministry and has not yet got a stipend teaches us."

"Will it be only you and me or will your sister be there too?" Rory asked.

"She will. Father wants her well versed in the doctrines of John Calvin. What she picks up besides is not important. Although I think, in her case, James was wrong."

"Who's James?" Rory asked.

"King James VI of Scotland." George's tone raised a decibel. "If Queen Elizabeth dies without children, he could become King

James I of England. He said, *making women learned and foxes tame has the same effect. It makes them more cunning.*" He hesitated. "At least that's what I think he said." He fiddled with the cord of his robe. "Rory, teacher will dislike anybody who is neither Calvinist nor English. Be sure you are present before class begins."

Rory wished he'd leave so that he could sleep.

A long silence developed before George spoke again. He sounded tentative. "Teacher is supposed to start lessons an hour after breakfast, but he sometimes starts earlier. I think he might do that tomorrow."

Oblivious to the warning, Rory had begun to snore.

Chapter Two

Once a week, just before going to bed, Sir Walter went to the chapel to examine his conscience and to pray. He knelt in his pew in front of the altar table and savoured the quietness of his simple surroundings. The dry wood creaked as he knelt. He noted absently that the *Book of Common Prayer* near him looked largely unused by its owner. The chaplain, Sir Walter shared with three surrounding estates, would be displeased if he knew.

He put his head in his hands, his mind troubled and wondered if he was becoming more like his father, if he was compromising his beliefs for political expediency. Would he persecute his co-religionists if asked to by Her Majesty?

As he lifted his head, he raised his eyes upwards. Queen Elizabeth would never accept *The Ecclesiastical Ordinances* as the primary law of the state or *The Institutes of the Christian Religion* as the primary law of the church. How simple it would be if she did, how happy it would make him.

Although her array of handsome puppets amused her, Queen Elizabeth refused to share power with any man. She dallied with Sir Henry Sidney, Sir Walter Raleigh, Richard Deveraux and countless others but always at a safe distance. When one of them tried to become her husband, Her Majesty no longer favoured him. Neither would she allow a pack of zealots dictate to her.

He knew that he should be more careful in his intercourse with those who attacked the church or the bishops. Elizabeth decided who got important church positions. Critics of her appointees indirectly attacked her; support for them would not help him remain close to the queen.

Malcontents everywhere had adopted Calvin's belief that if the state *overrode private conscience*, it was moral to rebel against it. Sir Walter thought of the Netherlands where, under William of Orange, Calvinists had rebelled against Philip II of Spain, a Catholic. The Huguenots in France were fighting a civil war against the Catholic house of Valois. Presbyterians had rebelled against Mary Queen of Scots, a Catholic. He was not surprised that the queen was sensitive to the wealth of emotions stirred by religious beliefs. In England the people still referred to her half sister as *Bloody Mary* because of the Protestants she had put to death.

Papists still believed that because Queen Elizabeth's father divorced Mary's mother to marry hers, it was not a real marriage. By their reckoning, Queen Elizabeth was illegitimate with no right to the throne. Anglicanism, Catholic in its ceremonies, Protestant in its doctrine, was an effort to appease both sides. If people in England and Ireland were loyal to her, his queen was indifferent to which way, if any, they worshipped.

He agreed with the queen when she deemed any kind of religious persecution foolhardy. If the Irish wanted to be true to the pope, let them damn themselves; he would not start a rebellion over it but Chalk Hall was not Ireland. Here he could live up to the missionary faith he professed. Rory Maguire was in his charge, and he was a Catholic. The English would support him against his uncle Eoin and set him up as an English baron under their direction. It was only right, then, that Rory should enforce the true religion. Example was the better teacher. Sir Walter disapproved of force.

His conscience mollified, he decided to discuss it with Duncan Erskine early the next morning. He would leave it in his hands.

Before he rose from his knees, he contemplated the former classmate of John Knox employed in his schoolroom. Duncan Erskine had come back from Geneva brandishing a severe brand of Calvinism. Sir Walter still found it difficult to believe that a tailor's son from Shropshire had returned as a respected teacher. He hesitated, he remembered, before he had accepted him as a tutor. In the end, he had chosen him because of his intelligence and because discreet Calvinists were hard to find.

It was not for the comeliness of his person he had employed him, Sir Walter thought, as a picture of a pallid complexion, topped by a clump of black hair swelling from a round head, rose before him. Duncan's large nose and big stomach added to his rough appearance. There, any resemblance to a buffoon ended. Duncan Erskine had transcended his humble origins.

Reminding himself to talk to Duncan Erskine about Rory, he rose, stiff kneed, from his humble posture.

On his first morning at Chalk Hall Rory left the dining hall after breakfast, wiping his mouth hurriedly. Earlier in his room he had grabbed a quill and scribbled a communication to Cormac informing him of his safe arrival. Time was too short to tell Finola about his journey; his note to her simply read: *I wish I could go home.*

Now he handed the missive to Sir Walter, saying. "Must go Sir. I want to be in the schoolroom on time."

However, when he arrived, George and a younger girl, he supposed was Jane, were already scratching away with their quills. A faint smell of ink tinged the air. Wondering why they had they started so soon, he squeezed his lanky body into a small desk.

"Maguire you are late," Duncan Erskine said in a careful aristocratic tone, which, despite his best efforts, held traces of his lowly Shropshire origin. "Your first day and you come late."

"I thought I was early." Rory felt genuinely surprised. "I went as fast as I could. I had to write to Cormac to tell him we had arrived. And then I included a word for Finola. Otherwise she'd say I'd forgotten her already."

"Cormac. Finola? Irish, no doubt."

"I lived with them at Mulahinsa."

"The people with whom you lived before you came here are not of interest to me. You are late. That is my concern. Nothing else." The tutor paused. "What have you to say?"

"Nothing."

Duncan Erskine's expression suffused in a dark glow and his lips closed tighter as he discerned Rory's assured air.

Rory felt the venom behind his gaze but failed to understand it. He knew that the tutor expected him to do something, but he was at a loss as to what.

The tutor clasped and unclasped his hands several times. In a loud voice he said, "You will kneel by your desk until the lesson is over."

Rory thought he had misheard, that the strangeness of Duncan Erskine's pronunciation had caused him to mistake what he had said. He stayed sitting. If he remained still, he'd leave him alone. Jane raised her head and looked curiously at him.

The tutor licked his lips and approached Rory's desk. Rory felt his breath on his hair. The tutor's eyes sparkled as, with an eager hand, he pulled hard on the short hairs above Rory's ear.

His eyes filled with tears; he could hardly breathe with the pain. Finola used to pull his hair but that was a twinge compared to this. He noticed a birch sticking out of the tutor's pocket.

"I will respect your ignorance and repeat another time, kneel by your desk until the lesson is over," Duncan Erskine said flatly.

As the heir of an Irish chieftain, there was no reason for him to be afraid. He had fled after Matthew's burial and again in fear of the grey merchant. No more. He recalled Brian's lesson on the English strategy of *Divide and Conquer;* he too needed a tactic. He would acquiesce outwardly to any orders he received while inside retaining his independent spirit.

Tentatively he put one foot out on the floor.

Duncan Erskine ground the heel of his boot onto Rory's sandal clad instep. His toes curling in pain, he gripped the desk. Blows from the birch rained on his knuckles. He knelt.

The thin material of his English hose barely protected his knees from the bare floorboards. Jane's gaze was now sympathetic. Rory twisted in mortification and pain. He was only beginning to feel the full effects of the birching. Yellow-black bruises appeared across the back of his hand and the ends of his fingers; he wondered if there were any bones broken.

Duncan Erskine moved away from him and swaggered towards Jane.

Rory studied him from behind. He wondered what he had done wrong and what it was this man wanted. But what ever it was he resolved there and then that he would learn all he could from Duncan Erskine and his ilk and then use the knowledge for his own advancement. This tormenter was going to like him. He was going to learn all he could with the least trouble.

When he realised that the bastard required an apology, he lowered his eyes and put up his hand. After what seemed like two minutes he was about to lower it when Duncan Erskine addressed him from the podium. "Yes?"

"I'm sorry I was late."

Duncan Erskine licked his lips with his pink tongue and gave a triumphant smile.

Swallowing his anger, Rory smiled back.

Duncan Erskine said, "You may return to your desk."

"Thank you Sir. I'm very sorry, Sir." How like a court jester he is. Rory's thoughts were mutinous. As he sat, he gripped the table. His foot hurt. His knuckles hurt. But through it all he managed to give Duncan Erskine another meek smile.

Lessons were over. The Carew family, minus Sir Walter, were eating their dinner in the oblong dining chamber. Anne sat at the top of the table, Rory and George opposite each other, and Jane beside her brother.

George announced that he intended to spend the time between noon and evening in his garden. "You can come if you want," he said to Rory, his mouth full of bread.

"Finish that wastrel," Anne said. "If your father saw you talking with your mouth full, you know what would happen."

George's eyes were sad. "He will not be able to see me from half-way to London."

"Watch your manners young man." Anne's kind tone belied her words.

Rory's sandals were the only mark of Irish apparel he still wore. He shifted his foot under the table. His instep ached where the heel of Duncan Erskine's boot had split the flesh. He contemplated the piece of jellied loaf on his platter; it smelled of pork, but it could as easily be veal.

As if reading his thoughts Anne left down her knife and said, "It's brawn Rory. You may be unfamiliar with it. It's an English dish. Cook made it today from a pig's head. Next week it might be a calf's."

Rory appreciated her explanation. He liked pork well enough. He sliced off a piece. It was halfway to his mouth when Anne interrupted. "What happened to your hand? It looks as if someone danced on it."

He expected Duncan Erskine to arrive for dinner any minute. If he told her, he'd get into more trouble.

George's expression was uncertain.

Jane seemed anxious, but her freckled face looked determined. She finished chewing. "Mamma," she looked at Anne; her voice came in bursts, "Duncan Erskine hit Rory with the birch, pulled his sidelocks and stepped on his foot."

Rory felt Anne's furious gaze upon him. "Is this true?"

What would he do? Tell the truth or lie.

Again, as if reading his thoughts, Anne explained. "Duncan

Erskine does not join the family at meal times. At his request, our maid brings a tray to his room. Otherwise he eats with the other servants." Her voice was gentle. "Is what Jane says true?"

Still humiliated, he longed to shout abuse at the bully they had in their school room, to scream at Anne that he hated being here with English people about whom he had heard only bad tales all his life, that he preferred ordinary pork to the mess on his platter.

But as quickly as his anger had arisen it dissipated. Feeling Anne's compassion he was tempted to throw himself into her arms, to cry deep heaving sobs into her shoulder. He wanted to tell her ...

He thought of his resolution earlier that morning. So instead he wrapped his injured fingers around his knife, and ignoring his throbbing head, said, "I was late. I should have been early." He chose his words carefully. "The lesson on punctuality was worth learning."

Jane just looked at him and shrugged. George appeared relieved. Anne, however, was sceptical. She paused a moment. Then, she pushed back her chair and rose. Her foot- steps were noiseless on the carpet as she went around to his side of the table.

She leant over the back of his chair and kissed the top of his head.

A warm feeling ran through him. A smell of roses engulfed him.

She held his hand. "There will be no cruelty under my roof." She returned to her chair. "Finish and, if you want to, you may go to the garden with George." She tapped Jane on the sleeve. "We have top stitching to do."

As he picked at his food, Rory felt mixed emotions.

George looked imploringly at him, begging him to hurry. Jane was already finished and about to leave the table. Then Anne rose and they trooped out. Rory followed George along the winding paths to the garden.

"I hope you do not expect too much of Chalk Hall, Rory," George said over his shoulder. "We have no deer parks. We do not even have a greyhound or a spaniel."

So everything in England was less than grandiose after all, Rory thought.

"My father uses a neighbour's when there is a royal visit. Queen Elizabeth is fond of hunting. She enjoys visiting her subjects."

Like in Ireland. It was the same idea as 'cuid oidhche.' The queen's lords fed and entertained her *gratis* and saved her expense. The *uirrithe* did the same for Cormac.

Despite George's warning, Rory still felt disappointed when he saw his garden.

"I am so lucky to have this square of ground," George said sensing his reaction. "I had to fight to get it, and I had to agree to have it surrounded by a wall. My father does not like display." His voice trembled.

Although the plot was small Rory had to acknowledge that George took good care of it.

"I sowed flowering plants beside the wall. When they were fully grown, I draped the blossoms over the bricks and changed a dull wall into a pink and white ornament. My dearest wish is to install a fountain or even a sundial but my father thinks it's a silly idea." George stabbed his trowel into the clay.

Rory had never heard anybody speak so passionately about a profusion of primroses, violets and gillyflowers. He half-heartedly offered to help.

"With your wounds?" George said. "You are like a soldier home from battle."

The air around them was heavy with the mingled scents of flowers. Rory positioned himself in the shade of an overhanging branch and lay on the ground. The only sound now was the digging of George's trowel in the flower beds. The grass felt cool against his head. Memories of the morning began to fade.

When he woke, George had put his tunic over him. "I thought you would get cold lying there," he said.

Next morning a servant moved a bigger desk into the schoolroom for Rory. "Orders from her ladyship," he said.

After lessons Rory asked George, "Do you know anything about my change of desk?"

"My mother thought your other one too small." He gave a little laugh. "You will be able to escape from Duncan Erskine if he tries to hit you again."

Rory began to feel close to Sir Walter's son; they were both outsiders, George in his family, Rory in a strange country.

Chapter Three

Ireland

Finola had felt the first of many changes since Shane's accident three years previously. Brian's sojourn in Munster, Rory's departure for England, Molly's entry into the household had all caused upheaval. On this October morning at the beginning of 1586, the quietness of Mulahinsa threatened to choke her.

She was sitting at a stout rectangular table, square cloths adorned by fancy stitching in a heap beside her. "I don't see why we need more of these." She held up a half finished piece between finger and thumb.

"They are a great protection for the furniture from yellow stains. It's easier to wash material than to scrub wood. Prevention is better than cure."Her mother raised her head from her own sewing, her expression disapproving. "You need to practise. You'll never get a husband with the kind of work you do."

Finola bit her lip. She didn't want a husband. What she had seen of her mother and father's relationship had failed to enhance her view of matrimony. People only married to cement alliances. That was why her mother discouraged her relationship with Rory. He had his uncle Eoin to deal with first before he succeeded to Glenone. However, when it came to romance, her father believed more in the fates.

Leaving her stitching aside, she rose from the stool, placed her hand on her mother's shoulder and left the room. She knew that if she looked back, Maeve would be sitting statue-like with her needle poised.

As she walked down the narrow steps to the bottom storey, her leather sandals rubbed against the stone, the sound charmingly melodic in the stillness. There was a musty smell in the storeroom. It was time for a cleaning and a dumping. More work for the already overworked servants. She felt useless and in need of air.

Emerging into the day, she walked the short distance to the hall. It was not yet time for the mid-day meal and an aura of waiting hung over the place. Grabbing her mantle she left the castle. The earth was soft from rain. Although there were no drops, she could feel the moist air on her skin. A lone jackdaw croaked from the wall of the bawn.

She descended the incline from the castle and passed by the dark houses of the tenants. Smoke curled through holes in the roof or through open doors. It must be hard for the tenants to keep themselves clean. She realised that she had never been in one of these houses.

Rory and Matthew had been allowed to play with Murrough O'Toole, but not her. Her family boasted of their love for the tenants. Cormac cited his willingness to allow his family to go to the booley with them. Yes, they sang with the churls on the way, but when they had set up their shelters there, they were as separate from them as at Mulahinsa.

Tenants were the workhorses at the bottom of society with Queen Elizabeth at the pinnacle. Then came the nobility in all its tiers. Her father would fit into the class of a lesser nobleman, Eochy O'More and two others being his only *uirrithe*. Eoin Maguire had Cormac and scores of others as *uirrithe* so he was a potent chieftain. Swordsmen, horsemen, *Gallóglaigh* and kerne, the lightly armed infantry, would be next.

But it was the poor Finola pitied, tenants, churls, cow keepers, horse-boys. There were two enemies in Gaelic Ireland, she thought ruefully, the English and themselves. One attacked from the outside, greed and snobbery from within.

She reached the hut that Rory played in with Murrough O'Toole as a small child. Grace, his grandmother lived here; she used to like her when she was younger. Breaking with the tenet imposed on her as a child, she decided to visit her.

When she stepped inside, she saw through swirling smoke that the place was divided in two. At one end hens scratched on the earthen floor. A pig lay quietly in a corner. At the other side of the room was a smoky fire with a bed on either side. Now she understood why the poor smelled so.

Kate, a cooking pot in her hand, stopped suddenly when Finola entered. No more than thirty-seven years old, work, hunger and pregnancies had aged her too soon. Like most peasants she was unable to read or write. Her only interests were her hut, her man, son and daughter, her grandparents and the settlement. Although Finola knew that her visit was unexpected, unwanted and untimely, it was plain from Kate's expression that it would never occur to her to refuse her entry.

Aoife, Kate's daughter, was busy washing platters in a tub and chatting animatedly to Kate.

"Whist girl," said Kate. "Don't ya know 'tis company we have."

Finola felt mortified as both women stared at her.

Kate removed a heap of eggs from atop a wooden box. "Won't you sit yourself?" As her movements floundered, two eggs slipped through her fingers and broke in a yellow mess on the mud.

"I'll leave. I should never have come," said Finola hurriedly.

"Sure 'tis as welcome as Sunday you'd be if I didn't have to feed my lot. 'Tis in from the fields they'll be in a few minutes," Kate said. She looked at the broken eggs on the ground, "'Twas about to cook them we were." She rubbed her hands on the skimpy material clothing her. Started on our patcheen did our men this morning. Soon as 'twas light. 'Tis fierce hungry they'll be."

Finola felt two inches high. She had come here to satisfy a whim. Their meal had been spoiled because of it. "I came to speak to Grace." Her voice was lame.

Aoife turned, her eyes glinting. "'Tis dead Grandmother is. 'Twas when you were over visiting at the castle yonder. She had the cough for a long time."

Then Finola remembered. "Old Grace died while you were away," her mother had told her. "I'll miss her for her remedies." Maeve had used the same tone as if she were talking about the death of a hen.

Shamed at her failure to remember, Finola recognised that she was not any better than the others. She drew herself to her full height. "I'm sorry," she said and left to return to the familiarity of the castle.

As Finola entered the castle, Shane was coming down the stairway. His legs had lengthened in the three years since he had been rendered voiceless by the injuries inflicted by the wolf. He was thirteen going on fourteen. A shaft of light falling on his face emphasised his perfectly formed features and the whiteness of his skin. It was a face that mirrored - Finola searched for a word - purity. But a little voice whispered that a whited sepulchre might be more appropriate.

Stepping aside, he let her pass. When she had walked a few yards, she felt his animosity burn into her back and she turned to encounter a stare containing an almost evil intent. But she was becoming accustomed to this of late. He followed her into the kitchen.

Brigid was kneading a lump of grey dough. "What do you want now, Shane?" she said. Flesh rippled across her back.

Shane looked at the spot where Molly was usually found lolling.

He's disappointed she's not here, Finola thought. She wasn't surprised when her father had been seduced by Molly's flirtatious behaviour but she found it difficult to understand how Shane had been so under her spell from the moment she had come, beaten and discarded, from Eochy O'More's castle.

Her brother fiddled idly with a whetstone he had taken from the table.

Brigid's voice was knowing. "The master wanted her," she said.

Shane gave a sneering look. With a cheeky gait, he went over to the vessel which usually held hazel nuts. When he found it empty, he gazed at Brigid.

"There are never any left because you scoff them all," she admonished. "Here, and away with you." She grabbed a fistful from the grain sack. "Mind, I'll know if you go near my new hiding place."

He left the whetstone aside, grabbed the nuts and touching his lips with the tips of his fingers, blew her a kiss.

Finola bristled as Brigid's face broke into a smile.

Outside the wind had not yet dried the mud on the ground. Shane threw the nuts into the mire. His expression had changed, becoming melancholy and dark.

Entering the castle by the back way, he climbed a spiral staircase, which wound past the lower levels to the living area on the third floor. Then he went up an additional flight of stairs that led from an alcove to the ramparts above. He paused a moment at the loading bay opening, through which heavy, cumbersome articles were lifted from the ground by pulley, and looked down the forty foot drop.

Moving away, he walked to the north side of the castle where he put his ear to the arched door and listened. After several seconds he turned the lock and went in.

The walls were, as they had always been, of naked stone. Cobwebs hung from the corners of the ceiling. The air reeked of sweat. A rug covered the crude wood. Shane fell to his knees. Using his fingers, he straightened the pile that the shape of Molly and his father had flattened.

That evening the family sat together to play cards. Finola sat on the form beside Shane. Her mother sat opposite in a box chair, her father in his favourite seat. The peat fire flickered in the middle of the room and threw leaping shadows onto the walls. Her mother beamed at her from across the table. There was a glow in her cheeks and her eyes were bright. Finola knew that her father's presence was the reason for her mother's contentment. She hoped he would indulge her tonight. They were with each other so seldom these days.

As her mother bent to collect the playing cards, Finola noticed grey streaks mixed through the blonde in her hair. Maeve looked so much older than she had a year ago.

Cormac, nursing his half filled goblet of *uisce beatha,* seemed unaware of his wife's adoration. "It's very hot in here," he said, leaving down his drink. He shrugged off his jerkin and threw it on the floor.

That's the fourth game I've won, Shane wrote. Want to continue playing?

"Count me out. I'll finish my drink and go to my bed." Cormac scratched his bared arm pit. Maeve, discomfited, reddened and averted her eyes.

Finola turned to her. "We'll have a game of chess. I feel wide awake."

"The board is in the usual place on top of the chest," Maeve answered. "And would you get my mantle? It's cold in here." She glared at Cormac's nakedness.

"I'll throw on a bit more peat." Cormac pushed out his chest showing more body hair. The *uisce beatha* has heated me."

"I dislike when you display yourself so blatantly," Maeve said, not smiling now.

As Finola left to do her mother's bidding, Shane had begun to draw something on his parchment. She found the mantle and the chess set. When she returned Shane handed her the drawing. It showed a man holding a sceptre, standing beside a prone figure. Underneath the sketch he had written, *the eldest son, chief of Mulahinsa.*

If the upright figure looked like Brian, Finola thought, the person lying down must be her father.

Cormac refilled his glass. Maeve drew her mantle closely around her. Shane sat with his arms folded and grinned widely at their disturbed faces. Finola had no real notion what the sketch meant, but she knew that Shane had written about something that was important to him. Suddenly sick of the hidden meanings and insinuations she said, "I've changed my mind. I'll skip the chess. I'm going to my pallet."

In the middle of the night she woke trembling from the effects of a nightmare she had partially forgotten. The words, "Don't Shane, Oh God don't," spoken in her voice, still reverberated in the chamber. After that, sleep refused to come.

Next morning as she sat bleary eyed eating her bowl of porridge she noticed a missive near her on the table. She reached for the note and read: *Why don't you like me Finola? You know that I want you to like me. I like you.*

There was no need for the *S* at the end. Nobody but Shane sent her letters anymore.

Chapter Four

Sir Walter Carew sat in the administrative section of Dublin Castle waiting for Sir Samuel Fenton to join him. When he had left Chalk Hall the morning after depositing Rory there, he had not understood that the queen would require his presence for so long. Neither had he expected to spend month after dreary month in Munster and Dublin arranging drafts for the parliament.

He patted the bag that bore the communication from Rory Maguire. It was faded, tattered and three years out of date, but he could not help that. Anyway he preferred to keep contact between Rory and his fosterers to a minimum. It would be better if the O'Hanlon family did not fortify Rory's barbarous heritage.

A portrait of Henry VIII looked down upon him. He shifted on the bench less from the effect of the kingly glare and more from the hardness of the wood. During the past months his weight had dropped; he could feel the timber against the end of his spine. To divert himself, he contemplated the Queen's attitude to events in Ireland.

The native population had been too weak after the Munster wars to put up any worthwhile resistance. He had convinced Her Majesty of that and had risen in her favour when he told her that rents he had received from the confiscated estates, would repay the half million pounds it had cost to suppress the rebellion.

He recalled Queen Elizabeth raising a ring-decked hand to her brow and pronouncing, "Our planters will protect us from a Spanish attack, and impose English law and civility. After we settle Munster, we will turn to Ulster. That is where your ward, what is his name ... Phelim Maguire will come in useful."

Though agitated by the mention of Rory's father, he had not corrected Her Majesty. She had measured him with shrewd eyes. "Everything has to be done legally. We are happy to entrust England's security to experienced officials like yourself and Sir Samuel Fenton."

He tilted his head back so his beard almost pointed towards the ceiling and closed his eyes. Yes, he had remembered everything of the interview.

Sir Samuel Fenton entered, carrying a register. Although the day was cold, beads of sweat clung to his forehead. "I have here," he said, "the list of people I summoned to the House of Lords." As he talked, Sir Walter found himself being sprayed with spittle. He stepped back, but Sir Samuel leaned forward and continued. "Twenty-six bishops and twenty-five lay peers."

"It will represent a bigger area than ever," Sir Walter spoke from behind his handkerchief.

"Representatives from twenty-seven counties and thirty-six boroughs are to be present in the Commons," Sir Samuel Fenton said. "There will even be two O'Reillys representing Cavan, two O'Farrells for Longford and an O'Brien and a Clancy for Clare."

Sir Walter shook his head doubtfully. "Are you sure they know that the purpose of the parliament is to pass an *Act of Attainder* against the Earl of Desmond and his followers?"

"Walter, Gaels constantly cut each other's throats." Sir Samuel Fenton wagged his finger. "It's time you accepted that these people are savages." He paused. "Past time. If my memory serves me accurately, when we met in Munster, you interceded for a rebel."

Sir Walter chose to ignore the barb. He said, "We are using the *Surrender and re-grant* clause, I presume."

"Of course. The Irish rebelled *ergo* they lose their lands to the crown. King Henry's strategy."

As they left the 1586 parliament that found the house of Desmond and eighty-one Munster landowners guilty of treason, Sir Samuel Fenton said, "I told you so Walter. Now it's your responsibility to return to England to persuade settlers to come and live on *our* land."

"Persuade settlers to come," Sir Walter mimicked silently wishing it were as easy as that, but he must keep a calm exterior. He would not disclose his proposed trip to Mulahinsa to Sir Samuel Fenton. If he found out, it would reinforce his view that he had an elevated view of the natives.

When Sir Walter reached Mulahinsa, he dismounted and walked, unaccompanied, towards the O'Hanlon castle leaving the six soldiers who had come with him, outside. Their horses moved skittishly. Knowing they were anxious to join the rest of their troop, waiting in Dundalk for their ship back to England, he had no intention of delaying.

He felt dishevelled. Mud stained his cloak.

Finola descended the stairs, her pace leisurely, her demeanour confident and greeted him. Sir Walter bowed slightly.

"Sir Walter," she said, "Let me escort you up to my mother."

By the time they had climbed to the third level Sir Walter was out of breath and would have liked to stop and rest but did not wish to appear weak. He disliked letting himself down in front of women especially a beautiful one like Finola and his muddied appearance was already denting his pride.

When Finola ushered him into her mother's presence, his confidence waned further. Maeve looked so controlled and serene as she sat behind her bureau, a parchment in front of her, and a quill in her hand.

"I'll leave you together," Finola stepped out of the room.

Sir Walter, tired from climbing three flights of steps, thought, "All this to deliver an out of date missive,"

Maeve left aside her quill and rose from her chair. "Sir Walter," she said sweetly and presented the back of her hand.

Her regard made him even more aware of how slovenly the loose travelling pants, he had donned to protect his hose, appeared. He doubled the folds of his cloak over to hide the dirt. There was mud on his hands.

Maeve waited.

He pressed his cold lips to her fingers. "I have brought a message from Rory Maguire," he said, straightening. "I will await a reply if you write it quickly."

Maeve went back to her desk. The pleats of her frock gathered around her, outlining her figure. She took one of two quills from the inkwell and dipping it in the ink, she began to write.

Sir Walter searched in his bag. The message had slipped out of its Maguire listing and lay with his personal necessities. Taking it out, he walked over to where Maeve was writing. Daylight filtered from the side wall and fell on her.

"Here is the letter from Rory. It is almost three years out of date and of little use." Why was he apologising to her? It must be this hellish pain in his head that was making him soft.

Maeve met his gaze and held it. "I know. That is why I began my salutations before you finished your search. You've been here for nigh on two years have you not?" Beneath his muddy cloak, he felt hot. The Irish. They had spies everywhere.

He remained silent. Maeve continued to look at him with raised eyebrows.

"I was in Dublin for many months. I am a busy man," he said feeling flustered.

She went back to her letter. Stray locks peeped from beneath her cap. His heart began to pound. Blonde, like Anne. It was so long since he had seen his beloved. An unexpected yearning ran through him and made him hunger to put his arms around this woman, to press her to him, to appeal for absolution for his curtness, to abolish her diffidence with his touch, his caresses, his ardour.

He bit on his lower lip as he felt his male organ swell. Turning his back to her, he tried to banish the feelings. How could he see a resemblance between his wife and this female? She was one of them. A native of this blasphemous country. A barbarian. They were *vermin, beasts*- images that helped him calm his arousal.

As he felt his manhood become soft and limp, he heaved a sigh of relief. He would do an extra hour of meditation tonight; that would atone for this misdeed. Composing himself, he turned back to Maeve as she applied her seal, willing her to hurry so he could leave.

The unsettled feeling returned. He had to get out of here; he moved towards the door. It would be boorish to leave without the communication but he could no longer ignore a new tingling. Different this time, a bulge but further down. There was something in the wide leg of his protective pants and it was creeping upwards. Feeling his skin being scratched, he shifted uneasily and thanked God for the protection of his hose.

The girl Finola entered carrying a parchment. "There must be some cheese about Mother." She was standing inside the door her head sideways, her alert eyes on him, her shoulders heaving. When she put her hand over her mouth, he suspected it was to hide laughter and her derision puzzled him.

"I think out resident mouse has discovered you Sir Walter." She giggled. With a rustle of taffeta she walked over to him and deftly ran her fingers down his leg. Sir Walter jumped back in fright of this female, Maeve's daughter. However she expertly squeezed the rodent down until it appeared pink-nosed on his boot.

97

Instinctively he kicked it, tossed it up and as it came down, kicked it squeaking up again. It went up and down until it hit the floor dead.

Hurriedly he snatched the missive for Rory from Maeve's bureau and ignored Finola's contemptuous look as she added something to hers before proffering it to him. Neither woman expressed gratitude as he put both letters in his satchel. Nobody showed him out.

He was back on his horse when he realised that he had not seen Cormac O' Hanlon or his sons. Maeve had looked unsure when she said that her husband must be out on the demesne. Distracted by his arousal, he had not pursued the matter.

It was fortunate that he was returning to England and the moral environment of Chalk Hall on the morrow. He would soon be home with his wife. After Wednesday, the night he had set aside for their weekly copulation, he would no longer be prone to sexual temptation.

It was early evening when Sir Walter and his troop neared Dundalk. The horses' hooves sank in the softness of the bog. Here and there furze bushes broke the monotony of the dun-coloured terrain. The air was moist and cold.

Thoughts of the dead mouse had triggered a memory of a distant past when he was seventeen. He should have killed the rodent that time too, but he had not and ... A censoring voice in his head whispered, "It was a tame mouse at Mulahinsa, not a large

predatory rat, nothing like that other time. You should have let it scurry back to its nest."

A corncrake called from the grass distracting Sir Walter. As he came closer, he spied the bird for a moment as he revealed himself in buff speckled splendour before disappearing again.

His head still throbbed. He remembered the woman, similar to Maeve, but in rags in her hovel. The touch of her was now on his skin. His mouth felt wet. If he did not concentrate on his riding, the horse would pitch him.

Soldiers were complaining to each other. He heard the words 'stinkin' bogs'.

He looked towards them and said, "We will soon be out of this dank Irish air." There was a moment of uneasy silence

"We will, Sir Walter," a lieutenant answered.

The memory edged its way back. A baby gurgling in a basket. The harlot saying "'Tis free it is this time," as she pointed to the pallet and looked lewdly at his young body.

His back jerked as his horse put his hoof into a trough. Quickly, he pulled on the reins steadying the animal. He must concentrate. This foul landscape could kill a man.

But still the memory persisted.

A rat in the centre of the room. Its narrow head menacing. Its tail like Lucifer's.

The harlot kissing him on his ear lobe, her body astride him, obstructing his view. He could have done nothing.

The sound of the corncrake was now the baby's cry in his head. He put his hands to his ears to block out the wailing. The reins dropped. The horse snorted and sniffed the sod. He could see the rodent tearing at the infant's dimpled chin.

"Are you ailing Sir Walter?" This time the lieutenant's utterance was low.

Sir Walter forced a smile. "No I'm not ailing Lieutenant. I have always disliked the sound of the corncrake."

Chapter Five

England

Though life at Chalk Hall was mostly a trial, Rory knew it was worth the bouts of loneliness, the religious indoctrination, the pandering to Duncan Erskine and the attentions from Jane he was becoming forced to endure.

He had learned much since his arrival here. In many ways he was different from the boy who, three years before, had made such gallant efforts to minister to Sir Walter Carew on the journey to England. The lessons he absorbed may not always have been what his mentor intended, but he considered them useful. He would need knowledge and restraint to claim his birthright.

Now he had come to realise that his strategy, to acquiesce outwardly to any orders he received while inside retaining his independent spirit, conceived in the schoolroom when he was eleven, had outlived its usefulness. Lately, he had begun to enjoy surprising Duncan Erskine with sporadic flashes of intelligent comment; he knew the tutor constantly reported his progress to Sir Walter so he wanted to convince him of his suitability to rule in Ireland.

At fifteen his shoulders had broadened and hair was appearing on his chin. His father's Roman nose and hard jaw were taking shape. The auburn hair of his earlier years had darkened and was now a burnished brown. His voice was deeply masculine.

Sitting at his ample desk in the schoolroom, he put aside his finished assignment. While George and Jane continued to work on theirs, he scrutinised Duncan Erskine who was intent on his own tract.

Duncan taunted Rory less now, but he was nevertheless still a bully masquerading as a pious scholar. His drooling over Jane had worsened in the past year, and she constantly stoked his interest by behaving amorously towards him whenever Rory was present.

But, Rory mused, despite his inappropriate attentions to Jane, he was a good teacher. He did not stick rigidly to the *trivium* of grammar, logic and rhetoric and the *quadrivium* of arithmetic, geometry, astrology and music, but also taught them English literature, History and Philosophy. Of course his view of the world was a Calvinist one, but he presented facts as impartially as he was able.

Rory reread his assignment and was satisfied. It was at an acceptable level of competence. He did not want to appear bright enough to be a threat to Duncan but yet wanted to lose the reputation for mediocrity he had acquired. Vanity would persuade him to accept that, under his guidance, Rory had escaped the natural backwardness of his countrymen.

He raised his hand now and said, "Excuse me, Sir, I disagree with this statement."

Duncan Erskine looked up, his expression darkening. "And what statement is that Rory Maguire?" he asked.

Rory read from his assignment.

"It says that if a country is not ruling itself well, a more powerful one should intervene. I know it is written in print, but that does not make it true. It carries only the same weight as the spoken word." Rory knew what he had said was a double heresy, considering William Caxton, who had brought the printing press to England, had been born in Kent and was much admired in the shire.

George and Jane looked at him, puzzled. Duncan Erskine flattened his hair with his palm.

"You have been expounding novel ideas of late Rory Maguire. You could turn out to be ..." He stopped himself. Then, donning a more benign façade, he said, "You have made a valid point. Now lessons are finished for this morning."

They filed out of the classroom. Anne stood at the door, waiting. Her voice slightly trembling she told them that Walter was to be home on the morrow. Then, as was her wont, she embraced each of them in turn. When she came to him, Rory felt her rest her weight against him momentarily, as if she were weary. Though he sensed that she was less than overjoyed by the prospect of her husband's homecoming, he felt unable to empathise; he welcomed the news of Sir Walter's imminent arrival.

It meant he would hear news from Cormac and Finola. He had waited so long for word from them. He began to imagine what they would say. Finola would tell him how she missed him. They would describe how Shane had recovered his voice and that Brian was back from Munster. That they hoped to welcome himself back soon. Danger had passed. There was nothing to fear from uncle Eoin any more.

Dreamily thinking these thoughts, he walked with the others towards the dining chamber. His stomach churned with excitement so he scarcely touched the roasted hare.

"Do you not like it Rory?" Jane sounded worried. "It's so tasty and tender."

"Eat it then and don't mind me." What a nuisance she was! He was sick of her bumping into him every chance she got, sick of the coy smile she wore as she caressed the part of her he had touched. He knew that if he tried to kiss her, she would run. Not that he had any interest in her. The thought of kisses and Finola were inseparable in his head. He wished the remaining months would fly by so he could go back to Mulahinsa. Thankful that Anne was absent so he could leave the table without permission and, ignoring the disappointed look on Jane's face, he went outside.

Usually after dinner, instead of going to the schoolroom with the others, he adjourned to the parlour to do the work Duncan Erskine had assigned him. He loved the glow of the flames from the open fireplace and the way they cast a mosaic of orange and yellow across his legs. He'd hold the script on his knee and study his assignment. Sir Walter would be intolerant of such a casual approach to homework. Today would be his last chance to indulge himself, yet he did not avail of the opportunity.

He needed to be outside, to feel the cold air on his cheeks, to forget book learning and refinement, to go back to the way he was before he had come to this boringly chivalrous country. If he stayed much longer here, he would become soft and inactive like George and life in Ulster was no place for a weakling.

Rory had absconded from the table before George, now breathless, caught up to him. "Will you help me to paint the railings in my garden, Rory?" he asked.

"I'll help you tomorrow. Today I feel like doing something more energetic like going for a ride."

"It's warm and there's no sign of rain. I'll ask mother. I'm sure she will let me go." George donned what Rory termed his old man stance.

"Don't delay. I'll go and get ready." In his bed chamber Rory pulled on his thigh high riding boots. In Chalk Hall it was customary to change into duds when going out on a horse, but today he would do like he would have if he were in Ulster and remained dressed in his everyday garments. Bolstered by this little act of rebellion, he whistled for the first time since leaving Mulahinsa.

In the coach house beside the stables he checked on the carriage with the ornate Carew coat of arms. He associated this coach with his arrival in Bristol so he liked to look it over whenever he went for a ride. The outside was newly polished and the interior grey lining still looked as new as it had those three years before. It was used only by Anne when she called on her friends once a fortnight or when she went out on her nocturnal expeditions with her cousin Francis.

"Examining the coach?" a voice said behind him. "Shining isn't she. All ready for *Her Ladyship* tonight." It was the coachman, Spence. Rory smiled. He had a special affection for him since their first meeting in Bristol. Spence gestured towards the Prussian leather that to Rory's eyes looked pristine clean. "Well when this is polished, it'll be all ready," he said.

They went through the dividing door that led into the stables. Here each of Sir Walter's five horses was kept in compartments divided by wooden partitions. With a half-door to the front. This abode is bigger than the cabin Murrough O'Toole lived in at Mulahinsa, Rory thought, and the straw is fresher smelling.

He thumped himself on the temple. What was wrong with him today? He was continually comparing his life now with the life he had left. News of Sir Walter's forthcoming arrival was making him restless.

As he walked along the row of horses, he chose a young bay, its nostrils flaring in anticipation of a spirited ride.

Spence's eyes twinkled. "Good choice. That beauty has good wind. She'll gallop as fast as you want. Here take this saddle. 'Tis foin and sturdy the straps are."

"No saddle today, Spence. I'm going to ride the Ulster way."

Spence shook his head in mystification.

Rory was leading the horse out when George arrived.

"I'm coming with you," he said. He called to Spence and pointed to a low sized horse in the last pen. "Saddle him."

"Are you sure you'll be able to manage him?" Spence's expression was impassive.

Rory's hunter stamped impatiently as George's docile pony was being saddled up.

Leaving the yard Rory said, "We'll go through the open fields on the other side of the house and then let the horses break into a gallop. I want to see how fast this beauty can run."

"I would prefer to canter around by the orchards and stop for apples or cherries. Then we can go by the garden and see if we need to paint the railings tomorrow. If you do not object."

"I do object. I haven't been on a horse for ten days."

George hesitated. He looked close to tears. "You go," he said. "I think it's going to rain. Mother hates me to get wet."

Weaklings, he was destined to live with weaklings who considered themselves superior to Gaels. He galloped across the fields urging his mount to go faster and faster, guiding him over the hillocks without slackening his pace. When he returned, the horse was slouching, his flanks heaved, and he was lathered in a white sweat.

"A good rub down is what he needs," Spence said, coming out of the coach house.

"I'll do it," Rory said. He felt more energetic than he had in months.

Later that evening, as Rory was going to the library, he espied Anne leaving her bed chamber. Her hair hung loose, her eyes were shining, and she bore an eager expression, making her appear, Rory thought, more like Sir Walter's daughter than his wife. He stood in the shadows at the end of the corridor to watch a moment. He was about to move again when Jane came up the stairway.

"Mama what have you done to your eyes?" she asked in an admiring tone when she approached her mother.

Anne said, "I outlined them with Kohl and put belladonna on the pupils."

"Can I do that to my eyes?" Jane's tone was hopeful.

Anne laughed. "I'll show you if you like. But your father is due tomorrow. It will have to wait until he leaves on another of his trips. You know how he feels about frippery."

Rory tiptoed away and when he returned sometime later, with

Edward Topsell's *History of Serpents* under his arm, he saw Geoffrey, in his role as footman, come out of the pantry to open the front door. He welcomed the waiting visitor, took his cloak and showed him into the waiting alcove.

Entering the parlour, curiosity assailed him and he stood a moment before closing the door. Anne was running down the stairway like a *girseach* to meet her visitor. He wondered where the carriage would take her and her beloved cousin tonight.

He was so absorbed that he failed to realise that George was sitting at the far end of the room, his lap covered with flowers from his precious garden.

"You must be wondering why cousin visits only when my father is away." George's tone became confidential. "My father dislikes Francis. That's why he arranges his visits to avoid him."

"I understand," Rory answered.

Again George resembled a seventy year-old man instead of a seventeen year old youth.

"My mother thinks it would be deceitful for us to meet cousin Francis in father's absence."

"I understand," repeated Rory. At that moment Jane entered the parlour and interrupted the conversation. "I'm off to the . . . library. See you anon." If he stayed he knew he would have to listen to Jane's giggles for hours.

As he sat again among the leather tomes and manuscripts, he realised that he went to the library less to escape boredom or Jane any more but because he enjoyed reading. He had found the Latin of Thomas More's *Utopia* and had just finished it. It was a refreshing and welcome change from English, a language he associated with oppression. Because of Philip Sydney's connection with Ireland, he would have liked to read his poetry but knew it was not available. Court poets believed that printed verse was less exclusive than the spoken word and so avoided the 'stigma of print.'

Neither could he get hold of Marlowe's play *Dr Faustus* which he'd love to study, as much because he knew Sir Walter would disapprove of the plot as from any real interest in sorcery. But the serpent book he had borrowed earlier was turning out to be a real pleasure.

He had just begun to read when he heard the front door open and close and the sound of carriage wheels on the path. Anne would, he knew, not appear again until morning.

Chapter Six

It was daybreak and Anne Carew was sitting at her dressing table. The gown she had donned had a high neck and loose fit, unflattering to her figure, and was very different from the ornate silk she had worn when out with Francis the previous night. "Bare shoulders or figure hugging materials lead to sinful thoughts and actions," Sir Walter had said often. Reaching to the back of a drawer, she took out the small looking-glass given to her by her cousin.

There were only two other looking-glasses in the whole of Chalk Hall. One hung in the corridor leading to the bed chambers. Sir Walter had planned that, in view of its prominence, nobody would submit to a temptation to preen. The other was in Jane's room. Her father was unaware of the existence of that one. Anne had bought it from a peddler and warned her to keep it a secret.

Looking at herself now, she saw that the darkness of the dress only emphasised her pallid complexion. Her eyes looked lifeless and her lips colourless. She tied her hair back into its habitual 'Sir Walter style,' and returned the illicit looking-glass to its hiding place. Taking a wrap from the closet, she threw it over her shoulders and walked from the chamber to the dining hall.

Rory, Jane and George were already at breakfast. She looked at them blankly a moment until her eyes rested on the primroses placed in a circle around her platter of beaconed herring.

"I thought you would appreciate them, Mama. I picked them this morning," George said.

She thanked him and reached for the bread.

Moved by her desolate air, Rory repressed a desire to reach out and caress her face. He had considered Anne plain when he first met her but today, inexplicably, he saw the voluptuousness of her lips as she smiled affectionately at him. He imagined Sir Walter's precise movements as he undressed her and felt an aching in his groin.

Then, as if she had just thought of something, Anne said, "I would like to see you all in the study after breakfast." Her voice softened to a whisper. "Since your father went away, I have neglected my duty towards your souls."

"But Duncan teaches us Mama," Jane said and then lowered

her gaze. "We know what is sinful."

"Nevertheless," was all Anne said in reply.

After they had eaten, the four of them trooped from the dining chamber into the parlour. In the morning light the room looked forlorn. Motes of dust floated in the air after the maid's cleaning. There were specks of ash from last night's fire in the grate, and the smell of candles lingered.

Anne gathered them in a circle round her. "Rory, could you move your chair nearer?" she asked.

He could feel her sensuousness and it flustered him. To cover his confusion, he took out a 'kerchief and pretended to clean his nose.

"I hope you're not getting a cold," she said and laid a hand on his arm.

His skin, where she had touched it, felt like it burned as if it had been touched by a flaring torch.

Anne began, "As I said, I have neglected my duty towards helping you to save your souls. Everybody needs to repent. Me, more than any of you, perhaps." She paused. "If you have hidden jealousies or lustful thoughts, you must seek to rid yourselves of them."

Rory's felt his breath catch. Could she know how he was feeling?

"Hell is an awful place," she continued.

"But, Mama, God decides before we are born whether we are going to heaven or hell. Nothing we do on earth can change that." Jane looked perplexed by all of this.

"Dearest Jane, you have no need of reparation. You do nothing wrong. I see I have no need to preach to you. Duncan has you well versed." She rose and kissed each of them in turn and left.

Though unsure whether he had learned anything from the sermon, Rory was certain that the touch of Anne's lips on his forehead set off tingling sensations in his body. If Jane were even a paltry shred of her mother, he would explore this new physical excitement further.

At evening time Anne stood in the rain, heedless of the staring soldiers, and waited for Sir Walter to dismount so she could welcome him home.

His expression was grim as he heaved his leg over the horse's neck and slid down his flank. On reaching the ground he silently took Anne by the elbow and guided her towards the house.

"'Tis good to have ya back Sir Walter," Geoffrey said, handing him a towel to dry himself. "Cook has prepared a repast. *Her Ladyship* had Spence on the lookout for your arrival."

"Thank you Geoffrey. You may tell Cook I am not hungry at present."

"Yes, your Lordship." Geoffrey's tone was indefinable. "I'll send out George and Jane."

"Do not disturb their routine. I will see them later at supper. I would like to change."

"I laid your clothes out for you. There is fresh water on the wash stand. Welcome home Walter." Anne leaned her cheek towards him.

He moved backwards. "Please Anne. You know how I dislike exhibitions of emotion. I will be coming to your chamber tonight. It is Wednesday. You can express your devotion then."

Though lust and longing surged through him, he hoped there had been no hint of his feelings in his words.

"Of course, Walter. She dug her nails into her palms. "I had forgotten the day of the week."

On the way to supper that evening Rory met Anne and she accompanied him into the dining hall. He felt himself dissolve beside her and was unsure what to say. He was a love struck swain incapable of rational thought.

Sir Walter was already there and had reinstated himself at the head of the table, on what Rory regarded as Anne's seat. Shortly after sitting under Sir Walter's gaze across the boiled chicken, Rory's feelings lessened. His nerve ends still tingled, but he felt more in control and dinner was proceeding calmly.

Anne now sat on the top right hand corner beside her husband. George had had to move down one place. Jane now sat opposite her mother with Rory across from George. It was not the change of location that made the difference, Rory thought, but their changed behaviour.

He was amazed how the presence of one person could imbue an atmosphere with such tension. Jane and George sat in front of their full platters, fiddling with the linen napkins, looking uncomfortable.

As she ate slowly and swallowed painstakingly, the sound of Anne's eating was audible in the stillness. Between bites she asked, "Did you achieve your aims in Ireland Walter?" Then another tentative question. "Did the parliament go as planned?"

Geoffrey set a goblet before Sir Walter.

"Yes. We found the house of Desmond guilty of treason." He filled the goblet with water and began to chew a piece of chicken. When it was well masticated and swallowed, he continued in a self-congratulatory tone, "Their lands are now legally ours."

Surrender and re-grant thought Rory. He felt fire in his stomach. He tried to form words but failed.

"Yes Rory?" Anne said, noticing, her voice gentle. "Did you want to say something?" She looked at him and he felt a deep pang.

Ignoring his sweating palms, he concentrated on her smiling mouth. He felt braver now.

"This is the second time *Surrender and re-grant* treaties have made it legal to put the Irish out of their lands and replace them with English tenants," he said. As he spoke, he became conscious of his accent reverting to what it used to be.

Sir Walter pushed away his platter and leaned back in his chair, his belly full, ready to give a political speech. "When people rebel they lose their lands. Those are the terms of the agreement." He hesitated. "We made mistakes in the first plantation of Laois and Offaly." He drank a mouthful of water. "We will not make the same mistakes in Munster. We planned this well."

Braggart, Rory thought, his politeness strained. "It was an ingenious plan," he said, trying to keep his voice steady.

"Of course," Sir Walter answered. He looked piercingly at Rory. "It is a God sent method for us to move in people of culture and courtesy. The natives, as I already revealed to Her Majesty, are too weak after the war to resist."

Jane gave an uninterested look at her father and said, "Would you excuse me please? I feel unwell."

"Bid goodnight to your father if you are going to bed," Anne said giving her a kiss.

"Good night, father."

Sir Walter looked at her over the rim of his goblet. "Good night."

Rory's anger at Sir Walter was rising and he could not continue this charade of flattery any longer. He had to make a deliberate effort to keep his voice even when he said, "Rents."

"I do not understand." Sir Walter's tone was inquiring.

"Money. The plantation. It will make money for the crown. I am sure the government will draw rents from the colony as it prospers. Ireland will no longer be a drain." Rory strove to use his best English and pronounce his words clearly.

"It is a pity that you are unable to see that it is our duty to impose English law and civility where we can, Rory," Sir Walter said, drumming his fingers on the table. "While we are doing God's work, our motives may be misunderstood, but I had expected, because of your time spent in Chalk Hall, that you would understand."

Careful, Rory thought. Draw back. He must not betray any more of his true feelings. "How many acres did you confiscate?" he asked, this time in a conversational tone.

"Nearly half a million."

"Who got the land?"

"You would not know any of them except, perhaps, Sir Walter Raleigh."

"Another Sir Walter," George said his tone eager.

"As I was saying before the interruption," his father gave George a disparaging look, "Sir Walter Raleigh got a twelve thousand acre seigniory. Edmund Spenser received an estate in Co. Cork. In Kilcolman, which, if we are fortunate, he will use as a setting for his poetry."

"I am sure Munster men will be honoured to have him live among them," Rory said.

Anne turned to Sir Walter. "Rory has read more than most boys of his age. Even more than George here, although George is that much older." To Rory, on her lips these words sounded like a declaration of passion.

"I am glad to hear it," Sir Walter said. "At least one boy in the household is knowledgeable."

George's face contorted as if he were about to cry. Anne put her arm across his shoulder, but he shook it off and jumped from the table, making it shake.

Sir Walter swirled water on his tongue as if he tasted a rare vintage and continued as if nothing had happened

"A Gael called Hugh O'Neill fought on the English side in the Desmond wars." He looked directly at Rory. "I mention him because, when he was a boy, he lived in the Pale and learned English ways." Seeming to measure Rory, he continued, "He received the title Earl of Tyrone as a reward for aiding us, and we continue to support him against his enemies." Then, from his perch at the head of the table, he wagged a finger. "If you follow in his footsteps, we will support you, too, against Eoin Maguire."

There was a silence. Rory's throat filled with unspoken words. His heart began to ache. Three years had passed since he had come to Chalk Hall, a lifetime in his mind. Yet the day Duncan Erskine had forced him to his knees on the schoolroom floor returned to him now, vividly and cruelly. Nothing had changed. Everything had a price. His presence in Chalk Hall was tolerated by Sir Walter only because he would be useful to him in the future as a puppet chief in Ireland.

As they left the dining hall, Anne left a gentle hand on his shoulder but so caught up was he in these thoughts that he could feel none of his earlier feelings, and he went to his bed chamber in a disconsolate mood. There he unrolled the parchments Sir Walter had brought him from Ireland and read again:

I write this in haste as Sir Walter Carew is here and will bring my reply back to you. Everybody is well. We're awaiting your return. You are a young man now. You will soon be back in Ulster. He that is born to be hanged shall never be drowned.

Though it was unsigned, Rory knew that it was from Maeve. His delight dissipated. Was this all? Was this what he had waited for, for three years?

He unrolled the second one.

When are you coming home? Kisses, kisses, kisses. Unlike you, this parchment did not wither and die at the touch of my lips!

There followed some scanty information about what had transpired in Mulahinsa since he left. Then Finola had written at the end,

I hope mouse killer will carry this to you safely.

He knew what she meant by the first comment. It was a

reference to how muddled he had become when she kissed him in the enclosure on the day he left. The scribbled *post script* puzzled him. Who was mouse killer? And why was there no missive from Cormac?

For the first time since he came to Chalk Hall, he was unable to stop himself crying from homesickness. But his weeping exposed deeper veins of grief – the killing of his father in the civil war, Matthew's suspected poisoning, the responsibility he shouldered to regain Glenone, his aloneness. The tears ran down his cheeks; he buried his face on the pillow and sobbed till he thought he could weep forever.

Chapter Seven

Ireland

"You are so occupied with yourself you neglect everyone else." Cormac shuffled as Maeve continued to upbraid him, her face white with rage.

Then he spoke, "Easy, woman. I've heard this every few months since God knows when." Cormac's impatience was tangible. "As you often say yourself, it's time to forgive and forget."

"You still refuse to tell me where you were that time Sir Walter Carew visited," Maeve's voice rose further. "And to think you let him leave without a word for poor Rory."

Finola shifted on her stool. Her mother had introduced the question she most dreaded.

She had her own suspicions as to where her father had been on that fateful day. Returning from a walk through the fields, she had seen a wicker wood crate being lowered by the pulley down the castle wall, a woman's red hair trailing over its side.

Sometime later she saw Shane sitting on the stairway, leading from the upper level of the castle a worried expression on his face. And in the middle of the night, she had heard him open the door of his bed-chamber and walk about the hallway.

It was daylight when her father had returned to his chamber on that occasion. Since that time, she had felt a tension between her parents.

Leaving the room, she went downstairs out into the damp air and headed once more for the tenants' dwellings. She was drawn in this direction so much these days because she was unhappy at home. The peasants seemed to lead uncomplicated lives.

As she entered the O'Toole hut, Eamon, the grand-father, Grace's widower and a cow-keeper for Mulahinsa, fingered his forehead in an awkward salute before fleeing to the sleeping quarters. She apologised for intruding but Kate told her, "Don't worry about auld Eamon. You're the excuse he's been needin' to grab a wink of sleep. He's not as lively on the feet as he used to be."

She took off her mantle, spread it on the low box that doubled as a stool and a storage space for eggs and sat down.

Kate continued with her work of winding bits of straw to make tethers for fowl. She looked absorbed, not in the mood for idle chatter with the lady of the castle.

After a while she lifted her head. "I'm thinkin' 'tis trouble like the rest of us the chief's daughter is havin'," she muttered.

Finola remained silent. A smell of smoke and offal made her stomach lurch.

She was about to leave again when the sound of rain came thumping on the straw roof, threatening to peel the layers of mud from the hut's wooden frame.

"Plastered this morning it was." Kate's voice was glum. "'Tis still wet." She looked upward. "Here's hopin' the roof doesn't leak."

At a loss as to what to say, Finola was conscious that she had never been in a position like this before where the walls around her were in danger of wearing away because of a cloudburst.

"You'd be as well to wait until it stops," Kate said. "Can't have you catchin' cold after you comin' to visit."

The atmosphere pressed down thick and suffocating, a smell of wood smoke mingled with the smell of mice droppings and pigshit. They sat in silence.

That was how Murrough found them when he came in dripping wet. He smiled at his mother, and took a cloth that was hanging on a rope and rubbed it over his face and neck. Without glancing in Finola's direction, he walked into the other room.

Finola felt her anger rise. She reprimanded herself for allowing this man with deep set green eyes and a head of long brown hair with a glib to make her uncomfortable. For the hundredth time she wondered what Rory had found to amuse him in this uncivil oaf. Or Matthew either, who should have had more sense.

Then she felt ashamed. Like the rest of her class, she expected respect from the peasants, even servility. She was finding it difficult to comprehend Murrough's lack of reverence.

As she made her way home through what was now a drizzle, she pulled her mantle tight around her. The mist clung to her face with a soft warmth.

When she neared the castle, she heard a woman's voice, soft

and sensuous, come from what they called the diamond, an area where the grass grew abundantly and stood out like a gem in the middle of the otherwise wispy enclosure.

"Darlin'," the voice crooned. "Come here darlin'."

Finola couldn't stop herself. She peered over the wall. At first she was unable to see anything. When her eyes became accustomed to the mist, she made out the outline of a man and a woman fastened in each other's arms.

The man, thin like a wraith, displayed a narrow back that tapered towards alluring buttocks. The female form rubbed against his manhood. She was kissing him, her hands moving over his body, drawing him closer. Her red hair stood out against the green of the lush grass. Of course! It was red haired Molly from the kitchens. Destitute after Eochy O'More had banished her from his house, her father had taken pity on her and taken her in.

It was her brother's blue jerkin on the ground she recognized. When she realized who he was, she wanted to disappear, become part of the haze, but she was unable to move.

"Shane.'Tis a grand animal you are. Come into me. Now. Oh! Yes. Yes."

No longer twisting away from her, his hands were at the back of her head and he was looking deep into her eyes.

Molly's hand gripped his penis. Then she stopped suddenly and opened her eyes. "'Tis dumb you are. In every way. That you are. Strutting about for the last year you've been, offering me your wares. Now you have the chance 'tis nothing you can do."

Shane stared back at her. A familiar malignant expression stole over his face.

He jerked her upright and pulled her to him. His hands caressed her hips and waist. She struggled. He lowered her to the ground. She began to tremble as he kissed her and fondled her breasts.

Then suddenly he turned her over and kissed her again, not on her lips now, but down the length of her spine. He drew back for a moment and stared at her naked body.

"Shane?"

Silently, he arched his body and plunged.

Trying to blot out Molly's scream, Finola ran, her eyes clouded by repulsion, towards the castle.

Finola shivered by the fire. Moisture dribbled down her face. She lifted her frock towards the flames more to keep the dampness away from her legs than to dry it. Her hair was pulled down over her right shoulder as she gazed into the flames.

"Why don't you take off those wet clothes Finola? They won't dry like that." Maeve came up behind her. "What were you doing out in this weather?"

There were shadows under her mother's eyes. "You look tired Mother. Are you not sleeping?" She'd forget what she had just seen if she concentrated on her mother's difficulties.

"You too lack luster." Maeve's smile was wan. "It's as if you've seen somebody commit sacrilege."

Finola returned to observing the fire. "Perhaps I did," she said quietly to the roaring flames.

"It's past time you found a husband." Maeve looked at her sharply. "This idea of refusing to meet any man, who asks permission to press his suit, is a mistake. I've let your father deal with it up to now, but no more. Rory has been gone four years and there's no suggestion that he will be coming back."

"Mother, I refuse to be a brood mare for any man. That was what my suitors wanted. Their mistresses could provide everything but legitimate children."

Maeve, looking pained, did not pursue the conversation.

Chapter Eight

England

Sir Walter sat astride his horse, ready to begin his journey across country to Cornwall to promote the Plantation of Munster. The younger sons of the aristocracy, who would be unable to inherit at home in their own right, were to be his main target. The refreshing breeze of the early morning had diminished to a mere breath of air that murmured among the pines.

He was looking forward to travelling through the rich pastures of Surrey and Somerset and seeing, at first hand, the dairy farms of Wiltshire. Sometimes he felt he should have been a farmer instead of a soldier.

When he first went to Ireland, he had been sceptical of the love the Gaels displayed for the soil. But not anymore. He saw now it was their reason for living. They found in the land what the English looked for in a woman ... fertility, obedience, power. That was why the Irish fought in rebellion. People like him came and took their property and settled strangers on it. It was like defiling their wives or lovers or deflowering their virgins.

Behind him his retinue was murmuring among themselves. He shifted uneasily in his saddle. They, too, were anxious to begin.

His fear had been that Anne would resent his leaving, and perhaps indulge in unfitting behaviour in front of his soldiers. Though he understood her regret that he was depriving her of his company, he hated emotional outbursts. His extended stay this time meant that they had slipped into a routine, and he felt mildly regretful to be spoiling it for her.

Returning home had been less than the pleasure he had expected. Anne was polite and dutiful. She supervised the servants with aplomb. Even the cook, who had been with the Carew family as long as he could remember and who, if the mood came upon her would be audacious enough to even chide *him*, worked well under her guidance, learning from her how to dry fruit, make quince jelly and prepare rose leaves for pot pourris. The sisters who did the house work also came to Anne for direction. He was glad to see she advised them with admirable patience. She was, however, a shade too familiar with

Geoffrey. It was always better, he felt, not to get intimate with servants.

She had abided by his wishes that George, Rory and Jane, despite his leaving this morning, had gone as usual to the school room. She had also conveyed to Duncan Erskine, without giving offence, that Sir Walter did not have the time necessary to go through a detailed account of their accomplishments. If it were an increase in remuneration the tutor desired, he trusted Anne enough to judge the request on its merits.

But of course all of these accomplishments were less important to him than her dedication to her spiritual duties. Each morning she made time for private prayer and meditation. More than once he saw her write under headings *Strengths* and *Weaknesses,* but he had not asked about their significance.

As his thoughts took a new twist, he shifted again in the saddle. Not once had Anne avoided her conjugal duties. Unlike his mother with her distressed smile listing her ailments, sore back, pain in her head ... His father had traipsed to her bed-chamber every night and left five minutes later shouting imprecations to the air. The boy Walter had turned over, thinking that what his father had wanted to do so badly with his mother must be disgusting to her.

In an attempt to make Wednesday nights as pleasant as possible for Anne, he'd finish his work early and, in the privacy of his chamber, he'd doff his garments and immerse himself in a tub of hot water. Once he had even filed his nails, an action he regarded as vain and superfluous. Another time, suppressing his aversion to such shallowness for Anne's sake, he had used the scent invented by Henry VIII, instead of his usual soap. It had been to no avail. Anne had still lain beneath him, her expression tortured, like a person in John Fox's *Book of Martyrs.*

Sighing he looked towards the house. His face shadowed for a moment as he turned and thought of the task ahead. In 1586 English officials had begun the campaign to lure people to Munster to inhabit the confiscated land. It was now almost 1589 and settlers were loath to come. He had decided Munster needed his presence if they were to attract more families.

The children and Rory were in the school room. His departure was working out admirably.

Anne stood at the door, dabbing at her eyes and squeezing her

118

handkerchief into a ball.

She waved as Sir Walter and his retinue made their departure, closed the door and went slowly towards her bedchamber. Sitting on the linen chest on which each Wednesday Sir Walter sat to remove his shoes before he clambered onto her bed, she wrapped her arms around a carved post and rested her forehead on the coolness of the oak. Her crying shook her whole body.

In the library Rory sat his elbows on his knees, his chin resting on his knit fingers. Although surrounded by leather bound books, their spines embellished by ornate handwriting, he was unaware of them.

A year had elapsed since his conversation at the dinner table with Sir Walter concerning Munster. Now he was more concerned with his own position and that of Ulster but, as often happened lately, when he tried to think strategically, thoughts of Anne seemed to intrude.

Her body, every contour from its ankle to its neck is flawless.

Eoin, his ogre since the civil war and Matthew's death, was a minor obstacle to his ambition; he could bribe some kinsman to kill his uncle. Ulster clansmen would betray if the reward were right. The realization dawned slowly.

He longed to see Anne as creation intended, unencumbered by her gowns, her limbs bare in the moonlight.

Getting revenge for his father and Matthew's death would not be enough to sustain him he knew; he wanted to repossess the land as well. Power and prestige would follow when he achieved that.

Sir Walter's voice still reverberated in his head. "As a reward for loyalty to England, Hugh O'Neill got the title he coveted. You follow in his footsteps and we will support you against Eoin Maguire." Again his anger stirred. In Sir Walter's estimation, he was a minion. But once he had gained ownership of land he would have *uirrithe,* rent, and political influence.

Anne's face, its clear skin so unlike Jane's, is that of an angel's.

He had begun to understand the practice of colonisation. Duncan Erskine often described how the conquistadors, Pizarro and Cortez, had, under the guise of civilising the Indians, divided their quarry, conquered them and snatched their riches. Plantation schemes were all the same whether practised in

Mexico, Peru or Ireland.

Making a further effort to concentrate, Rory looked around at the library that had given him sustenance and consolation for the past three and a half years. He knew he was lucky to be staying in one of the few houses in England to have a separate room solely for books. And, he admitted, Sir Walter had some good characteristics. They had forged a relationship that suited them both; Rory gave Sir Walter a reason to talk about his theories about Ulster; Sir Walter gave Rory facts about Ireland. Facts for which he thirsted. Yet, despite their association, he sensed that Sir Walter did not desire intimacy with him. He sometimes wondered if he suspected his ardour for his wife.

When he had left Ireland, his ambition was to gain the tools he needed to seek revenge for his father's and Matthew's deaths. As he told Finola in the *bawn*, he would regain his lands and live happily ever after. All that seemed so long ago. He pondered on the boy who left Mulahinsa, the boy who fled at a hint of trouble, who did not know books, who had almost burst with love when Finola pecked him on the lips. What an innocent he had been!

Three months had passed since Sir Walter's departure for the south west on his recruitment program. Rory was in the library reading a military history when Jane found him and proceeded to annoy him with mindless chatter. He wanted to rid himself of her attentions which had been more persistent of late. It was then he had spied George from the window, shears in hand, heading for the garden. Making an excuse to Jane about wanting to speak with him, he followed him there. He brought the book with him and lay on the grass reading while George busied himself with his pruning.

His heart jumped when he glimpsed her. Anne had let herself out the back door and was walking through the grounds at a leisurely pace. Pebbles crunched beneath her shoes and with each step her farthingale swung. An empty basket hung on her arm. She turned right and went into the orchard and strolled among the trees. She was beautiful, he thought.

The sun emerged from behind the clouds. The air warmed. He began to sweat. Anne undid the tie at the front of her over-all. As he watched, she raised the hem of her over garment and, gyrating her hips, allowed it to slip over the hoops under her gown.

Rory's breathing quickened. He turned to where George was busy trimming plants. "George, your mother is picking fruit in the orchard. I think I'll go and help her." He tried to sound nonchalant.

George's expression darkened. "I'll go with you." He waved the shears in his hand. "This is blunt. I will have to get the whetstone." He grabbed Rory's elbow, and kept pace with him into the orchard.

Anne turned and looked directly at them both, her eyes twinkling. "Rory." She paused. "This is fortunate. I need your help. I had forgotten these trees were so lofty." She gestured up at the tall pear trees, a teasing curve to her lips.

"I'll get some for you," his voice croaked. He climbed the tree and twisted off several pears, handing them down to her. As she bent to place them in her basket, her breasts revealed themselves pressing out of her gown. Like ripe pears, Rory thought. He avoided George's eyes. He felt peculiar, the feeling similar to the one he got when he rubbed his male organ in the night, a warm blurry pleasure which increased to a squeezing liquefying sensation as if his guts might dissolve. He would love if Anne made those sensations for him.

For weeks after he could think of nothing else but her. What used to be a minor incursion in his thoughts became an obsession. He would see her about the house bedecked in jewellery, never worn when Sir Walter was home, and desired to caress her. Like a tracker dog, he searched for her scent of roses. When she coaxed the organ to music, he listened spellbound.

One day she sat on a window seat gazing out at George's garden. Rory made bold enough as to sit beside her. She nodded towards the view. "It's hard to imagine the beautiful flowers behind the brick wall," she said. "Like it is hard to imagine what goes on behind people's faces." She got up abruptly. "I had better take my leave," she said. "Spence will be waiting for me. I am paying a call on the Marquis of Dooley." She rushed off, forgetting her gloves in her haste.

Each night since he had sat in his chamber picturing her, wanting her, touching her glove to his face, wondering what she was doing then, whether she was brushing her hair, pulling off her gown or lying down to sleep. She made him feel so comfortable, so wise, so much a man. Puzzling and exciting to him, she personified the wonder of the female creation and he hungered to know more.

Then one day as he was leaving the school room, where he had spent the previous quarter of an hour listening to Jane recite collects and psalms, George handed him a slim pamphlet. "I have something you may find interesting," he said with a knowing expression.

Rory looked at the cover.

"Calvinism? No thanks. I have had my bellyful on the subject since I came to Chalk hall."

George took the book, opened it at a spot he had marked and handed it back. Rory read:

Calvinism has a strict moral code. In Geneva the authorities drown a woman they find guilty of adultery. They behead males.

"My father is a powerful man," said George looking at a point above Rory's head. "I would hate to see someone I care about have his future imperilled because of him."

Chapter Nine

Sir Walter felt grateful that this was the last day of his journey. Summer had bedecked the route back from Devon with a profusion of primroses, violets and peonies. They filled many gardens and fringed many paths, bestowing colour across the land. But Sir Walter was uninterested in the landscape. He wanted to get home to Chalk Hall with the least possible trouble. Considering the air too laden with pollen for his sensitive nostrils, he had chosen to pamper himself and travel back by coach rather than horseback. Now the longest part of the journey was already over and he would be home by nightfall.

The clatter of the soldiers' horses and those pulling his carriage were the only sound on the cobblestones. He rubbed his hand across his forehead and removed his shoes, stretching his toes blissfully. Though conscious of the possibility of being robbed by a highwayman, he determined to trust his musket armed escort. Raising his head towards the roof of the coach, he flexed his shoulders before settling himself. Another reason he chose to travel by coach was his abject tiredness. It had been a difficult eleven months.

When he returned to Chalk Hall, he felt sure he would be hearing more from the palace, about the Armada of ships Philip II of Spain had sent to invade England.

Although he had nothing to do with the navy, their achievement delighted him. Compared to the clumsy galleys of the Spaniards, their English vessels were easily manoeuvred and their artillery superior. Vessels built for the calm Mediterranean had been no match for the channel.

He had heard that the defeated armada, what remained of it, had sailed up the east coast and around Scotland hoping to turn south into the mid-Atlantic to return to Spain. Gales had blown them off course until they had floundered on Ireland's western seaboard. He felt a foreboding that he would be hearing more about these flotillas.

It was easy for Queen Elizabeth's council to draw up extensive plans on the requirements of prospective planters but now that he had been in the middle of it, he knew how hard it was to put theory into practice.

Only a patient man like himself could have endured the rhetoric of spoiled younger sons of the aristocracy, poised to become wealthy landowners in Ireland. Some of them had treated his soldiers abominably. Imagine! The audacity to think they could treat soldiers of the crown the way they would the native Irish.

The swaying of the rig lulled him to a sleep where he found himself dreaming of Anne bereft of her dark gown and her prayer book. Anne, as he longed to see her, spread under him in abandon, letting him ... He opened his eyes suddenly. He tasted sweat on his upper lip, under his neatly clipped beard. God forgive me, he thought. Do I have to tarnish everything pure? The workings of the sexual act repulsed him. The messiness of pushing his penis, engorged and purple, into an opening between Anne's thighs was anathema to his civilized tastes. Yet he loved the feeling it gave him when he bucked, twisted and moaned uncontrollably and his sperm spurt forth into her.

Though he craved to do it again and again, her resigned expression as she lay rigidly beneath him, gazing into the middle distance, made him feel like a trespasser. She had been seventeen years younger than he, when they married. When she had accepted his suit, he had made a vow that he would not burden her with his sexual desires. He refused to be a rutting stag, his intellect would rule his bodily desires.

He thought of the love letters he had never given to her. Though he had re-written some of them several times to get them virtuous and pertinent, he had always felt they were still too passionate. She must not know how much he desired her; it would make her anxious. Having Wednesday as conjugal rights night had been his way of curtailing his lust, but he was unable to stifle his disappointment that today was Friday. He hoped God would forgive him his lustful yearnings.

Suddenly realising that many hours had elapsed since he had begun his journey, and that they must be near Chalk Hall, he rapped on the roof. The carriage jerked to a halt.

His lieutenant, seeing the coach stop, dismounted and opened the door. "Do you want me to detail a soldier to ride ahead to Chalk Hall to announce your arrival?"

Sir Walter nodded. He always did that. It was as if he feared what he would find if the household were unaware of his imminent arrival. But he knew Anne would not need advance notice of his coming. She would be waiting for him since early morning, and had probably used the vigil as an opportunity for meditation. His heart swelled. She was such a dutiful wife.

Some weeks later Sir Walter stood looking at the emissary from Queen Elizabeth's court standing before him. He waved the missive he had brought in the messenger's impassive face. His worst fears had been realised.

"I have lately arrived from Cornwall," he said, his voice rising in anger, "after arduous months spent praising Munster in an effort to entice potential planters there, and the council is now trying to return me to Ireland on the strength of this." Displeased with himself for divulging personal details to a subordinate, he looked back at the document. "They believe that the dregs of the Armada could organise with Irish chiefs and start a revolt? Their informants are exaggerating. The Gaels see two ships off the coast of Ireland and by the end of the day it is twenty-two. I assume this information *has* come from Gaelic spies."

The courtier's eyes burned with resentment. "I agree there is no race who can overestimate like the Irish," he said, "but we did not rely solely on traitors. The council made careful enquiries before they acted. It was the Governor of Connaught, Bingham, who reported the possibility of Spain launching a renewed attack on England using Armada survivors in Ireland.

"Are the Spaniards being aided by the Gaels?" Sir Walter asked.

"No, not in Connaught, sir. Bingham ordered the Connaught men to hand over relics of the Armada fleet. They assembled over three hundred Spanish prisoners in Galway and hanged them," the emissary replied.

"That means our policies are working."

"It's Ulster we are worried about Sir Walter. Her Majesty suggested that you were an authority on the province, you know the terrain and the people."

These Spaniards are castaways not invaders, Sir Walter thought to himself. But he would not disagree with Her Majesty. He would have to go to Ulster.

Giving a curt nod, he said, "Leave me for an hour. I wish to think. I will call you when I need you."

"As you wish, Sir Walter." The envoy's lips expanded in a

fawning smile and he withdrew.

Ireland again. In resignation rather than sorrow, Sir Walter shook his head.

Immediately following his return, he had been glad to be back. He enjoyed waking in his familiar bed, donning his favourite apparel and going to chapel. The sight of Jane and Rory on their way to the school room every morning pleased him. The routine and tranquillity stilled his restlessness and assuaged his fatigue. For the first time in months his persistent headaches had ceased.

As the weeks at home had progressed, he had become dissatisfied with George. He seemed to look to Rory for guidance. Rory was a Gael after all. And George was his flesh and blood while Rory was only his ... He deliberately discontinued the thought sequence.

He disliked the notion of his son remaining idle until he inherited Chalk Hall. Soldiering was a worthy calling and a tradition he should be honoured to serve. George had retched at the prospect. And now Oxford had accepted him as a student in a new branch of learning, studying plants. He was glad he had found some course of study that interested him, even if it did mean spending his days in the trivia of defining weeds.

Why then was he displeased with him? A feeling like guilt beset him. But, he thought, it cannot be guilt; he had nothing to be guilty about. Regret? No, that would not do either. Sir Walter Carew did not have regrets. Annoyed by his failure to name his feelings, he allowed them free rein.

His thoughts turned to Anne. Her attitude had changed of late. He began to list in his head the differences one by one.

Monday-Anne did not hand him the ewer of water when he wanted it.

Tuesday-she ordered the carriage without his permission.

Wednesday- she had a cold so he could not come to her bed.

Thursday- she contradicted him in front of Geoffrey.

Friday- her attention wandered as he told her about his fears for Ireland.

All this and much more had happened each day and without any fixed pattern.

The pain in his head returned. He no longer felt happy to be at home. He would be glad to leave.

Sir Walter left the document on the table and ran his fingers through his close clipped hair.

Fear of a Spanish retaliatory attack had spurred the plantation in Munster. A loyal colony there provided a cheap garrison against the Spanish. If this manuscript were true and men from Spain decided to use Ireland as a back door to England, the settlers in Munster would deal swiftly with them. But Ulster was different. It was time now to make Ulster loyal too.

Rory was sitting cross-legged on the window seat of the parlour, his favourite spot of late. Sir Walter's account of the end of the war in Munster, at last night's supper table, still troubled him. It was dreadful what Sir Walter had described. Men and women crawling on their bellies, sinking their heads into the grass, devouring it. He could almost smell the stink of starvation, see the sunken eyes and hollow cheeks, and feel their terrible apathy. Men like Cormac or Shane. Women like Finola or Maeve.

"Mind if I sit?" Jane sank onto the seat beside him, a flirtatious grin across her face. He moved closer to the side of the window. As she settled herself to do her needlework, the hoop of her gown rubbed against his leg. Of late he had been unable to deny that her plain gowns covered her long and shapely limbs with aplomb or that she was becoming tall and comely, more like someone from Ulster than a gentle English woman. Her doe eyes followed his every movement. If only Anne found him as attractive. He was about to get up and go, when he heard footsteps on the passageway.

Sir Walter entered his expression as firm as his footsteps. He glared at Rory, then at Jane. "I am returning to Ireland in a few days. If you have communication to send, prepare it now," he said.

"Oh! You will be going to Mulahinsa?"

"Yes." Seeing his expectant look, Sir Walter waited.

"From what you recounted last night about Munster you must control the province. And 'The flail of Connaught' is in control in the west."

Sir Walter gave Rory a straight hard look. "I trust you mean Sir Richard Bingham?"

. "Yes, that's who I mean." Rory's voice took on a guarded tone.

"And Leinster, as always, is a bulwark for the English."

"The Gaelic order survives only in Ulster."

Rory stood, almost equal in stature to the older man. "Even the Normans did not penetrate north of the river Bann," he said with a note of pride.

"Lakes, bogs and mountains," Sir Walter replied, "will not protect Ulster from invasion for ever. We have only made half-hearted attempts to build forts and maintain garrisons there up to now. That is going to change. We are starting to rearrange the political balance and of course I must remember we have you, Rory." There was a faint question in his tone. "A loyal subject of the crown."

"And Eoin Maguire?"

"Eoin Maguire! He raids and spoils in the old manner. Yes, your uncle has his uses. But when you rise to power the chiefs who are loyal to him now will swing to you."

"When will that be?" Rory asked the question that had so often trembled on his lips since Sir Walter's return from Devon.

Ignoring Rory's question Sir Walter answered, "Two days from now I leave for Ulster." He moved towards the door. Before he opened it he stopped and half turned, as if remembering something. "Come along Jane," he said. "I hear your mother calling."

In the days and weeks after Sir Walter's departure Rory and Anne talked every day, as they usually did. But it was always in the presence of the servants, or else that of George and Jane. Rory was unsure what he would do if the impossible happened and they were alone. His thoughts of her were becoming more and more sexual, but he knew he was unschooled in such matters. He would have to rely on her instruction.

Such were his thoughts as he searched among the library shelves trying to find something interesting to read. He had not read anything for a long time, had been unable to concentrate. Climbing the wooden steps he rummaged through the books on the higher shelves. He was flicking through the pages of a tome when he heard a noise and peered down.

Anne had glided in and was exploring among the shelves running her hand almost absent-mindedly across the books.

This was his chance. With a shaky breath, he squared his

shoulders. Awkwardly, he started down from his height, holding the book in one hand and leaning the other hand on the ladder. The ladder began to slide to one side. Instinctively he leaned backwards; he could see the ladder and shelves separating from each other but could do nothing now to stop it. He felt himself sailing backwards through the air until both he and the ladder landed on the ground beside Anne. The book was still in his hand.

For a moment he lay stunned and when he opened his eyes, he got a blurred impression of a body leaning over him. Through the haze, he could see her bosom almost level with his chin. He could have reached out and touched the breasts that rose and fell under her yellow gown.

"Are you hurt Rory?" she asked. "I did not mean to startle you. Let me have a look at you. You may have hurt your head. You are fortunate the book case was not any higher." She parted his hair and felt his scalp.

He felt her fingers ... like a lover's touch on his forehead. He clasped her to him wildly. "Anne," he gasped. "Anne."

Hungry with desire, his lips sought hers. His mouth opened, but, unlike what happened in his dreams, there was no answering pressure, no tongue touching his, only lips tightly sealed.

She forced him away from her and ran from the library. Rory understood now that she did not love him and felt ashamed. Leaving the library, he went to his bed-chamber.

As he lay on his bed, he tried to ignore the throbbing in his head. For all his reading, he understood nothing. He hoped to become a Gaelic chieftain, defend his lands, be a hero to his people, yet he was behaving in a manner that a love struck servant at Mulahinsa would have repudiated. What must she have thought of him? Bad cess to him. Her scorn was well deserved.

At his age his uncle Eoin had peopled Ulster with bastards and he didn't even know if he could perform like a man. His brain pounded. Another night of sleeplessness awaited him.

Then from the depths of his self pity an idea sprang. Cormac had given him *uisce beatha* for the journey to England. He had given some to Sir Walter, which he had spilled rather than drink, but there was still a drop left in the bottom of the flagon. If ever he needed it, it was now.

It was wrapped in a pair of trews that had remained unworn since he had adopted his English apparel. He drank in one gulp. The fiery liquid inflamed his throat and made his insides ignite. Like the dragons he had read about, he felt that if he opened his mouth, he would breathe fire. He wanted more.

There was wine from Jerez in a press in the kitchen quarters, he knew, that cook used in some of her dishes. Earlier he had heard Anne, George and Jane going for their supper. Now darkness had fallen and silence enveloped the house. Everybody had retired.

Leaving his bed-chamber, he tip-toed along the passageway and stepped down the main stairway. The sound of his measured footsteps rang through the silent house as he made his way to the kitchen where he opened the *sherris* press and, grabbing a bottle, caressed it and kissed it wetly at the mouth before sitting on the flagstones. The bitter tasting liquid made him more light-headed and increased the glow in the pit of his stomach.

The disaster in the library was becoming less dramatic to him. He had exaggerated everything. Images of him as he lay on the library floor and gazed at Anne with lecherous eyes were no longer tragic, merely amusing. The whole idea made him laugh out loud.

As he reached the dregs of the bottle, a mad thought struck him. He would go and share his cheer with Anne. Laughter was catching. The shock of falling had unhinged his mind momentarily would be his excuse. She would understand.

Slowly, he wove his way to his own wing. The torches were burning low and it was darker than he expected. Fumbling along he reached a bed-chamber door which he assumed in the near darkness must be Anne's. Standing for a minute, he steeled his nerve and turned the handle.

A blur of green faced him. Drapes obstructed his view of the bed. He pulled them apart and there he saw, not Anne, but Jane and looking like he had never imagined she could.

She was wearing a night smock that showed off her long neck and ample bosom. She looked young and erotic. Thoughts of conversation with Anne went out of his head. He felt powerful . . . like the first man about to ravish this new Eve.

Jane did not scream or move as she opened her eyes, heavy

with sleep, a bewildered look on her face.

For the first time Rory was alone with a woman in her bed-chamber and, even if it was not the woman he lusted after, his desire reached new heights.

Go slowly, gently, he cautioned himself as he lay on top of her. Mustn't frighten her off. "Jane how comely you are," he slurred.

"Do you mean it, Rory?" Jane's expression brightened. Her eyes took on a luminous quality.

"You're so beauteous."

"Shhh! Don't waken Mabel," she warned from underneath him. "She is asleep in there." She motioned in the direction of the withdrawing chamber.

He clasped her hand. If she didn't want to talk, she must want to ... pulling her to him, he kissed her lightly. She seemed acquiescent. But when he tried to prise her lips apart with his tongue, she protested.

"No, Rory. No! No! It is wrong."

She tugged at the night smock he had raised above her thighs and tried to yank it down. "Let me go Rory, let me go, it is a sin."

Silly Jane, he had done nothing yet. His tone was pious. "You are an angel."

Her body flexed. She drew him closer.

He struggled with his breeches, wriggled, trying to push them off without getting up.

"What are you doing?"

He was beginning to lose his patience with Jane, with himself, but mostly with his breeches which had twisted round his ankles. At last he managed to break free.

His penis was hard and gluey on Jane's belly and now he began to move it between her legs with one hand while propping the weight of his body with the other. He explored between her thighs without quite knowing what he was looking for, but feeling instinctively that what would give him pleasure was somewhere around here. In his mind was a moist inviting cavity but as he poked and stabbed, he found nothing but taut unyielding skin.

Feeling like an *amadán*, he still searched, in a mood of growing despair. Each time Jane said, "I still think it's a sin," she clamped her legs closer together. He felt like throttling her. Finally he gave up, dismounted and sat on the edge of the bed feeling sorry for himself.

Behind him Jane lay motionless.

Watching his slightly swelled penis subside to limpness, he realized that he was unable to perform the most basic manly imperative. Then Jane, as if sensing his hopelessness touched him on the elbow. "What you're looking for Rory, I know where it is," she said as she spread her legs and gestured.

Back on top of her his penis rose again. She guided him with her hand into her vagina and they lay still for a while. He felt so happy to have become a man, proud to have possessed a female, even if it were only Jane, giggly Jane. If it had been an old crone, he would still have been pleased to be there a virile man lying with a woman. Then he moved backwards and forwards, just a few times, came in a sad, exhausted way and withdrew.

Jane said, "You've made me all squishy inside."

In gratitude he flattered, and fondled her.

She let him do to her, what he did not know he knew how to do.

Her breathing became heavy and fast. His penis, with new hope, rose again and this time found its own way without her direction. She gave a low moan as he entered her.

"Hold me closer, Rory ... closer, I love you."

What was she braying about now? he wondered. Anchors seemed to weigh his limbs. Her hair stuck into his mouth. She needed to cut her toe nails. He untangled himself, dragged on his garments and left the room. Sleep! All he wanted was sleep.

Thirst woke him the following morning and he felt as if a smithy was shoeing a horse inside his head. Licking his lips he moistened them with his spit. Thoughts of last night tumbled back and he grinned, the grin of a man, recently satiated.

In the following weeks he found himself thinking not of Jane but of Finola. She would have waited for him as he had waited for her. Now that he knew what to do sexually, he would love her as she deserved. She would be almost past marrying age. Another reason for him to go back to Mulahinsa quickly and claim her.

That was if he survived Jane and ever reached Ireland. Each night as he lay in his bed he said to himself, "I will resist." But as he changed his position, in an effort to get comfortable, his resolution waned. He was a hot blooded swain. There was a filly

132

down the hall that was willing to follow direction.

He adored the feeling of Jane wanting him. Thinking of the risk he was taking caused his heartbeat to quicken. In a Puritan household such transgressions as this would be considered outrageous. Burrowing his face deeper into his down pillow, he closed his eyes. Images of white flesh, entwined in his, bedevilled him. As he had done several times since the first, he left his bed, pulled on his tunic and trews, and crept barefoot to her chamber.

She was waiting for him. Her body felt warm and exciting in his arms. He loved each embrace, each whispered endearment, each erotic touch, her lithe figure with its mass of fair hair. But each night, as he reached his most intense moment, he shouted 'Finola' in his head.

"You do love me, Rory?" Jane implored.

Her whine always jolted him into the realisation that she was not Finola. He kissed her nipples and played with the tufts of blonde between her legs. "How could I feel your body and not love it?" he quipped.

On his way back to his own chamber, he experienced his habitual feeling of self-reproach.

As he lay in his bed drifting into sleep he thought about Finola and longed for some communication. He scolded himself for not having sent a letter to Mulahinsa with Sir Walter, but he had been too besotted by Anne at the time.

He would never let himself be love-struck by a woman like that again. His infatuation for her had been childish. Now that he was a man he found his obsession for her difficult to comprehend. If Jane were less clinging, he would be happy to mate with her until he returned to Ireland. As it was, he had begun to look, with seduction in mind, at the servant sisters Mabel and Elise.

Chapter Ten

Ireland

In the O'Hanlon household all was not well. There was bad feeling, Finola felt, between Shane and their father. It concerned Molly she was sure. She had been troubled for months by what she had seen on The Diamond.

After churning it around in her mind, she decided to confide in Niall. She found him sitting at his desk in the school room and, without preamble, told him her worries. "Shane's face was so full of revulsion that day," she finished. "I'm afraid something bad is going to happen."

Niall thought for a minute, then said, "He's not full of revulsion now Finola. He's full of passion. At least that's what it seems like to me. And Molly is relishing the experience. Now passion comes in many different forms. It sometimes expresses itself in ..."

"I know Niall. I have some myself ... passions I mean." Was there anything he was unable to give a dissertation on?

She wished Rory were here. He would know whether she should tell her father or not.

Niall said, "Shane is old enough to have a sexual relationship if he wants one Finola. Henry VIII was married when he was eighteen and Essex was ..."

"Yes Niall but they aren't my brother and you didn't see what I saw." She walked away before he could question her further.

That evening at dinner Finola eyed her father across the table. Since he had stopped going to the loading bay area, he had been in bad humour. The atmosphere in the room was tense. Shane sat beside his father ladling stirabout into his mouth. Their mother sat opposite drinking a goblet of whey.

Even Brigid was sullen and preoccupied as she gathered the dirty platters from the table. When she left with her arms full of ware, Maeve said, "That woman has to work like a pack horse. I wonder is there any tenant's child ready for service."

"There's always Molly," Finola said ironically, "I wonder if she does much. Of course she could be killed working and I wouldn't know." She studied Shane's face for a reaction but got no response. Just then her father stood up, scraping his stool on the stone floor, his face white and he left the hall, his food half finished.

Later Finola made her excuses and left too. She went towards the loading bay where she suspected she'd find her father. As she approached, she heard voices.

"He's a good fuck," Molly's voice was shrill. "He does things to me. I like it."

Her father's voice was low but unmistakable. "He's just a boy. Leave him be ..." Finola recognised from its cadence his terrible anger.

"Jealous are we?" she purred now. "'Fraid I won't be able to keep the two of you satisfied?"

"Get out of here. You're nothing but a trollop."

"Cormac, darlin'," the voice was wheedling, "sure 'twas joking you I was. Me and Shane! That's a laugh! Poor mute animal that he is."

"Don't refer to him as an animal. He's an O'Hanlon and from a long line of chiefs. You are dirt under his feet, a receptacle for his sperm, nothing else."

"And you're an old goat."

"Lower your voice. We don't want the whole castle to know what a slut and a liar you are."

"Or what an old goat the master is."

Finola ran, the sound of Molly's derisive laughter ringing in her ears.

In a few weeks Finola had pushed all the problems about Shane, her father and Molly to the back of her mind and was looking forward to Brian's homecoming from Munster. On the day he was due she was filled with excitement and found it difficult to be still. At first light she went out to climb the hill behind the house. She had walked as far as the outfields and was now retracing her steps.

Brian had broken both his arms in Munster. She had heard it had something to do with the death of MacCarthy. It would take him some time to recover and his return would be delayed. But today was the day! She thought she saw a figure coming towards her in the distance, and she shaded her eyes from the morning sun. Her heart leapt. It was indeed her brother striding towards her, a lopsided grin on his usually sombre face.

She ran towards him, heedless of the dirt splashing her frock. "Brian!" she exclaimed. "How I've missed you! Did you see the others yet? Are you better now? Who told you where to find me?"

"I've missed you too." Gently he held out his arms. "Yes, I've seen father and mother and Shane, they haven't changed. Brigid told me where you had gone. She thought you might be hungry." He unwrapped some hazel nuts from a piece of linen.

As Finola crunched on the nuts, she studied her brother. He had changed since he had left Mulahinsa. At twenty five there was intensity in his expression and his eyes glinted with a purpose unlike that of other men his age.

"Has your return anything to do with the ships from the Armada that are coming in on the coast?"

When he did not answer, she continued, "Who broke your arms? One I can understand but two. Or can these new fangled guns break limbs too? A bow and arrow would never do that."

"No, you're right, an arquebus cannot break limbs. But an angry Englishman, supported by a soldier carrying one, can. I was lucky that he didn't beat in my head as well. A comrade of his had died of the ague and he blamed me for the Munster climate."

Silence followed. Brian stood motionless. Finola chewed on another nut.

"A more ruthless crew than the English I can't imagine," Brian continued. "They killed defendants of forts, even if they were women and children. Survivors were petrified after the war. That was why they were unable to resist being thrown off their land."

Finola's eyes smarted. "We'll sit for awhile," she said motioning towards the shade of an elm. The grass felt rough under her legs as she stretched them out.

Brian sat upright, his knees bent. "They hanged MacCarthy," he continued. "They saw him as a leader who could rally people."

She felt a sick feeling rise in the pit of her stomach as she listened to Brian describing the horrors he had seen in Munster. She was unfamiliar with this Brian, his face dark as slag, his lips shaking with emotion. He sounded sure that they would have to go to war. It looks like Rory will have more than Eoin to fight to regain his land, she thought.

"I'm back in Ulster to muster help for the Armada survivors," he said. "Do you think Cormac will help?"

"Don't dwell on it for now," Finola replied, taking off her mantle and making a pillow of it on the ground. "What you need is rest."

Brian lay back and was soon dozing in the early morning heat. Finola sat gazing out across the land. Her mind was full of starving people, dead babies, shipwrecked Spaniards and the horrible premonition that Ulster would be next for devastation.

Chapter Eleven

Sir Walter sat in the chill of his quarters in Newry while his lieutenant hovered outside the partially opened door, pacing the rushes. Let him wait. He had some serious thinking to do and strategic decisions to make.

Any threat from the Spanish fleet he considered to be imaginary and that it was foolhardy to have been forced to return to Ulster. Nevertheless he felt more at ease than he had at Chalk Hall. Here he was a military commander; he knew what his duties were. At home he was constantly at a loss as to what was expected of him. Anne had been dry-eyed on the day he left, his children relieved at his going. Rory was still an enigma to him. That reminded him that he had to visit the O'Hanlon family at Mulahinsa. But before that there was much to do. These rumours of a planned invasion of Ireland by the Spanish had to be dealt with without delay.

He did not blame officials for regarding the ships now being bashed against the stormy Atlantic coast, as a planned offensive. From his informants in the Spanish court, Sir Walter knew only too well that an invasion of Ireland had often been discussed. King Philip had proposed it merely as a subsidiary plan if the Armada's invasion of England were to fail. Sir Walter did not believe that the ships being blown against the Irish coast was such an invasion. That was just accidental, but all the better to keep the Irish occupied. Booty not rebellion was what interested the natives now.

The parchment in his hand told how a ship from the fleet had drifted onto a reef at Tyrconnell, beyond the inlet of Lough Foyle and was on the verge of sinking. He summoned his lieutenant to enter. "Have the crew of the scuttled ship come ashore yet?" he asked when he appeared.

"No Sir. God help them when they do."

"Be that as it may, we will let events proceed as normal." He rose from the chair. "I'm going to the scene to observe." He made himself sound decisive. "And from what I see there, I will formulate further policy."

"You don't want us to interfere?"

"Correct. We'll watch from the rocks and see if indeed any of these dramas have been planned."

The ride was long and arduous and there was a strong October wind with a cutting edge to it. Passing through lowland country, a thick fog slowed them down. His muscles ached. They stopped only to water their horses and eat. In the evening they reached O'Donnell territory and went to the inlet of Lough Foyle and continued on for a few more miles.

"This is the place," the lieutenant said sounding very sure. Sir Walter thought some praise might be appropriate. Pointing to the map in the man's hand, he said, "It was a feat to read that correctly." The other soldiers looked at each other in surprise. Sir Walter enjoyed the moment. Doing the unexpected kept them alert.

He decided not to rest but to go directly to the strand. The wind that had dogged their journey whistled eerily through the reeds. Their timing was perfect. After a few minutes the Spaniards, their brown faces and dark eyes full of fear, came struggling through the surf. Some of the men were younger than George or Rory.

A few peasants, who had been picking plankton on the rocks, stopped what they were doing and went to meet the castaways. They greeted the Spaniards warmly shaking their hands and gesturing towards the land. The Spaniards made attempts to bow. Sir Walter was troubled by this warm feeling between them. If the Spaniards allied with these barbaric Irish, they could cause an abundance of trouble.

His trusted lieutenant came to his side. "A scout has reconnoitred and found an English fort within a mile of here. He has procured a pallet there for you. The men will set up camp in the clearing beside it."

Sir Walter felt the salt wind cut through him. He gathered his cloak closely around him and with a backward glance at the gathering on the beach, said, "I've seen enough. It'll be getting dark soon."

Tallows flared in the fort when he entered and he went immediately to his pallet. His head ached. The pillow beneath his head leaked feathers. A thick yellow mucus had dried between his lips and his nose. That's why he felt so poorly. He'd caught a cold out on that rugged shore.

For hours he twisted on his pallet, thoughts circling in his head. The Spaniards would need food and rest and then in a few weeks they would be able to help the locals against this very garrison. Her Majesty would be displeased with him if such happened. His emissary would tell her of his conviction that the Spaniards were harmless. He wondered if it were possible to lose a title. He tried to block out his fears and finally fell into some kind of sleep.

In his dream wolves were howling. The Irish were beheading him. He could see King Philip II entering Dublin Castle. The victors shouted, "Death to the English."

He heard his name called. "Sir Walter!" He woke with a start, stroking his neck with his fingers.

"Sir Walter!" His lieutenant was calling. Why was he being disturbed at this hour? This was what happened when you doled out praise. Conceit was what had his lieutenant knocking on his door so early. He opened it a crack.

"On the shore. Come and see. The Spaniards they …"

He was sick of thinking of the Spaniards and the Irish together, sick of what his miscalculation would mean to his future, sick of the sight of this lieutenant. "I will see for myself," he said. "Whatever it is, is clearly beyond your ability to relate." He had a sudden overwhelming feeling that he had to do this alone.

The sound of the breakers against the shore told Sir Walter that he was near the place where he had stood the previous night. Seeing a pass between the rocks he made his way towards the strand.

What had his lieutenant been raving about? Perhaps the Spaniards had armed themselves or built an arsenal already. He knew all about the gunrunners in the towns who supplied arms to the rebels. With gold from the ships, the insurgents would be able to buy many weapons. He continued walking.

When he reached the rocks from where he had watched the shore last night he recognised the spot where the Spaniards had emerged from the foam. The breeze became colder and the clouds began to spit rain.

Then he came upon the shocking sight.

The Spaniards lay on the sand, naked, their faces frozen in surprise. Black bruises adorned their temples like misplaced beauty marks. The murderers had piled the corpses on the shore line for the water to wash. Some had obviously tried to flee. A ring embossed with a heart glittered on the knuckle of one young man. A scavenger had attempted to pull it over the finger. Sir Walter stooped and pushed it back. In all he counted thirty-two bodies. Feeling sorrow for these dead men who had believed the natives were friendly, welcoming, he instructed his lieutenant to arrange for the burying of the dead.

Then he plodded back to his chamber. Along the way he saw women, baskets in hand, filled with gold chains, jewels and medallions. He was foolish to have doubted his original estimation of the situation. If the wild beasts couldn't co-operate and unite with each other, how could they do so with foreigners? He sometimes forgot the Irish were savages, and such lapses frightened him.

Chapter Twelve

Twilight had shadowed the parlour at Mulahinsa. Cormac had placed his chair under the narrow window above him and was busy with his accounts. Brigid had lit three candles and placed them in the wall sconces but still eyes were strained. She had turned to stoke the fire when Brian came in. "'Tis welcome back you are Sir," she said.

He smiled half heartedly at her and, taking a stool, went over and sat with his father. "Father I must speak with you." His tone was serious.

Cormac abandoned the accounts.

"A Spanish ship has floundered off Beanna Point," Brian said. "I want to ask you to succour them."

"In my humble opinion every province should aid them," Cormac said.

"I was so uneasy about asking you."

Cormac gave a satisfied grunt. "Thought you might be." His tone lost its levity. "But when we help these Spaniards, we risk every life at Mulahinsa."

"When we help. Does that mean you will?"

"I've been considering it since yesterday. Before you came. The stories we have been hearing from the south has horrified all of us. It will be a chance to strike a blow against England. Your mother agrees. I have already got the servants to bring straw in from the fields. I thought it would be better to be prepared. We'll have to leave the cattle out at night for a while."

"Yes."

"We'll leave for Beanna Point in the morning."

"We'll have to keep the venture secret, "Brian said, "I know how plentiful informers are."

Cormac agreed. "We will have to tell the kitchen servants and Shane, of course. It would be unfair to hide it from him."

"The fewer people who know the less there are to suffer if anything goes wrong." Brian spoke in a low voice.

"I hope the Spaniards are still alive," Cormac said. "My *uirrí* was afraid for their safety."

Next morning the kitchen was buzzing with the preparation of food for the forty expected starving sailors. Brigid stirred a steaming pot. "'Tis handy this cauldron of chicken brawn will be," she told no-one in particular.

"Tell Dara," Maeve said to her, "that when he finishes the thatch, we need three more pigs slaughtered. We'll have to hang extra hooks as well."

Molly's face glowed with excitement. She was slicing bacon into thick strips.

"'Tisn't forgetting what the mistress said you'll be Molly," Brigid said, eyeing her. "A secret this is."

"'Tis a break for me, 'tis, Brigid. The mistress would leave me turning the spit forever." She put a hand to her face. "And me skin is getting blotched."

Brigid's response was edgy. "'Tis too much time you spend with the master and Shane I'm thinking. Hurry with those vittles. Dead with hunger these men will be."

The surviving Spaniards had walked some distance inland, hungry, footsore, their clothes torn to rags. The path through the bog was soft and their feet sunk in the spongy ground. Their spirits were near breaking.

When Brian saw them approach, he left down the sack of food he had brought and waited. Cormac sat on a clump of bracken.

The Spanish leader stepped forward. He was a low sized man with curling black hair and dark eyes with a hungry glint. On his gaunt body he had fashioned a type of Roman toga. Despite his dilemma, his confidence appeared intact. "I am Antonio," he said in Latin.

"My information is that there were forty of you," Cormac answered in the same tongue. "I can only count twenty-two."

Another man stepped forward. "My name is Don, and I will tell you what happened to the rest of us. They are dead. They died from the flux or were killed by savages. We have nothing left but our lives. Your people stripped us of our jewels, our coins and even our relics." He ceased to talk only when Antonio turned to him and gave him a cautionary glance.

"Trust us," Cormac said. "We will protect you. We are no friends of the Queen of England."

The Spaniards looked at each other. Meeting the rock of Cormac's will, they were in no mind to resist. Some shrugged, but most were impassive as they limped forward. A few looked despairing.

"Our castle is ten miles from here, but we have brought some food," Brian said.

He and Cormac took fish, milk and oatcakes from their sacks and bid the refugees eat. Cormac and Brian sat on the quagmire and joined them. After they had eaten, they trekked slowly to Mulahinsa.

When they arrived, Cormac showed them where they would be staying and warned them not to leave the protection of the *bawn*. "There are always men who will inform for a price. You will get us all killed if you do." The women, he told them, would make apparel for them. They would be fed from the castle. He would try to get them on a boat to Scotland. From there they would be able to get back to Spain.

Each night the Spaniards slept on straw. Every day Brigid and Molly brought them food and water. No other servants were trusted. After a week Antonio's eyes shone when Molly approached. One morning as she dished out his porridge, their hands touched. Her breath quickened.

Brigid noticed. "'Tis all the signs I do be seeing that you know that Shane and Cormac are tiring of you. Leave Antonio be," she warned.

"'Tis a handsome man he is, and that's the truth I'm sayin'. Marrying me he'll be and sweeping me off to his big castle in Spain." Molly's eyes were wide.

Weeks sped by. The men began to get restless. They saw Antonio and Molly slink away at twilight each evening and return in the early hours. It was dangerous, they knew and they were afraid, for him and for themselves. "We have no wish to be suspended from a rope," they said. "He is in command only because so many of us were murdered. We will all be killed because of him." But Antonio didn't hear.

Then one morning shortly after breakfast Finola heard Brigid's excited voice from her mother's bed-chamber. "'Tis Sir Walter Carew ma'am. 'Tis below he is. I saw him approach with his soldiers. I ran up the rear stairway. He didn't see me." Her voice came in pants. "There was no time to prepare."

"Thank you Brigid," her mother said. "You may help Caitlín clear the dishes in the hall. I'll deal with this."

She passed Finola on the landing. "I'll rely on you to maintain normality," she said, squeezing her shoulder in an unusual gesture of affection.

Her tone was falsetto when she met Sir Walter. "You're welcome. Please come in."

"I thought I should pay you a visit before I returned to England."

Finola peeped down the last flight of stairs to see Sir Walter closing the door. Maeve stepped back from him. "Please follow me." She led him to the parlour.

"I have something for you," Sir Walter said in a tremulous voice. He fumbled in his sack where he found his parchments but not what he was looking for. "I have some devices with which to kill mice."

Maeve studied the haughty Englishman with his head stuck in the sack like a horse at his feed bag and looked less anxious that the Spaniards would be discovered.

"I have found them. I was afeared I had left them in Tyrconnell." Sir Walter pulled several contraptions out of his sack and chose one from the pile."Attract them with a piece of cheese and as they nibble on this part here, the spring will break their necks."

"More merciful than kicking them to death surely."

"Quite." Sir Walter gave no indication that he understood that to which Maeve referred.

She swiftly changed the subject. "Rory, what of him?" We expect him back soon."

"It depends on Her Majesty and her plans for Glenone but I'm heartened that the Irish are not helping the Armada survivors. That will convince the queen they have potential for loyalty.

"You're generous with your compliments Sir Walter." She looked away from him. "But I hope your new respect persuades you that Ulster is ready for the newly civilised Rory Maguire."

Finola wondered what she could do to minimise the danger of their being discovered harbouring the Spaniards. Her father and Brian had gone to Dundalk to arrange to have the refugees shipped to Scotland. They had been gone three days. Only Shane was available and he didn't have any love for the survivors.

If the Spaniards stayed where they were, they would be safe. Finola was grateful that the men from Spain were out of sight of the castle entrance. But she was also aware that they could view its doorway from afar and so knew what had transpired. She hoped they would remain calm despite the soldiers' presence. She had to explain the situation to them. That it was mere chance that had brought Sir Walter Carew.

In their makeshift abodes the men were sitting arguing among themselves in Spanish. "We did not expect a visitor Seõrita," Antonio said. "You are welcome." As he spoke two of his comrades circled her.

"I have come to reassure you that the man visiting with my mother is a ... a friend," Finola began, starting to feel nervous.

"The lady is unsure whether he is friend or foe," Antonio's voice was smooth. "It is an English army. They will kill you if they find you sheltering us."

"He does not know that you are here. We will not betray you."

Another man said, "With a club above my head, an Irishman forced me to doff my garments and give him my coin. I wonder what you have in store for us this time." She sensed danger. These men felt tired of the idleness. Their stomachs were full, but they were frightened and distrustful.

"We will not let anybody butcher us again Señorita. Your people welcomed us to your country, beguiled us with false smiles, then murdered us." He reached underneath the straw where they had hidden the stout stakes used for penning the cattle and handed them round to the others.

Antonio peered out at the waiting soldiers.

"They say every man going to his death unburdens himself," he said.

Finola felt her heart lurch. "They don't know you are here. Wait quietly and they will leave in a short while."

Antonio eyed her and said, "The lady lies beautifully."

Finola felt her blood rise. He was a lecher. "Why do think they're waiting? Do you think they know you're here and are waiting for you to shoot at them? Be sensible."

"They are waiting for their leader to give them orders," Antonio answered. "The English do not function well without orders. That is the only virtue we share with the Irish ... hatred of the Saxon."

"We have nothing to gain by betraying you." She made an effort to be seductive by looking admiringly at him from under her eyelashes.

Antonio let some quiet seconds pass. He looked towards his men. "Agreed then. We will wait a little and see. But if you are telling untruths ..."

Chapter Thirteen

Finola watched Sir Walter Carew leave the castle and walk slowly down the track to his waiting soldiers. He stopped suddenly and turned. "He's forgotten something." She tried to keep her voice steady.

Nobody moved. The Spaniards gripped their clubs.

Then Maeve hurried down the path carrying a parchment. An epistle for Rory. Nobody would think from her mother's serene expression that their lives were hanging in the balance. Finola was under no illusions about Sir Walter's ability to order their executions.

He took the document and turned to his lieutenant. "We can head for Carlingford now. We have nothing left to do here. We may meet Cormac O'Hanlon en route. He has gone to Dundalk to report Armada survivors he spied some twenty miles from here."

Her mother had used the excuse to explain Cormac's absence. She had stuck so close to the truth she had allayed suspicions and lulled Sir Walter into a belief in their loyalty.

As the soldiers rode away from the castle, the Spaniards slapped each other on the back, raised their fists in the air and blessed themselves.

Another day passed. Finola was worried. She had come to the dye house to divert herself from her concerns. Cormac and Brian had not returned from their expedition. She hoped the English had not discovered their mission. Also Brigid had reported that Molly had been absent since the previous day. She had just begun to organise herself in her dyeing when Brigid ran in, exclaiming. "'Tis coming up the track your father is this very minute."

She rushed out. Brian and Cormac were riding abreast. Brian looked gaunt and anxious. Her father was pale and strained. The kernes who rode behind had set faces. Without dismounting Cormac said, "We heard in Gowla that Sir Walter Carew and his battalion passed this way. We thought you'd all be dead."

"He discovered nothing," Finola said.

Cormac leapt from his horse. "The Spaniards will walk to Larne in the morning. We'll ship them to Edinburgh. There's a Catholic contingent there who has been petitioning King Philip for a brigade against the English for years. They will look after them well."

Maeve walked sedately down the path towards them.

"You look like you have fought a battle," Cormac said, admiration in his tone.

"A verbal skirmish," Maeve said, her eyes meeting Finola's. Both of them laughed. It had been so long since Finola and her mother had shared a common adventure.

"Mother is a real life heroine," she said to her father. "I'll let her recount the story of Sir Walter herself." She gave him a gentle push in her mother's direction. He took Maeve's arm and linked her inside.

Finola went over to Brian still on his horse. "Come down out of there, Chief exalted. I want to tell you about my part in the drama."

Neither of them noticed Shane standing over by the side, a strangely withdrawn expression on his face.

The Spaniards washed themselves and their apparel. All the servants lugged tubs of springwater to them. The sound of singing, talking and scrubbing came from behind the eight foot wall. They would soon be in Scotland and they sang about it in Spanish. In Latin, the aristocrats expressed their gratitude to their hosts. To the common soldier Latin was as strange as Gaelic so they smiled their thanks.

That evening Finola went to say good bye to the Spaniards. When she noticed that Antonio was missing she asked Don where he was. "We haven't seen him since last night," Don said. Then he muttered something about "Señorita Molly" and walked away.

"There is something you are not telling me," Finola called after him.

"Antonio was trifling with this Molly." He turned. "That is all I know."

"He'd better hurry back," she said seeking to hide her disquiet, "or you'll have to leave him behind."

She'd better tell Cormac of Antonio's disappearance. There would be no need to connect Molly's name with it.

As she was leaving, Brigid came running towards her, "Holy mother of God!" She blessed herself when she reached Finola, "it's the divil's work."

149

"Yes Brigid, what is it?" she asked.

"We've found her, your mother and me," she said. "Molly and she stone dead."

Finola wrapped her arms across her breasts.

"'Tis not the only corpse neither. Brace yourself." Brigid pulled her by the arm, impatient to show her the spectacle.

Though she was unsure why, Finola was unsurprised that the bodies were near the loading bay. A slight drizzle was falling. Molly lay, her legs askew, her frock ripped; dark marks were clearly visible about her neck. Antonio lay beside her, a bloody opening on his head.

Maeve didn't look up, just concentrated on unfolding a pair of white sheets. "These will have to act as shrouds," she said.

Numb was how Finola felt. Only a few days previously she had seen Antonio ready to attack Sir Walter Carew's soldiers. Now he was dead himself.

"For God's sake help, Finola," Brigid, forgetting her servant status, said, "don't just stand there."

Molly's head was at a peculiar angle. Finola tried not to think about it as she lifted the red hair from the dirt. She and Brigid lifted her upper body while Maeve did the same with her feet and together they hoisted the body onto the white sheet. They did similar with Antonio and folded the sheets over. "Does father know?" Finola had been putting off asking the question.

"Yes, Shane 'told' him first. He saw Antonio attack Molly. By the time he had run down the stairs, he had squeezed the life out of her. In a fit of rage Shane killed him." Her voice lame she added, "Look before you leap I cautioned him all his life."

"Is he speaking the truth?" Finola found herself asking. Her lips were stiff with shock. "Shane I mean."

"See what happened for yourself," Maeve's tone was harsh. "Shane is very shaken."

When Finola went back to the castle to see Shane and Cormac, she was trembling. They were sitting together on a bench. Her father seemed to have grown smaller since this morning and his skin was grey. "We must bury them as soon as possible," was all he said.

She looked at Shane. Fortunate for him that Molly was a scullion and Antonio a foreigner.

For an instant the clever blue eyes focused on her, and then returned to their usual slackly lidded state, unperturbed by her scrutiny.

Chapter Fourteen

England

Back at Chalk Hall life for Rory had become dull. George had decided quite suddenly to forego his place at Oxford and pursue a military career. He had chosen to join the Kentish allotment that trained at the local military headquarters at Canterbury. "If nobody volunteered, England would be defenceless," he had said. "Anyway father loves the military life and I will come to like it too." But on the day of his departure, as a tearful Anne hugged him close, he had blurted out, "I have to go. Can you not see? It is the only way to make father proud of me."

Rory had felt envious that morning, as he watched the carriage roll away. Not of George or his destination, but of his getaway. If only events would overtake him like they had George. He too would have to think of a plan that would speed his departure from Chalk Hall. At nineteen, the Carews were still guiding his life. And it was choking him. If Sir Walter's edicts about behaviour were not so strict, he could have some enjoyment but he even disapproved of bowling, for god sakes.

For nigh on eight years, he had been in training for his return to Ireland. Now that Sir Walter was back he would have a purpose at least in tolerating Jane's foolishness towards him. Her father would not countenance a marriage between an Irish yokel and his daughter and would do anything to keep them apart.

Jane was sitting in the parlour, as he knew she would, on her favourite chair by the wall, holding a square of embroidery. Jane and her infernal stitching were inseparable. Wanting to get the pretence over quickly, he sat beside her. "What is that you are doing?"

She said, "It is a handkerchief for George. You know how he likes flowers on his cloths."

He did know and he thought it silly but he said, "What a good idea. You are so good to everybody, Jane."

"Oh Rory, I do love you." And she left her head on his shoulder.

Later that evening as they sat at the trestle table for their evening repast, he let his hand linger on Jane's arm for a fraction longer than was necessary and felt a glow of satisfaction when

151

Sir Walter gave a disapproving glance in his direction. "Rory," he said, "to my surprise the Irish behaved admirably in their dealing with the escapees from the Armada. Behaved true to their nature."

"Oh, yes?" Rory queried.

"As the Spanish hobbled ashore, the natives fell on them. They attacked them on the rocks, beat them with clubs, and slit their throats." Sir Walter detailed the happenings all the while staring intently at Rory.

Rory felt the blood rush to his cheeks. "The government ordered the Irish not to help any Spaniard," he said staring back. "Bingham proclaimed he would treat anyone who billeted them for more than twenty-four hours as a traitor. The penalty death."

"Is this true Walter? We ordered the Irish to murder defenceless people?" Anne asked.

"Let's eat," Sir Walter ordered. "This conversation is not helping my appetite."

There must have been people who helped them, Rory thought. Somebody would have had the sense to realise that Ulster would need Spain's help to keep what belonged to it. The stony face of Sir Walter reminded him that it was not in his interests to thwart him too much. Expedience began with knowing when to retreat.

He stroked Jane's ankle with his own causing her colour to heighten. She cast shifty eyes in her father's direction. "Stop it, Rory," she whispered.

Sir Walter's pallor changed. He shifted on the chair. Somehow Rory knew that Gaelic-Spanish relations were not the reason for his discomfort.

After supper Sir Walter went to his study and read through the most recent dispatch from Her Majesty. Since Elizabeth had succeeded as queen, her policy towards Ireland had swung between combat and compromise. Neither was wholly successful. The cost of ruling Ireland enraged her. Like her father Henry VIII, she was tight with the purse strings. The missive concluded with the edict:

We must rule Ireland more cheaply. Members of Her Majesty's council are at present considering a new policy they foresee will be more effective.

When he had read the dispatch, Sir Walter, deep in thought,

opened the door leading from his study and climbed the steps to the chapel.

In the gloom, he picked out his pew and fell to his knees. He pondered on Her Majesty's missive and then suddenly the solution came to him. Looking upwards at the altar, he prayed aloud. "Thank you God for giving me this gleam of a solution."

If he acted quickly, he could still win. He would write of his idea while it was fresh in his mind. As swiftly as he knelt, he rose and walked away from his place of worship towards his bureau. He extracted a parchment from a drawer and began to write:

It may please your Majesty to know that my ward Rory Maguire is now a grown ...

Chapter Fifteen

Sir Walter had cornered Rory in the library. "Rory," he said, his expression funereal as he motioned him to a chair. "Come, sit with me here. I see my daughter has become very friendly with you."

"Yes." Rory thought that, at last, his plan had begun to work

"She is unworldly. Religious, a good person. An unspoiled girl like her will meet a Protestant gentleman someday."

It was as he envisioned. Sir Walter did not want him wooing his daughter. A reformed papist and a barbarian were not what he wanted for a son-in-law.

"I am almost nineteen now," he said. "I am beginning to care a lot for Jane. You are right. She would make a good wife."

Sir Walter's expression was pained. Then he said peremptorily, "You are to visit London to present yourself to the queen and her council."

Rory merely nodded and walked slowly towards the door. In his bed-chamber, unable to contain his delight any longer, he pulled the bolster from his bed and, holding it in his arms, danced around the room. Victory! Sir Walter wanted him out of his house and lost in the desolation of Ireland, far away from his chaste daughter. He would hazard going to Jane's room tonight. To celebrate.

On the morning of their departure for London Sir Walter, instead of his usual sombre apparel, sported a green velvet doublet attached by laces to his breeches. Underneath, he wore a white ruff shirt the frill of which, high about his throat, accented his face.

For the first time Rory saw the loose pouches under Sir Walter's eyes. Lately, he had also noticed that Sir Walter's hair had thinned on top. The silk hat he was wearing now for the trip, covered the patch and made him appear younger, but his beard was completely grey. Anne still looked much younger than him. He must be at least fifty.

Sir Walter's change in clothing did not surprise him. Rory knew that while he was in London he would pretend he was a lukewarm Anglican. Elizabeth was not a zealot herself and did not like excessive religious zeal in others.

Over a well fitting doublet and trunk hose, Rory himself wore a cloak which emphasized the breadth of his shoulders. The mantle he had worn coming to Chalk Hall was too small for him now. Out of earshot of Sir Walter, he whispered to Jane, "Well Janie, how do I look?"

"Oh Rory." Her voice was thick with tears as she whispered her devotion wetly in his ear.

"I shall pine for you," he said. He was going to London, and then to Ireland, he could afford to be generous.

She fished in the pocket of her gown for another handkerchief.

"Stay indoors," Sir Walter ordered as he kissed Anne on the brow. "It is cold outside."

Anne touched him on the arm. "Be vigilant." Her eyes were anxious. "A man of your lineage should not undertake such a journey with only one other for company. Do as I beg. Take Spence with you."

Sir Walter pursed his mouth. "Anne. We have discussed this already. We will go faster and be less conspicuous on our own. I abhor travellers who bring their household with them. Do I have to remind you of my hatred of pageantry?"

"No, Walter."

He turned to Rory. "Let us go."

Anne kissed Rory on the cheek. Jane sobbed and ran in the direction of her chamber.

Sir Walter's eyes followed her retreating figure. "Come along Rory," he ordered.

Spence stood holding the reins of the horses, his hands blue from the cold. Yet his humour was benign. Since the first day he and Rory met at Bristol, they were allies.

"You should have stayed in the stables," Rory said, "It would have been warmer."

"Expected you every minute, that I did," Spence answered, "No harm done."

"Someone misinformed you," Sir Walter stated. "I said we would leave early. It is early."

"Yessir." As he held his chestnut steed steady for him, Spence winked at Rory.

Turning his horse's head towards Canterbury for the journey to London, the thought ran through Rory's mind that his life up to this had been a preparation for today and for what was to come.

The sporadic drizzle, that fell more as a reminder of the season than any real risk of rain, dampened his enthusiasm. Through miles of flat countryside he and Sir Walter rode side by side. The pits and sloughs were similar to the pot holes in Ireland. They rode carefully, Sir Walter deep in thought. Rory remained silent, absorbed by the wagons and pack-trains that travelled too along the London Road. When they reached Canterbury, he broke the silence. "George is here, he said. "May we visit him?"

Sir Walter was irritated by the request. "You expect me to spend the day searching for my son when I could be half-way to London? To what purpose? To greet him? We will stop at this inn to water our horses and perform our ablutions, that is all the stopping we will do."

Tight-lipped, Rory went to the privy as Sir Walter talked to the ostler. Back on the road again, he found it hard to concentrate on his riding. It had been morning when they left Chalk Hall. Now evening approached. His horse sweated. Hunger pangs gnawed at him. He needed to go to the privy again. If they did not stop soon, he would have to say something. He gritted his teeth.

Finally Sir Walter said, "We will stay in an inn for the night."

Rory's face was rigid as they reined in.

A servant, a short man with black hair and a thick beard took their horses. "I will walk them 'till they get cool Squire, then I will rub them down and give them to eat." His voice was high pitched.

Darkness had begun to fall. The passages smelt of must as he followed his guide through the flickering shadows.

When he entered the room, the servant left his luggage on the floor and kindled the fire. The flames had begun to dance, when he said, "There Sir. Now the boots I'll take, if I may Sir. Clean them for you."

"They are clean enough."

"Very good, Sir." The man hesitated a moment. "Is it far you're travelling?

"We are going to London."

"You don't say, Sir."

"We are to meet The Queen."

The servant's eyes narrowed. "That is an honour indeed, Sir. To meet *Her Gracious Majesty.*" As he headed towards the door, he lifted Rory's bag, held it, and left it down again.

Rory reflected on how friendly the servant was, a pleasant change from Sir Walter.

The candle on the night-table, with the grease congealed on its sides and on the holder, shed little light. The drapes were faded and the carpet was threadbare. But the bed linen looked newly washed. Every muscle in his body ached. The water in the pitcher on the wash stand was ice cold. He eyed the bell pull. His eyes burned. He would wash in the morning. Doffing his apparel, he laid his head on the pillow ...

He threshed in the bed. Then he heard a loud knocking. It could not be morning already. "Who is it?" he asked. His voice was thick with sleep as he called through the planks.

"It's Sir Walter." The announcement came crisp and clear. "We are leaving."

Rory rubbed his eyes and pulled himself out of the bed. What was wrong with him now? The sooner he would be rid of these Carews the better. "I have to wash," was all he could think of to say.

"Now," Sir Walter said. "We are leaving now."

When he went out, he found Sir Walter standing like a sentinel next to his door, his baggage beside him.

"What's wrong?"

"Later. I will tell you later."

The entrance hall was empty except for a scrawny cat who sniffed at their boots in hope of a meal. Carefully Sir Water deposited a shilling on the table. A board creaked under Rory's feet. "Quiet," Sir Walter said. "We do not want to waken anybody."

In the stables, the ostler lay curled on the straw, asleep beside the horses. "Do not make any noise," Sir Walter said again. "The quicker we get away from here the better."

When Rory raised a questioning eyebrow, Sir Walter said, "You told your servant you were going to London."

"Yes! I mentioned it."

"Did you notice if he took an interest in the weight of your bag?"

"Yes. Why did he do that?"

"Wanted to see if it contained coin."

"Similar happened to me."

On hearing Sir Walter's admission, Rory felt less foolish.

"He was unaware of *my* destination." Sir Walter said. "I overheard him tell his highwayman friend *your* direction. We would have been robbed if we had waited till morning. If only you had kept your counsel ..."

Uncomfortable, Rory bit his lip.

"You cannot find all your knowledge in books," Sir Walter finished.

But Rory knew how true that was. That was why, discerning as Sir Walter thought he was, he had not seen through his plan. If he had, he would not be in such a hurry to send him back to Ireland.

They rode through the night and by dawn had covered a long distance. Soon *The Hillock Inn* came into view

"We will breakfast here," Sir Walter said. "The ostler will feed and water the horses."

An aroma of cooked fish greeted them. The host, a genial man joined them at the table. "The Queen is to make one of her progresses through the city today," he told them. "Merchants have built causeways across the marsh and clay belts."

Rory did not open his mouth except to eat the dish of white herring set before him.

"Good," replied Sir Walter. "We will be able to ride faster from here on."

Out on the road again the rest of their journey passed quickly and soon they were dismounting at Bayswater.

"We have arrived at an opportune time," Sir Walter said. He took Rory by the arm. "We will line up along the street with these good citizens."

Rory caught a glimpse of the queen's open carriage. Her retainers rode before and aft. From the centre of her seat, she waved to the crowds on either side of the road. She was wearing a gown under an ermine cape. A little girl near him tugged at her mother's sleeve and said innocently, "Her la'yship is made o' gold."

"Aye, made o' gold," said the mother, "wit' a heart o' gold."

Though the queen waved in a typical regal fashion, Rory saw that her expression was one of genuine enjoyment. Men and women staged pageants in her honour while children explained their meaning in verse.

Gesturing with one hand, the queen silenced the crowd so that she could hear the boys and girls speak. That's what it means to have power, Rory thought. As she passed from his view, she carried a sprig of rosemary a subject had pressed into her hand.

"Indeed she has her father's attraction for the people," Sir Walter said.

Rory remained silent letting the surroundings filter through. He had never been in a place like London before. The maze of streets, so different from the rolling hills of Ulster or the chalky countryside of Kent, filled him with wonder and even a little dread. If he had come here from Mulahinsa without having learned the lessons of Chalk Hall, he would have run away.

Chapter Sixteen

Sir Walter walked Rory through several streets. "That is the royal Palace of Whitehall on the river front," he said. "To the west of it is St. James's. The Queen has several palaces within a day's ride of London," he added by way of explanation. "Her Majesty likes to move her court from one royal palace to another." He pointed in the general direction of the Thames. "Behind the river, on the other side of the Strand, is my town house."

17 Cowlminister St was at the end of a row of houses, its gable end facing onto a side street. Weeds peeped through the stone of the courtyard. The stables needed a coat of whitewash. Black paint peeled from the front door. The butler answered eventually. A maid bobbed a curtsy and took their cloaks.

"Tell the cook I wish to partake of supper in an hour," Sir Walter said. Then he motioned Rory to the sitting room where famed men of the day and of times past hung on the walls. Sir Walter was not as pure a Calvinist as he pretended considering they regarded portraits as articles of human conceit. He would peruse the paintings until it was time to eat.

Portraits of Henry VIII and his leading ministers by Holbein covered one wall. Rory imagined what Cormac's reaction would be if he saw the esteem in which the originator of *Surrender and re-grant* treaty was held. But then Rory would not have any right to Glenone if his grandfather had not accepted the English terms, a fact that surfaced in his mind at the most peculiar times.

A series of miniatures of the Dutch writer Erasmus hung on the opposite wall alongside one of Martin Luther by Lucas Cranach. Then a small picture on the fourth wall drew his eye. A young man, ordinary among the other figures, stared out at him. He moved closer. When he found himself searching for the scar that had been on his father's chin, he laughed at his foolishness. It was ludicrous to think that Sir Walter would own a portrait of Rory's father.

He looked again. Of course! How asinine of him. It was a likeness of a much younger Sir Walter. But as they both answered cook's call to eat, Rory turned to gaze another time at the likeness.

They ate in silence until the butler entered carrying a silver tray with a dispatch placed upon it. He bowed and proffered it to Sir Walter.

Sir Walter opened the message and read it. Then lifting his head, he said, "Rory, Her Majesty has summoned you to appear before a small group of the crown's most trusted advisers. Wednesday. You are to meet them in the blue room at Nonsuch Palace."

Rory looked up from his food.

Sir Walter continued, "They will convene in the blue room at eleven o'clock. We must be well prepared."

At eleven o'clock on Wednesday, Rory was sitting in the vestibule outside the blue room waiting to be cross-examined. Would Elizabeth really be there? Sir Walter had been unsure.

A smell of polish from the oak floor mixed with the odour of marjoram and made him feel slightly nauseated. He had resolved in bed last night that he would not be overawed by what was happening but, alone with the hammering of his heart, he was finding it difficult to remain calm. He was afraid that when the doorman beckoned him through the pilaster flanked door, his legs would be too weak to carry him.

At the top of the room, five men sat at a table, a clerk at a smaller one on the side. The clerk gestured him to his appointed chair.

He recognised Sir Francis Walsingham and Lord Burghley. He had read about these men. Sir Francis ran an efficient spy service for the queen in England and overseas. Lord Burghley had survived the flexible policies and changes of administration of Edward VI and Mary Tudor. They stared down at him from their rostrum. He felt their eyes run from his thigh high boots to his head and tried not to fidget.

Lord Burghley introduced everybody and motioned to the clerk to begin taking notes. The clerk looked at the ornate clock beside him and held his quill aloft with a flourish.

"This is an interesting enterprise," Lord Burghley said, "in so far as it concerns the nephew of Eoin Maguire. This young man, Rory Maguire, has been a guest in the house of the venerable Sir Walter Carew for the past eight years. I wish to affirm the council's admiration for Sir Walter. He took this boy into his family and taught him how to live civilly. We respect him for undertaking this task."

He must remain impassive and leave the button on his cloak alone.

You are nephew of Eoin Maguire," Lord Burghley said, addressing Rory.

"Yes Sir, he is my uncle by blood."

Lord Burghley said, "I will allow Sir James Perrott to take over."

Sir James was a portly gentleman with damp skin and eyes so big for his little face that God should have created them for someone else. "Our Lord Deputy had to make many forays into your uncle's lands. The man is impudent."

They were unable to defeat him. That was their problem. "I am sorry to hear that Sir," Rory lied.

Sir James exchanged a glance with Lord Burghley that asked if he should continue. Rory felt his misfit eyes examine him. "You are loyal to England?"

"I have lived here for eight years Sir. It is my home."

"You have not answered the question," Sir Francis Walsingham, a cadaverous man with narrow lips, interjected.

"I was never disloyal."

"Hardly had the opportunity. You were a boy when you came. If you got the chance, what then?"

Lord Howard interrupted, "Rory is not on trial here. What my colleague wants to confirm is that you are a loyal subject of *Her Gracious Majesty*."

Lord Howard, with his direct gaze, was the pacifier. He continued to speak, "We hope to set up permanent garrisons around the perimeters of Eoin Maguire's lands."

So they would be better able to invade his territory. "That would be an interesting task for the right person," Rory said.

The fifth person, a small man on the right of the group from whom Rory had sensed animosity, did not speak at all. He was Arthur Petrell. He had a son, Sir Walter told Rory, a soldier of twenty one, missing in Ireland for the past three years, believed dead.

The council put their heads together and talked in low tones. If Sir Walter spoke truly, the purpose of this interview was merely to acquaint him with the situation in Ireland, and their expectations of him. Lord Brughley turned to Rory. "We have decided to allot the task to you."

"It will be an honour to serve the crown. I will do my utmost to be worthy of your trust."

Lord Burghley continued. "We will give you an army of eight hundred men." He looked straight into Rory's eyes. "Of course given that you are only nineteen years old and have no formal military background, you will be under Sir Walter's guidance. He will train you to take command. Sir Walter will also provide your purse."

"Thank you Sir."

"You are on bad terms with your uncle Eoin, I believe."

"I am very grateful for the chance to right the wrong that my uncle did to my family."

Lord Burghley became expansive under Rory's innocent regard. "When you defeat Eoin Maguire, the collateral branches of your family and the smaller clans will hold their lands directly from the crown."

Now he understood. He swallowed hard. It was a clever plan. They did not like Eoin Maguire's power, but that suited him. He felt relieved that the show was over.

Rory felt a mixture of interest and worry about his audience with Elizabeth. His experience with the council had been intimidating yet he had endured. He would be meeting The Queen on his own, which pleased him.

"When she has the time, Her Majesty likes to give young male visitors her undivided attention," Sir Walter told him. "She will not require my presence."

A footman escorted him through the long corridors, far from the blue room of his earlier ordeal, to the royal apartments. As he listened to the sounds and murmurs of the courtiers, emissaries, petitioners and court ladies, he thanked God Ulster was so removed from the pomp of court life.

The décor, too, was a world away from the stone castle where Cormac and Maeve reared him. Colourful cloths hung from the walls; panels of decorated leather sided the doors. Persian and Indian carpets covered the floors.

Waiting in the ante chamber for the queen's summons, the fluster was the same as in the corridors outside the blue room. The refined voices of the ladies-in-waiting floated around him.

Delicately garbed, their bosoms peeped over their Spanish farthingales; their cane hoops kept time with their dainty steps. Before he had time to become too apprehensive, one of them ushered him into Her Majesty's presence.

"*Your Majesty!*" Realising he should have said that as he bowed, he inflected his voice with sincerity, hoping it made up for his lack of style.

As her penetrating eyes examined him, Rory subtly did the same to her. She appeared older than the day he had seen her in her chariot. Up close he could spot wrinkles that the jewels circling her neck failed to hide. But she was ornately dressed in a white taffeta gown lined with crimson and sewn throughout with pearls and rubies. Pearls were the symbol of virginity. He knew the queen was born under the sign of Virgo and this was September. Also he spotted a set of tapestries on the wall showing the wise and foolish virgins.

At his feet was a colourful Persian carpet that ran through the centre of the room, its warmth contrasting with the coldness of the marble. Then Her Majesty held her hand aloft for Rory to kiss her coronation stone. As he raised his eyes from her ring, he felt a nervous desire to laugh. Finola would have fun if she could see him kissing Lizzie, the queen's feline namesake. Cormac had given the cat her name. "They both purr if they get their own way," he had said.

"You are son of Phelim Maguire, nephew of Eoin Maguire. We are aware of the facts surrounding your case." Her eyes were shrewd. "Our counsellors have made a proposition, which you accepted. We like to meet someone before we give them our trust. A fleeting expression can reveal what words do not. We are satisfied."

The Queen rose from her chair and walked to a table where an astrolabe rested, gesturing to him to follow. She said, "Geminus made this for her royal highness. We place importance on astrology at the court." She traced the craftsmanship with her fingers then pointed to the star map that showed twenty-nine stars. "Astrology ... if only the stars could assure us."

Rory had expected to talk about Ireland, not how the movement and position of the planets affected behaviour. "I know little of the subject *Your Majesty.*" He saw her eyes dim and realised he needed to do something creative. Remembering that even cats like stroking, his eyes caressed her. "The book by Copernicus on celestial spheres is the nearest I have come to studying," he stressed the last two words, "heavenly bodies."

He saw infuriation at his audacity and pleasure at his tribute mingle on Her Majesty's face. Her expression revealed that he was not the illiterate Gaelic clod she expected. She smiled coyly, "You have benefited from your stay with us in England," she said.

Rory was disappointed. He had failed to convince her that she had underestimated the Irish after all.

Chapter Seventeen

Rory would have liked to sample the delights of London but Sir Walter was in a hurry to get home. "We will leave for Ireland as soon as possible," he had said. "I will accompany you with the army, and train you in your duties."

But there was recompense for returning to Chalk Hall early. Jane would be there. Rory's blood rose at the thought. The doxies on the streets of the city had stimulated his appetite, and he felt ripe for her body. It would not be long now until he could appease his desire.

The night of his return he made his way to her bed-chamber and tried to open the door, pushing and heaving for many minutes. He wondered if she had put a padlock on the hasp inside, but then dismissed the thought. The door had stuck, that was all. However, tired, he returned to his bed and fell asleep.

The Jane who met him next morning was paler than usual. She needed the help of beeswax. But, he knew, in deference to her father's aversion to beauty preparations, she would not wear any in his presence. If the thickening waist under her hooped gown were anything to judge by, his absence had only increased her appetite. She offered no explanation for her rebuff of the night before.

This was how things continued. As the weeks passed, he and Jane scarcely saw each other. She spent her time in her bed-chamber with an ailing stomach. And he was too busy learning his duties as commander of a new army to trifle with her.

He spent days in Sir Walter's den sifting through correspondence, one was from Elizabeth's court. It said She expected him to carry out his duties to the crown faithfully, referred to trouble caused by the Campbells and said that She would expect his royal army to move against them. She had signed it *Your loving sovereign, Elizabeth R.*

His appointment depended on his willingness to do The Queen's bidding. He knew he would be unable to evade this assignment. A time would come when he would not have to accept Her Majesty's orders.

While studying lists of the type of soldier he would command in Ireland, he discovered that some of the eight hundred men would be volunteers. Others would be veterans of Elizabeth's continental wars. The majority however would be pressed men; recruiters habitually snatched thieves from prisons, ruffians from taverns and vagabonds and rogues from both city and country to serve in Ireland.

When he expressed his abhorrence of this practice to Sir Walter, he said, "We will persuade the officials that it is not in their interests to resort to these measures. I will compile a background of each soldier and keep a record of desertions." There was a cautionary note in Sir Walter's voice, "Deserters sell arms to the Irish. Be particularly careful who *you* hire."

Rory resented the implication that, because he was a Gael, he would be careless. Sir Walter had become irascible of late. There were times when Rory felt him staring belligerently at him and was puzzled. He had thought that, through working together, he and Sir Walter had come to an understanding. He was even beginning to like him. If it were before his visit to London, he would suspect that he had found out about his assignations with Jane, but he had not been near her since his return.

Anne was acting out of character, too. She snapped at servants and talked in sombre tones to Sir Walter.

But his primary concern had to be his return to Ireland so, with this aim foremost in his mind, he focused on matters at hand.

Sir Walter buttoned his robe in readiness for his return to his chamber. It was Wednesday night and he was hot and sweaty from their coupling.

Anne was lying on the bed in her plain night gown. She said, "I have sought all evening to find words to explain to you about our daughter. There is no other way but to say it outright Walter." She looked at his bent head. "Jane is with child."

He pressed at an artery on his temple. "Are you sure?"

When she nodded, he remained very still. In a mumble he said almost to himself, "It is God's judgement. The seed is passed on." He knew Rory Maguire was pivotal to the situation, but it was too horrific to acknowledge openly. Instead he prevaricated. "A marriage in affluent families is barter like any other. A pauper can choose to marry the girl he loves. Distinguished families like us expect their children to marry pedigree and family fortune. If love is there, so much the better. It alleviates suffering from wifely duties."

"Yes Walter."

"That the man is a gentleman and a Puritan is important."

He noted Anne's hesitation before she said, "Rory Maguire fits the first of these." He will be a landowner of modest means in Ireland." She leaned over and took his hand. "Men will not saturate Jane with offers of matrimony."

Snapping his hand back, he rubbed his temple. "I may not have made myself clear. Rory will leave for Ulster shortly. He is intelligent enough to realise that someone like Jane is out of his sphere, if you are not."

"I do not want a Gaelic son in-law either." Anne added under her breath, "Jane may be grateful to anybody who will marry her."

"Rory Maguire is going to Ireland, Anne." Sir Walter staggered towards the door, his temple throbbing.

Chapter Eighteen

Mabel, Jane's personal maid, and her sister, Elise, were in Jane's bed-chamber at the appointed time. "Tell us again what happened this morning Mabel," Elise was saying

"I tol' you afore. I was awaking Miss Jane and pullin' back her bed curtains when she jerked me by the arm. Like this."

"Hey, steady on."

"She asked me to meet her here at midday, after we'd eaten, and she tol' me to bring you."

"Mabel, Are you sure she dina tell you why?"

"No, but I think it's to do with Master Maguire. Altho' this morning I met him on the corridor, and he didna say anything." For a moment Mabel looked dreamy. "He's why I'm here. Not for Miss Jane at all. He was good to me when I was a scullery maid. I do not wanna get into trouble with her ladyship."

"I know. You told me enough times."

Mabel said, "If they wan' us to be witnesses in a secret marriage, we could get into trouble."

"Rory dinna lie with her since he came back from the city," Elise said. "He's been with me only. 'Tis not him atall who'll be marryin' her." Her face sparkled.

Mabel looked confounded. "There was somebody in her bed-chamber a week ago. It was the same voice I heard a few days after Rory left for the city. I could have been dreamin'." She looked at her sister. "As you've been dreamin'. A gentleman, even if he's from Ire ... Ire ... wherever the bleedin' place is and the likes of you!"

"We'll soon know." Elise turned towards the door.

Duncan Erskine entered first, all dressed up for the occasion. Over his doublet he wore a black cloak with silver lace. Designs, more appropriate to an aristocrat's apparel, than that of the son of a poor tailor from Shropshire, decorated its insides.

Jane, too, had replaced her Spanish farthingale with the more fashionable French version. Rolls of material, around her waist, pushed the skirt out at right angles. That morning Mabel, with nimble fingers, had brushed her hair and parted it in the middle, with an ivory comb, so it fell loosely around her face. Tied in a soft knot at the nape of her neck, the style made her look less severe and very vulnerable. She had plastered over tell tale signs of tears with a white powder of ground alabaster and painted her lips red.

She pulled Duncan Erskine to her side. "You know the words," she said to him. "You start."

He looked at her proprietarily. The daughter of a great English house with its own coat of arms would, in normal circumstances, be out of his reach."I take you for my wife," he said solemnly.

"I take you for my husband." Jane's voice was toneless as she answered quickly.

He produced a ring from his pocket and placed it on her finger.

"My father cannot prevent our union now," she said, almost triumphantly. "Ecclesiastical law says these promises are unchangeable." She looked down at her frontal bulge. "When they accompany certain circumstances. And the ring on my hand is my present. We have fulfilled the requirements."

Elise coughed and looked at Mabel. "The mistress will want us in the kitchen," she said and they exited hastily.

The physician, whom Anne had summoned to her husband's bedside, washed his hands. A skeletal man with tired eyes, he looked flushed from his ride from Margate. Taking a towel from the wash stand, he dried his face and neck and turned towards Anne.

"This hard to judge." He paused to measure his words. "I always recognised Sir Walter as a phlegmatic. In a few months his constitutional balance has changed. He now has a presence of heat and dryness, the properties of fire and the choleric man." He looked questioningly at Anne. "What distressed your husband like this? I have never seen such a change in a patient before."

Anne did not give him an answer, nor did he appear to expect one.

He continued, "He is not to eat white meat, fruit or spices."When the movement returns to his paralysed side, he will need to take exercise. If he walks every day and is careful of his diet, he will recover within a few months." He paused. "I think." He lifted his bag.

"Thank you," Anne said. "Geoffrey will see you out."

As he was leaving Rory knocked and entered. He had heard

the commotion from his chamber where he was looking over particulars of the journey to Ireland given him by Sir Walter. The amounts of provisions needed jumbled chaotically in his head with the number of soldiers requiring each. He knew he would be unable to do any constructive work if he remained in his chamber.

Anne went to him and he felt her arms enfold him. He broke away quickly. "What happened?"

She explained the symptoms, but not the reason for the attack.

He was so shocked he took refuge in dealing with practicalities. "Have you sent George a communicat?"

"No I am waiting for Jane to come first. I cannot think where she is or what is detaining her."

Rory looked at the diminished figure in the bed and found it difficult to recognise the Sir Walter who'd cast so colossal a shadow over his life. His skin was ashen. Sweat was breaking out on his forehead, trickling into his beard. His eyes were closed. The character had left his face.

The chamber, heavy with the fetid odours of sickness, made him yearn for the cooling air so detrimental to the sick room. He wanted to escape, but it would be wrong to leave Anne alone. He had never envisaged wishing for Jane's presence, but now he longed for her to appear.

When Jane did come at last, Anne embraced her tightly. Over her mother's shoulder, Rory felt her gaze. Stepping back from Anne she asked in a thin voice, "What happened? Is father very unwell? Geoffrey told me his physician has attended. What did he say?"

"Your father had a slight attack and will be better soon."

"Soon, what does he mean by soon?"

Duncan Erskine, who had entered the chamber almost unnoticed, went to Jane's side and put a reassuring hand on her arm.

Anne said, "He hopes for a complete recovery in a matter of months."

"Thank God." Jane's lower lip quivered.

"He will have to eat prescribed foods and take daily exercise and remain calm." Anne wrung her hands. "In all the years of our marriage, I have seen him agitated only in the last weeks."

She stared at Jane.

Jane turned to Duncan Erskine. "We will tell them now."

"Is this the right time?"

"I cannot bear to wait any longer."

"We should wait until later."

"Wait until later for what?" Anne asked.

Duncan Erskine squeezed Jane's hand. As she pulled it away, Rory noticed it was a blackish yellow, as if someone had slammed a door on it instead of caressed it. His eyes were shifty as he said in a low defiant tone, "Jane and I pledged ourselves to one another. We intend to marry in a church as soon as they read the bans. I will support ..."

"What?" Anne said. "You and Ja ... I thought ... you are not a gentle ..." she stuttered in disbelief.

Duncan Erskine's eyes glittered."I know I am not worthy of her."

Anne crumbled her lace handkerchief. Jane looked forlornly at Rory, a look that said he was her only anchor in a world set adrift. Blankly, he returned her anguished look. What did she want from him? What would he do if she confessed her dalliance with him? There was enough trouble with Sir Walter ill. She loved Erskine. She was a garment he had once worn with pleasure, but had now outgrown.

Geoffrey entered with a warming pan and placed it under Sir Walter.

The group fell silent. "The physician suggested that the heat would stimulate the circulation," he explained. Sir Walter's eyes opened slowly.

When Geoffrey was gone, Anne turned her attention once more to Jane and Duncan Erskine. "You want to get married? You have already pledged yourself?" she asked as if she hadn't heard correctly.

Sir Walter looked at the errant Jane, his expression impassive. Lifting himself off the bed, he pointed in the direction of Rory. As though the words were wrenched from him he said, "Ror ... and Jane can ... cannot have a bab ... Kill them first."

Anne hurried to soothe him. "There now, time to go back to sleep."

"Tell him Mama," Jane cried.

Anne looked perplexed. Then she blurted out, "Jane and Duncan Erskine are betrothed."

The helpless anger seemed to leave Sir Walter's eyes. "Say ... say tha ... again."

"Jane and Duncan Erskine are betrothed," Anne said firmly.

"Ag ..."

Slowly, Anne repeated what she had said.

Tears ran down Sir Walter's cheek. "Del ... del ... lighted with the news. Thank Go ..."

Each day Rory expected George's return, but the days passed without sight of him. Although Sir Walter had improved steadily, he would be incapable of resuming his duties for some time. When he mentioned George's absence to him, Sir Walter just smiled aggravatingly.

When white-haired generals came to visit him, Sir Walter told them he had important work to do for the crown. His important work was Rory's training. For an hour each day, he informed him about army life and army protocol and warned him of resentment he would face as an inexperienced campaigner and a native.

With difficulty, his tongue thick in his mouth, he persevered until he gave Rory an outline of each file and where he had deposited each list. The records gave information on men, supplies, fodder, weapons and ammunition. "They are approximate," Sir Walter used to insist, but his idea of approximate differed from Rory's.

Rory watched Sir Walter, despite his poor health, fill his diary every day and wondered what prompted a man to have such a fixation for detail. The rest of his memoirs, filled annually, were in a drawer in his bureau. However he was grateful for Sir Walter's obsession. The data would make his change to Ireland easier, especially now that *he* was in full command.

Chapter Nineteen

Ireland

For days now Finola had felt restless. She would take a piece of embroidery, loll on her pallet and sew. A few minutes later, discontent would boil up inside her again and she would throw it aside. The events of the past months had unsettled her. She had witnessed Brian throw Molly's body into a hole. Her name was no longer mentioned. At least Maeve had gained something. Since the loading bay incident, Cormac was attentive and faithful.

But Finola had begun to feel strangely trapped after it all. And to see all those around her as trapped. The servants were trapped in the strictures of their birth. Shane, trapped in his silence. Resentful. Unhappy. Brian, trapped in his fears for Ulster? Niall, locked in a delicate body, feeling he could do more with his life.

Herself, trapped, by her feelings for Rory? When she had warned him not to forget her, she had expected his return to Mulahinsa shortly. That he would be incapable of enduring England. The weeks had dragged into months and then years. This was his eighth year in England. Time to forget someone she had last seen as a boy. If she married one of her suitors, she would escape from Mulahinsa.

Something to stimulate her before gloom made her distraught was what she needed. If anybody saw her lying fully dressed on a pallet in the middle of the day, what would they say? She'd go for a walk, visit with Kate O'Toole.

Murrough might be there. She felt a slow blush rise from her neck. What was wrong with her? He was nobody. A peasant. She'd just walk by the house. Maybe the door would be open and she'd sit and talk for a few minutes.

The line of huts was quiet. Smells of cooking wafted from open doors. As she reached the O'Toole dwelling, she heard a low mewling sound coming from nearby. She stood and listened a moment.

She had wanted a quiet walk, but the sound was so pathetic she could not ignore it. At the rear of the hut she saw the youngest member of the O'Toole family exhausted from persistent crying and now unable to expel more than a mewl, beat her feet on the grass, her eyes straying towards the hurt.

As she leaned over, she saw that she had caught her right hand under the spring of a discarded mouse-trap. The snap, made to break a rodent's neck, had done its job. Slowly lifting the spring, she eased the little one's hand from under it. Then picking her up, she ran with her to the O'Toole hut.

Murrough was standing drying his tunic in front of the fire.

"It's the baby," Finola gasped, holding the infant's hand up. "I think her fingers are broken."

"Jesus, Mary and Joseph! 'Tis *cipíní*, you'll be needin'." Immediately Murrough rushed out leaving her to pacify the sobbing child.

Finola placed the baby on her shoulder and patted her on the back. The crying stopped and she laid her head on her chest and closed her eyes.

Murrough was back in seconds with whittled sticks and strips of cloth. He knelt in front of her, gently unfolded the baby's injured fingers and supported them with the slivers of wood. Then he wound the cloth about them making a firm splint.

Watching him Finola felt suddenly reckless. It was akin to the feeling she had experienced in the *bawn* with Rory so many years ago. Yet it was also different. She would be too cowardly to kiss this man as she had Rory. She was a woman now, not a girl and he was not an innocent boy.

Thoughts of suitors who came to the castle to speak to her father and ask for her hand surfaced in her mind. Some, like Campbell, were interesting and intelligent. Yet none of them would have been as quick thinking as Murrough was in this situation. Oh she knew he would be inept at cheek kissing or chess playing and his voice, used to shouting over the lowing of a herd, would be incapable of polite murmurs. But, with his hard jaw contrasting the softness of his green eyes, hair hanging to his shoulders, his potential for brute force, his tenderness, he touched her as nobody else had since Rory.

Discomfited by these thoughts, she quickly dispelled them and handed the sleeping baby to Murrough. Then muttering something about more urgent matters requiring her attention she quickly left the hut.

This incident, however trivial it was, became an important

milestone in her life. Realising that she had a vocation to heal and care for sick people, she studied her mother more as she ministered to yet another of Caitlín's burns. She also remembered how her mother had nursed Shane after the wolf attack and tended to Cormac when he had broken his ankle.

When the servants became ill, she began helping to look after them. Over the months she learned how to use herbs effectively to cure ailments. She made broths and restoratives for weak stomachs. For common complaints she prepared cordials and physics. She bandaged cuts and counselled cleanliness. Learning how to make the herbal concoctions of her mother was the easy part. Developing perseverance to make the patients take them took longer. One day, when she had gathered enough knowledge, she hoped to build a shelter like the ones at the booley. There she'd meet with the tenants and talk to them about how they could remain free from disease.

Some time after the incident with the baby Finola was out walking in the early morning. The air was fresh and sharp and her spirits were lifted. When she espied Murrough sitting on a boulder on the side of the track, she was unsure whether to feel annoyance or pleasure at meeting him.

He was bent over a page deep in concentration. It was early for anybody, except tenants trudging to the fields, to be out. When he looked up, she could see that his expression mirrored her own feelings of displeasure and gladness.

"What are you doing? Shouldn't you be at work?" she asked, sounding awkward.

Murrough stood up. He pulled at his hair. "'Tisn't working for your father I am this morning."

Like a gauche twelve-year-old, she twirled the tassels of her mantle between her finger and thumb. On impulse she crouched down beside where he was sitting and looked at the scripts he had left there.

His face went red. "'Tis practising writing I am."

It was very unusual for a peasant to have even the rudiments of the skill, Finola thought. Printed matter of any kind was scarce enough among her class but it was almost unheard of among the tenants.

"Why don't you ask where I learned such grandeur?" he said

then, his tone getting bolder.

His audacity unnerved her and she jumped to her feet. "I haven't time to ask questions. If ... if I don't hurry back to the house, I'll have a few of my own to answer. I left without eating a breakfast."

When she got back to the castle, the hall was empty. But Brigid had set the tables the previous night and everything was in its place for breakfast. Shane entered from the kitchen. His hair was in disarray, windblown like her own. He looked disturbed. Surely, he hadn't followed her and seen her talk to Murrough.

He sat opposite her and began to write feverishly. When he was finished he passed the note to her, his expression severe. She put out her hand to receive the missive she knew would contain contempt.

Why were you talking to Murrough O'Toole? You're the same as Matthew and Rory. They taught that fool to read and write. I should have told Father then.

No good will come from peasants with learning. As it is, that fellow acts conceited.

I suppose you're going to help him now.

Finola felt a sinking feeling. So it was Rory taught Murrough to read and write. He had never told her. She would not have expected Matthew to confide in her, but she thought Rory used to tell her everything. Maybe they were not as close as she had foolishly imagined. Her hunger disappeared. Had she mistaken their relationship?

Each morning after that Finola trod the same path as on that day. When the first light shone through the slit in her chamber wall, she jumped from her pallet. Sometimes she did not wait to heat the water to wash, just broke the ice on the top of the ewer. She would decide the night before what frock she would wear. Then she would lay it across the night table and by morning the creases would be gone. Usually as she got ready, she would wonder in her head what Murrough would find difficult in his lessons that day.

From Matthew and Rory's boyish teaching he had learned enough writing and reading for his needs, but nobody had exploited his talent for figures.

"I'll show you how to add and subtract," Finola offered one

morning.

"Then a grey merchant won't puzzle my head with lordly lines of figures. That he won't."

Week followed week and their meetings continued. Murrough lost his shyness. With picturesque detail, he told Finola stories of his childhood. She laughed at tales about his grandfather and the fun Murrough had when he helped him take care of the cows. He reminded her of the ewer she used to leave behind the enclosure to collect rain water. He used to watch her rinse her hair with it. One day he almost talked to her, but Shane had come along and hunted him away.

"Shane's able to make himself understood without saying anything, that he is. Yet 'twas always trying to 'talk' to me himself he was."

"What do you expect from the future?" she asked him suddenly once as they sat on a hillock.

He looked at her dully.

She realised, too late, his lack of choice.

"I'm better off than anyone else in the hollow. 'Tis the readin' and writin'. They respect that. 'Tisn't always to the priest MacCavell, they go now." His voice sounded unusually serious. "My kin sometimes blame me for aping you folk. You think me a lout with no hope." He fidgeted with the string of his trews.

As the weeks sped by, Finola borrowed manuscripts, written in Gaelic by monks of earlier times, from Niall. She would bring them to Murrough to read. When he found a story that interested him, he would read aloud slowly. Finola, listening to the cadence of his voice and looking around at the wild countryside realised that she was more at peace in those moments than she had ever been since Shane's misfortune and Rory's departure to Chalk Hall.

One clear morning Murrough was by her side reading aloud to her. She was looking towards the mountains, where dots of sheep nibbled between stones. Suddenly, on impulse, she reached out and clasped Murrough's hand. He stopped reading, leaned towards her and brushed her lips lightly with his own. It felt to Finola like dew drops on morning leaves.

"'Tis spoilin' me you are for the local maidens," he said. "'Tis as beautiful as a bluebell you are."

For the briefest moment, hope of a life with him flickered, but, just as soon as it was lit the hope guttered. She jumped to her feet once more and rushed back to her castle.

However, she could not get the thought of that kiss out of her mind. When she opened her eyes each morning, when light fell on her pupils, even before she affirmed that she was Finola O'Hanlon and that another day had begun, she thought of Murrough O'Toole. Then she would think of her mother.

Without naming him, Maeve had made it clear that she would reject a daughter who copulated with inferiors. She had said, "I know you have your father's nature, but rise above it. Shane must not be troubled. You will not get an offer like you have received from Campbell again."

It was the first time her mother had referred to Cormac's infidelities in her hearing. She felt demeaned by her comments, that what had been pure and wholesome between her and Murrough was somehow tainted.

She had waited for a feeling like this all her life, but now that it had come, she wondered if she were strong enough to persist. Strong enough to live in penury, scorned by society. Being with Murrough would mean living in an oval shaped mud hut beside the castle, giving birth to his children on a bed of straw, washing his apparel and cooking his meals. She'd have to forego any prospect of living in Mulahinsa and its environs and content herself to a life anticipating seasons that dictated the food she'd have in her belly.

Without warning she felt ugly. Her coronet of black hair, or the bright eyes that stared at her from her looking-glass, failed to reassure her. Did she want to meet Murrough at all? If she failed to meet him this morning, she would not get the courage to see him again. She washed and pulled on her gown.

"You're going for your usual walk, I see," her mother said coolly. "Better be alone than in bad company. That's all I'll say."

Finola shrugged, tilted her chin and held her head erect. Her mother was treating her like a child. And she wished Shane would stop spying on her and reporting what she did. She ran down the path only to career into the arms of her father.

"Slow down Finola," Cormac said, holding onto her. "I've news that should interest you. I've just heard from Rory. He's preparing to come home."

She shook off his restraining hand. It was too late. The feeling she had for him was gone. It had been a childish fantasy.

"I'm sure, he'll be anxious to reclaim his inheritance. He'll be busy when he returns. He is more an Englishman now," she said, with perfect composure,

Cormac studied her face and rubbed a finger gently along her cheek. "Mayhap I should have done as your mother wanted and chosen your husband for the weight of his purse and the expanse of his land," he said, a slightly rough edge in the kindly voice. "And then ordered you to marry him," he added a little more firmly.

Chapter Twenty

Finola was glad when Brian had returned from Tyrone. She felt he was the only one she could confide in about her feelings for Murrough. Although she found it difficult to imagine a life with him, she found it equally difficult to imagine an existence without him.

But it was harder than she expected to get time with Brian on his own. The estate was taking up nearly all his time. He had begun to call meetings of the *uirrithe* in order to provide a forum for them to voice their grievances. Cormac was not enamoured by the idea but succumbed when Maeve sided with Brian. Finola noticed that men, who had been reluctant *uirrithe* before this, now became allies. Brian was preparing for war.

Then it happened quite by chance. She was in the dining hall on her own, drinking a goblet of balleyclabber, when Brian's shadow fell on the table beside her, and he sat. "What's this I hear about you losing your affection for Rory?" he asked. "I thought that you lived for the day when, in the best tradition of courtly love, he claimed you for his bride." Though trying to sound light-hearted, he failed to disguise the edge in his voice as he added, "Or have you another claimant?" He placed a piece of paper before her. "I found this discarded note."

She recognised Shane's scroll:

Brian my rival is back. Finola still frolics with that churl. There is nobody who understands me except my mother. I wonder does Finola tell Murrough how she hates me.

"Should I pay attention to his ramblings?" Brian came and sat by her.

"I love Murrough O'Toole." Finola felt shocked at the sound of her own words. It was a moment of self revelation.

Brian looked directly at her scarcely able to hide his anger. "He is a helot, a tenant. In the war he will be a person who does the dirty work around the camp, even prohibited from fighting." He lowered his voice. "Tell Rory about him and he will tell you the same. If he was even a swordsman or a kerne itself, but ... Finola, I thought Shane was just being his malicious self when he wrote this." Brian rose from his seat.

"You'd think he was less than human," Finola said, sounding petulant.

"He just about meets the requirements. I was ignorant of the extent of your commitment to this ... peasant. Give it up Finola. It's lust. I'd tell you to go and satisfy it, but you might end up bearing his brat ... Or die ridding yourself of it."

She felt soreness in her chest. What right had he to talk of Murrough like that? "Brian ..."

"It's hard to lay out such facts with kindness. You'll break your mother's heart, force your father to evict the whole O'Toole family, and die yourself after birthing seven or eight infants. If you proceed with this recklessness," his voice cracked, "everyone, suitors most of all, will ostracise you."

She remembered Murrough's kiss and tried to match the picture with the person Brian was depicting. Campbell and all her other suitors, with their cavalier attitudes and warlike ways, all paled before the one whom Brian considered now so unworthy of her.

He started again, this time more hesitantly, "I told you I'd changed after the southern wars. I've realised that everyone is out for their own gain. Even your adoring cow-keeper. What an advance it is for him to be on speaking terms with a gentlewoman. He must be in demand among the neighbouring girls since he got to know you." He looked at her shrewdly. "Or are you too smitten to notice?"

"Stop it, Brian. You've said enough."

He reached out to touch her but she cowered away from him. He rose from his seat. "I'm sorry to have to be so forthright."

"Leave me be now, please," she answered. "I have to think about what I'm going to do."

Finola waited a week before meeting Murrough again. When she told him about the conversation with Brian, he listened attentively, almost amused. Then when she finished he just held her close in his strong arms. She looked up into his open face, and felt a familiar heat envelop her. She knew that if it had been possible, at that particular moment, she would have gone a Maying in the woods, like the lowliest of servants, without benefit of priest.

That night, as she tossed on her pallet, she wanted to unburden her heart to her mother, but she had never shared anything like that with her before. She was afraid to involve her father for fear of what Brian had predicted would happen, and he banished the O'Tooles from his demesnes. She desired Murrough yet she wanted to maintain her position in society. It was one thing to be a benefactor to the less fortunate but to live among them was something else.

She imagined herself surrounded by fowl, eating a meal from shared pots and drinking beer from the chipped tankards she saw in the O'Toole shack. She hated the pungent odour of pigs that greeted her in the hovel. The pinched faces of the children in their scant clothing made her want to turn away in distaste. Murrough's mother, her figure shapeless from too many children and her expression resigned, was a symbol of *her* destiny with Murrough.

Many peasants drank the beer as quickly as they brewed it and became bloated. Murrough without his trim anatomy and Adonis looks was unthinkable. She wondered if Brian was right when he suspected Murrough's motives. Where her feelings led, she was too cowardly to follow. She must admit that or she would never find peace. If Murrough were a chieftain, even a minor one, she would not be faltering. No, it was all a mistake. He was not for her.

She thumped her pillow filled with down not straw as in the huts. Here, too, the rushes were sweet-smelling, the walls whitewashed. She resolved to deny any emotions she had for him and return to her proper role as his superior.

Towards morning she slept. When she woke, her tongue was thick in her mouth. As she dragged herself out of the bed, her mind went back into tumult. She would see him one last time. She owed him that. The water she splashed on her face did nothing to dispel her inertia. All she wanted was to tunnel into the covers and never get up again.

"'Tis being dramatic you are," Murrough would say if he knew what she was thinking. He would be correct. Practical Finola O'Hanlon had disappeared, had become scuttled in the last year. From having played the deserted damsel to Rory to becoming the indecisive female to Campbell's continued suit, she was now playing Delilah to Murrough's Samson.

Such were her thoughts as she descended the stairway and walked to their meeting place still undecided what to do. She knew that she would have to rescue them both from this limbo.

But she got a reprieve from her indecisiveness. Murrough, was absent from his usual place. He was most likely helping his grandfather herd the cows, she thought, he would be there tomorrow morning.

Chapter Twenty One

When Finola reached the castle she met Maeve coming towards her, a worried look on her face.

"There has been an accident," she said. "With a cow. I think it's bad."

Even as Finola rushed to investigate she knew it was Murrough and that it would be serious. He lay on the ground, his face white, a large red gash across his head. Beside the wall some men were holding a cow, usually the most gentle of the herd, by a rope. The cow snorted and stamped, her hump up.

Murrough groaned weakly. His wound was bloody and dirty with straw and mud. That needs to be cleaned immediately, Finola thought.

"I'll run to the castle and get some cloths and water," she said to the men. "Don't move him until I clean that cut."

But when she had left, the men took Murrough by the arms and legs and carried him to his hut. Murrough's grandfather had already gone ahead to tell Kate of the calamity.

By the time Finola had rushed back, Kate was standing in the doorway of the hut a rag in her hand. "We'll clean him up and 'tis alright he'll be. Sit yourself down won't you?" She offered Finola a stool before ministering to her son. "'Tis myself who'll do it," she said, squeezing the rag out in murky water. She wiped the blood from Murrough's forehead. He made no movement. He had stopped his moaning and his heaving chest had stilled. Kate continued to rub the wound.

"Get me a piece of glass," Finola suddenly ordered to no-one in particular.

Someone went into the other room to do her bidding.

Finola grabbed the piece of glass from her and put it to Murrough's mouth. There was no breath. The lips that had kissed her so gently were lifeless now. She felt a nervous laugh begin to rumble deep within her as she backed away in disbelief.

The group stood in silence staring at the corpse. She suddenly felt she didn't belong here, that she should go back to her own and let them mourn in their own way.

As she walked towards the door of the hut, she said, "If there is anything we can do, remember to ask. Of course Cormac will be along to see you."

"Very good of him, I'm sure," Kate said, but Finola sensed the hint of antipathy in her voice.

Over the following few days Finola was able to pretend she was calm and barely disturbed by the death. She joined in the discussions of the terrible happening, everyone wondering how such a tragedy could occur a second time at Mulahinsa.

The peasants in the settlement said it was *na síoga* with their darts. The little people wanted to claim grandfather O'Toole for their own, they said. They had got a better bargain than they anticipated. A strong young man to grace their lands instead of the crumbling figure they expected. They told of the arrow that had provoked the normally docile milker to such fury. "Sure 'twas with me own eyes, I seen it," the servant Dara told Cormac. "Then 'twas gone."

"The man is dead," Cormac said. "In my humble opinion the animal became briefly enraged, that was all. No more talk about arrows. That kind of chatter can lead to trouble. Now we must make a coffin and get some beer for the wake."

Inside Finola wanted to cry but knew she couldn't reveal her grief. She felt a screaming inside her head. Seeking to keep busy, she went to help in the kitchen. As she emptied slop buckets, the filth on her hands reflected how she felt inside. Later when Molly's replacement looked askance at her, she understood once again that she must stay within the confines of the society into which she was born.

The night that Murrough was buried Finola lay awake thinking of the life she could have had - would have had - with him. She loved him, but she was unsure whether she could have spent each day with him but she was sure she could cope with her heartbreak. Fortune had done its worst.

As dawn broke, she knew what she was going to do. Her decision to marry failed to lift her heart or free her from the feeling that she was in some way responsible for Murrough's death. Shane came to her mind. As he had stood watching proceedings following the cow's attack, he had his hand behind his back as if he were concealing an object.

Enough of pessimistic thoughts. Forcing herself to smile she rose to start her life anew, not anymore as the daughter of Cormac O'Hanlon but as the wife of Andrew Campbell.

She gathered together her belongings, but when she came upon the bow that Rory had given her before he left she did not notice that it was without its attendant arrow. She was too preoccupied with thoughts of a new life with Andrew Campbell and the grim realisation that soon she would be leaving Mulahinsa to live among strangers.

Chapter TwentyTwo

England

Rory knew that the Ulster to which he would return had changed little in the years of his exile. The Desmond wars had raged in the south of the country while the chieftains of the north looked on uninterested. They had watched while the English desolated Munster, butchered its inhabitants and confiscated the lands. The invader did not threaten them they thought. But Ulster's only hope of salvation was the emergence of an enlightened leader who realised that Ulster would be next for confiscation. A leader who would be strong enough to break the local mould of tribal conflict.

In Europe, Spain's Philip II, Sweden's Gustavus Adolphus, and England's Elizabeth had started to unify their countries. Individuals were becoming aware of themselves as part of nations. But in Ireland the local supremacy of the clans that Rory had experienced as a boy still held true. He knew this was short-sighted and foolish. His task would be to break it.

During the week prior to his expected date of departure, Anne came to him to say that Sir Walter wanted to see him in his bed-chamber.

Though still confined to his bed Sir Walter's humour was permanently buoyed since Duncan Erskine's announcement. He was happy Rory knew that it was Duncan and not himself that was to marry Jane. Everybody in the household was in good spirits - everyone except Jane. For somebody who waited for her church wedding, she did not appear happy. Heavy with child, she slouched about the house in silence.

Rory, too, was thankful that it was Duncan Erskine who had fathered her baby when it could have been him. That she had flitted from one bed to another had not surprised him. She always used Duncan's attraction for her to incite his jealousy. Then while he was in London, she had missed him, he assumed, and their newly discovered pleasures of the flesh, and had used Erskine as a substitute. He too was looking forward to satisfying his desire with a harlot when he arrived in Dundalk. Now that he knew how to enjoy the delights of the flesh, he would savour coupling with different women.

"I left you in a predicament," Sir Walter said to Rory from his bed where he had been reading his breviary. "Therefore I have arranged for George to take my place." He put down the book. There was more hesitancy than usual in his voice. "You are twenty I know, but he is two years older. Twenty-two is still young for such an undertaking but being the same nationality as the men, he will command respect." He reached out and took a letter from the bureau beside him. "Here is the official word."

Rory took the letter and read:

Sir Walter informed Her Majesty of his unfortunate malady. In the circumstances we deemed it appropriate to send his son George Carew in his stead. We order you to obey him as you would his esteemed father.

Signed, E. R.

Rory suspected that the carefully worded directive concealed the intent behind it. Sir Walter was unable to come. Instead, they were sending someone who had his trust. Someone who would keep an eye on him as Sir Walter would have done. What George lacked in experience, he made up for by being his friend. To Sir Walter Rory was still a native and untrustworthy despite how long he had been under his civilising influence.

In all his speculations on what Sir Walter's illness would mean to him, Rory had not considered this. Sir Walter, he would have been rid of after a year. The son was more of an indefinite assignment.

Rory was trying to minimise the difficulties of the new arrangements. Although this kept him busy, he felt there was something amiss in the relationship between Duncan Erskine and Jane. Nobody had thought to ask why she was in the kitchen paring spinach when the knife slipped and almost severed the tip of her finger. Why should he? That the drape rail slipped, hit her on the head and left a gash, also puzzled him. She was Erskine's responsibility now. It was to him she had plighted her troth. Duncan would surely know if she needed special care. Perhaps women were prone to accidents when they were carrying.

The morning of the nuptials dawned wet and bleak. At three o'clock, the household gathered in the chapel. The church, a box chamber, was warm with a lingering scent of incense from the last service.

In a polished pew Rory sat facing Anne and Sir Walter who sat among pews opposite.

He missed the statues and the ornate altar with its tabernacle of his childhood. When he was a boy, he and Matthew used to go with Maeve to the nearby monastery. It had been allowed to remain open by Henry VIII as it had no land attached, and the building was in such decay it had not been worth restoring as a home for an Englishman. How he remembered the little silver compartment that sat in the wall behind the altar. To his childish mind magic happened whenever the priest opened it. The people left their seats to gather around the altar. They stuck out their tongues and received the thin circle of bread they called God. Their faces took on a serene look and their lips moved in prayer.

But there was no tabernacle today and no magic. There was only the chaplain, standing waiting behind the simple wooden altar table, his waxen face matching the candles.

George came and sat beside him, resting his head in his hands. Anne continually cast anxious glances towards the entrance waiting for the bride to appear. Sir Walter looked almost euphoric at the prospect of this marriage.

Suddenly Rory noticed Anne's anxious expression turn to one of perplexity. She looked back from the entrance and leaned towards Sir Walter, her whisper audible in the hush of the chapel. "It is Duncan. Something is wrong." With an intake of breath, she jumped to her feet and ran as fast as her gown would allow from the oratory.

Baby boy, Quintin Walter John, was born to Duncan and Jane Erskine on the sixth of August 1592, on what was to have been their wedding day. The mite came into the world leaving his dispirited mother sickly.

"If it was not for her wide hips, she would have died," the midwife had confided to Anne.

Rory went to see the newborn. It would have been more sensible to visit Jane in her sick room, but he felt sorry for the babe. He knew that when Sir Walter had seen the infant, he had said, "Yes, handsome fellow. He is healthy I hope. Hear too much about the nearness of the cradle to the grave nowadays."

He had not asked to see him since.

The nurse, a thin woman of fifty with a solemn expression, reluctantly allowed him in.

A current of hot air met him on the threshold. Trickles of sweat swamped his arm-pits. A wooden cradle, with deep rockers, stood beside the fire. The infant was lying on a feather pillow underneath a mound of blankets. All Rory could see were two blinking eyes and a red face topped by a close cap.

He felt an impulse to snatch him and take him home to Ulster, away from the strict rules of the Tudor nursery. He hoped Duncan Erskine would discard the theory that a baby was a child of wrath until his conversion and had to have the devil beaten out of him. Although they had become easier in recent years, the rod found many users especially in Puritan households.

Sitting on a box chair, he rocked the cradle with his foot. The nurse looked on, her mouth folded in an expression of disapproval.

Aware that he was less than welcome, he put his hand on Quentin's forehead before quietly walking towards the door.

As he closed it, the nurse's disparaging hiss rang in his ears, "Foreigners!"

Not for much longer. Tomorrow he and George and their army would leave for Ireland. He would be among his own.

PART III

1592- 1595

Inferiors revolt in order that they may be equal, and equals that they may be superior. Such is the state of mind, which creates revolutions.

- Aristotle - Politics, Book 5.

Chapter One

Rory placed his hand on the sternpost and watched the shore line recede. It had been a hard ride to Bristol where he had met up with his soldiers, under the custody of their recruiters. He was thankful to be on his way home. Life was beginning. He had to admit that he had learned many lessons in England, some good, some bad. But he had been cosseted by the Carews for too long. The time had come for him to mould his own destiny, to put his many ideas into practice, to regain what was his.

He gazed out at the waves. It was inevitable that he would have to conquer his uncle Eoin. But to consolidate his power, he would have to co-operate with the English in their plans for his uncle. The English looked on him as a tool for their expansion. He had no choice but to pursue the course marked out for him. They expected it of him and self interest demanded it.

During his stay in England, he had learned that if Ulster were to remain independent, the tribes would have to rise above personal gain. Now that he was back, he realised how difficult it would be to break the pattern of raid and counter-raid. His smile was wry. Already a desire for revenge and acquisition had seduced him. Sir Walter had told once how Hugh O'Neill, the boy educated in the Pale, had won England's trust by fighting for them in the southern wars. Rory wondered if *he* had felt these emotions when he returned to Ulster, or had the English dominated Pale rid him of his youthful idealism.

The sea was calm and a breeze filled the sails, but there was no repetition of the outward journey's storm. How innocent he had been when he had last stood on a ship's deck. He remembered his longing for Finola as if it were yesterday, and his dream that she was on board with him.

He wondered whether Cormac and his family had changed much since he had left. He understood that they found it difficult to write; he had not communicated much himself.

Part of the reason he had been such a poor correspondent was that there would have been little to interest Cormac in the stultifying atmosphere of a Puritan household in the heart of England. Cormac, in turn, it seemed, found it difficult to describe Ulster. Puzzlingly he had said in his last communication.

You should have returned before this.

There was no explanation. It was almost as if he regretted penning the words, but yet did not rewrite them.

Rory had left Ulster a boy, and was now returning as a young man. For nine years he had forged an existence independent of Cormac. The experiences that had formed him in those years were alien to the people of Ulster. He felt isolated by that realisation; he had not expected to feel like this when he docked.

George came and placed a hand on his arm. For the first time since he heard about his appointment, he was glad George was with him. He was his link with the life he left behind, the only person who made his past real.

In the moment he lost his usual forethought and impulsively said, "Come with me to Mulahinsa, George. I would like to show you an Irish castle." He immediately began to regret the invitation but continued, "Maeve and Cormac will welcome you. They know I have stayed in your house since I left. It will be a chance for them to return the kindness. Finola and Brian will be glad to meet you, too." He hesitated. "And I nearly forgot Shane. Remember I told you about what happened in the forest. Shane is the one who is unable to speak."

"It is well you reminded me of Shane. You've not mentioned him for years. Are you sure it would be appropriate to leave the men on their own?"

"They will not be on their own. Soldiers already domiciled at the garrison at Ennistoomey will meet the boat and escort your men back there. Appoint one of the captains to take command in our absences."

"If you are sure." George looked grateful. "I will do it now." He went to the lower deck and approached the men who were playing dice amid the spare sails and wooden spars. They looked up, mistrust on their faces. With his aristocratic bearing and his delicate features, George looked very different from these pressed men.

"I am sorry for intruding. I ... ," he began.

"Roll the dice," said one and they resumed their game.

George hitched his trews. "I want to talk to you. Would you cease playing?"

"You lucky bugger. Six was it?" The game continued.

"I will not be accompanying you to Ennistoomey garrison."

George tried to sound authoritative.

The soldiers looked at each other with smiles of derision.

"I am going to Mulahinsa with my second-in-command." He faltered. "To discuss tactics."

"Mulahinsa? Not a whorehouse?" Someone whispered audibly. The others laughed.

George looked at an ascetic looking man, hovering in the corner, who was not taking part in the gambling. "Percy Sidney will be in charge until I return," he said.

"Aristo like himself." The same voice spoke. The same mocking laugh from the others.

George said, "I will let you back to the vice of the dice before we dock." And he walked away, his head high.

When they returned, Rory was absorbed watching a man on shore. As they got closer he knew it was Cormac and thought how much smaller he looked than the Cormac he remembered.

A broad shouldered giant of a man, about the same age as Rory, his eyes flitting around uneasily, stood by Cormac's side.

As he descended the gangplank, he felt nervous and cold. Clouds, swollen with rain, hovered overhead. Cormac waved to him and pushed his way through the crowd. When he hugged him tightly, Rory was back again on the day he left and hearing Cormac tell him that he must look on his trip to England as an opportunity to learn.

"I saw you from the deck," Rory said. "I recognised you instantly. Did you know it was me? Am I the same as when you saw me last?" Realising he sounded infantile, he felt suddenly shy. "I suppose I have grown a little."

Cormac stood back to look at him. "You're still the same Rory. Broader in the shoulders, more stubble on your chin. The auburn hair is the same."

"You have not changed at all," Rory said. "Maybe a bit." Remembering George he drew him forward by the arm. "This is George Carew." An awkward pause.

"I knew your father," Cormac said coldly.

Rory began to be sorry again that he had invited George to Mulahinsa. He sometimes forgot that inoffensive George was an 'enemy'. He looked at him expecting to see a hurt expression, but his attention was riveted on the man accompanying Cormac.

"This is my son Shane," Cormac said.

"Shane. So you are Shane." George rolled the name round on his tongue.

The two men clasped hands.

"And you know Rory," Cormac quipped.

Shane gazed at him with a detached air.

Rory ignored the expression and put out his hand. He was back in Ulster. Nothing was going to spoil that. He smiled and said, "Tell me about Finola. Is she with you?"

Shane stiffened more.

Too late Rory realised he had forgotten Shane's inability to speak.

Cormac intervened, "It is time to collect your belongings. You will come to Mulahinsa for a few days. In my humble opinion, you need a rest."

"Is it suitable for George to come with me?" Rory asked. "I told him, he could."

"The same old Rory," Cormac said, but his tone was warm. "If you want him to come, he can come."

What did he mean the same Rory? He was not the same. He had worked at not being the same. He was now astute, clear thinking and a planner. The child Rory had long disappeared. This homecoming was not turning out as he expected.

Cormac turned to George, "You have delegated someone to take charge of your men. *You* are the commanding officer."

But George was too engrossed in Shane to hear him; the two men walked close together, George talking, Shane listening.

"They are going to Ennistoomey to the garrison there." Rory's tone was harsh. He was still irritated by Cormac's assessment of him and he now bristled at the assumption that George was in charge. He wondered how Cormac knew so much about the queen's army with them. If Cormac had heard about it, Eoin had heard about it.

Cormac had tied two extra horses to a tethering stake a hundred yards from the dock. Now his horse-boy brought them forward.

It took Rory some time to re-accustom himself to riding without stirrups. "The horses benefited from the rest at the dock," Cormac said. "We are making good time." Then the clouds fulfilled their threat and heavy rain fell, drenching him in his English hose. Up ahead George seemed to be enjoying Shane's appreciative glances at his attire. Rory should have felt disenchanted by it all, but the prospect of meeting Finola to whom he had given his most prized possession when he was a boy, exhilarated him.

"I felt the journey was much shorter than when I rode the opposite way nine years ago, Rory said to Cormac. "How long more is it to Mulahinsa?"

"Oh, we're nearly there. Another ten miles or so." Cormac, sounding distracted, rubbed his horse's mane. Then he said, "Rory, I have something to tell you before we reach home." He halted suddenly and grabbed the bridle of Rory's chestnut.

George and Shane were deep in 'conversation' as they trotted ahead along the stretch of ground that led to Mulahinsa.

"Rory," Cormac began. "You should have returned before this."

Anxiety welled up in Rory's stomach. "Yes, what is it?" He raised his head to look at Cormac.

"Finola will not be at the castle."

"Oh! When will she be back?"

"Rory. Finola is married."

"Married? But she can't be. She's too young."

"A couple of months older than you, that's all."

He drew his cloak tighter around his shoulders. "I will catch up to the others," he said. He dug his heels into the horse's flanks and urged him forward. He had to escape before Cormac described Finola's husband and completely unmanned him.

It had not struck him that Finola would be with another man, that she would not have waited for him. Like his return to Ulster, she was part of his destiny. He jerked his horse to a walk.

He felt suddenly so alone. Even the landscape was unwelcoming. Ulster was so unlike Kent. No buildings surrounding a town square. No orchards. Nothing divided one field from another. There was just bleakness and rain. Even the people had changed. He was a stranger in his own country while George, the true stranger, was being treated like a native. He was grateful when Cormac passed him out and he could continue his journey in silence.

When they arrived at the castle, Cormac, Shane and George had gone up the stairway to the parlour before him. Half-way up the stairs he heard Maeve's exclamation of surprise and pleasure that Rory had brought a friend. Usurped again. She had clearly forgotten her antipathy to the English.

As he dawdled, reluctant to intrude on the happy group, the three blithely descended the stairs. "We're going for some vittles," Cormac said. "George must be starving." He turned to Rory. "Go up to see Maeve and then join us."

Maeve, sitting on a stool beside the fire, looked up when he entered. She appeared somewhat older than he had remembered. There were red patches on her cheeks. "Rory." Her voice was bland. "It's good to have you back." She proffered her hand as if she were expecting him to prove his civility by kissing it.

He took it in his but, feeling it limp, let it go.

"Brian is in Dublin," she said. There was a strained pause. "Cormac told you that Finola is no longer with us."

She made it sound as if she were dead instead of married. In a way she had departed. From him. "Yes. He told me."

Brigid had lit candles on the top table. Nothing had changed. Gristle lay on the ground at the end of the hall but the earth under the table where Cormac, George and Shane were sitting was clean.

George was holding a biscuit rather tentatively, a reluctant expression on his face. He took a bite and then a sip of ballyclabber.

"You don't like it Sir," Brigid said.

Cormac looked towards Brigid. "Bring something else. Our guest dislikes oatmeal biscuits and ballyclabber."

"'Twas for Rory, I did 'em," Brigid answered. "They being his favourites."

Rory took the platter from in front of George and, sitting opposite Cormac, he demolished three oatmeal biscuits.

"It's good to have you back, that it is Sir," Brigid said, with renewed confidence. She looked at George. "Now, what's that you'll be wantin' Sir? A bit of puddin' from the cow we bled yesterday? Or," her face lit with inspiration, "I'm thinkin' there's some pig's crubeens still in the mistress's cauldron. 'Tis only a week they've been there." She eyed his frame. "Fill you up as befitting they will."

Dragging himself away from watching Rory eat, Shane jumped from the bench.

Cormac fluttered his tongue against his teeth in light-hearted censure, but he looked worried.

Within a minute Shane was back bearing a piece of cold beef on a wooden platter and, wearing an expectant smile, placed it in front of George.

George stared at the platter and swallowed hard, his Adam's apple about to break through his neck. A slimy fluid ran down the side of the shank. A fly landed on top of the meat.

Rory felt a twinge of sympathy for him. Maeve would not have served such a joint to anyone.

He cut a slice and began to eat. As he chewed, his face turned a peculiar shade of green. Suddenly Brigid ran back in. "Holy Mother of God. That's Setanta's dinner you've eaten." Rory's heart lurched more at the name of the wolfhound, a pup when he left, than at the blunder made by Shane or any impairment to George's stomach.

Since the debacle with the vittles and lest the same mistake be made again, Shane had ordered Maeve to supervise each morsel destined for George's plate. For the first time in his life George was being pampered so he lacked an incentive to move from Mulahinsa.

"The soldiers are awaiting our presence at Ennistoomey," Rory said one evening as they ate their meal in the dining hall. For reasons he did not care to acknowledge, George's behaviour troubled him.

He simply answered with his sweet smile.

Maeve filled the silence, "Do whatever you consider necessary, George," she said.

Cormac, however, was more forthright. "In my humble opinion," he said, "to stay here any longer would be a desertion of duty. I'm not a lover of your queen, but this endless shillying-shallying is tedious. I don't like shirkers, be they Gaelic or Gallic."

George turned to Brigid who was serving food to Shane. "Remember to include my brown doublet when you pack my bag," he said. "Last time I saw it, it was destined for the tub. Perhaps, it is still drying."

"I'll see Sir."

Shane spluttered over his food. A pout appeared on his lips.

He reached for his quill. His hand shook as he wrote: *Ignore them. You can't leave me.*

"My father put me in charge of an army. I must do my duty. You understand?" George asked.

Shane shook his head vehemently, his fair curls dancing. He wrote again: *You're like the rest of them. I never come first.*

"We will see," George said as he rose from his stool and moved towards Shane.

Two days later Rory was bidding good-bye to Maeve and Cormac.

"I wish you came alone Rory," Maeve said. Then she added as if by way of explanation, "We would have been able to devote more time to you."

The sentiment sounded false. Maeve only had devotion to Shane and Cormac.

In soft voice Cormac said, "Stay out of danger lad."

"I will be in Ennistoomey not England. It's riding distance."

"Distance is not what's troubling me," replied Cormac.

As Rory went to the *bawn* to load his belongings on his pack horse and saddle his mount, George came behind him. His face was pale. "I will stay here a while longer," he said.

This delighted Rory. George's absence from the garrison would better suit his political aims. He did not want him around to report his activities to Sir Walter. Yet he was unable to banish disquiet at the thought of him remaining at Mulahinsa.

Chapter Two

When Rory arrived at Ennistoomey the soldiers had the garrison like a chicken coop. Discarded goblets, stained by dregs of *uisce beatha*, lay under pallets, on dirty platters and in the privy. Wood shavings strewn about bespoke the laziness of the soldiers who passed the time, between drinks, whittling sticks. He felt irritated by it all but happily a chamber had been cordoned off for his use. The simple furnishings of wooden bed, table and stool were adequate for his needs and after a servant had changed the smelly floor rushes, he used the space and free time to think and plan.

He made two lists - people worth wooing to his side, and those who would remain loyal to Eoin - for the present anyway. Many lords were loyal to the memory of his father and grandfather and would support him if he got power. As the grandchild of Con Maguire his position encouraged treachery. He had not forgotten the lesson of the sticks and the strategy of *divide and conquer* so favoured by the English, but he knew that if he played the idealist, he would fail.

Next day he set off into the hills to tell anyone he considered useful to his cause that a new overlord for the land of Glenone was on the horizon.

On a piece of high ground he stopped to let his horse rest and nibble at the grass. He looked down at the huts of the peasants, snuggled for protection around the castles of their chiefs. Ireland's land system was outmoded. Mere tenants, *Uirrithe,* Overlords. *Uirrithe* suppressed the tenants so that they did not think of improving their lot. Overlords suppressed *Uirrithe* so that they did not think of becoming Overlords themselves. Ulster was as disunited as when he left for England. He thought of O'Neill and the rumblings from Tyrone. Would O'Neill be strong enough to lift Ireland from its morass of medievalism?

Of course *he* was the same as those he was judging so harshly. Here he was riding over the mountain to Gallagher's stronghold to woo an *uirrí* loyal to Eoin. Perhaps he was starting a civil war. This time uncle against nephew, instead of brother against brother. All for his own aggrandizement.

Fingering his arquebus, he was conscious that he was taking a chance riding alone like this.

On arrival at Gallagher's fortress, Gallagher's wife welcomed him in the traditional way, with a kiss on each cheek.

Inside at the trestle table in the hall swordsmen and horsemen lolled about, chewing on chicken legs, gulping beer and peering suspiciously at him.

When he saw Rory, Gallagher, from the top table, ordered, "Feast's over, men."

Midst grumbles and curses the room cleared, nothing remaining of the revelry except the mess.

He and Gallagher went into an alcove where they sat on stools, facing each other across a roughly hewn table. They discussed past harvests, surmised about this year's and the prospect for the future.

When the subject turned to herds of cattle and the danger of raids, Rory felt his throat dry and longed for some libation. He said, "For the past three years any dues Eoin has got from you has been through force."

Gallagher produced a cask of wine, more than likely from the hold of an Armada ship. "You owe Eoin many cows so a raid is due," Rory continued, knowing he had harnessed Gallagher's interest.

He paused. Should he promise to protect him from such an incursion? He knew the cradle of his power would be his ability to defend his *uirrithe* against attack. The connection would link them to him and him to them. "I may not be able to prevent Eoin from raiding you now, but if you are loyal to me, I will assure your future."

Gallagher scowled, "You tell a good tale."

Rory thought quickly. "In a few months I will be able to confiscate your lands in the queen's name." His voice trailed.

Gallagher's eyes narrowed.

Rory hoped his meaning was clear. With or without Gallagher's help, he would defeat Eoin. "That will not happen to anybody who proves faithful now."

They talked until he allowed Gallagher conclude with a limited compliance. "I won't obstruct you. That's as much as I can pledge."

They talked on into the night until they finally both lay in a drunken sleep on the stone floor.

The next morning after a breakfast of griddle-cakes, Rory rode northward beside the mountain range of the Jora where mount Bis ascended on his right. In the castle of Dogherty, Gallagher's neighbour, he spent six more hours pleading his cause. He knew, as he left, that he had achieved what he wanted. The chief would do his will, albeit unwittingly. Dogherty was a talker and Rory knew he would run immediately to the Lord Deputy with the story of Rory's planned treachery.

Tired from his political manoeuvrings and the over indulgence in alcohol he felt like going back to Ennistoomey and making the trip to Aoedh O'Cassidy another day but decided that when he was this far he may as well go on.

Aoedh O'Cassidy produced more *uisce beatha*. After a few goblets it was easy. Rory buttered him up and listened to him reminisce about the raids he saw as a boy.

"There was nobody who could steal cattle like your grandfather. Con Maguire was a man that men respected."

Rory praised Aoedh's women and patted his dogs. Then in the midst of O'Cassidy's words and expressions of fidelity, he made his offer. "I will give you a third reduction in your rents, effective immediately. In return you must muster your forces if I need you."

At sunrise, the *uirrí* stood at the castle door, satisfied. As Rory rode away, he knew that these *uirrithe* had talked to him because of his grandfather. He would have to do a lot more to gain their loyalty for himself. It was easy to mouth compliance. Fealty was more than polite words. O'Cassidy had merely replaced subservience to Eoin with subservience to him. And he was unusual in that a lessening of his rent was the extent of his ambition.

Two weeks later, he was still drained from his visits to Eoin's *uirrithe,* and his stomach had scarcely recovered from his feed of *uisce beatha* and wine. So he was not in any mood to meet the Chief Secretary whom he knew to be Sir Samuel Fenton's trusted assistant. "I hear you are making great efforts to turn Eoin Maguire's allies against him," he said sitting on the one cushioned chair that Rory had. He was glad he had swept the floor and cleaned the place that morning. He did not want this Englishman to see anything that would give credence to his belief that the Irish were dirty savages.

So Dogherty informed as I knew he would, Rory thought to himself. As far as the English knew, he was following orders. They were unaware that he was positioning *himself* and not the government to take over from his uncle.

"The Lord Deputy feels that nothing is being done to protect the Pale from robbers. I wish to discuss the extortion practised by the Irish on Palesmen with you," The Chief Secretary continued without waiting for Rory to reply.

Rory studied his harelip. The Irish believed that anyone with a harelip was a bringer of bad luck. What he needed was good luck.

"How are you getting on with these clowns? Have you anything to show for our investment? I thought not. I told the Lord Deputy only the other week ..."

Rory bristled.

"Never mind. We have a plan. No need to concern yourself. I will give the orders." He tickled his chin. "Is the Englishman George Carew here?"

"No, he is not," Rory answered.

The Chief Secretary shifted his feet. In a neutral tone, he said, "Campbells are playing the knave as competently as they always did. The Lord Deputy ordered that when the rest of the battalion arrive, you are to proceed against them. I have details of their location on this dispatch."

If the English were postponing their plans for Eoin, Rory thought, the black renters must have upset somebody important in the Pale.

"I will contact you, the Chief Secretary continued. "We will plan our strategy as soon as the reinforcements arrive. Before that I have further orders that will interest you directly." The Chief Secretary took a handful of gold coins from his purse and let them fall with silvery clinks on to his opposite palm.

Rory had never seen so much money.

"I have here one hundred pounds," he said "You are to hire an assassin. Eoin Maguire's henchmen guard him well so you will need to get someone who will not falter." He waved the fistful of coins with a flourish. "You will find many willing takers for these."

Rory felt shocked. Hatred for his uncle had become diluted over the years. But then he remembered Matthew's demise. His uncle, and indeed other chieftains like his uncle, regarded poison as a permissible weapon. Phelim and Matthew had been obstacles to Eoin's ambition. That was why they died. Eoin was now an obstacle to his ambition. That was why *he* must die. Suddenly feeling much older than his actual age, he reached and took the money from the Englishman's hand.

Chapter Three

Finola studied herself in the looking-glass in her bed-chamber. She had braided her hair into a coil on top of her head and it added a few inches to her petite stature. Around her neck she wore a cluster of pearls, a new present from Andrew. Another atonement gift, she thought. But she felt no rancour. Without him, she would not have her son Andrew Óg. He came rushing in now squealing, "giddy up." She smiled at the tousled head and the blazing dark eyes.

"I'm Drake," he giggled. "This is my horse."

"Shouldn't it be a ship?" Her voice was teasing.

"Oh, I know that," he said with solemnity. "But I prefer a horse."

They were the model of the happy family, full of flamboyant gestures, rich presents, erotic love, and affection for their son. She feigned belief when Andrew said he loved her. He did not press her about her feelings for him. What was not in doubt in their make believe world was that they both loved their child.

She knew that her husband had a sensual allure that had nothing to do with age or class or education. Other women envied her. Yet when she lay with him, Murrough's sweet face replaced her husband's.

Since Murrough's death, she had changed. In the past, she had been greedy for life's bounty, now she felt prepared to give more to others. She had lost the opportunity to give to Murrough, but she had a second chance in her son. There were times when she longed to throw her husband's gold bracelets and jewels back at him and seek a divorce but concern for their little boy stopped her. She had been about to disavow love before, she would not do it again.

At these moments, she remembered how scornful she had been of her mother's tolerance of Cormac's infidelities. Now, she realised that love, whether it is for a child or a man, made people accept more than they should.

Later that morning Brian came to visit. He told her of Rory's return. "A retinue of soldiers and Sir Walter Carew's son came with him. I met his father, Sir Walter, in Munster." Brian's expression darkened momentarily. "I have been away from

Mulahinsa since Rory's arrival. No doubt he will have left by now and will be with his soldiers at Ennistoomey."

The thought of seeing Rory again, after so many years, excited Finola. What would he look like? Did he remember her?

"You want to know what he looks like," Brian said. There was laughter in his voice. "I know you too well. Let me think! From what I could see from a distance, he was fat and had a bald spot on his head and carbuncles on ..."

"You're a divil Brian. Don't taunt."

"It does my heart good to see you laugh," he said. "Since that Murrough ..."

"That's enough Brian."

Andrew Óg came and climbed onto Brian's knee and snuggled into him. "I omitted to tell you something, Finola," Brian continued. "Niall intends to visit you. Since his mother's death, he feels dejected. He misses you in Mulahinsa and is reluctant to return there. Shane is too old for a tutor now so there is no reason for him to stay." He looked reflective. "Did you ever think of giving him a post?" He caressed Andrew Óg's head. "This lad here will need a tutor soon." He paused. "I'm sure Andrew can afford it. Rumour says he captured much booty lately."

Finola did not comment on the reference to her husband's cattle raids, which he refused to discuss with her. She said, "I'd love to see Niall. Tell him I miss our conversations."

Campbell and his brother Edward reined in with a herd of horses just as Finola was saying farewell to Brian at the *bawn*. Some more of his thievery rashly brought home, she thought. His clan's nickname for him was Andrew the Impulsive. If he would only content himself with the life of a normal chieftain, they might have some hope of happiness.

As Campbell jumped from his horse and came over to her and Brian, Edward remained mounted. He walked stiffly, rubbing the base of his spine, "Getting old," he said jokingly. "Have seen too many corpses with their guts spilled. Death looms and makes me weary." His eyes sparked. "A border raider must keep himself alert."

"Andrew Campbell you would be unable to afford your gambling and expensive scatter rugs were it not for the thousands of cattle you rustle from the Pale. That's why your herds are so big," Brian jested. "Though you must admit the rewards for your precarious life are manifold," he said then, looking around at the neatly kept houses of his tenants.

"Must go. Haven't time to waste. It's as well you're leaving. Business to attend." Andrew hurried away into his dwelling.

Finola knew that the Palesmen paid him what they called *black rent* three times a year, to stop him raiding their cattle. If someone were behind in his payments, Andrew stripped him of his herds. The Pale could not withstand his attacks.

She was also aware that Palesmen frequently harassed the government for protection from this corruption. Aid was slow, meagre, and usually too late. And, thankfully, Andrew was as crafty as the Scottish mercenaries from whom he was descended. Intuition told him when to push and when to withdraw.

A mere six hours after his visit home with the stolen horses, Andrew and his men were riding into the fertile land around Dublin's Pale. In a low voice, he said to his brother, "The two lately arrived from England in Dempsey's place might expect us. Third time we've been back."

He stopped at the home of one of the landowners. His henchmen gathered round him astride their horses, armed with muskets and javelins. He shouted through the open door. "Your last warning. No money for us. No cattle or crops for you."

The landowner came out onto the steps. In a voice as thin and weedy as his body he said, "Robbers. Stealing our livelihood from us."

Andrew was surprised at this display of defiance. Then he noticed over to the right, the English guns pointing at them. He had to think quickly.

The tinny voice continued, "When I came here, my agreement was that if thieves interfered, I could request the aid of the Lord Deputy." The little man moistened his lips. "I am giving you fair warning now. We will kill the lot of you."

"You've no right to the land," Andrew shouted back at him, but carefully eyed the soldiers. "No right to the cattle. They belong to the Irish." He turned to go, his expression unusually sombre. Signalling to his men to retreat, he urged his horse into a gallop.

Back in Andrew's fortress, his brother Edward asked, "Why didn't we fire? It is we who usually make the threats. Today *he* threatened us."

Campbell warmed his hands at the blaze. "No dupe is this new man. Guns trained on us from the beginning. We had no chance. Must think this one out. The Lord Deputy mustn't come against me."

"Brother, if you can't manage him I'll marry an English woman."

"There's only one promise ever I was incapable of carrying out, Edward." Andrew's tone was sorrowful.

"Eoin Maguire, I suppose," Edward's voice filled with irritation. "Why are you still seeking revenge? Sinéad is dead ten years now. It wasn't Eoin Maguire himself who put her to the sword."

"Didn't do the dirty deed himself, you mean, but he's responsible for men in his command. Never got close enough to kill him. Feud has simmered so long now, it'll never boil." He got up to put on more logs on the fire. "From the cast of events, my revenge will take ten years more." His voice filled with foreboding. "The upstart we had to deal with today will keep us busy for a while."

"You have Finola and Andrew Óg now," Edward spoke carefully. "It's not fair to them that you are always thinking of Sinéad." His voice became compassionate. "I know you loved her, but you have to forget her."

"First woman I loved. Can't forget her," Andrew mumbled through his fingers, his head in his hands. "Haunted I am, God help me." Suddenly, he shoved his stool back from the fire and left without another word.

He rode at the head of his men back to his territory and his safe land. As he passed his tenants, they greeted him warmly. They loved their buccaneering chief, with his new wife and baby son. In these lands there was no shortage of food on the table. Even when the harvests were bad, the laird made sure they had enough to eat. No matter the source of their bounty. Interlopers from England had no right to plenty when natives were poor.

Chapter Four

Finola lay wide-eyed underneath her husband. He pulled at her night apparel, impatient and breathing heavily and explored her legs and thighs. She wondered why he invariably used the same hand. During these quick couplings, he rolled on top of her until he quickly came, gasping and thumping. She remained dry and sore. The days when she became moist with desire at the sight of Murrough were so long ago, they had the mien of a dream.

He moved from on top of her, and lay on his back his breathing gradually returning to normal. Opening his eyes, he said, "Better go before I fall asleep." Then he was up and off – to another raid, she supposed.

As she took control of her body after the invasion, she wondered if this were all there were to lovemaking. If she didn't long for another child, she would abandon it gladly. Andrew would have to satisfy himself elsewhere. It wasn't as if he loved her.

She was still on her back an hour later feeling too lethargic to rise. When she realised that Peg was waiting to go to a settlement wedding feast, she dragged herself out of bed and made her way to the kitchen to get Andrew Óg.

"Is it sick you are milady?" Peg asked when she entered the kitchen. "'Tisn't well you're looking. 'Tis here I'll be staying today I'm thinkin'," she said unable to hide her disappointment.

"No, Peg. Go. Hurry or they'll leave without you."

"If 'tis sure you are."

Finola smiled as she watched the girl escape through the door. She touched Andrew Óg's head nestled in her skirts. "Come with me." She took him by the hand. "Mother is going to have a little rest. You can play in my bed-chamber."

She lay on her bed while Andrew Óg sat on the floor and amused himself with the blocks that Andrew had hewn for his birthday. When she woke, she realised that it was too quiet and sitting up she saw the blocks thrown on the floor but no child. "Andrew, Andrew Óg," she called. "Where are you? Andrew Óg I'm not playing. Answer me." Her pitch rose. "Do you hear me?"

He would be too big to fit in the clothes bureau. The lock on the walnut chest in the corner was secure. Arising, she left the bed chamber and went into the kitchen.

Nothing seemed out of place except for the honey jar on the floor. She stooped to pick it up. It was empty, and the lid was missing. As she searched in every corner, she imagined the worst.

Then she removed the lid of the flour vat and looked inside. She was unsure whether to laugh or weep. There Andrew Óg sat, delighting in how the honey made the flour stick all over him. "Look Mother," he said a mischievous grin on his white face. "Me snowman."

As she scrubbed flour and honey from her son, she felt so tired she regretted giving the servants the day off and wished Andrew would return to keep Andrew Óg absorbed. She sank onto a form and put her head in her hands. She craved sleep.

Later she endured watching Andrew Óg as he smeared peat onto his face. His father had told him a story about *na sióga* who had taken a beautiful child and left a changeling instead. He wanted to look ugly like the changeling he said. As she washed off the brown, she felt tears well up.

The light was fading as she bundled him into bed fully clothed. It was the first time he had gone to sleep so neglected, but she had lacked the strength to persuade him to don his night clothes. Later she checked if he were still awake. As she looked at him, curled tight as a leaf bulb in the bedclothes, his face angelic in slumber, she wondered had she only imagined the times he had been mischievous that day. Would Andrew come home tonight? He hadn't said when he left this morning and she had neglected to ask. For herself, she felt well pleased by his absence, but he would be a help with the high spirited Andrew Óg.

Too sluggish to remove her gown, she fell into bed. She wished she could put her weeping down to being with child. But no. Her bleeding had started on the thirtieth of the month. That was a week ago. She had lain awake for nearly two hours when she heard Campbell come in and go to his dressing room. She continued to stare at the ceiling, waiting for him to appear. Tears started again.

When Campbell saw her distress, he took her into his arms."What's wrong Finola?" he asked. "Is it Andrew Óg? Is he sick?"

"No, he is well."

"What is it then?"

"I feel tired and I cry for the smallest aggravation. See!" She held up a sodden piece of cloth. "I've used all the lace handkerchiefs you brought me last week."

"You need rest Finola. You take full care of the child. You're like a peasant woman the way you carry him around. Didn't say anything. Knew it made you happy. But you need rest."

She brightened at his concern.

In a gesture of affection, unusual in that it was not a prelude to sexual intimacy, he kissed her on the lips. "They talk in the cabins about their chief who plays with his child. I'll give the hags more to gossip about. I'll take care of him for a few weeks. You go to visit your family at Mulahinsa. I'll watch over our son. And plot tactics."

A few days later, Finola rose from the trestle table, where she was threading garlic, and went to meet Niall. He had entered the hall escorted by Peg. "Brian told me you were coming, but I thought it would be later." She was delighted to see him, but she was disappointed that she was about to leave. "I'm going to Mulahinsa in a few days, but I can change the plan."

"Mulahinsa will do you good. I want no talk of plan changes."

Niall had not met either Andrew Óg or his father before. Neither had he seen her since her marriage three years ago. Yet, there was no strangeness or awkwardness between any of them.

When the sun shone, the four of them strolled out by the hedgerows. She plucked flowers and gave them to Andrew Óg who made a garland for his hair. His father and Niall bowed to him as they joined in his game of 'I'm lord of the castle.' When he tired of that, he ran about after the butterflies shouting "beautif' colour." As she looked at the two men bending over the child, engrossed in his chatter, she thought of water freezing into ice in winter and wished she could solidify the moment in the same way.

"You're leaving tomorrow Finola," Niall said, "While you're gone I'll have a chance to get to know this divil."

"If we need relief, his grand-parents are close," Andrew turned to Niall. "Finola will tell you that the Scots of the Isles stick together."

She said, "All his soldiers and farmers are related to him, it's true. Now with you here also, I know Andrew Óg will be safe."

Finola felt a flutter of anticipation as she neared the borders of her homelands. She had spent most of her life here and, despite the sad memory it held of her departure, she was glad to be back.

She was unsure whether Brian had informed them at Mulahinsa of her intention to make the journey; she had been indefinite about when exactly she intended to come. Dismounting at the *bawn*, she turned to her escort of horsemen and told them to go into the kitchen for vittles when they had foddered the horses.

From the outside, the castle was unchanged. It would still keep them safe from attack if there was, as was rumoured, a war with England. Her mother stood at the front door, embroidery in her hand. "News of your arrival came through from the kitchen," she said with only a hint of excitement in her voice. "I interrupted my work," she added then descending the steps.

Cormac emerged next and rushed to Finola taking her in his arms. "What a surprise!" he exclaimed.

Maeve let Finola embrace her. Her eyes sparkled, but her remote expression, for so long a mask, was now part of her. The once fair hair drawn back from her face was almost entirely grey and gave her skin a luminous quality that added to her other-worldly demeanour.

Shane stood in the background looking surly. Finola gave him a sisterly hug but he barely reacted. Then Finola saw a young man, whom she had never met nor expected to be there, come and stand behind Shane. She looked enquiringly at him.

"You are Finola?" he asked.

She nodded.

"You are everything he described and more," he said as he straightened from a bow and gazed at her with a strange fierceness.

Shifting her focus she met her brother's gaze, chilly as the air about them. Nothing changes, she thought, and returned her attention to the stranger.

"Are you curious about who discussed you with me?" he asked.

"I'd like to know who you are first." She felt too tired after the long ride to play guessing games. "Nobody introduced us, Sir."

"I am George Carew. The person I alluded to is Rory Maguire." He looked contrite. "Forgive me for presuming on your good-humour, but I felt I already knew you. I have heard your praises sung eloquently and often."

Finola was immediately sorry for her sharpness. He seemed after all a likable man.

He took her hand and touched it to his lips. "Let us forgive each other," he said.

She entered the house on his arm, unaware of Shane's malevolent expression.

Chapter Five

After a week at Mulahinsa Finola began to feel refreshed. When the rest of the castle rose, she turned over and slept on. It was a novelty to be able to have a bed to herself without the possibility of Andrew encroaching. When she did rise, she'd wash in cold water from the basin and don her most comfortable dress. Here at Mulahinsa there was no need to beautify herself for the sake of others. In her Campbell home, strangers on horseback were constantly calling with sealed missives for Andrew. Her husband liked her to be suitably attired. But here, although she missed Andrew Óg, she felt as carefree as she had felt in the months at the booley with Rory so long ago.

She spent her days helping Maeve with the dyeing and even tried weaving, but gave it up in despair after an hour.

While talking with George and listening to him, in his light hesitant voice, tell her about his garden, she marvelled that a soldier of the crown would engage in such a conversation. Shane, however, disliked it when she monopolised George's company. Whenever he was about there was hostility. But this was the only cloud on her contentment and she was determined to ignore it.

Another week went by. She began to wake early. The cold water on her skin in the mornings chafed; she must ask Teresa or Caitlín to heat a pot of water. She began to take early morning walks but they took her past Murrough's hut and she felt unable to face the memories that invoked. Her heart ached for Andrew Óg's presence. At times she even missed big Andrew's warmth in the bed beside her.

Then one day a messenger arrived with a missive for Cormac. He read it aloud for Maeve and Finola in an excited tone. "There is to be a feast at Eoin Maguire's abode. He has invited me." He looked from one to the other. "In my humble opinion, this is the most interesting and unexpected happening this year."

"Eoin Maguire wants to kill you," exclaimed Maeve.

"Have sense woman. Do you think he would have to invite me to a feast to kill me?"

"That's what he did to Matthew. Or have you forgotten?"

"I'll be careful about the food and drink. Before I leave, I'll eat a wholesome dinner and enjoy some *uisce beatha*. That should keep me spry for the duration. Anyway," he went on, "Rory will soon have an army of men at his disposal." He took a deep breath and sat. "It must have alarmed Eoin. He's afraid Rory is back to claim his own. He wants to offer me an inducement to support him." Cormac grinned. "Why would I refuse such an opportunity to have fun?"

Finola said, "I could do with a bit of fun myself. Can I come?"

"Why would you want to go to Eoin Maguire's?" Maeve sounded incredulous.

"The prospect of visiting the lair of the ogre of my childhood excites me," Finola replied. "And I need a diversion to keep me from missing Andrew Óg. I know exactly what I'll wear, too."

Delighted to have an excuse to doff her dreary frocks, she went to her chamber and donned the gown her seamstress had recently put together for her. It was a European style she had designed herself. She looked in the mirror. A woman dressed in a scarlet satin gown, embroidered with threads of black, stared back at her. "Sensuous but dignified," Andrew would have said. She threw a mantle of black, lined with the eye-catching satin, over her shoulders and placed a ruby and diamond necklace around her neck.

Suddenly and inexplicably she felt Murrough's presence at her shoulder. Then she heard a voice, "You look beautiful Finola." But it wasn't Murrough's. George, flanked by Shane stood in the open doorway. "My mother wears gowns with long sleeves puffed at the shoulders like that. I like the style." Though her heart had longed for the voice to be Murrough's she, nevertheless, felt pleased at George's compliment.

"What do you think of it Shane?" she asked, with sudden boldness. "Do you think your sister looks beautiful?" But Shane turned his back and, placing an arm around George's shoulder, ushered him away.

Chapter Six

The dispatch that the Chief Secretary delivered at Ennistoomey was addressed to George Carew, though George was not due to visit until the following day. So Rory felt validated when he broke the seal and read that another shipload of soldiers would be leaving from England on the eighteenth to act as reinforcements. They would be needed. The soldiers already at Ennistoomey were indolent and tough to manage. But he knew it was not in his interests to antagonise the queen's army. Perhaps he would need their support for his own plans in the future. As Maeve would say, "It is better to have more than one fetter on a lively donkey."

The following morning a distant thudding of hooves and George's voice ordering his horse-boy to dismount and knock on the door, alerted Rory. He came outside to see George sitting astride his horse. The sun shining on his face gave him a princely appearance that infuriated Rory. "Won't you come in?" he said a little coldly, he felt.

"I am hurrying to get back to Mulahinsa."

Rory did not answer.

George continued with a question. "The men have settled into their new quarters?"

Rory nodded. He knew he should be more courteous but felt unable right now. He handed George the dispatch.

George examined the name on the outside. "You had no right to open this."

Rory allowed a long pause. Then he said, "The Chief Secretary would have given the dispatch to you if you had been here. When do you intend to join us?"

"I will remain at Mulahinsa for the present." His tone was curt. "Please arrange for Percy Sidney to take the soldiers on manoeuvres. To keep them vigilant and prepared for conflict. The veterans from Britanny will soon be here. I took my father's advice and refused permission for them to disembark at Plymouth lest they desert. Meantime, I will trust your judgement."

When he rode away, Rory's stomach began to whirl in a brew of apprehension. Tomorrow he would do the Chief Secretary's bidding and hire an assassin. To while away the hours until then he did as George ordered, and arranged for the men to go on manoeuvres in a week's time.

The following day Rory went to see O'Cathán, Eoin Maguire's brother-in-law. O'Cathán was the sole brother of Eoin's newly acquired third wife. Although O'Cathán was an outlaw, his seventeen-year-old sister trusted him, and Eoin, in the height of sexual bedazzlement, granted her every wish. Rory found it intriguing that his uncle, ten years older than him, was such a sot for a woman. He was profiting from other's foolishness these days. First there was George's unwillingness to leave Mulahinsa and now Eoin's readiness, to have renegade O'Cathán at his feast.

As he trudged the low hills on foot, the terrain being most unsuitable for riding, his boots sank into the mire. Blinding rain battered his face. He felt sick at the thought of recruiting an assassin. However, he was determined to carry it out and had hired two kerne to accompany him for safety on his mission to O'Cathán's abode.

In truth, his return to Ulster had lost its gloss. All his life he had wanted nothing more than to regain his lands and avenge his father and Matthew's death. But, at this moment, he felt he had no right to the lands of Glenone, he felt no affinity with his ancestors, the fearless leaders of Gaelic Ulster. Maybe his uncle Eoin had been telling the truth all along and his father was an O'Reilley not a Maguire after all. Maybe he was the grandson of a wheelwright and not of Con Maguire, a Gaelic chieftain, honoured by his people and written of by poets.

He had confided this to Sir Walter once. Sir Walter had told him not to believe Eoin. Yes, it was true that his father Phelim had been illegitimate, but he was the natural son of Con Maguire. Sir Walter had known his grandmother, he'd said. Phelim had been six months old when she had married O'Reilley. When her husband died, Sir Walter had helped her to *name* Con Maguire as the rightful father. It was fitting, he felt, that the child should have an inheritance and that Con should pay for his dalliance.

Rory had asked Sir Walter what his grandmother had been like. Strange that he could still recall Sir Walter's reply. "She was as beautiful as Helen of Troy." For a moment Rory thought he had begun to look wistful. Sir Walter wasn't given to such extravagant statements.

Rory's mind was a vortex of depressing thoughts. He missed Finola, gone from him forever now, it seemed. His own people and his English masters both regarded him with suspicion. His future was uncertain.

O'Cathán had built a bothy for himself in a wood four miles from castle Uí Laoi and a half day's ride from Ennistoomey. It was unusual for outlaws like O'Cathán to stay in one place for very long. However because of his marital link with Eoin Maguire, other chiefs ignored his presence on their lands. If the authorities came looking for him they would deny any knowledge of his being there. Tenants gave him milk and dry clothes when his makeshift shelter leaked and generally he was well looked after.

Rory found the hunchback sitting on smelly rushes in his shelter. Wrapped in a pelt, he was drinking *uisce beatha* from a goblet. A square of sky was visible through the roof; a fire, more a heap of ashes, stood in a small pile in the centre of the floor; a platter and a spoon lay on the dirt beside it. The girl who came to the doorway, a can in her hand, saw Rory and scurried away.

O'Cathán threw some *uisce beatha* from his goblet onto the ashes, causing smoke and smuts to rise and splutter. Coughing, he reached for the gun beside him. "'Tis the son of Phelim you are. My friends told me 'twould be coming you'd be. Invited you to his feast has Eoin Maguire I'm thinkin'."

Rory did not intend to reveal anything to this man. He would not tell him about the three hostages Eoin had offered to assure Rory's attendance at the feast. Eoin obviously badly wanted him to be there to make such an offer. Being alone at Ennistoomey, the men being out on manoeuvres, Rory had sent one of them back with a message of acceptance, and locked the other three in the cellar.

"What do you want with me?" O'Cathán continued in a menacing tone.

Rory felt the covering of fine hair on the back of his neck stand upright. No need to prevaricate with O'Cathán.

"I want Eoin Maguire killed," he said in a voice bolder than he expected. "The way you do it is your affair. The result is my only interest. There is forty pounds in it for you."

"Is it me to murder? 'Tis out of your mind you are." O'Cathán feigned incredulity.

"The Chief Secretary told me that you killed an Englishman in Larne last year. The dead man's wife and daughter will testify. They may be mistaken, of course. If that is the situation, you will not mind coming back to face an investigation."

O'Cathán cleared his throat and cocked his firearm.

"If you co-operate, that naturally will not be necessary." Rory waved to the two kerne on each side of the shelter. They came to the doorway and trained their guns on O'Cathán. Between them they would have killed him before he fired a shot.

He handed the weapon to Rory.

"I will control it from here," Rory told the mercenaries. He handed them a pound each. He turned back to O'Cathán. "I will kill you if you betray me to your lord." He knew he would not have to do it personally, of course. He would get soldiers to do it for him as he was getting O'Cathán to kill Eoin. He stifled his guilt pangs. This had official approval. The Chief Secretary had ordered it and he represented the Lord Deputy who in turn represented Queen Elizabeth.

O'Cathán pulled his glib, "Fifty and it's a deal."

Rory tried not to show his satisfaction. He had expected him to hold out for sixty. He calculated. When he subtracted the two pounds he had spent on the kerne with the guns, he would have forty eight pounds left. He would use it to buy weapons when the time came. "Twenty-five pounds now. The rest when you do the deed."

O'Cathán took the money without another word.

As he left the shelter and descended the hill, it crossed his mind that he was taking a chance exposing his back to O'Cathán. Another saying of Maeve's came to mind, "Ill doers are ill thinkers."

That night Rory could not sit still. A hundred times he rose from his stool and walked around the circular room at Ennistoomey that had become his lair. His life had become one ordeal after another. The long boring days of Chalk Hall were a distant memory; he had longed for excitement then. What he would give now for a few days' rest. But it was not to be. The night of the feast was approaching. And it bothered him. He did not like the planned cold-blooded murder and his part in it.

The queasy feelings returned. He could not allow himself to capitulate to an attack of doubt at this stage. The deed was set in motion. There was no going back.

He wondered about Eoin's motives in inviting him to the feast. Perhaps he was wary of his English aid. Perhaps he planned collusion with Rory. Better to share his lands with his nephew than to give it all to the English.

In Ulster there was unease, murmurings. There were rumours from Tyrone that O'Neill was not as loyal to the crown as he had been. Ulstermen had, at last, begun to absorb the lessons of the Desmond wars. He did not expect conflict to break out immediately, but like all Ulstermen, he was wary of the future. Perhaps some of this anxiety had pierced Eoin Maguire's hide also.

The feeling in his stomach worsened. He undressed and laid his head on the pillow. Now that he had arranged for it, the full treachery of his murder scheme hit him with all its force and clarity. He stared into the darkness fearing sleep would elude him this night.

Chapter Seven

Finola's face was flushed with excitement as she stood before Eoin Maguire in the dining hall of his castle. He held an amenable expression. She saw no resemblance to his nephews in his brown eyes and the refined shape of his chin or his full lips.

Taking her hands in his, he drew them to his lips. Such audacity! For a mad moment she entertained the idea of kicking him in the shins but, fortunately, the sound of his voice and the content of his words stopped her from indulging in such infantile behaviour.

"You look spectacular," he said. "How foolish of me not to have sought your company before this."

"I came in place of my mother tonight," she said. In spite of herself her voice quivered. She had heard about his reputation with the ladies. Although she determined not to let him charm her, she found herself disliking him less than she imagined she would.

He let go her hands and turned to Cormac beside her. She felt a little slighted at the sudden loss of his attention.

"Cormac. It is an honour to have you under my roof. I trust you will take pleasure in the feast."

"Thank you for your invitation." Cormac made an effort to be civil.

"I have other guests to welcome. My servants will seat you." Eoin's voice was silky.

Finola and Cormac took their places at a long table. Finola looked about her and saw that she was not the only one who had taken trouble with her appearance. The women were all resplendent in their gowns and jewels, the men handsome in their jackets of velvet and tight trews. The conversation was animated and witty. The lords and ladies were obviously ready for a spry evening.

Up on the podium the *reacaire* began to recite a ditty of greeting, accompanied by an old man on the eight-stringed harp. Finola felt a current of exhilaration flow through her. Despite her remembering that Matthew died here, she felt care-free.

A mendicant friar said Grace and the feast began. Finola

reached for a draught of the mulled wine beside her. Her fingers had just wound around the goblet when Cormac, from across the table, put his hand on hers. "Don't drink anything until you're sure that the other guests have drunk first, and from the same vessel as yours."

She felt disturbed by the caution; in such a congenial atmosphere, it was hard to imagine any kind of perfidy. Tonight was not a night for dire warnings and dramatic gestures. It was so long since she had been to a feast. Wanting to feel young and carefree, she raised the goblet to her mouth and felt the liquid warm her body and relax her mind. Minutes later she beckoned for a refill. Unlike her father she had eaten nothing before she came; now as she felt the effects of the alcohol she regretted that she hadn't.

Glancing in Eoin's direction she saw that he was looking at her and admitted to herself that he was sufficiently handsome and elegant to make rumours of his many female disciples credible. He gave a slight bow in her direction and a faintly derisive smile.

She finished her wine and was so intent on getting the attention of a hireling for a refill, she failed to hear her father when he spoke to her.

He reached for her hand again. More dire warnings, she thought. "Eoin Maguire is not going to propose anything tonight," Cormac said. "This is just part of a reacquainting process." He eyed the *uisce beatha,* sorry now that he had resolved to remain abstemious.

"Eat and drink, Father," Finola said, surprising herself by her asperity. "Eoin wants to woo you not kill you."

Cormac reached for his goblet. Finola sat back and revelled in her surroundings. Everyone was in festive mood. The *reacaire,* accompanied by the harpist, continued to recite praise poems to Eoin. The light from the candles cast a soft glow on the laden platters of food.

Suddenly Eoin was seen to push back his stool and walk towards the door.

"More guests have arrived," Cormac said. "They must be important when he interrupted his meal to go and greet them."

Finola spilled a dollop of wine onto her gown causing a large stain to appear in a grotesque contrast to the crimson of her dress. She was frantically rubbing it with her handkerchief when a loud shot could be heard from outside the dining-hall.

Cormac jumped up. Another shot rang out. The crowd rose to their feet looking at each other in bewilderment. Cormac turned a questioning face to the lord beside him, but he just shrugged. Slowly the crowd sat again.

There was a clamour at the door. One of Eoin's *Gallóglaigh* stamped into the hall. "Someone shot the chief," he uttered hoarsely, to nobody in particular.

There was a gasp and the lords and ladies jumped to their feet again.

"He's alive for a' that." The *Gallóglach* assured them. He looked at Eimear O'Cathán, Eoin's wife. His tone softened when he said, "Donal O'Cathán was shot too. He's not badly injured tho.'"

Eimear sobbed.

The young man then looked towards Cormac. "'Tis with a purse someone parted ta arrange this." His voice was harsh. "The rogue escaped. God willin' O'Cathán will know him when he sees him."

At that, two of Eoin's henchmen came and stood behind Finola and Cormac. One placed an indelicate hand on her bare shoulder. "You are to come with us," he said.

Unsteadily, she got to her feet. Cormac, stepping to the door with his own escort, looked at her, a frown on his forehead.

They were ordered into the dungeons. A warden who proved to be talkative was placed at the door. A shot from the darkness had injured Eoin Maguire after he had gone to the doorway to speak to his brother-in-law, O'Cathán. O'Cathán himself had been shot in the leg.

"Somebody promised a hefty purse," the man said, repeating the words of his comrade in the hall.

"We had nothing to do with it," Finola protested. "Why would we come to Eoin Maguire's abode if we wanted to kill him?" She paused. Her words sounded faulty to her own ears. All their lives hadn't they wished Eoin dead? At Mulahinsa she had grown up with a hatred for Eoin Maguire. In her new home Andrew refused to talk about him with her. But with a woman's intuitiveness, she knew that they were enemies. "Wishing and doing are different," she muttered to herself.

She had found Eoin attractive and interesting and was now unsure whether she wished him harm. Perhaps there was something of his nephew about him after all. As she settled down to wait for whatever was to come, her thoughts centred on Rory. He would consider them foolhardy for walking into the lion's den like this.

At dawn the warden opened the door and entered. He looked at Finola. "'Tis to release you, I am. Cormac stays."

"I will remain with my father. Where he goes, I go." Finola felt her cheeks redden.

The man was taken aback by her display of bravery. So much so that he failed to notice Cormac come behind him, his stool raised high. He brought it down with a crash on the man's head. "Let's get out of here," Cormac urged.

They headed for the door and checked the passageway. There would be a sentry at each end. These henchmen would be less gentle than the unfortunate warden Cormac had hit. They huddled in the shadow of the door. Behind them their victim was beginning to wake. When he did he would raise the alarm.

A third man arrived on the scene. "The two of you will not escape," he said in a low voice. He spoke like George Carew. What was an Englishman doing in Eoin Maguire's dwelling? And why did he seem to be helping them?

His hand on Finola's wrist was smooth. "It is your father they want to question," he said. He looked at Cormac. "You would be dead if they really believed you had something to do with the attacks. Eoin Maguire will wish to talk to you when he is able." He paused. "Maybe concerning his nephew's intentions. Do you suspect Rory Maguire of being responsible for this act tonight?"

Cormac ignored the question. He took Finola's arm. "There will be no need for you to escape. You'll walk out the door as you walked in. An O'Hanlon will not scurry from a Maguire abode. I'll stay and face Eoin." He turned to the man. "I expect you to see her safely home."

The man looked at Cormac with a new respect.

The warden had by now recovered consciousness and holding his musket, he came and took Cormac roughly by the arm.

"Orders are not to harm him," the Englishman said to him. He turned to Finola. "Come with me."

She walked with him past the sentries and out of the castle. A hush filled the night air. Only her leather shoes and the swish of her chiffon made any sound. A horse waited. The horse-boy, open-mouthed at the sight of her dressed in such finery, hoisted her onto the horse. Her escort mounted in front.

They proceeded at a slow pace. The night was mild enough for them to hear each other when they spoke. "Am I correct in saying that you are not a native of Ulster?" Though she could not see his face, Finola sensed a hesitation in his answer.

"How perceptive of you. I am not an Ulsterman."

He was different to the commonplace bodyguard with whom Eoin Maguire usually surrounded himself.

"I am Arthur," he said. "Arthur Petrell. Called after my esteemed father."

She was too drowsy to pursue the conversation further. As they neared Mulahinsa, she said to him, "We're almost there. We have a man from The Queen's army staying with us so he will know what to do." Let him bring that information back to his master, she thought.

At the mention of military, she felt him tense. His previous good humour disappeared. He stopped some distance from the castle and dismounted before deftly helping her down from the horse. Then, uttering a hurried goodbye he rode quickly away leaving her standing in the middle of the track, the castle in darkness behind her.

Chapter Eight

Lying in his bed, Rory wanted to die or he wanted to sleep and not wake up. The tearing stomach pains were back. Since yesterday evening, he had been leaving a trail of vomit wherever he went. It covered the dirty pillow now and had hardened on his hair. He was too weak to clean the mess.

The last time he had the strength to move was when he had brought food to his three hostages in the cellar. He had found them lying on the floor, each in a bizarre pose of his own. He had not needed to smell the foul air or see the mess on the floor to know that they were ill. "The meat," one of them said. "Don't eat the meat. 'Tis the meat that's to blame."

It was too late. He had already eaten a hunk of the pork. When he had returned from his assignation with O'Cathán, he had been hungry.

He had left the cellar door unlocked after him as he would be unable to go to Eoin's feast. The men would no longer be needed as a guarantee of his safe return.

Now as he too lay in disgorged pork, he felt like weeping. Since he left Ireland, he had only cried once and then he had been still a boy. Soon he heard voices; the hostages had recovered. Death by poisoning was not to be his fate but they would doubtless kill him. He did not care.

They came into his chamber but taking his life was far from their minds; Rory was not their enemy, but Eoin's. Killing in battle in a fair fight was one thing. Leaving a food poisoned man to die in his bed was not their nature.

One of them lifted his head from the pillow. It was the older of the men, Ulick. He was carrying a goblet. "Drink this. It's bilin' water. It's thirsty you'll be getting."

Rory let the man put it to his dry lips.

"Slowly, now."

He did not drink much of it, but he felt better.

Another man, shaky on his legs, came in with a bucket of water, took away the ewer and cleaned the pallet. The third was still in the throes of sickness himself, they told him. They cleaned him as best they could and left.

Soon he fell asleep. He did not know how long he slept, but he did know that he was glad he had not slept forever. When he woke his mouth was dry and his tongue felt swollen but his stomach was more settled.

He rose carefully and swung his legs over the side of the bed, listening for sounds. All was quiet. The prisoners must have fled. Why did he feel disappointed? He would have let them go anyway. But as he staggered to the basin to wash himself, he heard their voices from below; they had not absconded even when they could.

There was a new voice, not like the others. Rory lifted his head from the basin.

And then George tiptoed into the room

"What brought you back?" Rory asked. "I thought you intended to stay at Mulahinsa forever."

"The men downstairs told me you all ate putrid pork and were sick," said George ignoring the question.

"Yes," Rory said, "and I do not feel like reliving the nightmare."

"They had offered themselves as hostages to guarantee your safe return from Eoin Maguire's feast. Is that correct? What a suggestion! I wonder what Maguire had planned? He would have expected you to refuse to go."

Rory did not wish to tell George of his original intention to accept Eoin's invitation.

George said, "Rory, I have something to tell you. Eoin Maquire invited Cormac to the same feast. He and Finola were foolhardy enough to go."

Rory's stomach lurched again. "And?"

"Somebody tried to kill Eoin."

"Tried? They didn't kill him? Did they find who did it?" Rory felt relieved.

"No. But Finola and her father are unhurt." George sounded puzzled. "Is your interest in your uncle so overwhelming that you forgot about a woman you claim to love?"

"Must be the effect of the sickness." Rory was surprised by George's forthrightness.

"Finola was allowed to go free, but they are holding Cormac for questioning about you." He is in no danger, according to Finola but you never know with these people."

Rory knew George was waiting for a response, but he remained silent, thinking.

George continued, "The culprit could claim that Cormac was

involved. To safeguard himself. "

Rory was still too deep in thought to answer.

"Shane did not want me to come. Having to disagree with him distressed me," George said.

"I know how you feel about confrontations," replied Rory, still thinking.

"I have yet to tell you about the circumstances of the shooting," said George. "Eoin Maguire went to ..."

Rory raised his hand to stop him. "I have something to do before I hear the full story. I will be back as soon as I check on my friends in the cellar. I'm sure they are preparing to leave. They'll make fine hostages alright – for Cormac, not for me. From under the bed he retrieved his arquebus and put it under his arm.

In the cellar the stink of vomit was still in the air. It was windowless except for six vents near the roof to let in air and light. A dirt floor kept the air cool.

The three hostages, Eoin's most trusted outriders, were picking up their mantles and searching for their packs, getting ready to leave. Rory felt sorry for them. If Eoin's intentions for him at the feast had always been benign, they would have been safe. His uncle had been thinking strategically. An arrangement between him and Rory would benefit everybody but the English. Wishing to keep the Chief Secretary and Lord Deputy's support, Rory had let his plans to assassinate Eoin go ahead. Now Cormac was embroiled in the affair. Though he did not expect Eoin to harm Cormac, he could not gamble on it. They would have to stay a little longer.

Ulick saw him first. "'Tis come to bid farewell our host has." He went over to Rory and left his hand on his shoulder. "Are you still ailing?"

Rory shook off the hand. "I'm sorry," he said. "A complication has arisen." He looked at their surprised faces. "I have to go," he added. This time he locked the door behind him.

He climbed the stairs feeling dispirited. Since he had returned from Kent, he had involved himself in nothing but intrigue and counter intrigue. His heritage was his ball and chain. He had hoped to stop inter tribal conflict, betrayals and killing, but instead of upraising and improving his people, he had joined in the melee.

When he returned he sat on the bed and rested the arquebus against the wall. He turned towards George, "Tell me the details of Cormac's imprisonment now."

George recounted what Finola had told him of the events at the feast.

"O'Cathán was shot too?" Rory asked.

"He got wounded in the foot." George looked puzzled. "Strange that he escaped so lightly when Maguire got hit badly."

O'Cathán was cleverer than he had acknowledged, Rory thought. He must have shot himself, after shooting Eoin, to draw suspicion away from himself.

"We must get Cormac out," he said. "I'm reluctant to involve myself openly in negotiations. You have been a guest in Cormac's house for several months. It will appear natural if you send a soldier to Eoin's fortress. He can tell my uncle that we will shoot his men unless he lets Cormac free before cockcrow.

George inhaled sharply. "It is now noon," he reminded Rory.

When George had left, Rory stretched himself the length of the bed and pressed a cold cloth to his forehead. There was no sound from the men. He thought of Finola in the dungeon at Glenone. Thank God she had been freed. He remembered her now as the girl with his first weapon, a bow with an arrow, clasped in her hands on the day he was leaving. Since his exile he had not met her once.

He dozed. In that half world between sleep and waking, he heard a knocking on the outside door. Raising himself on his elbow, he eased onto the floor. The noise became more persistent.

When he opened the door, there stood O'Cathán, his foot in a makeshift bandage.

He pointed to his injury. "'Twasn't to kill him I did, but I did me best. I was thinking 'twould be giving me the rest of the money you'd be, what with me being shot in the leg."

Rory got his purse from the pocket of his tunic and handed him twenty-five pounds. Best be shut of him, he thought.

O'Cathán grasped his reward. No further words passed between them.

Chapter Nine

George had been gone a long time. Rory was feeling sickly and anxious; he slept awhile and woke again longing for news. George's words rang in his ears. "You would never know what could happen with these people."

"My people," he muttered. "Fool." He should have asked O'Cathán for details of Cormac's detention. If Cormac suffered for an offence he had nothing to do with, how could he live with himself? The empty garrison pressed in on him.

Time passed. It was evening. Soon the light would fade and night would fall. Then it would be dawn. Unable to bear his own company any longer, he got out of bed, went to the bureau in the kitchen, rummaged in the shelves and found what he wanted. Armed with a pack of cards, he descended the steep stairs to the cellar.

The three men below had become more familiar to him. There was Malachy and Ulick, who had given him the lifesaving drink of water. Gearóid the most unwell of them all, had sometimes reminded him of Matthew lying sick on his pallet.

When he descended, however, all three greeted him with suspicion. Rory explained to them the reason for their imprisonment. That they were hostages for Cormac, who was innocent of the accusation against him. "I have sent a communication to Eoin," he concluded. "I expect it to be an easy exchange." They were, of course, unaware of the threat he had issued - Cormac released before daybreak or he would have them shot. When he produced the playing cards, their wariness left them.

"'Tis weary we are of nothing to do." Ulick looked at his companions. "What would you say to a game?"

"You can share the fur with us. 'Tis cold down here." Gearóid made room for him on the rug that Rory had supplied.

At one point Malachy laughed and said, "'Tis like carrows we'll be after this. Playing for hours we've been." He pointed towards the openings near the ceiling. "Look the sun has gone down."

Rory began to sweat with dread that he would have to kill them. He had not seriously considered the possibility of their dying. Expecting Cormac's return in a matter of hours, he had issued the threat with what he now realised was bravado.

Looking around at the eager faces, he hoped that Eoin would not put his pronouncement to the test.

A short while later he heard someone upstairs.

"I went myself to deliver the message," George informed Rory. "Imagine my surprise when I heard that you had accepted Eoin Maguire's invitation to the banquet but did not go. I can understand why your uncle's men are suspicious."

"You saw my condition yourself. I was too sick to move," Rory defended himself.

"They disbelieved me. They think you hired somebody to kill Eoin. That you planned not being there when he did it. The hostages would be your alibi when they came looking for you."

"If I had done that, I would have gone to the feast to allay suspicions of my involvement. Even a sceptic would have believed me innocent if I were there to play the ministering nephew at Eoin's bedside."

"They suspect Cormac and you of involvement," George said. "Eoin is too ill to trouble himself with this. It is all a botch. Whoever arranged this attack ought to feel shame. To kill in a war is different to shooting someone at the door of his dwelling."

"Even if the purpose of the war is to steal the land from its rightful owners." Rory filled with anger as he thought of the Munster plantation. But badgering George would achieve nothing. He calmed down again. There were more important problems to consider and the time was creeping towards daybreak.

"Prepare some vittles for yourself," he said to George, a little more kindly. "And get some sleep. I have some thinking to do."

Without quite knowing why, he felt himself drawn to the cellar again. It was only right that the prisoners should know of the danger. Perhaps one of them would have a solution. As he reached the door, he heard Ulick say good-naturedly, "Come back to trounce us, he has."

"'Tis winning I have been since you left," Malachy said when he entered. But when he saw the expression on Rory's face, his bantering died.

"What's wrong lad?" Ulick asked.

Rory felt vulnerable enough without being called lad, but,

perhaps it was because Ulick was older than all of them, he did not resent the designation.

"They think I arranged Eoin's shooting. They are refusing to release Cormac. I threatened to kill you three if he is not free before cockcrow." He saw the shock on their faces, but he could not stop now. The worst had yet to come. "Cockcrow this morning."

Somehow they did not believe he would carry out this threat; they had come to know each other over the days and nights of sickness and a sort of bond had been created between them.

Ulick looked at him with an authorative air. "He'd believe me," he said.

"Who would?"

"Eoin Maguire. Your uncle."

Rory had to act quickly. He realized the chance he would be taking if he left Malachy and Gearóid with only George to guard them but the alternative was to allow Cormac to die.

Within the hour Rory and Ulick were riding among the wet scrub into Glenone lands. The morning air was raw and Rory felt it cool and damp against his face.

As he neared the home of his childhood, several eyes followed his progress from lookouts within the castle. A groom was waiting outside the dwelling to take their horses.

Inside they met an Englishman who gestured to Ulick to accompany him. A deserter from the army, Rory assumed and more than likely a gunrunner. At least now he knew where Eoin got his supply of arms. A man like that would have allies in Manchester and Birmingham able to bribe the port inspectors to ignore the suspicious looking hogsheads and casks filled with 'merchandise.'

Rory sat waiting for a long time. Just as he thought Ulick might be betraying him he heard a door open from far up the twisting staircase. Then the same door shut and footsteps descended slowly.

The 'gunrunner' entered and beckoned Rory to follow. He found himself in a high, deep-walled room, where Eoin lay on a large wooden construction, being nursed by his wife Eimear O' Cathán. She stood when he entered and disappeared into the ante-chamber.

234

For the first time since he was a boy, Rory was alone with Matthew's killer.

The bullet had torn his stomach. Agony lines etched his lean face. Flesh had gathered under his eyes. As he looked into his uncle's sick face, Rory regretted that he hadn't shot him himself.

"I am here to bargain for the release of Cormac O'Hanlon. A barter. Two lives for one." Behind his back, he crossed his fingers. He hoped Malachy and Gearóid were still at Ennistoomey and not on their way back here, George dead behind them.

Eoin stared back at him too weak to speak, drifting into sleep. Eimear glided back into the chamber in an array of silk. She threw him a look that reminded Rory of the type of woman he would avoid unless he was in a whore house.

Moistening her lips with her tongue, she made a noise deep in her throat. "'Tis confirm your story about your sickness Ulick did. 'Tisn't worrying a strappin' lad like you should be." She stroked his arm. "'Tis home Cormac will be goin'. 'Tisn't any use to us he'll be."

That evening a fire glowed in the soldier's common room at Ennistoomey warming Rory and Cormac. On the table between them was a vessel of *uisce beatha* and two goblets.

Now that the crisis was over, tiredness had returned to hit him like a punch. George had ridden to tell the Mulahinsa household of Cormac's liberation. Malachy and Gearóid were on their way back to Glenone.

The past days had their lessons. Rory had experienced the humanity that linked everybody. As Malachy, Gearóid, Ulick and himself lay retching, none of them had cared that they were on opposite sides.

"I'm returning to Mulahinsa tomorrow," Cormac said, "So I'm in the mood for a drunken spree. Seldom I escape from Maeve these days."

Rory thinking he may never have the chance again to talk to Cormac about Finola, decided to ignore his fatigue. "Finola will be glad to hear you are free." He felt his colour rise as he said her name.

"Pity you both had to leave Mulahinsa so suddenly, though with Maeve's abhorrence of adultery, there would have been no

235

seduction." Cormac, his tongue loosened by a third goblet of *uisce beatha* slapped his leg and let a burst of a laugh. "Finola may have been willing to become your paramour. That husband of hers still loves his dead wife Sinéad." He put down his goblet and looked at Rory. "I'd have liked to have you for a son. If you returned two years earlier, she would have been waiting," He pondered for a minute. "But perhaps I'm mistaken. She would be loath to deprive her son of his father and that's what would happen if you were discovered." He stumbled towards the blazing heap in the centre of the floor oblivious to the effect of his words on Rory.

So Finola had a child. It could have been his son. But he was being presumptuous; he had only his childhood experiences by which to judge their relationship. They had understood each other then, but she had married and loved someone else. Perhaps, his love for her was false also. It was merely that his pride had been pricked when she had not been there to welcome him home. He would forget her.

Gazing into his drink, he tried to empty his mind and enjoy the evening but failed. He wanted Finola in his bed and in his life. Or was it the dream of her, he wanted? He did not have time to waste on imagining a girl he had not seen in reality for years. "I'm going to bed," he said.

Cormac stood abruptly, knocking over the bench as he did so and the now empty tumbler clattered to the ground. "Sit down there Rory, the night is but a pup. You must hear this." Liquid ran down his chin. "You were impressive today. The hostages were a timely notion. I knew you'd be smart enough to think of that. When I heard that Eoin had invited you to the feast as well, I knew he would have to give you assurance of your safe return." He rubbed his sleeve over his mouth. "I wasn't important enough to merit an offer like that."

Rory let him ramble on. It was easier than contradicting him.

"Pity my man had such a bad shot," Cormac continued. "I ordered him to aim for the heart. Sorry for the other man, too. Shot in the foot wasn't he?" He spat into the fire. "Still, Eoin will be out of action for a few months. Give you time to build your power."

Rory flinched. So it was Cormac who was responsible for Eoin being wounded. How O'Cathán must have laughed as he held his fifty pounds in his sweaty fist. It would not be long before Donal O'Cathán was in Eoin's antechamber with information to sell.

He could see it all. Money would not pass hands, but O'Cathán would expect payment in kind, would describe how Rory went to him with a bribe that he refused, would assert that Rory had induced another to do the deed. The reprieve he believed he had obtained when O'Cathán had only injured Eoin was gone.

Chapter Ten

Rory had been summoned to meet with officials from the Privy Council at their headquarters at Dundalk. He had not seen The Lord Deputy, Sir Samuel Fenton, since the failed attempt on Eoin's life, but he had heard that he had had an audience with the queen. Everyone knew that when Elizabeth called a Lord Deputy or his next in command The Chief Secretary, to London his career was in danger. Rory knew that his notification meant the same, but he meant to go down fighting.

He sat at his table in Ennistoomey and quilled a note:

Lord Deputy, I commend myself to you. I do not care to enter Dundalk today, fearing that danger awaits me. Eoin Maguire lies wounded in his bed, afflicted by a gunshot wound. I do not intend to invite a similar attack. One of my captains will escort you to me at Dromtirim wood on the morrow.

Yours in good faith, Rory Maguire, Ennistoomey garrison.

The Chief Secretary would have consulted Lord Deputy Sir Samuel Fenton on the attempt on Eoin's life yet the Lord Deputy would deny any official knowledge of Eoin's 'accident.'

Rory folded the missive and gave it to his horse-boy to deliver. He then chose the soldiers he wished to accompany his 'envoy.'

When his horse boy returned, he gave Rory an account of what happened when he made the delivery. Sir Samuel Fenton had 'foamed at the mouth' first at having to go to meet Rory and secondly that the meeting place was beside a wood.

Rory had hoped that the presence of trees, behind which anyone could hide, would make Sir Samuel feel uncomfortable. He was getting old and more easily disconcerted.

Never had a day passed with such excruciating slowness. Never before had Rory begrudged the daylight and welcomed the darkness but he dreaded the meeting with Sir Samuel Fenton and longed to have it over.

The following morning Rory and his cavalcade waited on the edge of Dromtirim Wood. Soon he spied Sir Samuel Fenton riding towards them with fifteen horsemen. Intent on hiding his discomfiture, Rory sat more erect on his horse.

He went to meet Sir Samuel; he had dictated the meeting's

location, so he could afford to be magnanimous. Over the jangle of harness Rory said, "I hope you fare well, Sir Samuel."

Sir Samuel wore a fixed smile. His horse was skittish and he held the reins tight. "I am here," he said in an unemotional tone. All the while his eyes swept the wood. Then he leaned across and gripped Rory's reins close to the bit, so that he could not move. "We decided it was appropriate to inform you of our displeasure," he said through clenched teeth. "You will soon have an army of eight hundred men from Queen Elizabeth yet you spend your time making alliances with your neighbouring chiefs."

"You are well informed," Rory said.

Sir Samuel ignored the interruption. "You have two duties to perform. Establish garrisons on Eoin Maguire's lands. Now that he has an injury, it should not be beyond your capabilities." He paused, and then added resolutely, "and put a stop to the Campbells' plunder of the Pale."

With some grimness Rory replied, "I remember my orders."

"Obey them or we will disband the Queen's forces." He flung the reins from him with such ferocity that Rory's horse bucked, neighing. "I wish no ill to you but you hinder me at your peril." And turning, he and his fifteen horsemen galloped away from Dromtirim.

Four hundred men, the second part of what Rory considered to be his army, but was nominally under George's command, marched through the Welsh hills on route to Bristol and a boat to Ireland. Their armed recruiters flanked them making sure none deserted. At this end of their journey the recruiters were in command and they wielded their power brutally. They were a varied crew, not all pressed men. Among them were young blades who took Irish commissions out of love of adventure and a chance to make money. Men of this character regarded the Irish with contempt.

Richard Dolman was one such man. The third son of a wealthy English merchant, he had jumped at the chance to go to Ireland. The authorities would have hauled him before the magistrates on a charge of aggravated assault if he stayed in England.

He was given to borrowing quotes from the jurist de

Sepulveda on the conquest of the Indies and applying them to Ireland. "To summarise," he was fond of saying, "The Spaniards have the right to rule over the Indians. Indians are naturally inferior. We were born to rule the Irish. The Irish were born to serve". His public school education and his ability to philosophise had prompted an English general, who shared his views, to give him command of a company.

"It is better to hang at home than die like a dog in Ireland," the conscripts muttered as they trudged the Welsh hills barefoot and in rags. "Where is our 'coat and conduct' money? They have even cheated us of that."

"Hush your complaining," Richard Dolman's cultured voice counselled. "You are fortunate they only cheated you out of a few shillings. They could as easily have taken your lives." A chorus of grunts followed his censure. "Think of the ploughman they hanged yesterday for trying to desert."

The exchange halted when an armed recruiter came behind Richard Dolman and butted him between the shoulder blades with his gun.

"God damn you," Richard Dolman muttered, "I am a soldier of the crown."

"Old Sorrey may have given you command of a company, but he is a doddering fool impressed by a grand accent. I know that if you had not come with us you would be in prison like more here. Stop giving yourself airs," the burly conductor added icily, "that is if you want to reach the port alive."

Many nodded in agreement but did not speak. It was more than their lives were worth to make an enemy of Richard Dolman. Although they were not innocents and could cut a throat like the next man, there was something even more callous about him.

For four days and nights the soldiers bickered among themselves, extorted food passing through towns and drank in taverns. It was not in the recruiters' interest to stop them. They might complain to the authorities about their hunger and the disappearance of their rations.

Bearded, tired and dirty the 'army' rushed towards the waiting caravels at the port in Bristol. On the ship there would at least be enough stores to stay alive. As they boarded, the wind was high and rain poured down.

"Weeks it will take us if this keeps up," a red faced man with a swollen belly said. "The corn we stole for the beer will be sopping."

"Worry about biscuit and bread first," his friend told him. "From what I have heard we will not get many victuals in Ireland.

Three weeks later, they docked at Dundalk and though the rabble that descended the gangways in different forms of disarray did not impress Rory, he was glad they had come. He hoped their presence would prise George away from Shane.

A week after their arrival, George came to Ennistoomey and inspected 'his soldiers'. He immediately identified Richard Dolman's sway over the men and was satisfied to leave him in charge of the company. Then he returned to Mulahinsa.

Over the next few months Rory failed to notice that Richard Dolman was selling leave of absences to his men, falsifying the roll-calls and embezzling their earnings. He failed to notice the desertions, too. When Dolman would look him in the eye and say, "The dampness and the rain defeat them. The army has thinned because of sickness," Rory believed him. He knew he should investigate the depletion in numbers, but he did nothing. Later he would realise what he could have averted if he had been doing his duty.

Chapter Eleven

When George returned to Ennistoomey he had Shane in tow. They had become inseparable. It was not this that disturbed Rory so much as the way Shane reminded him of Finola. His facial structure, the way he turned his head or softened his expression to look at George, reminded him so much of the day Finola kissed him.

Before he was compelled to enforce Sir Samuel Fenton's orders, he had to rid himself of thoughts of her.

He prepared to leave for Mulahinsa. On the morning of his departure he conferred with George on the manning of the garrison and the time of his expected return. George cautioned him, "Rory, you would be foolish to ride unescorted".

Rory insisted that he wanted to go alone.

"I am correct to urge caution. In Tyrone, somebody tried to kill your hero Hugh O'Neill."

"I know," Rory answered. "The English are not as certain of his loyalty as they were. We can presuppose who instigated the attempt."

"A good reason to bring a couple of the men with you," George said. "There is much unrest in Fermanagh. The chieftain there has risen against us because we put a sheriff in his territory."

"Perhaps, you are right. Since the English hanged O'Rourke at Tyburn for helping the Armada survivors, everybody is tense."

George changed the topic. "What decided you to go to Mulahinsa? Even if Finola is there, Maeve will disapprove. She'll assume your aim is seduction."

Was that the reason George had brought Shane to Ennistoomey? Rory ignored the thought.

"I must find out if my image of Finola is real. My time of emotional inaction is over." Even to his own ears, he sounded unlike the hard-headed person he was striving to become. Hauling himself onto the horse, he sped away without looking back.

As he neared Mulahinsa, Rory was glad he had set out alone. His blood was racing, too heady a feeling to quell with armed escorts. A light breeze ruffled the unchamped grasses. He found it hard to believe that danger could lurk in so beautiful a countryside.

In the distance, he saw the dim form of small black cattle out after the winter. The booley would soon move to the mountains. The cry of a goat sounded in the distance.

The country was green, soft and fresh after the winter rains. There was a sense of promise in the air. He was Jason in search of the Golden Fleece, young, healthy and excited. It was so long since he felt like this, as if he were indomitable.

He came around a turn in the track and there was the castle. How different it was from Chalk Hall. And how different his feelings for Finola than they were for Jane or the doxies he had copulated with since his return. He would disregard that now. As Maeve would say, comparisons are odious.

He gave a quick intake of breath as he spotted Finola walking in the distance. She looked so breathtaking; he knew that she was the presence for which he had been longing. It would be futile to look further, to equate or compare her with other females.

He feasted on the sight of her figure in her red dress. It enhanced her shape and her hips moved seductively beneath it. When she looked in his direction, her face took on a confused, puzzled expression.

Snatching a glimpse of breasts protruding from under their covering of linen, he was about to wave and call out when he saw her turn and rush into the castle. He was perplexed, unsure if she had thought he was an outlaw of some sort or if indeed she had recognised him and refused to meet him.

Rory continued towards the castle and was immediately greeted by Cormac.

"I expected you sooner," he said to Rory as they climbed the stairs to the parlour.

"I did not know whether to come or not. I ..."

"Come and sit. You look dazed."

They both sat on a bench. Cormac asked him, "Did you see that daughter of mine?"

"Yes, I saw her."

"Well, you certainly look smitten." He threw his arms across Rory's shoulders. "Good luck, you are going to need it."

Maeve's face was pale, her hair a pallid grey. "You're welcome

Rory." She spat the words. "You must eat with us. I'll get Brigid to bring you a drink." She hesitated before adding, "You will stay. Of course you must. Your bed-chamber is vacant." Then she swept away as quickly as she was able.

He was not doing well with the O'Hanlon women today. "Cormac, why is Maeve so opposed to me? I thought she liked me. As a child I believed she loved me."

"Nothing to do with you, son. Nothing to do with you," Cormac answered.

Finola sat in her bed-chamber, shaking. The tranquillity of the past weeks had been cancelled out by one glance at Rory's face. Nothing had distressed her as much as this. Murrough and the accident. Her marriage. The birth of Andrew Óg. The shock of Eoin and his brother-in-law's shooting. Her father's detention. She found it hard to believe that her second's brush with him could have wrought such a change in her.

There was a gargantuan rage inside her. But not at him, at herself for being so foolish. Rory had stayed in England for years. She had become embroiled in a forbidden love. When tragedy ended that, she had run into the arms of what she thought would be security. But, she now realised, she had been trying to replace her feelings for Rory. She put her head in her hands. What she dreaded had occurred. If only he had stayed away a few more days, she would have been back with her family and she would not have to live with this revelation.

For the duration of his stay, she would avoid him, would go home knowing that she had done nothing to complicate the situation. Her son was too precious to jeopardise in any kind of familial tussle. She knew with certainty that Andrew would not consider letting him go. A body could only support one love of the size she bore her child.

In the dining hall Rory was renewing his acquaintance with the newly arrived Brian and trying to forget that Finola was so nearby. Though she had not appeared for the evening meal, he was finding it difficult to concentrate on Brian's conversation. He was drawing a detailed picture of the southern rebellion, but it was his summation that finally interested Rory. "If they can," he asserted, "the English will find an excuse to confiscate our lands here in

Ulster as they did in Munster."

"They will use *Surrender and re-grant* again," Cormac joined in, his voice brittle. "What a legacy that left."

"They'll find a way to make it legal," Brian said. His tone was factual. "We'll have to defend ourselves. If they crush us, they'll have law on their side. It is a dismal prospect."

The heady feeling Rory felt when he spied Finola had long since disappeared. Dispirited that she had avoided him, and tired after his long ride, he drank the last of his wine, excused himself and made his way to bed.

And then on the corridor he saw her again. She was walking towards him her long gown swishing in the gloom. She stopped. They stood in silence studying each other.

"Why are you here?" she said at last.

She had not lost her directness. Rory hesitated. "I wanted to see you."

"Why?"

"There is something I want to ask you." He longed to caress her. She was just tall enough to reach the bottom of his heart.

"Well! Ask it." She folded her arms across her bosom.

"I cannot here."

"Why not?"

"Later, tonight."

It was near daylight when Rory left his chamber, after sleepless hours of agonising, and descended to the kitchen. In the dry light of dawn, he sat and continued to think hard. Was he about to throw his years of hard earned discretion away by behaving irrationally? He felt cold as he sipped a goblet of whey. Unexpectedly, the quietness of the kitchen was disturbed by a knocking on the door. When the rasping persisted, he went to open it.

Richard Dolman and five horsemen stood on the threshold. "I have a letter for you from the commander," he said.

Rory got the distinct smell of cloves as Dolman handed him the letter.

Rory read:

As you are aware, Lord Deputy Fenton has returned from his visit to the Queen. She was displeased with our progress against raiders of the Pale. Our reinforcements are here. I am doing my utmost to prepare them for battle. We are to attack the Campbells, the main culprits, immediately.

The Lord Deputy will support us.

Failure to follow these instructions will result in the immediate dismissal of our force.

Sincerely,

George Carew.

Rory looked questioningly at Dolman.

"The Scots have led one plundering raid too many on the Pale," Dolman said by way of explanation.

"Your meaning?"

"When a newcomer from England refused to pay *black rent* to the scoundrels, they attacked him. Hence the urgency in mounting a counter attack."

Dolman was much too self-important. Rory looked witheringly at him but it had no effect. "A slippery eel is that Campbell fellow. We must net him while there is an ebb."

"That is for me to decide," Rory said. "Go to the stables and curry your horses. You may need them soon."

What would he say if he woke Cormac to ask his counsel? That he intended to refuse a direct order and antagonise the English so he would have time to play the amorous fool. Again he saw the way Finola's eyes caressed him, her movements belying her curt questioning. Her head had tilted proudly as she moved away. How could he leave her to return to her husband? To forget him.

Somebody, besides him, was up early. He turned to the opening door and saw Brian enter.

Rory said, "I have to leave in a hurry. I hope to see Finola and Cormac before I go."

"That will be impossible. Finola left last night." Then Brian added. "She was in a hurry, too."

He knew he must not think of her rushing home to her husband. The thought would undo him and he needed his mind clear for his foray against Campbell.

Chapter Twelve

Finola had left Mulahinsa, partly to avoid meeting with Rory again. She did not want to endanger her marriage, regardless of her feelings for him latent as they may be. But she had also received word that Andrew had moved the family to *Oileán Na Stoirme*. He had been told by informers that someone unknown had lined up with the Lord Deputy's forces for an attack on his clan. Andrew knew there would be a serious challenge to his power. As his fortress was considered the axis of his supremacy, speed was important. The sooner he removed his family from their home and had them transported to safety the happier he would be.

He would have preferred to remain until Finola returned, the messenger had told her, but speed was of the essence. The only action he could take was to send him to Mulahinsa to inform her of events and hope she would reach them before they sailed.

News of the evacuation had failed to alarm her at first. Similar withdrawals had occurred previously. They were another reason why Andrew's kin had nicknamed her husband Campbell *the Impulsive*. But now she used the news as a further excuse to herself to flee Mulahinsa.

The island would be pleasant in late April. Natural buffers of colossal rocks protected the piece of ground itself. But the uncertainty of the weather was the only feature about *Oileán Na Stoirme* that caused disappointment. She often wondered about the appropriateness of its name. Once, when she and five others of the Campbell clan and the children, had planned to spend a day there, a storm had blown up out in the bay and lasted for several days. No boat could make the journey, so she had taken Andrew Óg home with the others. She felt that it was the bay, that contained it, should be called *Bá Na Stoirme*.

As the distance between Rory and her grew, she diverted herself with motherly concerns and domestic trivia. She felt regret that she had been absent for the mass departure. Her husband's preparation would be hurried and hopeless. He, Niall and the servants would take good care of Andrew Óg, but none of them would know the correct garments to take for him. The wool on the seat of his blue trews was thread-bare. His favourite red tunic had been washed so much, the dye had begun to run.

She had put them out of sight in a chest, but she was certain they were the first garments he would discover.

A sigh slipped from Finola when she arrived at the pier to find her family had already boated across and that a strong wind was blowing out on the bay.

"We won't be able to follow," Finola said, sick with disappointment.

"Nae ta be sure. If this storm lasts, ya won't be able to get through. You ken these waters yourself." In spite of her obvious disappointment, the soldier continued in his Scottish burr. "You could be lucky and get a lull, but you'd have ta always have a boatman standing by. Auld Ronan likes to keep busy mending his nets when he canna fish. Nae, you'd be better off staying in Ronan and Ellen's and keeping an eye on the sea."

Finola was still unaccustomed to the easy relationship her husband cultivated with his retainers. This soldier was a Campbell, a namesake as well as a distant relation of Andrew's. She nodded at the man's advice, acknowledging sense in what he said.

The wind thrashed her face. Standing motionless, she listened to the roaring of the surf against the pier and watched the waves jump across the open bay. The island would be a cocoon of tranquillity, beaten by harsh winds from the sea, but protected by its layers of rocks. However strong the winds blew, her family would be safe. "It's God's own parable," she remembered Andrew Óg's grandmother describe it. "A lesson ta the wind that no matter how hard it blows it canna affect all it touches."

Despite knowing all this, she suddenly was afraid. Andrew Óg was just a few miles away and she was unable to get to him. Turning, she made her way to the house of Ronan and Ellen; she would stay the night and go to the island when the wind had abated.

She knocked on the door of the dry stone house, which the elements had fissured and eroded but not penetrated. Ropes, holding the rushes steady, were testimony to the frequency of gales in these parts. There was no reply to her first rap. She tried again. Someone came out of the 'sleeping room.' Finally the door swung open and a wiry woman stood in its frame.

"I'm Finola O'Hanlon wife of Andrew Campbell."

"I know," the woman said. "I'm Ellen. 'Tis welcome you are. Your man said if it got stormy 'tis staying with us you'd be." Her voice contained none of the humility of the tenants of Mulahinsa. She wiped her hands on her dress and led Finola in.

The furnishing was similar to that in Murrough's house. The sleeping quarters were divided from the living area by a flimsy partition. A pile of logs and brushwood stood in a corner. Two three-legged stools of bog timber were located in the centre of the floor beside the fire. A chest was positioned in the corner. Against the whitewashed walls a number of pallets, stuffed with straw, were lined up. Several children lay sleeping, huddled together.

"Grandchildren," Ellen explained. "Ten of them. They stay here when 'tis bad the weather gets."

Finola sat to eat the meal of cheese and bread offered to her. Her eyes smarted from the smoke that the wind drove back through the hole in the thatch. The smell of bad tallow sickened her. She ate the bread, but the first bite of the heavy yellow cheese stuck in her throat. She pushed the form back from the table. "This storm is hard to take. After my night ride, and the thought of my home deserted and my family scattered, I feel gloomy."

The dark eyes stared at her, but there were no words. The fisherman and his wife were unaccustomed to strangers. They did not know what to do with her.

Finola was at a loss what to do with them either. An air of unreality surrounded her. Better sleep. She was no use to anyone in this condition. "I'm feeling tired," she said, her voice quiet. "May I go and lie down?"

They had moved their own pallet out from behind the partition, so she could sleep comfortably. She remembered how, on cold winter nights Murrough slept side by side with his family around a fire. She lay down, unsurprised by the straw that scratched at her back. She had seen it all before.

Her head filled with pictures of Andrew Óg as she had last seen him. Though tempted to go out and ask Ronan to bring her to the island now, common sense won. This evening she'd try again. Perhaps by then the storm would have died.

Chapter Thirteen

Rory did not wish to go on an expedition with the Lord Deputy against the raider, Campbell, but he felt obliged to obey orders. Hugh O'Neill, his kindred spirit in Tyrone, using tactics similar to those used by Campbell in the Pale, had defeated the queen's forces at the *Battle of Clontibret* in early 1595. Because of the reservoir of anti-English feeling that Gaelic victory had welled up in the country, Rory knew the Lord Deputy, Sir Samuel Fenton, would keep a wary eye on him until he proved unswerving loyalty.

As he approached the garrison, he found it difficult to believe the changes that had occurred in the short time he had been away. Shelters in the fields around Ennistoomey evidenced the increased number of soldiers. Sutlers had supplied an abundance of food which the quartermaster had doled.

He looked at the three guns primed for action. Following the Lord Deputy's orders, the soldiers had hitched the saker, the biggest of them, to a train of oxen. If Rory had his way, he would leave the cannon where they stood; the idea of dragging them through the bogs and scrub of the Ulster countryside was absurd. But he would not create any difficulties, for him this was tantamount to a forced battle; he was careless of who won or lost as long as The Queen considered him loyal.

Between the Lord Deputy's army and their own there would be ten companies of foot and four of horse, totalling over two thousand men. He was not familiar enough with the company officers to trust them. George had high regard for a soldier called Percy Sidney whom *he* considered a fop. The two field officers leading the infantry were appointees from an earlier time. George, visibly ashamed of his previous dereliction of duty, had spent the night getting the men and supplies in order. He was glad this time it was George who was in charge and not him.

He left his horse in the care of his horse-boy and went into the garrison.

George had donned his boots for his morning ride.

Rory smiled when he noticed the shine on George's footwear, then the smudge of blacking on Shane's hands. An English affectation. He thought of the dirty brogues of the Ulstermen.

"Rory, I will not be taking part in today's proceedings." George concentrated on his boots before looking up. "In truth it was the Lord Deputy Sir Samuel Fenton, on recommendations from London, who decided that I should not fight. The men have good equipment." Indecision lurked on his face. "The Lord Deputy has sent half his army, but he is not going to take an active part in the fray either." He clasped Rory's shoulder. "You are on your own, and on trial. Good luck."

Rory looked at the band of men. The more robust in the infantry carried their pikes at shoulder height, the rest had calivers. Although for a pound of powder, a musket could fire ten balls within a range of over a hundred yards, there were four times as many calivers. A musket was cumbersome, and had to be fired from a rest. Some carried halberds and swords with round shields for close fighting. Although he did not want to fight, these men depended on him. They must capture the Campbell stronghold with as few deaths as possible on each side. He had no animosity towards this man and knew nothing about him, except that he was demanding *black rent* from Palesmen. And he had no desire to find out more. He found it less difficult to fight against a stranger.

"I will sound the Diana," a subaltern shouted. The fresh faced volunteer, a recruit from Cheshire, looked as if he regarded the looming battle as a frolic.

A heavy set man, who had fought for France's Henry IV against Spanish forces in Calais, spat on the ground. "Make sure you pound the drum with both hands. You may have only one coming back."

From the maps Rory had studied, and from the information the scouts brought back, he knew that the route from the garrison building to the Campbell fortress was good ambush territory. There was likelihood that they would be attacked on the way.

Contrary to what George would have told them, he knew that the soldiers would be unable to march in the usual route arrangement of company by company in columns of five. They should have been prepared for surprise attacks. Trying to manoeuvre marching troops from this order to battle formation took time, especially if the enemy were raining shot and javelins in their direction.

"I want all the pikes side by side in the centre and the shot in divisions on the flanks. We must be ready for unexpected assaults."

"Why can't we march the way we usually do?" Grumbles, curses and spits supported a soldier's question.

"Because this is Ulster. You're not used to the terrain."

"Bloody sure we're not. This country is worse than hell."

Rory's voice hardened, "I will march with the infantry. We move out in an hour."

They left Ennistoomey to the camp guards. George and Shane had not returned from their ride. To the beat of a drum, the cavalcade of footmen and horses meandered its way through the hills, the reduced army measuring three furlongs from the front to the rear.

They had thirteen and a quarter miles to go. The sun shone weakly on them as they walked. With the help of God, it would not rain. In line with his expectations, as they approached an area sided by woods, the sound of gunshot came from somewhere in the middle of the cavalcade.

"You are not to return fire unless under severe attack," Rory shouted. He turned to Richard Dolman. Why was he always beside him? "Make sure the lines know the arrangement."

"Yes, commander."

As the order rippled through the men, shots from the dykes and scrub found their targets. Rory felt a glimmer of fear as balls picked off two men from his flanks leaving them dead. Metal clashed on metal. The air filled with the smell of blood and sweat.

He primed his gun. The attackers from the brush spread out as he led his men forward. Again vegetation stood between him and the enemy. As suddenly as the rout began, it finished. The Scots withdrew among the willows and oaks.

They marched on. Rory handed his gun to his horse-boy walking bedside him. In exchange, he took a ring hilted sword and a shield. From the way the hostilities were progressing, he would find these weapons more useful.

While drumlins provided cover for Campbell's men, Rory's soldiers tripped and sank into the muck on the marshy and uneven ground. Water from the bogs seeped into their footwear.

Since his return, the cold and damp of Ulster had given him chilblains which ached when they came in contact with the icy water. Thickets of holly scraped their faces and ripped their tunics. All this made it easy for Campbell's raiders to move nearer to them. The intermittent wooded areas were a perfect hiding place.

A couple of miles further on, Campbell attacked again. Rory's cavalry knew that their horses would break their legs if they pursued him. They struggled on and endured like the men on foot. Rory, seeing there was no plan to the Scot's positions, became more hopeful. If they could get to Campbell's stronghold with their army reasonably intact, their troubles would be well nigh over. The big guns would see to that.

When their assailants disappeared again, an uneasy silence fell upon his men; even the groans of the wounded stilled. "Use your fire at the next attack," Rory ordered. He was not sure how useful it would be to hail shot at figures who were dodging behind tussocks and swinging among trees, but they had to take some action. Campbell's men sprang up again. This time Rory's soldiers returned their fire, wasting their shot. The enemy had a natural shield of vegetation and undergrowth.

The drummer fell to the ground, a ball through his chest. Rory felt the scales drop from his eyes and the truth, tired of denial, hammered home. It was Rory Maguire who was here with a sword and shield in his hand, not anybody else. He should not be here. Self interest had prompted him to proceed against the Scots; he had wanted to keep his army and the blessing of England. His ambition to recapture Glenone appeared trivial.

Eoin's peace initiative, the activities in Tyrone and rumours of a Catholic confederation had influenced him more than he realised. If they killed him now, he would die at the age of twenty-four, trying to stop Scots from claiming *black rent*. This, while his province and perhaps his country was on the verge of deciding its fate for centuries. Sweat dampened his hands. He took a deep breath. He must see this through he resolved, as the first drops of a rain began to drip.

They plodded on. The rain turned to a deluge, churning the mud into mire. The saker got stuck. As they tried to heave it, the Scots attacked again. Rory's head felt as if it were about to burst. His men wasted their powder. Did they not know that the terrain was their first enemy? They should save their lead for the siege.

Soon his vanguard came into sight of the Campbell stronghold. More open scrub country-side stood between him and its capture. He could feel relief in the men. "We are used to sieges not ambushes," Richard Dolman said. "The rest will be easy."

There was a mile to go when Rory realised that, midway along the boggy path, horses were missing their footing and were falling kicking and neighing to the ground, men broken beneath them. Rory held his sword aloft. Nobody charged him. He did not assault anybody. If someone attacked him, he would defend himself. If he were fighting for something worthwhile, he would have behaved differently.

The Scots had laid traps, holes in the ground covered with rushes and grass to make them blend with the short rough stubble. Cavalry and some infantry were victims of the apertures. Riders, concentrated trying to spot stray balls, failed to see the vacuum beneath their horses' hooves until the horses floundered on the ground, their legs broken. Foot soldiers panicked at the sight of maws opening in front of them and retreated.

In the middle of the rout, a voice with a hint of a Hebredian accent shouted, "Irish cur. Fight for the foreigner against your own, would you? Take that for Sinéad." A caliver shot followed the diatribe leaving Rory's horse-boy dead at his feet.

This Campbell must think it is his uncle Eoin Maguire he is fighting, Rory realised.

The Scots defeated his vanguard. His men were collapsing all around him. He must act quickly to bring about some kind of dignified abandonment. "Horsemen, protect your foot-soldiers and fall back," he ordered.

The men, stepping over corpses, angled back from the centre of Campbell power. Blood was flowing from each one. Some pressed their hands to their stomachs to keep their intestines intact. His orders, even if they obeyed them, could not change the outcome.

Rory felt relief that the conflict was over but was humiliated at being on the losing side. But he was not totally devastated. Gratitude that he was alive and unharmed was his foremost emotion. He looked back to see if there was anybody living who needed help. Bodies lay with contorted limbs and bloody chests, their faces fixed in stares of horror. He grabbed his horse-boy by the legs and lugged him after him.

The Scots had no fresh supplies of men to slaughter the retreating remnant. Besides, they would be eager to return to their homes.

Rory had done his duty, he had served *His* Queen. It would be the last time he would do it. He had buried his horse-boy. Now, three days later, he was sitting at his bureau writing to Queen Elizabeth.

He had magnified the numbers of Scots in the battle and overdone the flattery.

Thousands of disloyal raiders descended upon us, as if out of hell. The devils used underhanded methods to upend our army.

It ended with the words

How could a humble servant such as I not continue to carry an image of her Glorious Majesty in my mind? Since the day She granted me an audience, and I saw her glory with my own eyes, the loveliness of Gloriana has spurred me whenever my determination flagged.

Yours in good faith, Rory Maguire, Garrison at Ennistoomey.

Chapter Fourteen

What remained of Rory's army were a bedraggled lot. They had lost their feeling of superiority. The Irish could no longer be viewed as figures of fun. The Irish could kill as viciously as the Spaniards. It was a solemn revelation.

Through the calculations and recriminations, Rory remained unmoved. The Lord Deputy had withheld some of his men. One thousand soldiers had set out on the expedition to defeat Campbell. There were about two hundred and fifty men killed and three hundred wounded. Some one hundred and twenty men deserted. That left a remaining army of three hundred and thirty fit men. He informed George of developments. In turn, George told him of the anger of Lord Deputy, Sir Samuel Fenton, and agonised over the best way to appease him. Sometimes he forgot that George was an Englishman.

Later that day as he was passing by Richard Dolman's chamber he heard him speak in a raised tone to one of the infantry. "We should not let a rabble grind us into the mud," he was saying. "We must teach these savages a lesson. But what could we do? After all we were led by a savage."

Since the ignominious defeat Rory had been listless. These words of Dolman failed to arouse his antipathy. Maybe he was correct and he was not the right man to lead this army.

Then a few days later George came to him saying, "Rory, I am to inform Richard Dolman that I am sending what is left of the army, under his charge, around the coast to Lough Foyle to join with the Lord Deputy's forces and help enclose O'Neill in Ulster. I would give Percy Sidney the command, but he is still not healed of his wounds."

Rory nodded absently.

"You should perhaps show a little more interest," George said, somewhat irritated. "This is my attempt to appease the Lord Deputy after your failure against Campbell." He turned and walked away before Rory could reply.

A week later, Rory watched as the army sailed down the Knock river. Two flat bottomed vessels transported a hundred men at a time. The men looked subdued and anxious. Many would desert before they reached Derry. A vague apprehension crept into Rory's mind. He asked, "George, why are *you* not commanding them?"

George's fair skin coloured. "Shane is sickly. I cannot leave him."

It was not his concern, but if George were not careful he would bring a disgrace on his family of gigantic proportions. He shrugged. What did he care?

He felt washed out and threadbare. The simplest of tasks were arduous for him. The bilge he had written to Elizabeth disgusted him. That there was no admonishment from her was because she wanted him on her side against O'Neill, not because his penmanship had impressed her. The English were like quicksand. Inexorably, they would suck him into a war against Hugh O'Neill, the only Gaelic hope of uniting Ulster.

Dreams came back to trouble him. He saw women with spears brandished high, white bulls milling around them. Sonorous voices called to him in various dialects: "Don't forget your birthright," they wailed. They appeared to him as images of Queen Maeve and then as Finola. They walked on a turbulent sea and grappled with the wind, condemning him with their eyes and with their voices. They stuck spears into his stomach. His entrails spilled on the ground. He saw Finola in the arms of a shadowy figure, Finola walking towards him, Finola fading into the mist.

He woke. If only Finola were here now. She would calm his spirit like she did when they were children together. During the dark hours he moved from the bed to the floor and back to bed again like a man under a spell. Finally towards dawn he reached a decision. It was time to start dealing with his troubles and the first was Finola.

He would go again to Mulahinsa. This time he would ask Cormac about her husband and where she lived. The shadow in his mind would become a flesh and blood lawful husband. There was no choice. It would be better that he lay with his face in the mud, a ball in his back from a Scottish assailant, than continue to live in this emotional limbo.

After a fitful sleep in Ronan and Ellen's dwelling, Finola got up from her pallet and went out to the living area. She smelled fresh fish. Ellen was boning a trout for supper. But the thought of food sickened her. Her longing to see Andrew Óg had

257

magnified. *Oileán Na Stoirme* was where she wanted to be.

"Ellen," she said, "where is Ronan? I want him to take me across to the island. I'll see that my husband rewards him handsomely." She was prepared to ask politely first, but if that failed she would use her influence as Andrew's wife to get her way. Independent as these people were, they wanted to maintain her husband's friendship.

"'Tis too strong the wind is. Drowned you'd all be." Ellen frowned. "Worse than ever now, it is. It cleared for awhile when you were sleeping but himself knew the calm wouldn't be lasting long." She crossed herself.

"Where is your man? I want to talk to him."

"Skinning a hare at the gable. I'll get him."

Ronan was courteous but firm. He shook his head. "'Tis too rough. God bless us and save us, we'd all perish. Those other fools would have just about reached the island without drowning."

She didn't know to whom he was referring by 'those other fools.' "Will you come with me to the strand? I want to see for myself."

"Right. I'll humour you," he said. "But that is as far as I'll go."

They walked to the beach, the wind howling about them, pushing them back. The waves were mountainous and treacherous.

"Come on girl," Ronan said, "with God's help, 'tis better tomorrow it'll be." Ellen took her arm as she had done when she welcomed her into her house.

But Finola was unwilling to leave the shore. She knew she was being senseless, yet her instincts told her to go to her son. Jerking her arm, she drew apart from Ellen. Let them make their way home without her.

By Rory's reckoning, he was half-way to Mulahinsa. He had chosen his swiftest horse and had decided to take the longer route around by the coast, for safety.

Racing by the sea's edge, he exulted in the freshness of the evening. The ground began to rise. A nip crept into the air. He reached the brow of a hill and found himself with an unbroken view of the strand and across the bay to *Oileán Na*

Stoirme. He had heard of this place from Cormac so he dismounted.

In olden times, a warring tribe would leave the mainland for a few months to let their rivals calm themselves. In the seclusion of the island, they renewed their strength. Ireland was always the same. Wars, cattle thieving, betrayals, perpetually divided.

From his vantage point, he could see the squally sea, its waves tipped with white, thrashing under the darkening sky. The weather had changed. He saw figures on the beach below. Nobody could be going out to the island tonight. Why, he wondered, would anybody consider braving a sea the like of this? It was not as if there were inhabitants on the island.

He was about to remount and ride on when he noticed a slight figure standing alone. The others were leaving and going back to their abodes. Her mantle was wrapped about her; her long frock blew between her legs. He wondered at first if he were seeing a mirage, then he realised she was corporeal. Staring, his excitement overcame him.

"Finola, Finola," he called out. He was afraid she would not hear him above the roaring sea. "Finola, Finola." He shouted even louder. "Finola, it is me, Rory." His screams drifted away with the breeze. He made one last effort. Filling his lungs, he shouted. "Finola."

Below on the strand Finola was about to traipse after Ronan and Ellen when she heard his cry. It sounded like her name, but that was an impossibility. Andrew was off fighting a battle somewhere. Nobody else knew she was here. She looked towards the island. There it was again. Faint and distorted. But there was nothing but a raging sea and a bleak strand. She'd go back to the house and wait until morning, daylight, and hopefully calm. The storm was getting worse.

She had turned to leave when she spotted a figure slithering down the slope towards her without any care for safety. The land swept downward from where he came for a hundred yards until it climbed again to the right and ended in a precipice. To the left it undulated gently to the beach.

Flat stepping stones were scattered on the ground. The

belief was that *síoga*, not wanting to muddy their feet on the slime underneath, had strewn them there. In the old days, people believed that this water, with its volatile temper, held enchantment. Some believed it still.

Finola, too, suspected bewitchment as she saw Rory pick his way down to her. Her hands shook. Her legs were weak. She felt a mixture of relief and trepidation. The relief stemmed from a new understanding of her feelings. Her desire to cross the bay to her son had been so strong, she felt it was her maternal instinct telling her he was in danger. Thank God she was wrong. It was intuition that had prompted her to escape from certain seduction, not an affective belief that it was unsafe on the island. She should have known. Generations had regarded *Oileán Na Stoirme* as a safe retreat.

Chapter Fifteen

Finola stood rooted to the ground. She whispered, "God give me strength to resist my feelings." Even as she said it, she knew she was not in earnest.

Rory was running towards her, heedless of the slippery sand beneath his feet. The wind ripped through his hair. Through the half-light he came, his expression one of delight. She found herself responding with a smile as he took her hand and led her to shelter among the rocks. They squeezed between the boulders and, under an overhanging rock, they entered a house of granite.

"I was afraid the gusts would lift you from me," Rory whispered.

The rocks dwarfed them. Their bodies touched. She felt herself tremble. A loose tress of hair flowed over her forehead. There was a tightening around her heart that told her she would be weak. Recklessness took hold. Rory wound his arms around her waist. She leaned back.

"I waited for you to come home to me," she whispered. "Why did you leave it so long?" She searched the grey depths of his eyes with her own. "I thought you loved someone else."

He unwound his hands from around her and placed a finger on her lips. "Mo ghrá, my love, let us not break the spell. This is a magic place."

Indeed she felt beguiled. The anxious Finola of a short time before had been replaced by a teasing sensuous woman. She nipped at his finger tip. He swept her into his arms, her face against his face, the length of his body against hers.

Whispering endearments to her, he told her of his longing. Thunder exploded above their heads. He touched her breasts so tenderly that the reverent caress made her gasp. She felt as if she were falling over a precipice, she was past caring.

Slowly he undressed her and warmed her with his body. They lay on the sheltered sand, his touches driving her mad. Crying in indescribable joy, she searched for completion, kissing his hair, his eye lids, and the hollow of his throat. She ran her tongue around his ear and crooned to him as they lay like primordial spirits, destined never to separate, isolated in the middle of darkness.

Flashes of lightning streaked the sky. A sudden wailing, then silence. She thought she had imagined it. Again a shriek rang out, sounding sacrilegious on their sacred air. They sat up.

"It sounds as if it's coming from across the bay," Rory said. "From *Oileán Na Stoirme.*"

"My God!" Finola said. "Oh God, no no. Not from there. My son."

Rory clutched her to him and stilled her trembling. "What is the matter Finola? What is wrong?"

She shook him off and jumped up. The shrieks stopped. Standing still, she listened, terror rising inside her. Enchantment had turned to sorcery.

"The Lord Deputy," Finola said. "I thought he might have sent some men over to the island. Andrew Óg and my in-laws are there. But now I realise that would be impossible. Nobody has been able to cross in the past hours."

"Andrew Óg?" Rory queried.

"My son. It was only my imagination, but when I heard the scream ..."

"Why would the Lord Deputy want to harm your son?"

"That was the reason I left Mulahinsa so hastily. My husband knew that the English were going to attack him and he took these precautions."

"Your husband? Precautions?" Rory's voice rasped.

"Yes. He arranged for all the family to go to *Oileán Na Stoirme* for safety.

"*Who* would harm women and children?"

"You were away during the Desmond Rebellions in Munster, Rory. The English held nothing sacred. Even babies ..."

"You need not worry about Andrew Óg. The people on the island are safe." He held her hand. "Do you trust me? Tell me."

"I'm so frightened. Why are you so certain nothing is amiss?"

"I know the Lord Deputy is in Derry with half his army. The other half was defeated by Campbell. He will not be sending his soldiers to attack anybody for a few months."

"That's good news. Andrew was afraid the English forces would defeat him this time. He heard a rumour that somebody was helping the Lord Deputy. It must have been lies. Thank God, Rory."

Rory looked at her. He was unsure how to say this or even if he would. "It was not lies," he said then. "The rumour was correct. I was helping him." He hesitated. "I am the one who fought Campbell. Andrew Campbell. He killed my horse-boy."

She felt her colour fade.

"I was unaware that he was your husband. I didn't want to know anything about the man you married. I found it easier to bear that way. He had what I desired."

"I would be unable to bear it if you had killed him. He is the father of my child. Rory, you should have told me."

"Nobody harmed him. We had to retreat. I'm sure he will tell you about it. You can celebrate his victory."

Knowing that her concern for another man, so soon after their coming together was hurtful to him, she said, "Rory why did you stay so long in England? For years I treasured the memory of you giving me your precious bow and arrow. Then I imagined you with Jane Carew and felt foolish. I thought you had forgotten what you regarded as a childish friendship. Andrew came along and asked me to marry him. I accepted." She was unable to mention Murrough. "We had a son." She stopped. "Rory, you're sure nothing could have happened to him?"

"Sure," he said. "He is not in any danger from the Lord Deputy and that is who you are troubled about." Then he said, "Finola, you cannot go on living with Campbell. Leave him and marry me. I want you as my wife."

Tears threatened; she had seen so much of what her mother ignored. Her father's concubines had been plentiful, albeit not in the past years. She would not be a mistress. "I'll marry you someday," she said.

"Someday. What does that mean?" He took her face in his hands and kissed away the wetness. "Tell him tomorrow. No, it is today now. Tell Campbell today that you are going to divorce him and marry me."

Again, she felt uneasy about Andrew Óg. "Have you forgotten I'm going across to the island at dawn?"

In the morning, Rory and Finola bade each other farewell. She would go to the island with Ronan. Rory had no place there, not yet, he would return to Ennistoomey. He climbed away from the seaweed strewn beach, walking among uprooted trees and splinters of wood. His head was full of Finola, his senses reeling from her. The churned earth beneath his feet could have been paved with gold for all he cared. In the clearer light of morning Finola had been so beautiful. He was even more certain now that he wanted her for his wife.

During the night, amid the sighing of the wind and the slapping of the waves on the shore, they had filled the blanks of each other's lives. Later, as the gusts died down, they talked in the blessed quietness. She had wanted to rouse Ronan then to go to the island, but he had persuaded her to wait until daylight.

He felt different with her than with any other woman. They all had beautiful bodies, welcoming bosoms and sensuous mouths but a slight figure and lively mind was unique to Finola. He had revelled in her caresses and her abandonment to their pleasure. Here was a woman who was different. Not for her the caprice of the coquette. She told him simply of her feeling for him. Nor did she deny her affection for Andrew. She made no elaborate promises.

What was her son like, he wondered. Would he like him? How would Campbell react to his erstwhile attacker cuckolding him? He wished he had returned sooner. That he had kept in contact with her. That she had not given herself to somebody else.

Finola had told him that Andrew had a life-long feud with his uncle Eoin. One of Eoin's soldiers accidentally slew his first wife.

"The Maguire clan is destined to lock horns with 'Scots' one way or another," Rory had said to her. "I hope Andrew's victory will encourage him to let matters rest where they concern me."

He had no ill will towards Andrew Campbell politically. It was fortune's jest that he had chosen Finola O'Hanlon as his second wife. It was enough now for Rory to keep the English appeased, while he avoided taking the field against O'Neill in Tyrone. He had finished as the lap dog of the English. From now on he would make his own decisions and his own mistakes.

Not for the first time he wished for a crystal ball that would tell him whether Hugh O'Neill could unite Irishmen to fight for more than mere short term gain. Whether the Armada would have repercussions and Spain would come to the aid of the Gael.

The early morning sun slanted on him as he reclaimed his horse. The mare raised her head and shivered, still frightened from the storm. He loosened her reins from the post, and let her chew on the sparse grass. For the first time since the rout against Campbell he felt hungry. He took a lump of bacon from his pack and devoured it. The horse ate what she could find. As he relished his vittles, he wondered how the journey across the bay was progressing for Finola.

The fishing boat was small and Finola thanked God for her short legs and lithe frame. She knew there were better vessels than this, but she didn't complain. She had upset the good folk enough by having behaved in such an ungoverned way the previous night.

Ronan was silent in his disapproval. They were an ordered people and a woman should not stay out all night on her own. He expected families to lie down to sleep together shortly after darkness fell. It saved the candles and ensured everybody would be fresh in the morning. The old man and woman had lain awake all night expecting her return. When she had knocked on the door this morning, he had clamped his lips into a straight line and they were clenched since. Ellen tried, but couldn't soften his dismay. All this and he was unaware she had been with a man.

She had been selfish. He had been anxious about her. She was back now. Time for him to come out of his sulk. Whether he did or not she was too happy to feel unduly concerned.

Often when she slept in her empty bed or beside her husband, she dreamed of a night like last night. How could she humour this simple man with his idea of right and wrong when she was aglow from Rory's lovemaking and a consummation that felt so right.

Her needs were simple. She wanted to make love, to confide in someone who confided in her, to laugh and cry with someone. Her only bond with her husband was Andrew Óg. She guessed why men outside his clan dreaded him and why the Lord Deputy and Rory had proceeded against him, but he never told her of his activities. She would ask Rory the next time if her suspicions were true. They had too much to talk about last night to let Andrew intrude on them.

If only they had come together before she had married Andrew or better before she had met Murrough. It was too soon to tell Rory about him. It was acceptable to contract a loveless marriage within your own class but not to love outside it. The day she told Rory about her feeling for Murrough would be the day she consented to marry him.

"We are going very slowly." She looked the old man in the face. If there were a younger oarsman and a more sea worthy dug-out boat, they could move faster. Without warning an ominous feeling overcame her. There was a bad aura about the day, an indefinable atmosphere of doom. She felt the same as she had on the strand, before Rory had appeared. Perhaps it was the pain of separation now that was making her fretful.

When they came abreast of the land and into shallow water, Ronan tensed. He sniffed the air. Finola smelled it too. It was the unmistakable odour of burning.

The beach lay in a narrow cove on the eastern side of the island. Ronan knew the terrain well. An assortment of hefty boulders guarded its sides and protected the island from storms. This was the only way in. Elsewhere submerged rocks would tear at their boats and they would not find a break in the granite wall big enough to anchor.

He steered carefully over the pebbled floor. On the beach a battered boat half full of water lay on its side. Ronan stiffened. "The fools."

The reference to the men who crossed before the storm jolted Finola. The Lord Deputy was in Derry. There was no need for alarm. Doubtless, they were harmless visitors. In the middle of a storm? She did not stop to examine the scuttled boat. She had to find her son.

Running along the beach, she reached the path to the centre of the island, all the time gulping in air. It was eerily silent. Morning, it was early and they were all asleep, she told herself. The discarded boat had been there for weeks. The elements hadn't touched it although it was directly in the eye of the storm. Fooling herself with lies, she reached the island's living quarters, her lungs about to explode.

No clay and wattle houses greeted her. No golden buttercups decked the grasses. No colours of spring here. There were just hillocks of grey ashes, some small, some bigger and all smoking. Ronan caught up with her, breathing heavily. They did not speak as they looked at the devastation. At every step, they expected to see people.

"The caves," she said. "When the Lord Deputy burned their houses, they would have gone for shelter in the caves." Her voice shook. "Who else could it have been but the Lord Deputy?" She looked at Ronan, her expression desperate.

"'Tis to break up we should," he said. "You take the near ones and I'll be taking the ones over there." He patted her shoulder. "God bless you."

She ran to the far edge of the island stumbling and tripping on the coarse knotty grasses. "Andrew Óg. Where are you? Are you there? Niall? Answer me." Her voice thin and high rang out in the silence. Each time she stumbled, she picked herself up again. She had fallen many times before she reached the first cave.

Ridged along the borderline, the caves were like little limestone houses. After the brightness, the half-darkness inside was a balm. She smelled the damp air and heard the sound of water trickling, the only noise. "Grandmother? Grandfather? Where is everybody?"

As she scrambled to the third cavern, she tripped over what seemed to be a human form. Horrified, she looked down. Her stomach somersaulted. Seamus had died in the act of fleeing. A ball to his back had killed him.

She heard Ronan calling to her and turned again to run to him. He must have found something.

"Don't go in," he said. He was standing at the mouth of the fourth cave. He shook his head. "'Twill do you no good."

She looked at him, not in confusion and horror, but in knowledge. "Andrew Óg?" she whispered in someone else's voice. "My son?"

He did not look at her. "Some are alive," he said. But she already knew the truth.

She entered the cave. Walked among stalactites and stalagmites oddly beautiful against all this ugliness. She saw grandfather and grandmother sitting, staring. How dare they be alive when her son might be dead? They were old. And Niall. He had burns on his face. Blood streamed down his tunic. She turned away not wanting to see what he held in his arms. Later. She'd look later. She walked among the corpses. Some were alive among them. Three boys and two girls, with crazed eyes, clung to each other. She hugged each child in turn, touching their blisters with her lips.

She turned back to Niall. Having to know, she took the bundle from his arms. Andrew Óg's face looked unmarked, he had escaped the flames but not the thrust of the knife in his ribs. He was wearing his red tunic. His mouth hung open. She noticed that he had grown a new tooth since she last saw him.

Ronan rowed back to the mainland for reinforcements to clear the island of its dead and bring back the living. He rang the rusty bell in the church belfry. They came out of their houses, the women, the children and the old men. The husbands had gone fishing further up the coast, but were still within hailing distance.

The children skipped happily glad of an excuse to leave the confinement of the house. The old men sucked on their teeth, their faces resigned. The sea had claimed their loved ones before. The women gathered in groups, taking succour from each other. Relief mingled with compassion on their faces when they heard the news. None of their own had drowned this time. It was sad all the same.

Every available boat within miles of the island came. The water, now still after the storm, rippled from the onslaught of oars. Following in their wake, the seabirds seemed to sing a dirge. Nobody spoke as one by one the fishermen helped the wounded to the boats. They went where they were told, looking sporadically towards the open sea fearing another attack.

"I won't go without Andrew Óg. He can't go with the living," Finola whimpered. "I'll stay here."

Ellen gathered some kindling, took a flint from her pocket and managed to get a spark. Pursing her lips, she blew on it until it caught fire.

Finola was still shivering

Ellen squeezed her shoulder and settled to wait with her. Later that day Ronan returned for them. With her son in her arms, Finola sat in a trance in the curragh.

Three of Ellen's grandchildren, one of them a man of twenty two, rode to the Campbell fortress to tell them that their enemies had wiped out their clan. "'Twas when the storm quieted for a couple of hours yesterday they crossed. They returned in the early hours of the following morning."

An Irish chronicle recorded their deaths. It ended with the words:

Upon a more pleasant isle the sun never shone. Pity to see it befouled by the caked blood and ashes of so many aged, children, women, babes ... Herod left their bodies strewn on the grass. Ochón ... ochón ... bewail the slaughter of the innocent.

Chapter Sixteen

Rory felt trapped and isolated at Ennistoomey. George had retuned to Mulahinsa with Shane. It had been easy to be full of bravado when he felt the touch of Finola's skin on his. Easy to determine that he would be 'Chief Autonomous' one day. But back here he was finding it harder to put his resolve into action. Having learned caution in a bitter school, he found it difficult to set it aside. Expediency was winning out over any desire of his to support O'Neill.

This did not stop him dreaming of the day when permanency of land tenure was re-established and his country modernised. Such day-dreaming helped to divert him from thoughts of Finola's reunion with her husband and the scenes that must have ensued. He had not heard anything from her since his return to the garrison. Nor did he expect to. His presumption was that she had reached her family safely and that her husband had joined them later. He felt a rush of jealousy each time he imagined her making her way home with her family.

He must concentrate on his dreams for a new Ireland. The Gaels could make many changes if O'Neill were strong enough to unite them. Ulster's land was fertile. New improved methods of agriculture would improve yields. He could be O'Neill's second in command after he had achieved a military victory.

Though uninterested in being a soldier, he would relish being in charge of economic and social problems. Together they could enforce an O'Neill–Maguire dogma and save the country from falling back into anarchy. He would be a successful sixteenth century Wat Tyler and lead a peasant's revolt against ignorance and superstition. He would encourage that every dwelling would have a space for books ...

Did she kiss him when he came for her? Did they make love? Did they ... This was futile. He would have to trust her. When O'Neill was ...

"It worked." Richard Dolman burst into the room. Richard Dolman was the last person Rory wanted to see. From his swaggering demeanour he looked more like a man who had spent the previous day in a brothel than in arid discussions with the Lord Deputy, Sir Samuel Fenton, in Derry planning how best to thwart Hugh O'Neill. More to get rid of him than from any real interest he asked, "What worked?"

"His nickname suited him. I knew the Irish deserved their appellations." Dolman strutted around the chamber.

In spite of himself, Rory felt a stirring of curiosity. "What are you talking about?"

"Did you ever know anybody with a descriptive name?" Richard Dolman persisted.

"Who are you talking about?" Rory was beginning to get irritated.

"Andrew Campbell. Did you know that he hated Eoin Maguire?"

"Yes. I discovered that of late.

"Our Queen gave us an army to lessen Eoin Maguire's power."

"For that purpose Her Majesty gave George an army. Yes."

"Prior to the battle with Campbell the Lord Deputy ordered me to observe you closely." Richard Dolman's eyes were avaricious points.

Rory remembered how he had stuck to him like a burr during the battle."Say what you have to say Dolman."

Dolman puffed out his chest. "Eoin Maguire is dead." He paused. "Killed." He licked his lips. "His head is now on a spike at Dublin Castle."

Rory shook his head several times to clear it of the array of lights inside his brain. He should be glad; he had conspired to have him killed. Eoin was his uncle; he hated him. Did he hate him? Glenone could now be repossessed. No, the English would not allow it. It was them he had to overcome not Eoin. His uncle had tried to reach an agreement with him. He felt all confused at this news.

"What was your involvement?" he asked Dolman.

"The idiot did as I expected. I knew if I angered him, passion would triumph. I hit at his underbelly - his family."

Pretending calm he did not feel, Rory asked, "What are you talking about? Whose family?"

"He boated them across out of danger. They thought nobody would find the way in because of the surrounding rocks. Some men drowned when we tried the wrong entrance, but we persevered until we found the concealed landing point. We killed them all." He considered. "Perhaps a few escaped to the caves. They were pitiable." His tone was scornful. "Percy Sidney and his men disobeyed my orders. They did not have the valour for it. We ripped their bellies open with the others."

There was a stunned silence.

"It was all a plan and it worked." Richard Dolman rocked on his feet. "They heard the cries of the old men on the mainland. I spread the word that Eoin Maguire was responsible for the massacre on *Oileán Na Stoirme*. Andrew *The Impulsive* did not wait to confirm the veracity of the rumour. He already thought it was Eoin Maguire, not you, who had assisted the Lord Deputy against him. Believing Eoin Maguire killed his family as a reprisal for his defeat, he set out at once to seek revenge." A self-congratulatory chortle bubbled from Richard Dolman's mouth.

Rory felt an abomination of a kind he had not experienced before. During the battle Dolman would have heard Campbell blame Eoin for the death of Sinéad. Blood rushed to his head. He waited for the rest. Richard Dolman would be unable to stop now. He was too proud of himself.

"Campbell must have known that he could not get away with killing Eoin Maguire and live but he did not care. Everybody belonging to him was dead, his new wife, his son, his mother and father, everybody. Maddened by the thirst to even an old score, his thinking was cockeyed."

"What a cowardly rabble you were," Rory gabbed, scarcely aware of what he said.

"Campbell stuck his sword in Eoin Maguire's chest. He was weak from his previous wound. After Campbell had done the deed, one of Eoin's clansmen hacked him to death. True to their nature, they then cut Maguire's head from his shoulders and sent it in a basket to Dublin Castle as a sign of their loyalty to us. Barbarians, I always knew the Irish were barbaric. They used Maguire's demise to their advantage. Dead men have no power."

"Barbarians?" Rory's voice was falsetto in its horror. "You talk of barbarism."

"I was dong my duty as a soldier of Queen Elizabeth. We will take over Eoin Maguire's *uirrithe* and lands. We have accomplished what Her Majesty desired."

Stars appeared in front of Rory again. "His wife and son ... his wife and son ..." The words reverberated in his head in a morass of abhorrence. A muscle twitched under his left eye. The old urge to run seized him. Run, but where? The world was full of liars and deceivers and marauders of the weak. His stomach felt hollow. The smell of blood was in his nostrils. Now he knew why he had carried his horse-boy's sword since the foray against Campbell. It was for this.

Jumping up, he drew the sword and swung it. Richard Dolman was as quick. Their blades clashed. He kicked out at Rory and caught him in the stomach. For a moment Rory lost his breath and it took all his will power to stop himself from doubling up and sinking onto the rushes.

Fury distorted Richard Dolman's face as he straightened himself and attacked again. Rory's weapon ripped Dolman's tunic. He pounced. As he came in, Rory kicked him back. He tottered gasping. Rory leapt on him, knocking him to the ground.

Dolman wriggled to the right as Rory's blade descended, but he was not fast enough. It sank into his abdomen, twisting as it lunged. Dolman's eyes bored into Rory's as he reached up and grasped at his throat. With the last defiance of a dying man, he bruised and pressed the arteries on Rory's neck.

Rory felt his air current stop. As his head spun, he tried to prise the fingers away. Gradually they lost their pressure, turned blue and became limp.

There was a superficial sword wound to Rory's chest about an inch and a half long and a few minor bruises decorated his neck. He looked at Dolman's bloodied corpse lying on the floor before him - the first man he had ever killed.

When he called for servants to lug out the carcass, no one appeared. Only a fraction of his men had returned with Richard Dolman. Many had defected before the trip to the island. The rest must have absconded when they heard the fight. He didn't care what George would say about his lost soldiers; he was well rid of them.

They were less a mutinous army deserting their posts and more a gang of free-booters wanting to regain their independence. He knew if he stirred himself and went outside he would still be able to see them in the distance. They would be making their way towards the nearest town to beg or pillage or to Dundalk in search of a ship to carry them back to Wales.

The horrors of the massacre on the island would not leave Rory's mind. To blot them out he spent the days working feverishly. He mucked out the stables, polished his horse's harness until it shone, whitewashed the walls of the garrison and replaced the rushes. He got a spade and dug a dike around the fortress. He built a three foot embankment from a pile of clay, a useless exercise except that it helped dull his feelings.

Other times he lolled around and unfolded manuscripts but did not read them. When he tried to think, he was unable to marshal his thoughts. Twice he attempted to pray, but his words changed from a plea to a curse. He knew his apathy was due to disillusionment but the knowledge failed to help. Whether he was active or idle, a deep sorrow filled him.

His loss of Finola, when he had so lately discovered her, ravaged him. As the days passed, his slackness as a commander plagued him. It was George who had put Richard Dolman in control of the squadron and commanded him to go to Derry. That was no excuse. He had been too indifferent to question George's decision. A leader, or a second in command such as he, should accept blame as he accepts praise. Partial guilt rested with him. He should have assessed Richard Dolman's makeup. To have allowed him to leave with an army was unforgivable. The desolation wrought on that island was his fault. He felt unfit to live.

Then one early dawn he heard his name being called, "Rory, Rory. Are you there?"

The voice was familiar. As he stared at the stocky low sized man who had entered the garrison, he felt his tears brim.

Cormac's old eyes were equally moist.

Vaguely, Rory registered the change in him. His shoulders were hunched and there were new worry lines around his eyes, his hands trembled. When he opened his mouth to speak, no words came. The broad shape pulsated with a succession of sobs. He stood erect and tried again. "She's alive. Finola. The massacre was over when she arrived."

Rory devoured Cormac's words as if they were life giving.

Cormac added, in a pitiful tone. "Andrew Óg is dead. Her only child whom she adored."

His joy at Finola's survival was diluted by this.

274

Cormac said, "I wanted you to know." He wiped his arm across his eyes. "I must return to Mulahinsa. The women worry when I'm gone. Finola especially."

Silence stretched between them. He did not know how to thank him for what he had done. Cormac gripped his shoulders in a gesture of farewell and mounted his horse.

As Rory walked slowly back into the garrison, he felt strangely renewed. Though he felt guilt for the killing of Finola's in-laws and her son, he knew that self pity would achieve nothing. For the first time since Richard Dolman's revelation, he knew that he would survive. Let his ragged English army meet their sticky ends, he would convene an army of his own.

Chapter Seventeen

From the rumour and counter rumour that pervaded the province day after day Rory interpreted as much of the truth as was possible. O'Neill was keeping up a sustained opposition to the English. His spirits were raised a little by this. His periods of inertia became shorter, the spurts of energy less compulsive. Only the sorrow remained.

A week after Cormac's visit, Shane and George came to Ennistoomey.

Shane looked gaunt and sickly as, from astride his horse, he proffered a missive to Rory.

George, mounted beside Shane, looked abashed and unhappy. He was feeling guilty either for trusting Dolman or because he was a commander without an army. His choice, Rory knew, was to remain in Ireland as a deserter or return to England and make his excuses to the Queen. Sir Walter would shield him, if not for love of his son, to keep the Carew name unsullied.

The communication read simply:

Report to Dundalk immediately.

The signature was illegible. An official had signed for the Lord Deputy. Rory felt a sinking feeling. Killing Richard Dolman, an officer of The Queen was a serious affair.

Since its dissolution, the monastery at Kilmacmorris had been commandeered for government headquarters. The high stone building had had a special protective wall built around it and its tongueless bell slept unharried. Ivy rambled its walls and gave it a venerable appearance. A day's ride from Ennistoomey, it was next in importance to Dublin Castle as a centre of English power.

As he rode towards it now, Rory considered the choices the Lord Deputy had regarding him. He could deprive him of his army, but that was like robbing an old man of youth. He had lost the skirmish with Campbell; he could charge him with an inability to lead. Worse he could accuse him of being a traitor, but that would mean admitting his Anglicisation in Sir Walter Carew's house had failed.

Though Eoin was dead, they would still pursue their plans to force his *uirrithe* into submission and pay their rents directly to the crown instead of to another Irish upstart such as himself. The land his father and Matthew died for was what they wanted to control. No matter how effective they considered the civilising program in Sir Walter's house, they would not believe that it had invested a Gael with intelligence. They would expect him to assist his own downfall without demur. He touched the hilt of his sword.

As he entered the compound, Rory thought of the monks who walked these grounds, their cowled heads bent in prayer. The English had got rid of the pig pens, the bake house, and the inn for poor travellers, all the places he recalled from the monastery of his childhood. The stable where he left his horse was a squat stone edifice newly built. He handed the reins to the groom.

Inside the building, he climbed a winding stairs. Some of the rooms were used domestically, he knew. Since the beginning of overt hostilities, the Lord Deputy and his retinue preferred to sleep here, rather than face an antagonistic Ulster countryside to get to their homes. He knocked at a wooden door he presumed was the one to the Lord Deputy's office.

The reception room of the Lord Deputy rivalled the rooms Rory remembered from his visit to Nonesuch, the queen's palace in London. Tapestries adorned the walls and a portrait of Queen Elizabeth stared down at him. The rugs were luxuriant. A bowl of sweetmeats stood in the middle of the desk where the Lord Deputy sat.

Blood coursed to Rory's head as he looked at the man behind the bureau. Replaying the scene as if it were yesterday, he recalled the meeting outside Dundalk when he had last met Sir Samuel Fenton.

When he saw Rory, the expression on the Lord Deputy's face settled into a sneer. He slouched forward on the chair, leaned over his paunch and gestured to him to sit.

Rory manoeuvred his tall frame into the low chair.

Sir Samuel hauled his ample body to its feet, came from behind the desk and stood over him. "What I have to say has come from the highest level. Her Majesty is displeased with you. Richard Dolman caused the death of Eoin Maguire, the job we recruited you to do." Rory felt his animosity. "Now he is missing. Her Majesty's army is vastly depleted. What we achieved is in spite of, rather than because of, you." He leaned back against the bureau and continued, "Commander Carew is gathering the remnant of his army to fight the renegade ONeill."

Rory looked up at Sir Samuel and returned the stare. Inside he felt as if his guts had shrivelled. The army had not all perished or deserted. George had extricated himself from a bad situation by promising to fight O'Neill. He wondered how Cormac, Brian, or his precious Shane would like that.

"Sir Walter Carew wasted his energy trying to bring you to heel." Sir Samuel's face took on a darker hue. "We expect recompense for the opportunity we gave you."

In spite of his stay in England, he had not produced results helpful to the crown. Sir Samuel regarded this as a particular insult. He did not intend that he should go the way of O'Neill. Rory became suddenly alert to an unforeseen danger.

Sir Samuel examined his finger-nails. "My orders regarding you are disturbing, but there is nothing I can do."

Rory's heart pumped quicker. The fear he was feeling must remain hidden. Looking at the man in front of him, he knew his fate was irreversible. It was the castle dungeon for him.

Chapter Eighteen

Rory sat in the dark space of the prison ship as it sailed down the coast to Dublin Bay. A few hours previously he had been sitting in Sir Samuel Fenton's luxurious chambers. Now he was bound for prison sitting in the hold of a ship with three other prisoners.

He stretched and flexed his fingers and toes. A fat rat scurried to a corner. The vessel heaved to a stop. A soldier pulled back the canvas sheltering them, letting in a blast of air. "Time to leave. Be quick," he barked.

Rory and the three others rose from their narrow spaces and went above.

Once on deck he made out through a drizzly fog that they were within a stone's throw of Dublin Castle.

He felt himself being taken by the arm and whisked off by a group of soldiers, two marching in front of him and two behind. In that order, they marched through a chain of narrow streets and pathways. The reek of rotting entrails upset his already shaky stomach. Dogs scavenged among the putrid heaps. They passed a maze of mist-clothed hovels, finally entering the gateway of the state prison.

Besides being known as *the hole* or *the castle*, Rory knew this place as a *waiting chamber for the gallows at Tyburn*. Silken Thomas, Cormac's first cousin, had been held here before the English had executed him and his five uncles. He was thinking these thoughts when he felt his eyes drawn upward. Remembering what Richard Dolman had said about Uncle Eoin, he felt grateful for the mist that only allowed him to see the outline of his uncle's cranium.

The English plan that Eoin's decapitation would instil dread into anybody who saw it failed to work with Rory. Regret rather than fear surged through him.

Memories, which he had stifled since the day Eoin became Chief of Glenone instead of his father, surfaced. Now with a quarter of a century's experience of treachery behind him, he was beginning, at last, to accept Eoin Maguire's position. According to his rationale, Rory's father, Phelim, tried to steal his birthright from him. He fought a civil war to protect it and won. Matthew had been a threat so needed to be disposed of.

Then many years later Eoin had invited him to his feast, an overture towards reconciliation, perhaps a sign of political maturity, an awareness of the power of unity rather than the weakness of division where only the invader profits. In return, despite his supposed refinement and erudition, he had plotted to kill him.

The three other prisoners were lined up beside him. Rory viewed them with deliberate detachment. The boy nearest to him, no more than twelve years old, looked about to cry. He reckoned he was a pledge given by his father as guarantee of his own good behaviour. In saving his own life, his father had sacrificed his son to months, perhaps years of imprisonment. He did not have time to think about the other three as the soldiers pushed them through the castle door. The air in the chamber was as damp as what they had left outside.

A prison clerk, quill in hand, sat behind a table. He called out, "Line up." Then he turned to the sergeant of the military escort.

The sergeant took papers from his sack and gave them to him. "You first," the clerk said, looking at the youngster. Rory thought he saw a glimmer of pity in his face. He would be familiar with fathers who paid for the keep and provisions of hostages for the first few months and then forgot them until they died of neglect. "I admit Art O'Cathán, hostage for the good behaviour of one Donal O'Cathán, to Birmingham Tower," the clerk proclaimed.

The next man was a common malefactor who was not frightened of prison. The law accused him of stealing jewellery from the houses of English gentry. He had added murder to his crimes when he stabbed the watchman who arrested him.

When Rory's turn came, the clerk riffled through papers, pushed the documents aside and looked at him. "We have to talk to the constable about you Maguire. You are the ward of ..." He stopped. "You can go with the rest." He gestured towards the murderer. "Throw him in *the hole*. These two will have separate cells."

So they had no information on him, Rory thought. The Privy Council had not decided on his future, yet.

A fourth prisoner who emerged from the shadows was dressed in English hose and looked familiar to Rory.

The clerk, glanced at the paper in his hand, and gestured to him to stand to one side, away from them so they would not hear his offence. Then he rose and unlocked an interior door. After an exchange with the three military, he jerked a command with his head.

Rory and the other two filed down steep stairs to the lower rooms and the dungeons.

At the bottom of the stairs at the entrance to a long tunnel of cells, they were met by a low-sized balding warden who looked at Art and said abruptly, "Strip."

The boy began to shake. The other prisoner, the hairy giant of a murderer stared at his puny body.

Rory stood in front of Art allowing him to don the prison frieze.

"Ach, 'twasn't going to eat him I was. 'Tis a son like him I have myself," the murderer growled.

Rory took off his own clothes to put on the rags.

Another warder came in. His expression was harmless looking enough, but his eyes were like granite. None of them heard him approach until the clank of chains gave him away. He gave Rory and Art a number each. Rory's was 117, the numbers written in large figures. Then he gave Art 117 also, the numbers written in small figures. He said to Rory, "Since you feel so protective about the boy, you can have the long and short of 117. You share the same cell." They had met the jester of Birmingham Tower.

They entered a tunnel which was more suited to moles than to humans. Heavily barred spaces, with low ceilings, stood on either side. Rory found it difficult to look at the countless souls lying sprawled on the floors, their legs chained. Moans came from the darkness when the warder opened the door of one cell and pushed in the killer.

In their own small space, the warder pulled the chains tight on Rory's legs. When he had finished putting the irons on Art, he left. As there were two of them, they had even less room than was the norm. Neither was Rory able to stand to his full six foot one height. The white-washed walls were smeared with excrement. Beside the tick ridden mattress, there was a pewter chamber pot full of the prisoners' faeces. A pewter mug and platter stood at the far end of the cell. Low down on the wall there was a barricaded window.

"Isn't it terrible dark entirely?" Art said.

"That is because of the mist yonder," Rory answered. But he hoped he would not be here to test it on a sunny day.

As he looked at Art, Rory was saddened at the callousness that allowed this to happen to children. He felt suddenly isolated. Not so much by the bars that hemmed him in, but by the knowledge that people in Gaelic Ireland regarded this practice as normal. He must do something to help his country change these ways.

Eoin was dead, but he had not regained his lands. For the sake of his father and brother, that must be his priority "I am a prisoner of history," he said aloud. "I want to be a reformer not a destroyer." Then he thought that maybe sometimes to reform you must destroy.

The two warders came back and stood at the door of the cell.

"You'll get into trouble if you leave them together Jack," one said sounding emphatic. "We are not sure about the red-haired one. He might turn out to be important."

Jack turned the key in the lock and came in. Roughly he took off Art's chains, threw them over his shoulder with one hand and pulled Art out with the other. "Come with me, you." When they were outside, he pushed him in front and herded him further up the tunnel. Rory heard the grating sound of the key turn in another cell door.

His nausea had lessened but he did not feel like eating. It was as well. There was no food. The constable was probably now examining their records. In the morning he would decide what payment to demand for the provisions and keep of the new inmates. As in the Tower of London, the constable here could charge higher rates than the constables of other castles. If their kin paid the required stipend, the warders would feed the prisoners. If they did not, they would be dependent on alms they begged for through the bars.

As he lay on the bed, he thought about his position. He was here because he had disappointed Queen Elizabeth and resembled the renegade O'Neill, not because he had killed Dolman. Like Rory, Hugh O'Neill had been civilised in The Pale but had proved disloyal to England. Rory's imprisonment was meant to show him what happened to uppity traitors to the crown.

He fought back a childish desire to scream, calmed himself

and closed his eyes. Finola's silky touch was on his skin, her hand was on his brow, her words of endearment in his ears. He slept.

At dawn the prison bell rang and he woke with a certainty that his life was not going to end here just as he had known it would not end on the battlefield against Campbell. As he had not removed his clothes, he had nothing to do but wait.

On the first day, the warder gave him 'white meats' to eat and water to drink. They were not going to starve him or let him beg through the bars, but they did not intend to indulge him either. The cheese was mouldy and the butter was too yellow but he knew he needed his strength so he ate it. He was glad he did. It was the next morning before he received the same again. His only consolation was the thought that Art was getting even less than him.

On the third day he watched them remove Art to *the hole*. The authorities had decided that the chances of getting a stipend to nourish him were slim.

Most of Rory's days slipped into ennui. There was not much he could do with irons on his legs beyond performing his bodily functions. Sometimes he dozed. Other times he just stared and thought of nothing. As time went on, his ability to conjure pictures of Finola weakened.

Though he was unable to move, he knew he still had his intellect. He realised that by languishing he was letting them win. So he remained mentally active through reviewing Ireland's history and trying to make sense of it. He wished he had parchment so he could write about it. Very little of worth had been penned about Ireland. It would be heroic if someone were to write a description of the country that would add to the brief mentions of it made by Cambrensis, Sylvius, or Volateranus, venerable historians of antiquity. For a few days, to escape from the foulness and incertitude, he imagined himself writing such a history.

His fancy, with its limitations, could only sustain him for so long. On the seventh day despair gripped him. No matter what the cost he did not want to perish in this place The realisation had a sobering effect. He tried to eat the dire cheese but it stuck in his throat and he threw it into the chamber pot. Sleep evaded him, he felt forgotten.

On the tenth morning the bell rang again as it had done for the past nine. As he did each morning, he dragged himself from his pallet to receive his fare. The same face appeared in front of him, but this time the grin was replaced by a servile smile.

Comic Jack opened the padlock, entered the cell and stooped to open Rory's irons. The area where he clamped them ten days ago was numb and red. He said, "Follow me."

At last somebody had intervened.

They retraced the route they descended ten days earlier. Rory was given back his own clothes. Apart from the creases, it was the same tunic and trews he had doffed a week and three days ago. There was a different man sitting in the clerk's chair. From his demeanour, Rory could tell that this new man had authority. He felt sure it was the constable. The fourth prisoner, the one Rory thought was familiar, was there too, sitting on a chair. "Your father Sir Arthur Petrell has arranged for you to return to England," the constable was saying to him. "The Queen will decide your future. They are glad you are alive."

The young man looked resigned. "I'm sure they are."

Now Rory knew where he had seen him before. It was the man he met at Eoin's dwelling. The man he suspected of selling guns to his uncle. His name was Petrell, the name of his opponent on the council that had interrogated him in London. Sir Walter Carew had told him that his son was a soldier in Ireland. Missing, believed dead. But savages had not killed him. It was he who was helping the savages kill English men. He would like to be there when Sir Walter heard about this.

As the young man walked away in the custody of a guard, the door opened and, to Rory's shock and surprise, in walked the subject of his meditation. Sir Walter was as trim as ever. Only the dearth of hair told of his advancing years. Many men his age had died or at least had severely restricted movement. Not so Sir Walter.

His slower gait could have been the effect of the illness that laid him low before Rory's departure for Ireland. The dullness, Rory noticed in his expression when they left him in bed at Chalk Hall, was gone. There would be no sentimentality attached to this meeting. He was here for a purpose and Rory was it.

In crisp, sober language Sir Walter addressed the constable of the castle.

"The Queen has sent me from Newry to Dublin to clear up this misunderstanding. You have in your custody for the past several days my former ward, who should, at this moment, be helping my son George Carew defeat the defector O'Neill. This incarceration is foolishness of the highest order."

"Sir Walter, I receive my orders from the Lord Deputy."

"Are you aware that *Her Sovereign Majesty* has replaced Sir Samuel Fenton as Lord Deputy?"

The constable's voice shook. "No Sir. I was not aware of that."

"I am here to see Rory Maguire reinstated as second-in-command to my son. There can be no indecisiveness. I am returning to London this evening. I demand that this be resolved immediately."

Although the news about Sir Samuel Fenton's dismissal as Lord Deputy and the prospect of freedom had cheered him, Rory did not want to fight O'Neill. But neither did he want to stay in Dublin Castle. If there were a hint of betrayal, he knew Sir Walter would do his duty above all else. Where would that leave him? Rotting. Was it a time for honesty or would he prevaricate? The whole world was behaving dishonestly. Now was not a time to play the idealist.

Though his assurances to Sir Walter that he would fight to protect The Queen from Irish rebels sounded sincere, he felt ashamed of the subterfuge. Then before they left he thought of Art. At least there might be one noble act he could perform.

He told Sir Walter of the first night's happening when he and Art were unjustly incarcerated together. Knowing Sir Walter could not bear to see instructions flouted, he emphasized the clerk's orders to place him and Art in separate cells and stressed the unfairness of putting a boy through such upheaval.

"I will speak to the offending warder," the constable said. "It was unfortunate for the young man, but his position as a pledge remains."

Sir Walter's expression was rigid. "A few words alone," he said to the constable, tapping him on the arm.

Although they went to the lintel, Rory could still hear the exchange. "Produce this boy," Sir Walter said in his firm no-nonsense voice. "And I expect you to demote this cruel rule breaker."

So, at eight o'clock that morning, Rory and Art O'Cathán passed through the prison gates. Rory held his head high as he passed under the archway. His lips moved in silent prayer to a God, he hoped existed, for the soul of his uncle. He did not, however, look up.

A bright sun shone and after his days of confinement, he relished the fresh air on his face and the freedom of movement in his limbs. He longed to leave the confines of the narrow streets and be out in the open spaces. It would take him five days, perhaps more, to get back to the north. But first he had to get a mount for Art and himself. He did not hurry; Art was too weak to rush; he would use the time to plan.

Chapter Nineteen

England

Sir Walter spluttered into his water. The unusual luxuriance beneath him was aggravating his mood. He preferred a straight backed unadorned chair as Anne well knew. This new addition to the household furnishings had a soft seat and embellished arms. He took the pastel cushion from beneath his head and wrinkled his nose. It was hard to believe, but he smelled perfume. The fire sputtered and sent a hail of sparks up the chimney. It had too much fuel. He pulled at the neck of his grey doublet. Something adverse had happened to his wife in his absence. She did not usually hanker after luxuries like the chair on which he was sitting, or ostentation like the heaped fireplace. Nor did she question him like she was doing now.

"You were in Ireland three months and you did not find time to see your son?"

"I did not have time to meet with George, Anne. I received a missive from him saying that Rory was a prisoner in Dublin Castle. It asked for my intercession. The whole episode was inconvenient. It did not shed a good light on our son, or our erstwhile ward," he concluded.

"No doubt you came out of it smelling of roses," Anne's face was set and her tone abrasive. Standing by the new ornate clock, she left her goblet on the bureau and, putting one hand on her hip, raised her chin.

He lifted his eyebrows quizzically. "Are you feeling alright, dear? Perhaps you are fatigued. I hope you are not tiring yourself with too much needlepoint. We are not getting any younger."

She smiled a superior smile. "I am seventeen years younger than you or have you forgotten?"

His heart palpitated. He must stay calm. If he let her annoy him, she had won. When Geoffrey entered the room, he noticed the new livery, which made him look like the manservants of the rest of the nobility throughout England. As a devout Calvinist, he did not believe in the necessity for such glamour. He stared coldly at him. Geoffrey wilted. His expression strained, he looked to Anne for support.

"Yes Geoff," she said.

Sir Walter thought he would get apoplexy on the spot. He disliked such familiarity with servants.

"Supper is served, Madam."

What was this? There had never been formality at Chalk Hall. Usually they went to the dining chamber and sat at the table until Geoffrey served the meal without commotion.

As he sat in his usual position at the head of the table, he thought nostalgically about the time when he and his young wife went arm in arm to God's house to pray. "When we have finished eating our supper," he said to Anne, "let us go to the chapel together like we used to when we first married. We will find comfort in The Lord together." He felt better already. It never failed. Contentment came from making other people happy.

The smell of food drifted from the kitchen. He placed his napkin across his chest and waited for the nourishing fare to appear. He hid his impatience at the tardiness of the meal by pretending to savour his last drop of water.

"Tonight is Wednesday night," Anne said.

Would they have plain boiled chicken or undressed beef? Thank God highly spiced dishes were unknown at his table. "Did you say something Anne?"

She put the goblet to her mouth and sipped. As she put it back on the table mat, her laugh was mirthless. This time she pronounced each syllable flawlessly. "Tonight is Wednesday night, Walter. You will not be able to come to my bed if you are going to the chapel."

He pulled on his beard. This was an inappropriate conversation for the dinner table.

"Do not tell me you are going to be unpredictable and forego the pleasures of the flesh for the pleasures of the spirit."

Her contempt cut through him. He rubbed his hand across his forehead and hung his head.

"I am afraid I could not stand the excitement of either obligation. I must absent myself from both." When she rose from the table, she caught her goblet with the sleeve of her gown and spilled the contents over the table cloth.

The red stain seeping into the white cloth convinced him. The wine had her inflamed. Thank God it was only that. He could excuse her having a glass of wine to ease her loneliness when he was away. It was understandable that she missed him terribly. Such a dutiful wife, and she was missing supper to lie down. Sensible decision.

She swaggered towards the door. When she turned, she took him by surprise. "Jane was here today. She wants to come back here to live. Duncan feels Chalk Hall is more fitting to their rank than the house you found for them."

Though he abhorred nepotism, he had compromised his principles and used his influence to get them their small, but respectable abode.

"Quintin is older now and Duncan feels it is important for him to be known as Quintin Erskine of Chalk Hall. It would differentiate him as the illustrious Sir Walter Carew's grandson."

He squared his shoulders more in a symbolic defence against what was to come than from conceit.

"Doesn't it do wonders for your self importance," Anne scoffed. "No doubt about it. You are one of the elect. Everybody cannot be wrong."

"Anne, maybe you should refrain from alcohol. It changes you."

Her eyes were hooded. "You noticed." She left without a backward glance.

As he waited for Geoffrey to serve, he decided to enjoy his meal. Remaining hungry would achieve nothing. Geoffrey placed two dishes in the middle of the table. One contained a peacock, entire with feathers, head and tail.

"After cook roasted it, she sewed the skin back," Geoffrey explained. Beside it he placed a platter of *pomme de orange*, a dish containing seasoned pork liver with a sprig of parsley decorating its top.

His hunger deserted him. The events of the evening hit him like a hammer. He stumbled from the table, throwing his napkin down in disgust.

Sir Walter did not sleep much when he went to bed. He could not understand it. What was keeping him awake? His wife had wine. She was not accustomed to it. Temporarily, it had altered her temperament. It was lamentable, but he was sure she would be repentant in the morning. He turned in the bed and pulled the clothes up to his chin. She did not mean what she said.

Sometimes when people imbibed too much, they were insensitive.

He was glad that he had never indulged in liquor himself. Apart from his religious objections, he did not like the way people became sots when they had too many drinks. He remembered the wake of Phelim Maguire. *Uisce beatha* had made the Irish behave abominably. But he must be charitable. They were a primitive race and without Anne's advantages.

His covers were too warm so he put his hands outside the clothes. He still sacrificed his right to insist on his conjugal rights daily, and, to spare Anne, adhered to Wednesday night as one for pleasure. When he did indulge himself, he didn't prolong the agony for her. Sometimes his resolution not to give in to his base desires challenged him but he never submitted. He was proud that the only time he touched her down there was when his organ penetrated.

Suddenly cold, he put his hands back inside. Anne was his wife, he could not do to her what he had done to ... He felt his face colour at the memory. It was part of the past and he had repented. Why did it haunt him? Answering his own question, he mumbled, "because the living reminder of my sin remains."

Anne could not complain about him as a father. He had always provided for his offspring and did not interfere, did not question her orders. Perhaps he had counselled her against being too lenient with George. It was also he who had advised him to join the militia and give up his foolishness about flowers.

Perhaps he intervened in the boy's life a little more than he first believed, but it was for his good. There was nothing to trouble his conscience there.

Sitting up in bed, he adjusted his night-cap. If he had given more advice about the rearing of Jane, she might have married better. Would not have made a fool of herself by throwing herself at Rory Maguire. The daughter of Sir Walter Carew to stoop to such a level. Then to become impregnated by Duncan Erskine. He refused to linger on that, it made the ache in his head worse.

What was the matter with him? You would think from the way he was behaving that it was he who had done wrong. He had been his usual self all evening. It was Anne who had disgraced herself. While he lay awake, she was probably sleeping soundly.

In the morning Sir Walter returned from his ride to find Anne reading in the library. Here, too, there were chairs that had not been there when he left. Garish red velvet covered their seats. As soon as he had dealt with last night's behaviour, he would talk to her about it.

The ride had been a good idea. The fresh air had blown the cobwebs away. It also gave him an opportunity to rehearse his words to her. He determined to cause her the least possible discomfort. We are all fallible. He wanted her to know that he would not hold her conduct to be a character flaw.

When she saw him approach, she pushed a Thomas Lodge translation of an earthy Italian novel under a cushion and began to read Tusser's *Hundreth Good Pointes of Husbandrie*.

But all he noticed was the canary yellow gown sheathing her body, the creamy flesh of her breasts rising from her low neckline, the dainty ankles and trim feet peeping from underneath her gown. Feeling his manhood rouse itself, he was glad her book was engrossing her.

He waited for the familiar shame to wash over him. Nothing happened. There was no tightening of his stomach, no drumming in his head. It was incomprehensible. He would not have to get down on his knees and beg forgiveness to assuage his guilt.

He felt good all over. A voice sang in his brain. This was his wife and he wanted her. Not ritually, as he ate meals to ward off starvation, but for the closeness it would bring between him and the woman he loved. For the pleasure he would have without it being a sin. She looked so lovely.

Her Majesty must be informed that these frequent trips to Ireland had to stop. That he must spend more time with his beloved. They would continue to sleep in separate chambers, but he would visit her more often. Emotions that he had not felt since he was a boy of sixteen stirred in him.

The jewels on her neck were there to attract. The bright colour of her dress was so wanton, he could not be making a mistake. The fear of rejection that had plagued him all his life faded. She wanted him as much as he wanted her. He went over to her, took her book from her knee and laid it on the other chair.

She raised her head and tilted it. The house was silent with a wary expectant air that he suddenly found daunting. Something in her demeanour as she looked at him deadened the declaration of love on his lips. The words he had rehearsed came back to him.

Faltering, he said, "Anne, please do not feel bad about your little indiscretion last night. I have forgiven you." This was the wrong thing to say. His hands fiddled with the leaves of the discarded book. He was not used to being in a position like this. Sir Walter Carew was normally in control. His heart beat louder. There was heat on the back of his neck. At first he wavered but then in a stronger voice he said, "Anne, I love you." Her expression looked so troubled, he felt his heart plummet. His old fears re-emerged.

"I have something to say to you, Walter." Anne played with her lace handkerchief. "Maybe if I said it before, we would not be in this position. For years I devoted my life to you. You took my dedication and love as your due, as you took Jane and George's."

He must not get angry. "There is nothing wrong with Jane and George. I did not do them any harm."

"Your son's a soldier when he should be studying plants. Your daughter married an upstart, maybe worse. No, you did not do any harm." Her voice was weary. "You were always a good husband, never unfaithful, never demanding, always prayerful." She sighed.

His mind went mad. The earlier euphoria vanished like a puff of smoke. He could not stem the feeling that she spoke the truth. Through the years, Anne had been silent in the background, loving him, understanding him, ready to help. It was his pride that was at fault. Unable to bear the humiliation of rejection like his father, he had not wanted to burden her with his lusts.

Anne had always waited for him to return from Ireland; she read his moods and pandered to them; she comforted him when, after they had copulated, he woke shouting of his damnation; she accepted it when he no longer slept even one night with her. The guilt he had cultivated, too. Perhaps it would have helped if he confided in her. "What you are saying is valid," he said. "I will change. We will change." He gestured towards her gown. "Look, you have started already."

"With this dress? No this is me. I had changed for you. I knew you would think me brazen, so I played the submissive Puritan, the controlled lady, the holy woman. While you were home. I said nothing because ..." A red blotch appeared on her white cheeks. The 'kerchief fell on the rug. "There were the children. I hated what you did to them." She hesitated. "I could not bear that you showed preference to Rory Maguire at the expense of your own son."

Sir Walter drew a sharp breath.

"It is unimportant now." Her expression was unfathomable. "I cannot believe I used to hurt so much. It was when it became unbearable, I let Francis comfort me."

At the look of affection that flitted across Anne's face at the mention of another man's name, he thought his breath would stop.

"He appreciated me not an image he had conjured. I did not see him for months. I wanted to give our marriage another chance. But when you came home again I knew nothing would ever change."

"Who is this treasure? Have I had the honour?"

"How like you to ask that, Walter. Are you going to enter his name in your red book? He is not a peer of the realm so he will not be in your orbit."

He squirmed at her finality.

She left the room her step purposeful. There were no tears.

He remembered all the times he had chastened her for her sentimentality. All the times he wiped away the dampness from her kisses. The times he humiliated her in front of the servants. She was worth one last effort. He would try reason. "Do not do this Anne. Think of Jane and George."

"Jane will be here this evening. You will have company. I have written to George."

There was still emotion. He said, "I cherish you."

Her voice remained steady. "Good-bye."

She was surprising him, this wife of his. He had expected her to capitulate. Now, he knew, with an undeniable knowledge, that she would not. She had become a mirror of him, controlled, unbending, and merciless. He had been a good example.

Next morning he ordered a distressed Geoffrey to remove all traces of Lady Carew from his house.

PART IV

1595-1607

We hold it a very good piece of policy to make them cut one another's throats, without which this kingdom will never be quiet.

- Lord Mountjoy: 1601

Chapter One

"Finola could escape the scrutiny that other ambassadors would be subjected to," Brian told the circle of grim-faced men sitting on the ferns outside the castle at Mullahinsa. "I will arrange with my friend Antonio Borromeo, an enemy of Elizabeth's, that she come to the Escorial."

English supremacy in the Gaelic regions was diminishing. O'Neill's victory at Clontibret had encouraged many more people to join the struggle. From September 1595 the fighting had stopped and peace negotiations were dragging on from month to month. Behind the cloak of negotiations, both sides were really priming themselves for the next round of battles.

The Irish attempted to widen their contacts internationally. In particular they sought aid from Spain. They sent many envoys to the Spanish court, to seek military reinforcements but without results. Brian O'Hanlon advised that O'Neill's followers needed someone who had the swarthy looks of the Latin and who spoke Spanish well. Such a person could slip unnoticed to Spain.

Finola fitted the requirement and Brian had put her name forward. But he had little expectation of her being chosen. The rebels were not convinced Finola could accomplish much. The sea warrior, Grace O'Malley in Connaught, had appalled many with her masculine ways by sailing the seas and robbing male stalwarts of their treasures. If Finola were to be sent to Spain, it would have to be done clandestinely. To satisfy Brian and return him to his real work of negotiating a just peace they agreed to give her the mission.

After his months of persuasion, Brian confided the news to Cormac as they sat beside a glowing peat fire at Mulahinsa. All he had to do now was entice Finola to agree to go to Spain. He took a sip of his whiskey. "Of course, I wasn't impartial when I selected her for this adventure." He twirled the amber liquid in his goblet. "Since the carnage on the island and the deaths of the two Andrews, she is a shadow of her true self."

Cormac agreed. "She was always slender, but now she's gaunt. You could fit your fist in the hollows under her cheekbones."

"I know. She looks more like my daughter than my sister." Brian thought for a minute. "If that were the only change, I would be less troubled. But the disaster destroyed her spirit."

Cormac drained his goblet. "In my humble opinion, she should not be alone. We couldn't persuade her to stay here any longer. She misses Andrew although she was unhappy with him. And without the boy she is lost. Their home gives her comfort."

"I'm not underestimating her anguish," Brian said, "but I know she has the courage to survive. What she needs now is the challenge of Spain."

"I wish you luck." Cormac rose from the form. "I'm to bed. You'll be leaving early in the morning. Remember to quench the candle. And Brian," he stopped on the lintel, "tell her we are bereft without her."

It had taken Brian two hours to ride by fast horse from the castle at Mulahinsa to the Campbell fortress. As he rode into Campbell' territory, the tenants peered from their dwellings with dejected expressions. Children played quietly in the mud. The bridge was down. Unchallenged, he rode through. A servant took him to the hall.

In her widow's weeds and with a sweeping brush in her hand, Finola looked like a witch preparing for a jaunt on her broomstick.

"For God's sake Finola," Brian said, "this self debasement is unsuited to you. There are servants to do that kind of work."

Finola looked at him with deadened eyes. "You came here of your own volition, Brian," she said. "Go back to playing soldier with O'Neill and leave me alone." She swept a small carved wooden block out from under a press. "That's all men enjoy. Fighting and killing."

"I'm trying to end the fighting. I have slept less than five hours a night for the past three months."

As she looked at his yellow pallor and the bags under his eyes, she felt herself soften towards him. She could never be angry with Brian for long. They were different in character, but she knew she could trust him. It was reassuring to have a brother who would tell the truth as he saw it, yet be on her side.

Brian said, "We are not fighting for any romantic principle. We are fighting to keep our way of life."

"Way of life! You call killing children a way of life you want to keep?" She discarded the toy.

Brian's tone was level. "Yes, I'll say it again, to hold on to our way of life, or to be more precise, to maintain the best of our way of life and throw away the rest as chaff."

She shrugged, but he plodded on. "We want to keep the right to harvest our crops in peace, to go to the booley without having to listen to the English call us primitive, to have our wives and lovers without them calling us immoral, to hold our lands without fear of confiscation."

"I've never heard you speak so eloquently before brother." Though she mocked, she felt a flicker of interest.

"To accomplish what I've described, we need foreign aid. With help from Spain, we would defeat the English. We need you."

"Me? Why?"

"To get rid of the kind of people who killed Andrew Óg."

"You aren't playing fair."

"This is not a game."

"Oh! Brian."

"I want you to go to Spain, Finola. A woman may be able to sway King Philip towards our aims. You would pass unnoticed there." A hint of levity crept into his tone. "If you were still a child, and I was unsure of our mother's fidelity, I would swear an Armada survivor had sired you."

As she pushed back a strand of her sloe black hair, she knew that he spoke the truth. Her mother's fair skin and blonde hair contrasted hers. It was only now that Brian had drawn attention to it, she acknowledged her regret that she was the dark one. Perhaps now she could gain from what had always been an irritant.

"After the Armada debacle, Niall taught you Spanish, didn't he? There are also people at the Spanish court who owe us for saving them that time."

She thought of the dead Antonio.

Brian said, "I know that episode brings back sad memories. I'm asking you to put them aside." The note of appeal faded. His tone grew brisker. "This is your chance to make a difference, Finola. The choice is yours."

Expecting him to plead more, his new stance surprised her. She had been through a terrible ordeal; many a woman would have emerged from it without their reason. It was a blessing that he was asking her to travel to Europe. She could fulfil a purpose, would feel needed. Her son was dead. Rory was dead to her. Here was an alternative to eventually having to return to Mulahinsa. "I'll think about it," she promised.

Chapter Two

Spain

Finola was glad to have her feet on dry land. Though the Spanish built caravel that carried her from Tyrconnell had been swift, she sighed with relief when she reached the Spanish coast and anchored at Corunna. The motion of the carriage that was now carrying her to the palace of *San Lorenzo del Escorial*, King Philip's retreat in the mountains was less upsetting to her than the rolling of the ship. She was also glad she was going to the mountains and not to the court at Madrid. It would be less of an ordeal. Also there was a monastery attached to the palace where, in the solitude of its walls, she could perhaps regain some peace.

At first she had voiced her concern that they were travelling unescorted, but the driver assured her that the royal escutcheon on the side of the conveyance was all the protection she needed. After that she settled down and closed her eyes.

When she awoke, the first thing she noticed was the copious amount of dust that rose from under the wheels of the carriage. A hot sun glared down on the deserted *Sierra de Guadarrama*. They were twenty miles northwest of Madrid and an interminable horizon glittered before her. As they passed a dried up gorge, she missed the river Swift with its wealth of water.

Yet she was glad to be away from Ulster. It was good to feel energy replace inertia and thoughts of the living replace thoughts of the dead. For the first time since Andrew Óg's death, she could go through several minutes without thinking of him lying alone in the graveyard. At first she felt torn apart with guilt at forgetting him, for even a short time. But now the times between thoughts of him had lengthened and the guilt had lessened.

She knew that many at home were unenthusiastic about her coming here. Brian had told her story to O'Neill and arranged the trip more, she suspected, to give her a purpose than for any strategic reason. Also King Philip II was ill. If she had failed to come here before he died, her reason for making the journey would have been gone.

The Escorial did nothing to cheer Finola. Designed on the lines of the grid-iron on which St. Lawrence had been executed, its chilly facade gave it a solemn and remote look, characteristics she associated with King Philip who had taken a personal interest in its construction. When she alighted from the carriage, the driver carried her chests. She tidied her hair and pulled her gown straight around her legs.

A man, whom she assumed to be Antonio Borromeo, came out onto the veranda. While he looked pleased to see her he was also impatient to be away. "I have instructed Guillaume de Troy, a secretary to the king, to take care of you. He will do what he can to help your cause. I have to return to court immediately. Maria will show you your sleeping quarters."

With a courtly bow, the Castilian left her to the mercies of the footman who led her into a cathedral vestibule and departed, leaving her there alone.

The silence disquieted her; she sat on a red upholstered chair but immediately got up again.

To help calm herself, she studied the room. For all the outside severity, this division of the royal residence was magnificent. As she looked at the paintings, she admired how the canvases, with their coating of colour and oil glaze, contrasted with the marble walls. Guessing it was the work of Titian, court painter to Charles V, King Philip's father, she was surprised that the son liked Titian also; she would never have put these dazzling colours and King Philip together.

Perhaps it was the portraits of himself he liked, she surmised, as she looked at one of him as a young man. Titian had captured him very well. With his cold blue eyes, forbidding expression, bulging lower jaw and lip, few could mistake him for anything but a Hapsburg.

She turned and looked at the rest of the room. There were five doors leading off it and at one end was a colossal circle of stairs winding upwards. The floor was bare and sterile without a rug and her sandals looked decrepit against the polished marble. The coarse cloth of her travel gown was all wrong for this balmy autumn day; she longed for cool clothing.

From somewhere came the sounds of footsteps and clinking crockery. Shortly afterwards a dark-eyed woman, dressed in a light ankle length dress, stood in the doorway holding a small cup beneath her bosom. When she smiled her cheeks dimpled. "I am Maria. I am to look after you while you are here. You must be tired."

That night Finola lay between linen sheets under a cloth-of-gold coverlet in her four poster bed. As she stared at the ornate ceiling, she thought of home, thought of her mother and of Mulahinsa and longed to return there. She wanted life to be as it was before the massacre.

Finola was disappointed that her ally Guillaume de Troy was so unappealing. A thin man with an unhealthy pallor, hairs grew out of a mole over his top lip. His power lay in his closeness to the king. According to him, King Philip told him what was in each dispatch. Finola had met several secretaries who claimed the same privilege. Groups, who unlike her believed what Guillaume de Troy said, courted him. The attention did nothing for his humility. She also got to know the servants and the ambassadors and she walked the gardens endlessly.

At the Escorial the atmosphere was prayerful and ascetic. Each morning she attended Mass and spent sixty minutes on her knees, something she had not done in Ireland. If The King knelt on swollen knees on a hard floor four hours at a stretch, she could kneel for one. She did not pray. She tried to talk to nothing and found it impossible. Why would a God take away her son in such a brutal way? There was no God. There was the law of chance and Andrew Óg chanced to be on *Oileán Na Stoirme* that awful day. She stopped talking to Andrew Óg. He was incapable of hearing her and she grew tired talking to herself.

She went to confession to a Jesuit priest and confessed her doubts. "Traitors," he shouted. "Traitors from Ireland or traitors from the Netherlands, God will damn you all." As she had stumbled from the box, she realised that military and religious affairs were mixed in his mind with equal importance. He had assumed that her lack of faith made her a follower of Queen Elizabeth.

So now instead of going to Mass in the mornings, she practised her Spanish on Carlos, Maria's five-year-old son. She did not have to worry about grammatical errors or whether he understood what she meant; they concentrated on having fun. It

301

was the only time of the day that she laughed.

Her days of waiting gave her too much time for thought. It could be months before King Philip granted her an interview. She spent hours speaking about Ireland's strife to anyone who would listen. They looked at her blankly. Only the name Elizabeth interested them and then only as a butt for their venom.

Autumn became winter. She spent hours lying on her bed thinking of nothing, waiting for a summons from the king. It could be months before he committed to anything. She wondered how Ulster was faring while King Philip procrastinated. She was unsure whether she could endure any more of this idleness.

Then one day Guillaume de Troy knocked on her chamber door. "*His Majesty* has granted you an audience," he said. "Yours is a particular plea. The presence of a lady on such a mission is unusual. The death of your son moved him to compassion and *His Majesty* is seldom moved." He plucked at his mole. "Prepare well. You have an hour." He paused. "Are you competent enough to speak to him in Spanish or do you need an interpreter?"

"I'll speak to him myself." Why wasn't he more likeable? "I'll go and change."

She did not know what to expect. There were many stories about King Philip's inability to delegate responsibility. That was why she did not believe Gauillaume de Troy's estimation of his own power. In the short time she was here she had heard Philip's attendants mimic him on several occasions *Bien es myrar a todo* - it is well to consider everything. No wonder they called him Philip the Prudent.

She wished *she* had considered everything before she came. She had not anticipated that the ring of childish voices from the servant's quarters would constantly remind her of Andrew Óg, making her fancy that he was among them. Nor did she expect that when she lay on her bed in the evening and listened to the chant of the Hieronymite monks from the nearby chapel, that she would feel her loss of faith so acutely. Her need of a confidant surprised her. "*Bien es myrar a todo.*"

Waiting in the antechamber for her audience, she recalled the king's unenthusiastic reaction to Archbishop O'Hely's mission in

1593. That time King Philip's armies were fighting in The Netherlands, Italy and France so his coffers were empty. He was still short of money, but his hatred of Queen Elizabeth was such that if she were to persuade him that Irish noblemen posed a genuine threat to England, he would support them.

Guillaume de Troy, dressed in black hose and a striped black and white doublet, whispered to her, "His Majesty is feeling poorly. He has decided to remain in his bed-chamber and listen to daily Mass from there."

Though disappointed that her meeting with the king had been cancelled, she was not surprised. He liked to shut himself away and rule his empire by writing. The only sighting she'd had of him had occurred three weeks previously. She had espied him through a bay window overlooking the courtyard as he sat writing at a bureau. She had been astonished that he had granted her request for an audience so quickly, or at all.

Niall had told her a story about the king that seemed relevant now. King Philip lacked the skill to tell the difference between what is vital and non-essential. They said in England that while he was worrying about the sailors cursing on the Armada, Francis Drake had attacked the Spanish coast.

A week later, as she lay in her usual torpor, she heard Carlos's childish voice at the door of her bed-chamber. Her cheeks were smudged with tears. She told him to go away. All he was to her, in her present state of mind, was a reminder of her own loss. But the little voice continued its pleading.

She flung the door wide, ready to reprimand him but instead she held her breath as his wide eyes searched her face. When he handed her a posy tied with string and wrapped in green paper, she felt a melting inside her. A thought that had been hatching in her head for months broke forth. Now that she knew the answer, she would endure. Her healing lay in bearing another child.

Chapter Three

Ireland

A messenger from Spain came with the news that King Philip was terminally ill. Finola should act now, if she has any influence, Rory thought. There was a general feeling that his son King Philip III was more amenable to the Tudors than his father was. But if the king committed to sending aid now, before his death, there was a chance that his son would respect his wishes and carry them through.

The English deemed that O'Neill was fighting less for any romantic or chivalric concept, and more for his own personal aggrandisement; he wanted to be supreme in Ulster. Their objectives in opposing him had nothing to do with wanting to wrest his power for themselves. They were fighting to civilise a barbaric people! But this was a parody of a war; there were few battles. Instead when the English sought to supply their forts with stores of food from Dublin, the Gaels waylaid them and stole the provisions. And lest the garrisons eat the corn in the fields or raid the cattle, they destroyed the crops and drove the cows into the *bawns*.

It rankled that O'Neill did not fight according to English rules of warfare. Lord Deputy Brough called him *The Running Beast*. When he failed to defeat him through military might, he tried to accomplish it by murder and offered a thousand pounds to have O'Neill killed.

At the fort of Portmore O'Neill's men, without any siege artillery, sat outside and prevented any food from passing in. When the English tried to relieve it, the united armies of O'Neill and his ally Aodh Rua O'Donnell met and defeated them at the yellow ford of the Blackwater River. The Council agreed to a truce. One of the conditions was the withdrawal from Portmore and Armagh.

Both adversaries and supporters of O'Neill felt the effect of the victory. King Philip II sent a letter of praise to O'Neill. By December 1598 the Dublin Council could identify only two leaders in the whole country who had not gone over to the O'Neill cause.

Three leaders, if they included him, Rory thought, when he

heard the rumour en route from Dublin after his imprisonment. He still quaked when he thought of Dublin Castle. A man could go mad in that place.

He assumed that Cormac's *uirrithe* would have already gone to Tyrone to side with O'Neill. Eoin Maguire's would be in need of leadership. In need of him. Yet he was unsure how to proceed. Between snatches of conversation with Art O'Cathán, his new horse-boy, he rationalised his inaction and wondered why he found it so difficult to decide where his loyalties lay. He was beginning to think of himself as over-cautious.

It was in his genealogy to cling to the English ways. As a boy he had thought his father so brave to be fighting for what he believed to be his by right. Now he knew there had been nothing noble about the conflict. His father had sought to replace the Gaelic law of the *deirbhfhine* with the English law of *Primogeniture* so that he could grab land that belonged to the clan and have it for himself.

However, under the laws of kinship required by the *deirbhfhine* his genealogy also entitled him to be elected as the chief of the lands of Glenone under Gaelic law as his uncle had been.

His life had taken some strange paths and he felt he was at a crossroads.

The English must not be allowed to install him as a puppet chieftain in Glenone. However, he felt apprehension, even fear at the task that lay before him. He was only human after all and he was only one man. During the civil war, he remembered hiding in an oak and looking down at English soldiers burning Cormac's corn as a warning to him not to assist Eoin. There was little food for months thereafter so that all at Mulahinsa went to their pallets with hungry bellies. Though it was never talked about afterwards, the memory was still vivid.

He considered the concept he had thought of in prison. Sometimes you must destroy to build. Sometimes you must go to war to bring peace. Whatever the risk!

"Rory." George was sitting by the fire, pressing flowers into a book. "I have been at Ennistoomey for two days and have not seen you except at night. Why are you spending so much time with Eoin Maguire's retainers? It was I who asked father to get you released from prison, so I do not want you playing tricks."

"When war erupts after this truce, I want to be prepared," Rory answered.

"Why not go on manoeuvres with our own men? You cannot know with certitude that you will be able to persuade Eoin's *uirrithe* to fight for us against O'Neill."

"I will," Rory said. George's naivety made him feel guilty. George believed that Rory was training Eoin's men to fight on the side of the crown. Rory had deceived him into believing that. He could dress it any way he wanted, but that was what it was - deception, he was deceiving a friend who trusted him. He tried to end the conversation. "My clansmen still carry the weapons of their grandfathers," he said. "If they must fight with spears and bows and arrows, I need to train them well. They will not align with the modern artillery of the English otherwise."

George looked at him. "You know best."

Rory had spent months making militants out of all of Eoin's clan. There was no difference now between the blue-blooded fighting classes and churls. O'Neill's Confederation regarded all men of combative age as soldiers; their lowly nativity no longer deprived them of the honour of carrying weapons. He had gone against the norm himself when he had allowed his horse-boy to bear arms against Campbell and he had been killed. If there were no longer need of battles and loss of life, that would be the real progress.

"Damn!" he heard George say. Something had gone wrong with the flower pressing. A petal curled or crushed maybe, Rory thought.

"Something the matter, George?" he asked in a derisive tone.

George, to Rory's surprise, began to simper, "Do you remember the roses Rory? My mother loved roses. I always wanted a fountain. I spent days pleading for one, but my father would not let me have it. Nor pots for my special plants. He never liked my garden. I wonder what has happened to it, now that my mother has absconded with her lover." Then he burst into tears. "Imagine Rory, I thought he was her cousin. How could I have been so dim-witted?"

Rory had heard about the fountain on his second day at Chalk

Hall and countless times since. Anne's desertion was also a familiar refrain, but it was the first time George had cried like this. He felt sorry for him now and sorry for his earlier scornful attitude. Not because Anne Carew had left her passionless husband at last, but because George had taken it so badly. For him Anne's desertion had answered the riddles of his youth; all her changes of behaviour and mood were explained.

He imagined what Sir Walter's reaction would have been when he heard; he would have ordered the servants to remove her possessions from the house and never to mention her name again. "Her ungovernable appetites have disgraced her," he fancied Sir Walter saying.

George's persistent sobbing began to grate on him. He should learn to control himself more.

"I stepped on her favourite rose and squashed it under my foot when I was angry with her one day. Then I picked up each petal and threw them at her. Do you think she forgave me Rory? I know my father did not love me but she did. Was the rose the reason she left?"

His mother deserted his father because George threw flowers at her. Rory's contempt was returning. "I have not seen Shane lately," he said in an attempt to take George's mind off his remorse. "Is he still in Mulahinsa?"

"Shane has changed since we were defeated in the Battle of the Yellow Ford. He writes about joining O'Neill's cause," George sniffled.

Rory realised that he had not taken George's mind off his confusions, only centred his attention on his major one. Shane liked to be on the winning side so he was not surprised by his conversion to the cause. And O'Neill could do with all the help he could get. Neither would Shane's inability to speak hamper him. Perhaps joining up would banish Shane's dissatisfaction with everything. Give him a purpose.

After this revelation regarding Shane, George retreated to his chamber, almost like a snail retreating into his shell.

The figure of a man walking up the track towards them distracted Rory from his concern for George. It was the hump he recognised first.

Could it be who he thought it was? This man had cheated

him. Why would he want to face him now? People killed each other for less. Rory rose to meet him, too late recalling that he was without a weapon. When he had come back from training Eoin's men, he had left his sword in the garrison.

He checked O'Cathán's expression. It was as benign as his features would allow. There was even the semblance of a smile.

Suddenly Art, Rory's new horse-boy, came running from the garrison and rushed into the arms of O'Cathán. They greeted each other warmly.

"'Tis beholden to you, I am Sire," O'Cathan said to Rory, motioning to the boy. "'Tis a good son he is. Broke my heart to part with him it did." The tone was plaintive. "They would have put me in prison if I hadn't pledged him. Dead in a week I'd have been."

Art had been secretive about his parentage and his former life. It had not fallen into place until now that his new horse-boy and his erstwhile hired assassin had the same surnames. Rory did not accuse. Donal O'Cathán was not the first to send his son as a hostage, and he had cared enough to search him out.

"'Tis training men you are yourself, I do be hearin'."

Rory felt uneasy. If O'Cathán knew, it would not be long until the English knew.

O'Cathán added quickly, "'Twas the sister Eimear who told me. Nobody else." Red faced, he said, "She's married to MacRiocard now. It was from her I heard about himself." He caressed Art's shoulder.

Rory remembered the seductress and felt no surprise at her marriage so soon after Eoin's demise.

"Heard too that weapons are scarce.'Tis putting you in touch with suppliers of muskets and calivers I could be. There's powder coming in from Glasgow soon. Two shillings and sixpence a pound. They would be asking no questions."

Rory hoped that meant they were trustworthy. Not English agents planted to seek out rebels.

"'Tis to owe you, I do," O'Cathán said. "There will be no betrayal."

This was the contact for which Rory had hoped. An outlaw like O'Cathán, spurned by society and used by the government, gave allegiance rarely.

But it was not mistrust that made Rory hesitate. It was not the money. He had that prepared and waiting.

If he bought new arms for the freemen of the territory to fight for O'Neill, there could be no turning back. If the English imprisoned him again, even Sir Walter would be incapable of liberating him.

He had told himself that he would act when the opportunity arose. Now, wracked by indecision, he had to face his own flaw and deal with his tendency to be overly cautious.

Chapter Four

Spain

The more time Finola spent with young Carlos the more she was convinced that if she were to give birth to another child, she would recover from her melancholy. In Carlos she saw Andrew Óg as he might have been. She carved a wooden horse for him, a skill she learned from Campbell. She taught him how to say mother in Gaelic and in English. Each evening, after a day's roaming through the court, Finola returned Carlos to Maria. When she handed him over to his mother, she missed his chatter and the feel of his arms.

Summer was beginning. Campbell was dead a year and a half. It was also eighteen months since she'd seen Rory. As she played with Carlos, she imagined Rory by her side. But she then reminded herself that what she imagined was impossible. She had made it so by her vow. Her vow was not binding. She no longer cherished the deity to whom she had sworn not to join with Rory. The vow was to herself. To assuage her guilt and make life liveable.

She knew that she and Rory could spend little time together without being intimate. Even now as she thought about him she felt moistness between her legs. She bit hard on her lip, turned to the child and swung him off his feet. Shrieking with delight, he stopped only when he found himself entangled in a pair of muscular legs.

Startled, she found herself looking into the face of one of the king's secretaries. She had seen him once with the monarch strolling around the garden. Carlos reached down and began to playfully tie and untie the thongs of the man's shoes.

The secretary's smile was kind. "Will you join me?" He pointed to a bench. "I will sit and allow this little man to do his job in comfort."

She followed him along a sandy path to the resting place.

"I hope I am not taking a liberty." He hesitated. "I feel I know you. We have met before."

She squinted in the sunlight and suddenly became conscious of the cotton dress that clung to her breasts. A gift from Maria, the dress had been meant for the seclusion of the women's quarters. It was so hot this morning she had pulled it on with only ease in mind; she hoped that in a sitting position it would reveal her contours less.

Carlos was at the stage where if anybody had thonged footwear, he would sit for a half an hour tying and untying the strips.

While Carlos amused himself, the secretary turned to her. "I will stay still, so you can study me," he said teasingly.

She was too aware of him as a man to concentrate.

"You still do not know me. I am disappointed. Let me make a suggestion. Think back to 1588. Did anything startling happen to you around that time?"

Quickly she calculated. Eleven years ago. She was still at Mulahinsa. The most memorable thing that year was the arrival of the Armada survivors. She remembered the tension in the enclosure. The sight of Sir Walter Carew talking to her mother. Molly dead. Antonio dead.

"Don!" she said. "Don from the Armada!"

He bowed in confirmation.

"I did not expect to meet you at the palace of the king of Spain."

He wore a beard now, short and pointed and his body was fatter. She remembered his description of their tribulations on the ship. The sorrow he felt at the death of his friend. It was the voice that had finally convinced her. It had the same passion as then.

His attraction still lay in his dignity and aristocratic bearing. He tousled the shock of hair bent over his foot. "You must enjoy playing with this imp," he said. "I watch you often and envy your energy. I wish I shared it."

She could see the admiration in his eyes and it made her feel warm and a little flustered. Again she became conscious of her flimsy attire.

"Time for this young man's repast," she said, getting up suddenly. "His mother likes him to be on time for meals. I've got to go." That was untrue, but she wanted to gather her thoughts. It was so long since she had been in a charming man's company. She felt awkward. Retreat, she thought, and meet him again.

Over time Finola's daily meetings with Don became a pleasant

311

interlude in a mission that had become frustrating. Brian had arranged her presence here. She could not let him down. Her pride required that she be successful in her quest that King Philip send aid to Ulster.

No longer satisfied to wait passively for a royal summons, she crafted a plan. The king disliked face-to-face discussions. Her failed attempt at an audience had convinced her that these rumours were indeed correct. Verily, writing was his preferred method of communication.

Over two consecutive days she immersed herself in paper and wrote of her objective in coming to see him. She told him the news she had received, that O'Neill had won a magnificent victory at the Yellow Ford. She guessed that he already knew, but it was something to impart. Aid to O'Neill would help avenge the Armada. Afterwards he could use Ireland as a base from which to attack England. She sealed the missive.

Donning a white dress, one that caressed her in folds of soft linen and accented the colour of her skin and eyes, she put her feet into hide shoes and arranged her hair into a groomed but natural look. She left Carlos at the sandpit in the garden, and went towards the central courtyard.

"I came to meet you." Her regard was coquettish as Don moved towards her. His slim fingers brushed a coif of hair from her forehead. He smelled of nutmeg and sweat, a unique combination she found stimulating. Placing his hand beneath her chin, he raised her face to his. With his other hand he circled her waist. Through her light dress it felt as if he were caressing her naked body. He lowered his head.

Feeling his lips on hers, she closed her eyes and let a feeling of well being wash over her. She felt a storm crash over her head, but she was safe, safe amidst boulders ... safe with Rory.

His tongue probed.

She opened her eyes and drew apart.

He looked at her questioningly.

She produced the letter she had written to the king. It was inappropriate to hand it to him now, but she was unable to stop herself. After taking it from her, he read its destination. "You are using me as an instrument to get to the king." His tone was a mixture of incredulity and injury. "You should have told me that was my magnet."

312

She met his gaze with equanimity.

"And you, Don, should have told me you have a wife and sons in court."

He looked away. "I will do my utmost to assist you," he said.

From then on Don and Finola met regularly, but they knew there would no physical relationship between them. Their friendship had been established. Each found the other desirable, but Finola was not willing to become a mistress and Don's wife was a lady of influence who would repudiate infidelity. So their conversations now centred on politics and the sickly state of the king. Physicians continually bled his feet. Sleeplessness and pain wracked him. There were whispers that he was dying.

Aware that his days were tallied and that his son would succeed to an empty treasury, King Philip made peace with the Netherlands to lessen Spain's expenses. Finola became concerned that he would make peace with England too. When she handed her fourth letter to Don for the king, she said, "This will end with the rest of his unread correspondence in the archives of Simancas."

Don said, "No, the king reads each of your letters and writes comments on the side. Not that I think anyone can read them. His hand shakes."

She found what Don said difficult to believe and certainly was sceptical of receiving a response to her letters. Yet, that was what happened. Her heart hammered as she took the paper from Don's hand.

Wading through the complex prose, she attempted to discern its meaning. *His Majesty* seemed to be saying that he was unable to bring himself to make peace with the infidel Queen Elizabeth. It was not God's will that they reconcile. He regretted not being able to send a fleet to Ireland himself but he had ordered his son to do so when he became king. The Irish were fighting in the service of God. They would succeed. Spanish help was unimportant. The Saviour was on their side.

From what she'd heard recently from Ireland, Finola knew that God had divided loyalties. She also knew that there was nothing more she could accomplish at the court of King Philip II. It was time to return to Ulster.

Chapter Five

Ireland

The death of Philip II pleased the Queen of England as Rory knew it would. Now that they had a reprieve from the Spanish, they could concentrate on subduing O'Neill. Her Majesty abandoned her earlier military directives to spend as little money and apportion as few soldiers as possible to the Irish wars. Instead she instigated ways of gathering *the royallest army that ever went out of England*. The basic company contained thousands of foot and over a thousand horse. Every month there were plans to buttress these.

"O'Neill has cut down the sheaves of corn in the fields from Clandeboy to MacMahon territory. Any hope Her Majesty's army had of living off the land is gone. They will starve." Brian was exultant, shouting the news to Rory even before he dismounted.

"I hope you're right." There was a note of surprise in Rory's voice. "I thought the men Elizabeth is pouring in have plenty of supplies. Come inside. You must know more than I do."

"I have said farewell at Mulahinsa and am on my way to Tyrone." Brian dismounted. "Rory, Ireland is on the verge of a new era." He gave his horse to Art and walked with Rory into the garrison. He sat on the form, took off his boots and left them beside him on the floor.

"Make yourself comfortable," Rory said in a bantering tone. "Now, bring me up to date on events."

They did not mention the carnage on *Oileán na Stoirme*. Nor did Rory talk about his imprisonment. They discussed the lord who headed the queen's forces in Ireland. Brian felt that the Earl of Essex was going to seek an all-out victory soon. He also added that Queen Elizabeth found him attractive.

"So that is where the Sir before the Robert Devereaux came from," Rory said. "The Queen loves laying the tip of the sword on the shoulders of her favourites."

Brian laughed. "To knight from a sword on the shoulder, to death from a sword in the stomach. While he is here, he should not displease *Her Highness*. He has been her favourite since the death of Leicester, but of late they are not agreeing." There was distress in his voice. "A sack of rebellious Irish heads would make a nice reconciliation gift from Essex."

Rory said, "I have hearsay of my own. Sir Robert had no alternative but to accept the Irish command. His enemies put his name forward to get rid of him. I remember hearing that he went to university at nine. But do you know if he is a good general, Brian?"

"He is an experienced military leader. Yet, he's here since April and he has stayed away from Ulster; he has crusaded against Munster and Leinster only. The Dublin government tells him what to do and their main preoccupation is the Pale's protection. But he will march against Ulster to please Her Majesty, and we will defeat him. That is why I'm going back to Tyrone." Brian looked questioningly at Rory.
"You have some decisions to make yourself. Getting back Glenone will be difficult."

Rory sat very still.

Brian O'Hanlon was only partly correct in his prediction mused Rory several weeks later. The Earl of Essex had marched to the banks of the Lagan although he must have known the hopelessness of fighting against Ulstermen in their own territory. But Brian had been incorrect when he said that he would fight.

Instead O'Neill and Essex met at the Ford of Annaclint. There in the middle of the stream O'Neill outlined his conditions for peace with the Queen. Essex pledged to return to London to inform Her Majesty about them. Then, the two men announced a cease-fire.

Doubtless Her Majesty would be displeased by her favourite's inaction but then Rory felt unable to be that critical of his deeds. He was beginning to act like the Earl himself. It was a sobering thought.

George had ridden to Ennistoomey from the nearby English fort where his straggling soldiers were billeted since the debacle at *Oileán Na Stoirme*. He looked wind blown and agitated. "Rory I must talk to you," he said in a pleading tone.

"Sit and join me." A vessel of sweet milk and a platter of oatmeal biscuits, a taste that had remained with Rory into manhood, stood on the table in his room. "I will have finished with this script in a minute."

"I simply must talk to you," George repeated.

Rory put his reading aside when he noticed George's trembling lips and ashen face. "Has O'Neill won another battle? Or have you lost your only pair of breeches?"

"He left yesterday." The emotion in George's words made Rory feel ashamed of his foolish jesting.

"Shane?" he enquired

"I think a lot about the river Swift," George said. The abrupt change of topic bewildered Rory.

George rolled the word around on his lips. "What a lovely name. A lovely name for a lovely river. It is an alluring river. The waters are clear and inviting."

Was he missing something in this exchange? Rory wondered.

As if noticing his perplexity George changed the subject once again. He said, "I had a missive from my father today. Essex's negotiations with O'Neill displeased the Queen."

Rory felt relieved by the turn of the conversation. George's rambling worried him.

"So Elizabeth will send someone else to subdue O'Neill," Rory said, careful to maintain an appearance of indifference. He didn't want to alarm George with his doubtful loyalty to the queen.

"Father is coming over himself to inspect the force and make sure we do our duty." George paused. "Our duty means killing O'Neill's men. Do you realize that could mean Shane? I keep thinking that Shane is unkind. He can be rude and cruel." George wrung his hands. "Yet he is the only one who ever gave me attention. My father never bothered with me. You had Finola - and Jane ..."

He talked non-stop in a sorrowful tone, hardly breaking for breath. The word 'Shane' resounded until the air vibrated with his name. "Each time we touch ..."

"Quite," said Rory breaking in on him. He was not in the mood for revelations. It was hard enough to manage his own life. "George, I do not mean to be unsympathetic but there is little you can do if he is already gone. Brian is a follower of O'Neill. He will look out for Shane."

With a defeated look, George accepted his dismissal and

returned to his dreary quarters.

That night as he lay on his bed Rory pondered his conversation with George. Nuances of the dialogue, that had bothered him faintly at the time, took on an ominous significance. Why had he talked about the river Swift in such terms? George appeared troubled. Turning his face to the wall, he tried to sleep.

He was awake early. Since he had heard of Finola's return from Spain, thoughts of her graced his entry into each new day. But this morning was different. The disturbed feeling he went to bed with was still there. He could not banish images of the old George at Chalk Hall, weeding his garden, pruning and sowing his flowers.

When the sun was up, he rose. In the kitchen he refused the porridge that Art had prepared.

"'Tis mad you are to go out without a bite in your stomach," he grumbled as he watched Rory don his mantle. The propriety that usually existed between servant and master was absent between them. They had been equalised by their shared humiliation in prison.

"Get the horses and cease your moaning," Rory said.

"'Tis what's taking us out this hour of the morning that's making me wonder?"

"I am not sure myself," Rory muttered, as Art slammed the door in their wake.

As they rode, Rory was glad he had Art to accompany him. Art's father had also proved faithful. He had bought arms and ammunition with the English money Rory had given him.

When they were approaching the fort where George's soldiers were living, they spotted him astride his horse riding in their direction. All thoughts of the war disappeared from Rory's mind. He now realised what had brought him this way. He pulled his gelding to a stop; Art pulled up behind him. George jerked his steed in beside them and looked at them, puzzled.

Rory spoke first. "I was concerned about you. I thought you were distressed last night."

A look both of mortification and defiance came over George's face. "It is not like you to dramatise Rory. I was feeling despondent, that is all. Like you said, Shane is gone now. Fretting will not bring him back." He looked down the path. "I am going for a ride. It is a shame to waste such fresh air. Did you want to see me about something important?"

Rory shook his head. But he was still concerned. "We will be a piece of the way with you."

They rode in silence until they reached a fork on the road. George urged his horse into a trot and veered off to the right. When he was gone a short distance, he slowed, turned and waved his hat. Then he shouted something about water and roses.

Rory already disconcerted by George's impetuosity looked after him, perplexed. Then he and Art rode slowly back to Ennistoomey. Water and roses. Water and roses. The words echoed in his mind.

Chapter Six

It was already nearly noon and Rory was feeling as restless as a Puritan at an Irish wake. His outing to check on George had upset his routine. By this time each morning, Eoin's soldiers, under his supervision, would have had two hours of military practice over. But today Rory was still at breakfast and Art was just building the fire, pursing his lips to coax the sparks into flames.

As Rory scraped the last of the cold porridge in his breakfast bowl, there was a noise outside, then footsteps. Abandoning the bowl, he opened the door and there stood Cormac. He felt overwhelmed by Cormac coming to see him.

"Come, sit by the fire," he invited. "You left your horse in the stables? Art will take care of him. Make yourself comfortable." Rory turned to Art and said. "Leave that to water Cormac's horse." Then in a lower and more urgent voice he said, "Before you come back, inform Eoin's *uirrithe* that I have been delayed." He knew Cormac would react badly if he knew he was training an army to fight O'Neill. He filled a goblet of *uisce beatha* for Cormac and a smaller one for himself.

"That's welcome," Cormac said. He took the goblet from Rory's hand and raised it in the air. "O'Neill abú."

"O'Neill abú."

Cormac took a swig and looked into his goblet. He became thoughtful. "That was a mean trick the English played on my father when they persuaded him to sign the *Surrender and re-grant* treaty. They knew we were fools. They played us for fools. We were fools." There was anger in his voice.

Rory felt uneasy. Cormac was speaking as if it were yesterday his father signed the treaty rather than fifty-five years ago. Cormac twirled the liquid in the goblet, his expression pensive. "I never dwelt on the difference between the two laws before. This fighting makes us examine absurdities we thought we'd always have to endure. I had no brothers so *Surrender and re-grant* made no difference to me. If I'd an older brother, though, I'd have felt aggrieved."

He screwed his face into a scowl. "I considered it inevitable that Brian, would succeed me. Now, I'm beginning to question it. If O'Neill keeps winning, Shane could have his chance." He

319

banged the wooden tumbler onto the trestle. "We should never have accepted it."

Cormac was at least a decade younger than Sir Water Carew, but he was acting as if he were a decade older. He had heard all this before. Only the doubt about Brian's right to succeed him as Baron of Mulahinsa was new.

Cormac eyed him. "I know that you would not have any rights of inheritance from your father if your grandfather had refused to accept *Surrender and re-grant.*" Then he stopped and was silent.

"I have always had trouble about that," Rory said, "but nobody denies themselves. I want the land kept in the family under whatever law. I owe it to my father - and Matthew."

"We understand each other, Rory," Cormac raised his goblet. "Enough of the past. Let's think about the future."

He left down the goblet and rubbed his hands together. "I'm glad to have lived to see the English get their due." Then slapping his knee heavily for emphasis, he said. "Aw! He's a wonderful man. The Great O'Neill they call him now. It is well he deserves the name. They say he will be crowned at Tara as king of all Ireland." He smiled, revealing a top set of discoloured teeth. "I heard a woman say that when he has won the war here and wears a crown of kingship, he will carry it to England and kick The Queen off her throne." He smirked. "It's a crazy suggestion I know."

Rory sipped his drink. "I heard that Philip III and O'Neill will unite Spain and Ireland and draw straws for who will be King."

Cormac's withered face glowed with mirth.

More seriously, Rory said, "O'Neill got rid of the Earl of Essex in quick time. He was only here from April to September. Six months. Who will they send against him now? Queen Elizabeth will hate to have to spend more money."

"She has spent a fortune already. I enjoy seeing misers lose their crocks of gold. I heard that Charles Blount, or Lord Mountjoy to give him his correct title, is coming," Cormac said.

Rory knew that he had made a mistake about Cormac. He may look older, but his mind was alert. "Lord Mountjoy. No, I don't remember reading anything about him. Another of the queen's lap dogs?"

"In my humble opinion, he will have to do more than bark in

Ireland to affect O'Neill. The English should admit defeat and leave."

"Did you ever see the English do that?"

"No, I never did," Cormac smacked his lips, a new habit. "This time they might regret their tenacity. There are people fighting who never fought before." He repossessed his drink. "Shane is a follower of O'Neill now."

"I know." Rory did not want to be drawn into a discussion about Shane.

"Maeve is heartbroken, though she pretends otherwise. Brian has already gone. He believes that they are trying to take our lands off us altogether, that there is no option but war, a war of defence. Finola agrees with him."

"I know. Brian told me." Finola's name crackled in the air. He continued. "It was not my intention to mention her, but now that you have, where ..."

"She is unlike what she used to be, Rory," Cormac said quickly, "the two dying like that. First Andrew Óg and then his father. Enough to unhinge any woman. The only good that came out of it is that Eoin Maguire is dead. God knows. I can understand somebody protecting his land. But to kill Matthew. I never forgave him."

"But Finola ..." Rory began again.

"If she were weaker, she would have gone mad. The trip to Spain helped. Gave her something to dwell on besides her loss." His complexion paled. His eyes took on a distant look. "It was she who found them. Those snakes burned their bodies. Blood from the dying covered the ones who survived. Their ashes were ..." Then remembering who he was talking to, he stopped and straightened his shoulders. "Finola is back staying with us. Were it not for Niall, we would be at a loss as how best to deal with her."

"Niall?"

"Niall, you surely remember Niall."

"Yes, but he was on the island with Andrew Óg when, when ..."

"He survived. Badly wounded but alive. He dragged himself to a cave with Andrew Óg on his back. Some escaped that way but Andrew Óg died in the darkness there."

Rory sat rooted to the chair. He had learned about the massacre from Richard Dolman. Now he was hearing it from the victim's view.

"It must have been the survivors you and Finola heard wailing."

"Yes," was all he could say. Finola must have told Cormac about their being together that night.

"Bloodthirsty that's what the English are," Cormac declared loudly.

Rory found the sudden passion disconcerting. He had forgotten Cormac's lightning temper.

"I hope O'Neill and my sons kill them all."

With the word *savages* in his ears and the smell of burning flesh in his nostrils, Rory agreed. This time without ambiguity.

In February 1600, five months after the Earl of Essex's withdrawal, Lord Mountjoy, arrived in Dublin. What Cormac did not predict was that the queen would also appoint a new President of Munster. The new soldiers had come well equipped. Her Majesty had fixed that they must defeat O'Neill whatever the outlay.

The President of Munster was resolute, effective and fast acting. After arriving in Dublin, he went at once to Munster where he burned crops, razed houses and killed thousands of cattle.

In Ulster, too, Lord Mountjoy proved himself smarter than either Cormac or Rory had expected. He realised that they would not tame the Irish while the leaves were on the trees. O'Neill's tactic had been to take part in peace negotiations during the long dark months of winter while his armies rested in preparation for the summer fighting. Lord Mountjoy was the first English general to force the Irish to fight in the winter. He knew that the only solution to the hit and run warfare of O'Neill was to keep the enemy strained, to harry him pitilessly and to break his courage. To do this the English needed persistent and sustained attacks. During the worst weather, soaked by heavy rain and blinding hailstones, as his men cursed this godforsaken hole of a country, Mountjoy attacked and attacked and attacked.

For the first time since the wars began Brian had to leave his Tyrone bothy in winter and shiver in the bogs and woods. O'Neill no longer called the tune.

The new piper Lord Mountjoy allowed no truces; he forced O'Neil to keep his soldiers continually on the alert and constantly fed. This drained their resources. The English forced the Irish to fight on two fronts and made regular raids into Tyrone and Tyrconnell, burning crops and slaughtering cattle.

"The muscle of the crown is at work in Ulster," Brian said sardonically to his comrades. He was watching from the fastness as soldiers hacked the corn from its roots, and burned what remained uneaten. "We haven't enough powder to challenge every attack."

The vassals and collaterals of O'Neill and Aodh Rua O'Donnell deserted. Men who fought beside Brian in the past now fought for the English. "The deserters think England will defeat us," he told his stalwarts. "Wait 'till we start to win again. They'll all flock back."

Mountjoy knew, as well as Brian, that this was true. Loyalty was non-existent among the Irish. They followed the route of the most powerful. If O'Neill became strong again, they would change direction without a scruple.

George received orders from Lord Mountjoy; he was to build a fort on the lands of Glenone and prepare it for occupation by English soldiers. He was distraught at the prospect of aiding the enemies of Shane.

Rory consulted a dispirited Brian on the strategy he should pursue and was advised to remain neutral until help came from Spain. If he showed his hand now, the English were strong enough to wipe him out.

Initially, Rory felt relieved that he would not have to engage George in conflict, but as time went on he found it difficult. Now that he had resolved to fight, he longed to get into the fray. Like a carrow, holding his breath, waiting for the trump card, he waited for a Spanish fleet to sail around the northern coast. If that were to happen, the Irish could still win.

And he enjoyed the certainty that he would be part of the struggle. This second Spanish Armada would succeed where the first one had failed and traitors would defect again, this time back to the Irish side.

Nobody saw George leave the fort that morning and ride off into the countryside. However, when he was still missing by nightfall, Rory, as his second-in-command, was informed.

The next day, amid a deluge of rumour and guess-work and hear-say, he organised a party of soldiers to search within the far-flung environs of his fort. But he could not be found.

After a few days Rory went to Mulahinsa. He did not know what guided him, but he felt compelled to go. With the help of the servants and Cormac, he searched the woods there. Seeing the scenes of his childhood, made his heart heavy. These woods and this river held bad memories for him. He beat the grass with a stick and trudged through the forest, an arquebus under his arm. Suddenly he felt cold. But it was not the air in the woods but the thought in his heart that chilled him. The thought that George was dead.

The servants dragged the river Swift. They found an old shoe, a pewter can and lots of good skimming stones. Rory was relieved. Perhaps he had deserted, gone to a port town and returned to England.

Cormac was hopeful too. "They may have news of him at the fort by this," he said.

A woman had seen a man who fitted George's description, heading for Shanco the previous day. She remembered him because he had given her little girl a drawing of an attractive lady, he called Anne.

Shanco was a pretty town, full of brightly coloured houses and brilliant green foliage. Its walks, shaded by multicoloured creepers, would have enchanted George. Rory understood how his love of gardening would have brought George to this place. "Look at these blossoms, Rory. I'm not sure what they are, but they are beautiful," he imagined his light hesitant voice say.

It did not take him long to find him.

Silent, Rory rode over to him, dismounted and, within touching distance of his body, halted. Then he turned and gripping his stomach, he leaned over and emptied its contents onto the ground. The sight of George slumped over the fountain in the town square, his hand-gun by his side, his brains spattered over the last of the trailing summer roses, was too much for Rory. How would he tell Anne and Jane that their beloved George had shot himself? How would Shane be now that George was no more? Sir Walter would be dismayed, of course. Not fitting behaviour for the son of a peer of the English realm, he would think.

As he helped Cormac remove the corpse, Rory tried not to contemplate this new void in his life.

They laid George's body on an old door while they waited instructions on how to proceed. Two hours later soldiers arrived bearing a crude wooden box. Behind them came an aesthetic looking man, holding a book. "Orders are to inter him," he said.

George was carried to the graveyard on a slide car, his wooden box tied by ropes to the sides to keep it from slipping off. There in a corner of unconsecrated ground, they dug a grave and backed the slide car up to it. The soldiers undid the cords and the box slipped in.

The man with the book said some words.

Before the grave was filled in Rory picked some wild thyme and sprinkled it on the coffin. The man with the book pointed to it and asked, "What is the name of that? Sir Walter will want to know all the details."

Chapter Seven

England

Sir Walter sat on the floral covered bed in George's childhood bed-chamber. He traced the flowers with the tips of his fingers. With ruthless intensity, the words repeated themselves in his brain. "He should be studying plants not fighting; he should be a gardener not a soldier; he should ..." Why had he ignored Anne's words then? He shook his head from side to side. He was a good father; he was a good father; he was a good father; he ... He looked at the framed letter of congratulation on the wall.

I rejoice in the news that you have joined the militia. My hope has always been that you would follow the tradition set by your grandfather.

Your father,

Sir Walter Carew.

When he had penned that, he had been so proud. So proud, yet so foolish. He had been ashamed of his own father so how could he have expected George to be proud of his grandfather? Despising his parent, he had hated his hypocrisy in the reign of Queen Mary, hated his subservience to his sexual desires. Because he resembled his father, he hated himself. Yet George must have been proud to receive his congratulations; he had edged the letter with wood and hung it on a place of honour on the wall.

He picked up a trowel that Anne had crafted for the little boy. Always his mother doing his will. Spoiling him. Stealing his love away. Taking the tool in his hand, he ran his fingers over the surface where George's fingers had rested. A tear dropped onto the dried clay.

His head throbbed. A shooting pain jumped across his eyes. He closed them now and saw George and Rory. George pale, wan and sad. Rory confident, healthy and ebullient. It was his curse that he loved an Irish infidel more than his own son.

Enough of this sentimentality. His son was dead. By his own hand. *Prostrate over a fountain*, the report said. George always had a love of fountains. He remembered he forbade him to ...

He let the small gardening implement fall on the floor. His eyes roamed once more over the room where his son had spent so much of his early years. Then slamming the door he blotted it out.

Army administrators arranged to hide the fact of his son's suicide. His position as one of Her Majesty's generals and one of her peers merited that. The army had used its resourcefulness and buried George in Shanco with a tale of death in the pursuit of duty to explain his demise. It would have been impossible for George to be buried in Kent in the family graveyard; he was unworthy to lie with his ancestors.

Later that evening Sir Walter had the strangest of feelings. He imagined his heart was being over-run by maggots; the limbless larvae crawled about, smiling grotesquely. They were his family. His lost family. George lost to suicide. Anne lost to her lover. Jane, well Jane was Jane.

The maggots were coming again. He must chase them away, drown them. They would not expect whiskey to fall on them in Sir Walter's body. He would massacre them. Duncan had some in his bureau. Like a crazed man he found the bottle and, dispensing with the need for a goblet, he raised it to his lips. It tasted good. He swallowed more. No matter what, he had to kill those maggots.

Four weeks later, Sir Walter stood on the ground in Ulster where George was buried. A profusion of flowers edged the field, masking the presence of death admirably. He swayed on his feet. There was a drumming in his head.

Knowing that George had killed himself, Sir Walter was glad he had not seen the corpse. Anne wanted to remember him as a hero, but he could not. Jane, he did not know what Jane thought.

He looked down at the un-inscribed gravestone. In its isolation, the plot was conspicuous. Correct course to have taken. George could not lie beside good Christians who struggled on until God called them. Better to leave it anonymous. No reason to excite curiosity by putting the name Carew on it.

He would be dead himself soon. It would not matter to him. But his grandchild, Quintin. He must think of Quintin. And his other grandchild. Sir Walter shook his head. Why was he thinking of him? He did not even know he was kin.

The maggots started again but he had found a way to stymie them. He doused them. When they reformed and attacked, he drenched them again. He knew it was a life sentence, but it was the only honourable thing to do. Anne and Jane must never know that George was a failure. As he shuffled away from the plot, he extricated a flask of whiskey from his satchel.

Chapter Eight

Finola and her father were sitting in the parlour at Mulahinsa. Finola was talking about her sojourn in Spain. "Nearly every bit of land around the fortress is barren. People are moving from the country into the towns. Spain is less rich than it used to be."

"In my humble opinion, you're glad to be back." Cormac said, his tired eyes shining with delight at his daughter's return.

"You and your humble opinion," Finola said. "The day you're humble will be the day you die." Although she had said this in jest, as soon as the words escaped she regretted them. Death wasn't a joking matter anymore. In the past months, her father's movements had slowed; his hair had lost its thickness and hung in tufts on his head. The ankle he had broken three years previously had mended incorrectly leaving him with a slight limp. He spent much time staring into the fire, thinking. "There is something on your mind," she challenged him.

"Bring me over that mantle there." He pointed to the garment, thrown across the table, beside the candlesticks. "If you want to come for a walk with me, you can."

They closed the door of the parlour and came slowly down the stairway. "Maeve would worry if she heard what I'm going to say."

Finola felt her heart skip a beat. He wasn't philandering again, she hoped.

"If a Spanish force lands, I'll fight," he said.

She was uncertain how to respond so she posed the question, "What makes you think one will land? I wish I shared your hopefulness."

"Don't try to divert me Finola. I'm not a child. I've made up my mind."

"Why are you telling me then? If you have already decided."

"I need your help. I want you to persuade Rory to allow me and my tenants to join with him. My *uirrithe* have gone already. He'll only have a small band, too. We'd command well together. What he lacks in experience, I'll make up for."

"What you lack in energy, he'll make up for," she finished for him. "Father you're well over sixty. Will you be able for the hardship?"

"I'll ignore that." Cormac's colour rose. "Sir Walter Carew is older than me and is still active."

That puts you in your place Finola, she thought. "When do you expect this meeting to take place?"

"As soon as a battle site in arranged, Mountjoy and O'Neill will have a confrontation. It's inevitable."

"You want to be in the middle of it."

"I'm going to be. With or without your help."

On the morning of the twenty-fourth of September, 1601 Rory was sitting at the table in Ennistoomey eating breakfast. The early light shone through the narrow window and picked out the rings on the wood of the table. Absent-mindedly he counted the circles. He was up to twenty already. The trestle was only nine years younger than him. It would soon fall.

Art interrupted his count. "'Tis Feardorcha with a message from Cormac. Waitin' at the door he is."

The messenger followed Art inside. "Landed they have. Three days ago. The Spanish with their fleet." He swelled with enthusiasm. "That's all I know."

Art's face shone with delight. Rory jumped up from the table, his idle counting forgotten. He began to pace the room, his hands behind his back. "Do you know where they landed?" He stopped pacing.

"Upon my soul I don't, but Cormac is thinking 'tis to Sligo or Killala they'll come. 'Tis hopin' he's right I am. If Mountjoy treks to meet them, 'tis unprotected the north will be. We'll find our lost power." This was a long speech for someone nicknamed 'dark man.'

Rory said, "And if Mountjoy stays where he is, the Irish will rally around the Spanish. Both armies will attack him in the North." He looked earnestly at Feardorcha. "I would still prefer if they came ashore in Tyrconnell or somewhere even more north, say, Carlingford. The two armies could join with less effort."

"Yes. As long as they stay out of Munster," the messenger answered.

Rory agreed. The president of Munster had diminished the province. The Spanish could not count on support there.

Three days later he learned that his worst fears had come to pass. The fleet had anchored at Kinsale, a fishing village on the southern seaboard. Their leader Don Juan del Aquila had issued a proclamation to the Catholics of Munster imploring them to support the Catholic cause. But few lords had come forward to help.

Brian had told him this when he called to Ennistoomey on his way back to Tyrone after collecting ten horses from Mulahinsa. He had six men with him. Remaining on his mount, he had shouted down to Rory. "The Spaniards are two hundred miles away, in Kinsale." Under his wool mantle he gave a shiver. "It is winter. Ulster is over-run and will be defenceless if we go to help."

He looked more disturbed than Rory had ever seen him.

"We're sick at heart at the prospect of walking from tip to toe of the country, but we have to consider it. If we stay in Ulster, we'll never again be able to look for assistance from Spain." He turned to ride away. Then he looked back at Rory. "At last your time has come," he shouted.

A few days later Cormac stood in the doorway of the garrison. "Mountjoy mustered as many soldiers as he could and marched south to lay siege to the Spanish. O'Neill will have to take an army to Kinsale now."

"Come in and close the door," Rory told him from his seated position by the table in the common room. "It's freezing out."

"I've somebody with me," Cormac said. His voice held an impatient note. "I'll warm myself by the fire in the other chamber and let you talk."

When the 'someone' stepped inside, the arctic wind blowing from outside ceased.

At first Rory had difficulty finding his voice. "Finola," he said then. In spite of the cold, she stood before him bareheaded with a dark mantle thrown across her shoulders. If only he had expected her, he could have prepared. He stood and grabbed her hand.

Her withdrawal was swift. She backed away.

He repelled her, he thought. She still blamed him for *Oileán na Stoirme*. His guilt, alive like an ulcer, festered again. "I'm sorry Finola," he said. "If I could change what happened on the island, I would." Her eyes fell away from his. He felt the agony the same as when he heard the news of the deaths for the first time. "I killed him. Richard Dolman. I killed him myself. It was

331

the only action I could take."

"George should not have given him the command," she said. "If George were unfit for the responsibility, you should have taken over." She did not raise her voice. Her face was expressionless, her eyes fierce.

He felt her control slip as he watched the blood drain from her face and her eyes turn disconcertingly blank. "I found them," she said, her tone now rising. "Andrew Óg was in a cave, dead in Niall's arms. Blood was everywhere. He ..."

Rory looked into her dark face, tense with suffering. He leaned towards her and took her in his arms.

She began to shake but after a minute she gave herself up to his embrace.

His own ghosts reared their heads - his imprisonment, George's suicide, an impending war. He wanted to weep with her.

Then, as if possessed by a demon, she squirmed, twisting and pushing to be free. Slackening his grip on her waist, he took hold of her hands. "Finola." He caressed her name. "Finola," he said again.

She swallowed and smiled through her tears, weakly at first. "May I have my hands back now please?" she said.

"That sounds more like the old Finola." Rory was smiling now too.

"Enough sentiment," she said. "I came to talk about my father. He wants to fight the English. I want you to take him with you."

"Do you want to kill the man?"

"There been enough killing in my family."

He felt his cheeks get hot. "I did not mean ..."

"I'm afraid Cormac will die if he doesn't march with you. He wants to make up for what he thinks was Ireland's biggest mistake. You know his *Surrender and re-grant* refrain better than anyone. Give him this chance. It may be his last."

Rory pored over the calculations by the light of the candle. The cover on his pallet lay in a crumbled heap, damp from perspiration, in spite of the chilled air. No matter how often he did the sums, it amounted to the same.

They would have to walk about two hundred miles to get to Kinsale. If he allotted ten days to the journey, they would walk an average of twenty miles a day. If it took much longer, they may as well stay where they were; they would miss the battle.

But such a journey in the dead of winter, he thought, is foolhardy. Ulster is at its weakest surrounded as it is by English forts. What choice had they? As Brian said, they would never again get help from abroad if they did not go to Kinsale. Finola's work would have gone for nothing, if there were nobody there to help del Aquila.

He told Eoin's men of his decision. Standing in the cold he watched the various reactions. Some just shuffled away indifferently. Others remained and talked to each other in grim whispers. The younger men smiled. Many of them had never been outside the lands of Glenone. They were born here, lived here, and were it not for this lucky chance would have died without seeing beyond it.

He gave them a week to prepare. A messenger went to Cormac to tell him to assemble his men and convene in Glenone a week later.

As the days rolled by, amidst bedlam and confusion, Rory had little time for thought. The men sought him out continually with their worried questioning.

"Will the English attack us on the way?"

"Will we have enough food?"

"Do you think I should go?"

"Do you know the way?"

After a few days, the different voices merged into one. The men did not expect an answer. They were content that he listened to their doubts.

A peasant pleaded to bring his wife with him on the journey. "Twenty years on the same pallet your honour. How could I get a wink without her?"

"War involves sacrifice," he said, realising the moment the words passed his lips how preachy he sounded.

By now Sir Walter Carew would know of his treasonous activities. He felt a pang of regret, not at his decision, but at the need to hurt Sir Walter further. With Anne's desertion, Jane's unhappiness, and George's death, he had been through a lot of turmoil. There would be a lot more hurt before this war was over.

At ten o'clock on Saturday of the following week, the soldiers gathered outside the garrison. Rory had mustered one hundred and twenty men. Cormac came with twenty men of his own. There was one kerne to every farmer, ploughman, churl, and cow keeper. No professional *Gallóglach* marched with them.

Each man carried a rolled blanket tied with cord at both ends over their backs. They also had another bundle in which they carried a spare tunic, woollen socks and a pair of frieze trews. All the men carried a pewter mug on their belts. A horseman had to carry an extra set of shoes for his mount.

Rory doled out powder and shot to those who had firearms and put the remainder in a cartridge box and left it in the supply wagon with the meat, meal, bread, butter, salt, and four days' ration of water. The wagon, drawn by two horses, would have a hard time making it on the rough ground. They would be in trouble if it snowed.

As they moved out, a bevy of women from the huts came to meet them. One woman placed a wooden box in Rory's hands. "'Tisn't to let you go without anything from Glenone we will." The box contained a rooster and six hens. "Strangle and boil them is what you'll do when you need them. They're good and fat. 'Tis no harm starvation will do them."

"What's with you woman? They're me only hens," her churl husband scolded.

"'Tis waiting I'll be when you come back" she whispered. "'Tis more we'll raise."

A rooster and six hens would not add much extra weight to the supply wagon. Rory had a feeling the fowl would not last long.

"Winter weather has one advantage for provisions," Cormac said. "Our meat will stay fresh."

They had forty horses primarily for use in battle or to carry the wounded. One of them was for Cormac because of his age and lameness. The men had even begun to nickname him Cormac *bacach*. Six more were pack horses who would take turns pulling the supplies.

Art and four other lads were put in charge of the animals' feed and water. They would have less to do than when they were at home where they had to groom the horses every day. On this journey the horses would need to hold on to the natural grease that kept them warm and dry.

Rory fixed a method of food distribution. He wondered if he had been right to abandon the idea of letting each man carry his own. It would have been easier to manage, but it could mean that some men who were more circumspect than others would ration themselves and have food when everyone else starved. That could lead to discord, perhaps conflict among them.

"It is the quartermaster's responsibility to see that each man gets an equal share of everything or nothing. A situation where some men get bigger rations than others is quick to cause dissent," Rory explained to the men he appointed to distribute the provisions.

As they snaked out over the black bogs like a multicoloured ribbon, the men were silent and grim-faced. When they passed a peasant's hut, the atmosphere lightened; a woman, ten children around her, bade a farewell to her marching husband, "The divil go with you Virgin O'Doherty," she shouted. "'Twon't be carrying this winter I'll be." She crossed herself. "Thanks be to the Holy Mother."

Though he laughed with the rest, Rory was doing his best to hide his trepidation about the future.

Chapter Nine

Though his army was small, home-grown and straggling, Rory felt proud to be part of a common cause. All over Ulster men had left their lands and their homes to risk everything. This he felt sure would be the final contest between Tudor England and Gaelic Ireland. He longed for the time when the Irish would be able as a people to mould their own destiny, on their own terms, at their own pace.

Ironically, his grandfather Con Maguire had accepted the terms of *Surrender and re-grant*. His father had fought a civil war against Eoin to defend his claim to Glenone under the *Law of Primogeniture,* English law. Yet a Gaelic victory could ensure his stewardship of the land. There was nobody living who could claim a closer kinship to Eoin Maguire than a nephew. So, even if the chiefs re-introduced the Law of the *Deirbfhine,* he would be eligible for election by the clan. His debt to his dead family would be fulfilled in a way nobody would have countenanced.

They would suffer a lot before then, he thought, as he looked at his makeshift army, unequipped to face a siege and newly trained for a pitched battle.

After the first day's walking, some stragglers had disappeared. "They're going home," Cormac said to him. "They will still be able to find their way back. We will survive if more don't follow."

Two days more into their tramp, they passed through *Bealach an Mhaighre* the famous Gap of the North. Rory had heard that it was the *most arduous passage in Ireland*. Mountjoy had forged through it in May of 1599. If an Englishman could do it, albeit in spring, they could.

They were lucky. Although the snow was deep on the causeway and frost covered the bogs on either side, they managed to keep their footing and get the wagon through. Despite the bitter cold, Rory's spirit brightened after their triumph. They bypassed Dundalk and marched towards Westmeath. The men joked and sparred with each other and boasted of their energy.

He felt at one with them; he learned their names, where they came from, and what they did on their estate. He already knew many of Eoin Maguire's men, but he was just getting to know Cormac's.

Along the route women came out of their hovels and shouted, "O'Neill abú."

"Enjoy it while you can," Cormac advised. "If the Irish fail at Kinsale, they'll cheer for Mountjoy on our way back."

Rory started writing a diary along the route. He had no paper but he wrote on the margins of a volume of Livy which he had taken with him from Sir Walter's library. Since his stay in prison, he had become interested in the history of civilisations. Following his prison rumination on the work of Cambrensis and from reading London born Edmund Campion's *History of Ireland* he felt strongly that Gaels should start writing about their own country.

Wherever or whenever he got time, when the men rested sitting on tree trunks by the wayside, he jotted down passing impressions of the journey. At night by the light of the camp fire he'd add a few more lines, always commenting on the morale of the men. Although he knew he was considered odd, he persevered.

One day when he was writing, Cormac exclaimed in fake admiration, "What a deed it would be if we win the war and you become renowned as the first person to write an account of the march to Kinsale."

"If we die of starvation, I will not even be able to finish this half-written account." Suddenly mindful that what he said was true, he added, "I'm troubled, Cormac. We used too many provisions at the start. The first of the hens is on for the boil. I did not expect the country to be so ravaged."

They foraged in the fields for food. Of the cattle left alive by Mountjoy, Cormac said, "They are too thin to kill for meat. Leave them to the women. They might be able to make some use of them."

They passed through the south midland area of Laois and Offaly, what used to be O'More and O'Connor country before they had been dispossessed of their lands in the first plantation of 1556.

Children along the roadways picked seeds and whatever else they could from the winter bushes. The women and old men standing at the hovels called to them as they passed. "'Tis to trample and burn our crops the English did. Our men folk are gone with O'Neill and that captain Tyrell. God save and keep ye all and help ye win."

At night they lit fires, took off their mittens and brogues and toasted their feet. Rory's fingers and toes were a mass of red lumps that itched.

"'Tis chilblains you've got. From the dampness and the heat. Better to keep your hands and feet away from the fire entirely," Dara told him what he knew already.

As rations got smaller and smaller, the men appraised their neighbour's shares; they rolled dice for larger portions and then squabbled over them. Some stopped eating their rations in the evening, saving them for the next day. After their day's trudge, they chose to lie down hungry, wrapped in their blankets. Each morning they ate the beef or meal they should have had the night before, hoping it would give them extra energy for the day's tramp ahead.

They dragged their feet and prayed the wagon would not topple. Midday they stopped to eat a crust of bread. They had travelled seventy five miles, less than they expected.

As they plodded through the midlands, snow laden winds whipped about them. Underneath their trews, their legs were numb. Cormac's horse slipped and broke a leg. The nags drawing the food wagon slithered on the frosty surface and lagged. The remaining horses struggled through the deepening drifts, six of them lame.

"'Tis new shoes they are needin'," Art told Rory. "The wall of the hooves has got too big. 'Tis to trim them we'll have to. But it's too cold our hands are to do it."

Through the haze of white, they saw a clump of trees ahead. "We'll camp on the edge of these," Cormac spoke urgently. "That way we won't be targets if there are English lurking. The group is despondent. Their enthusiasm has waned. We should give them what's left of the fowl." He made an attempt at levity. "We don't want some goose to desert and bring the rest of the gaggle with him."

The men wrapped cloths around their footwear to protect them from twigs and boles. Yet many got frostbite on their toes. A man called Fiachra had frostbite almost from the beginning. Rory heard him call "Brigid" in his sleep and went to his side.

"Brigid," the man was saying again, "my wife Sire. Sure don't you know her? A servant in the kitchen at Mulahinsa she is. Knew you as a child she did." His face was as pale as marble. "'Tis burning off me these toes are."

Rory unbound Fiachra's rags. The five toes of his left foot had changed in colour from white to red.

When Rory told Cormac about them, he said, "I've seen damage like this before. We must get him off his feet. Otherwise, he'll lose the toes, perhaps the foot."

They made a type of litter out of branches for him in the form of a chair. That way it would need only two men to carry it through the narrow passes. Four would be needed to lug a stretcher.

Rory checked Fiachra's leg each night. The colour of his toes had changed again. This time the affected areas were purple and blisters were forming. His speech had become slurred. He complained of dizziness. Still they carried him onwards.

Each day his condition worsened. The blisters burst and each evening more pus replaced what Rory had squeezed out that morning.

"They have to come off," Cormac whispered at his elbow. "We've no choice."

"We'll wait one more day."

That evening Fiachra said, "'Tisn't to feel them at all, I can now." Beneath his mantle he looked weak and emaciated.

"We should act before it gets worse," Cormac said.

Reluctantly, Rory had to agree. He boiled water over the camp fire.

"I'll do it," Cormac offered.

As he held the knife in his hand, Rory knew that Cormac would be unable to hold it steady.

Fiachra lay on his blanket, his eyes balls of pain.

"Get the whiskey," Rory ordered Art. "For unforeseen happenings only," he said as he took the vessel from him and gave it to Fiachra. "Drink this."

As Fiachra drank deeply, Rory looked at the yellow pus sitting like cream on the skin of the toes. "Like rotten eggs that's what they are," Fiachra said. Smells like them, too. Take them off."

Rory's stomach quaked.

Cormac knelt on the ground his knife poised but his hand

shook. Rory knew he was torn between pride and prudence and was relieved when he said, "Rory, in my humble opinion, you'd do it better."

He felt skin, with its dead underlying muscle and bone, under the knife and tried to make believe that he was cutting a chine of beef. There was only a trickle of blood. Fiachra, intoxicated, remained still.

"May Jeysus guide your hand," a man said.

"Amen."

Rory found the encouragement comforting. He felt only bone. The knife was incapable of cutting through. Someone produced a hand tool, used for cutting wood.

"Boiling water. Quick," Cormac ordered, anticipating Rory's command. He cut quickly.

Cormac dumped the mixture of black skin and bone into a sack.

Rory washed the wound with the remainder of the alcohol and tied it tight with white strips.

Cormac tried to dig a hole in the snow for the sack, but it was too frozen so he covered it with leaves.

"Thank God he is still unconscious," Rory said, "let us hope he stays that way until morning."

Two hours later, Rory woke to check on him. He was still in the same position, but his heart had stopped, due to a combination of blood loss and cold, he guessed. The men needed their sleep, Rory thought. They would know of his death soon enough. Tears sprung to his eyes as he remembered Brigid's kindness the night they brought him home after the calamity in the forest. Next morning Cormac covered the body with snow and leaves as he had done with the severed toes. Liam led them in a 'Hail Mary.'

Rory followed the route Brian had recommended. They were wary especially when they passed through narrow glens, but they failed to hear a single shot or see a single English soldier. Aodh Rua O'Donnell was to proceed through Connaught and Limerick. O'Neill himself through Leinster. The further south they got the more they expected to be engaged in fighting with Mountjoy's men.

He hopes to divert some of Mountjoy's army, Brian had written of O'Neill's intention to attack the Pale on the way. Rory hoped he had succeeded, they needed good news.

One night when Rory took out his quill to write his diary, his hands shook. Though he concentrated with all his might and bit his lip to centre his energy on the simple task of writing one word, he made only a wavy line. He tried again but the pen fell from his numbed fingers. "Our enemy is the cold," he said to Cormac.

The men refused to change out of their clothes though each man had a second set of apparel. They couldn't bring themselves to bare all in woods and swamps rigid with ice. "'Tis too tired I am to change even if 'twas to freeze my balls off I wanted," a usually compliant Dara told him. "We know each other's smells by now, so what's the difference?"

As the eighth day of their trek began, Rory was washing his face in a fast flowing stream when he overheard a man called Calvach complain, "Working for the English that Maguire is - the spit of his father. He's leading us astray. 'Tis dead from tiredness we'll be before we do any fighting."

Rory ignored the comment but all that day he found it difficult to dismiss what he had heard. Later that evening he decided to pass around the only map he possessed. The place names on it were barely legible and most of the men were unable to read anyway. But as he saw each in turn bend over the flimsy parchment, their rude faces full of interest, he knew he had done right.

"'Tis only fair he show us. Not a soul can mouth then," Calvach said by way of an apology.

They marched on, the hailstones striking like needles at their faces. In Tipperary they crossed the river Suir, bridged with ice. From there they marched south and in another two days reached Bandon.

They came to an incline, a wide path through a forest filled with snow, which was powdery and deep. Horses struggled to drag the supply wagon but were unable to pull it forward. The wheels stuck solid in the bank of snow. With heaves and curses, Rory strained with the rest to get it clear.

"There are so little supplies in it, it is hardly worth the trouble," he said to Cormac.

"Think of the return journey. We might be able to collect

some food along the way."

They harnessed fresh horses to the wagon and, by pulling and lifting, managed to get it over the brow of the hill. From there they headed for Kinsale. As they neared their journey's end, none of them was interested in conversation. Their hands, chapped by the cold, trembled as they untied their bundles. Cormac was the only one who voiced an opinion on the forthcoming conflict and then only to Rory. "I'm too afraid of the deserting habit of the Irish to say anything," he admitted. "I don't want to awaken any doubts. We mustn't lose any more." In a low voice he asked Rory what he expected at the end of their journey.

Rory wished he would stop asking him the same question. He could only give him the same answer each time. "If only I knew Cormac, if only I knew."

The journey had taken eleven days in all. They were the last to arrive. The others turned out to welcome them with cheers and smiles.

"We need all the men we can get," Tyrell, the Irish captain, assured Rory in a welcoming voice. "Mountjoy is a crafty divil."

All the Irish divisions were weak and dispirited from their long trek and food shortages. Disease and lack of provisions had weakened the Spanish and Mountjoy's men as well. They had become edgy. Since they had met up with the rest, Rory's group had turned into a quarrelling ragged mob. When they rose from their watery ditches each morning, they chorused, "'Tis sick of waiting we are." They grumbled for the rest of the day.

"In my humble opinion, O'Neill should attack," Cormac said to Rory. "Why are we delaying? If there is no action soon, the men will desert."

"He should wait," Rory said. "We are on one flank of the English army and the Spaniards are on the other. Hem them in and starve them into submission would be my advice. It would be rash to fight a pitched battle. O'Neill has avoided an open clash for nigh on six years. Can we not hold out for six weeks?"

"Sensible Rory," Cormac's tone was scathing. "That way we could all starve."

Cormac's health had failed since the march. He would not let him goad him. Sensible or not, it was prudent to wait; events so far showed that it worked. Throughout the war O'Neill, because he lacked superiority in armaments and numbers, had chosen his ground carefully. Never had he pursued or attacked an English army who had not harassed or thwarted him. If delay could bring about victory, they should wait or else withdraw.

"There's a council of war tonight," Cormac said. "It will decide."

A day later, on the morning of the twenty-fourth of December 1601, Rory, his worst fears realised, found himself moving with the Ulstermen's main contingent from their location at Belgooly towards the English lines. Tyrell commanded the van of Meath, Munster and Leinster men. The rear was a mixture of all three kingdoms.

"We are going to take them by surprise," Cormac exulted as he limped along beside Rory, excitement in every stride. "Happy Christmas."

Chapter Ten

He must stay by Cormac's side. The old man would not turn back whatever the reasoning. As Rory saw a nobleman in a suit of plate armour, he regretted that he had made no effort to procure one for Cormac. But that was not the reason his heart was beating painfully against his ribs. It was because he felt this battle was all wrong. Since the Council he had tried to understand why O'Neill had allowed O'Donnell and the Spaniards persuade him to attack.

The sight of horses galloping across the squashy mud in their direction interrupted his thoughts. Mountjoy's cavalry were charging the foot-soldiers. Rory grabbed Cormac by the hand and dragged him just in time from under the horses' hooves. Cormac's bad ankle gave way. He stumbled and fell in the dirt. "Get up," Rory begged. "Get up." The urgency of his command harshened his tone.

Cormac's raised his face towards him. Though it was covered in slime Rory could see his anguished expression. Bending over him, he put his arms around his waist and clasped his body against his own. Like a shepherd carrying an ailing lamb, he hoisted him to the safety of a dyke and turned to view the state of the battle. The relief he felt that Cormac was out of danger dissipated when he saw how the English horse was crippling the Irish.

Calvach, the peasant who had accused him of leading them astray, fell, a ball through his throat; blood spurted from the hole in his neck. The portion of Irish foot taking the heaviest attack dissolved and disbanded.

Rushing back into the fray, Rory shouted to the Irish line, "Stand and fight." He did not know what else to say. Two of the divisions held the bombardment, but when the English came at them from the other side, they, too, ran.

"Where the hell are the Spanish?"

"What has happened to the men from Spain?"

"No wonder the English defeated the Armada."

"Did they come at all?"

"They'll slaughter the lot of us."

The unanswered questions sounded the tumult of defeat. The Irish centre attempted to hold its ground. The English killed all but a few score; the rest were in disarray. The English horse gave chase. At random, they slaughtered the Irish. The battle ended before it had truly begun.

Rory was unable to stay still. He threw more bracken on top of the peat. In the half-light, the camp fire glowed sullenly. "Ten days after the battle and I am still trying to make sense of what happened," he said to Brian opposite him. "It lasted no more than an hour. Between the Spanish army and our own, we had more men than the English. Yet they crushed us. They came from Spain and refused to fire a shot. It is hard to believe that yesterday Don Juan del Aquila surrendered and went back to Spain."

"I should rejoice," Brian said, warming his hands. "The English will curb the Law of the *Deirbfhine* permanently now. It will make sure that the elder son will inherit the land."

There was so much bitterness and so much irony in Brian's tone that Rory felt his own despair worsen. "Yes." He paused. "Brian, you told me once that the English would want our lands for themselves? That that was why we had to fight."

"I remember. I still believe it. I hope I'm wrong."

Rory felt the smell of peat mix with the sickening odour of defeat in his nostrils. What if Brian were right? What if the English stole their lands? He had to get his band back to Ulster alive. For what? His thoughts roamed back over the years of the confiscations. He felt afraid. Not just of the journey.

Then he thought of the scenes following the battle. Mountjoy's men waving white flags wrested from the Spanish, each with its red saltire, the crying of the wounded, Munster lords hurrying to Mountjoy to congratulate him on his victory.

If he were to see the north of the country, he knew that Ulstermen would be doing the same. O'Neill, prince of the north, had fallen. Their hope was gone. His only option was to retreat with what remained of his army, to inaccessible Ulster. "We will head home tomorrow. A further delay will gain us nothing," he said.

"I will remain with you," Brian said. "I'll look out for my father and help you get this despairing bunch back to Ulster."

"No sign of Shane?" Rory kept his expression deliberately impassive as he asked the question. He had not forgiven him his desertion of George. As he noticed Brian looking at him strangely, he added, "I hope he is safe."

Brian's face shadowed. "Shane will be disappointed at the defeat."

"Like all of Ireland."

"But he had no interest in politics previous to this. Suddenly, he spent all his time writing about it." Brian put his hand to his temple as if keeping his thoughts together. "For no obvious reason the English became his arch-enemies."

"Perhaps he read about the Desmond Rebellions," Rory said. "We are all entitled to a change of heart."

"Whatever he read, he believed that the Irish would win and we would have no interference from England again."

"That's what I hoped, too."

"This was different," Brian muttered.

There was nowhere to lie down. No dry place. As he lay in the muck, Rory mulled over recent occurrences until he felt he had an accurate picture of their situation. Thirty-five dead and eight injured from Glenone. Six dead from Mulahinsa and eight injured. One man had a ball in his head. Another lost an eye and had plugged the suppurating socket with rags. Three had knife wounds and one man had slipped and broken his arm. He wondered how many would be left after they had trekked back to Ulster.

Rory left Kinsale with a line of men defeated and footsore and without supplies. "We will walk as far as we can. If we can find our footing in the dark, we will. There is no need to preserve our strength for a battle," he told them. They found the countryside even more desolate than on the downward journey. O'Neill's returning army had picked the country clean. "Everyone will have to forage for food. There will be nettles. We will boil them and drink the soup. Any questions?"

They sank into a routine that felt comforting in its monotony. Each man foraged the wasted fields for food. They took turns carrying the wounded. The most they covered any day were five to ten miles, their usual was five.

Cormac was slow on his feet. He kept referring to "this damn ankle." When he lay down at night, he coughed constantly. Often he sat upright and threw up phlegm that left blood stains on the ground. His face was bony. He did not gibe at anyone anymore. The only time he showed vitality was when he talked of Maeve and the prospect of seeing her again. "I have had no woman but her since our refugees from the Armada left," he repeated in a flat tone like an incantation. He always added, "When will we be home?"

The best of each day was when the men came back from their scavenger hunts with an assortment of food. They collected honey, garlic, hazel nuts and once a scrawny cow that stumbled behind them for two days, yielded half a gallon of milk and then died. They hacked her up and ate each part of her carcass with relish. "If we can eat pig's crubeens, we can eat cow's hooves," Rory said when they reached the end of the animal. Boiled for a half day and flavoured with the remains of the honey, they were still inedible. Some days they could not find any ground or branches dry enough to light a fire, so they gnawed at the raw meat.

Rory lay beside Cormac staring upwards. Brian lay on the other side. To make it easier for the scouts to protect them, the men slept in small groups within a quarter of a mile of each other. There was no moon, but stars dotted the cold sky. He tried not to think of the hunger pangs in his stomach; he could feel his ribs protruding beneath his tunic and his backbone almost touching the ground. A hundred miles to go! If only they had won. They would still be cold and hungry, but their minds would be at peace.

A noise on the edge of the brush caused him to sit up. Perhaps a bramble had moved in the breeze. He listened again. Something was creeping towards the spot where they were lying. Where were the scouts? The ridge of grass sheltering them obstructed his view. Grabbing his arquebus, he held it to his shoulder.

A figure slid along the ground towards where they were lying. Then he stopped, lay back on the grass, and primed his gun.

Rory leapt to his feet, his firearm heavy in his shaking hands. By a supreme act of will, he flexed his fingers on the trigger and pulled with all his might. In the stillness the shot sundered the air.

Cormac woke, coughing. Brian sat and looked questioningly at Rory.

"I don't know why anybody would be trying to shoot at us," Rory said. "I hope I have scared him away." He walked the perimeter of the camp. The guards were like horses, asleep standing up. He shook them. "Stay awake," he warned. "There is an intruder about." As he issued the warning, he wondered why anybody would want to attack them now, after the battle.

He felt relieved to be approaching the borders of Ulster at last with the ragged remains of his army. His joy was short lived. On the road to Mulahinsa, a woman screamed out at them from her hovel, "All for nothing. My man died at the Battle of the Yellow Ford for nothing and now 'tis starving we are." Other women came and threw volleys of sods around their heads. Children joined in, pelting them with stones.

They began to avoid places of habitation and chose isolated paths. The contrast with the tumultuous farewell they received on their way to the battle dampened their already low spirits. Now the hush was so profound that the disturbance a short while previously appeared unthinkable, the war itself impossible. They had twelve miles to go.

But there was no repetition of the previous attack. He had killed or maimed a free-booter, Rory decided. That was all.

Chapter Eleven

Although invasion and calamity were all he envisaged from here on in, Rory felt happier when they crossed into Ulster. Exhaustion, hunger and cold plus the need to trudge on byways and hostile routes had added to their hardship. Now, as he recognised landmarks and realised they were nearing home, he smiled in hope. A spring came in the men's step. They would soon meet their families; they would not die in a strange province.

The air was soft with impending rain. He looked towards Cormac, walking beside him, huddled in his mantle, water running from his eyes, his clothes hanging in bunches on his body. "We will head for Mulahinsa first," he said to Brian. "It is better that we get your father to a warm place. The journey has exhausted him."

Rory had barely finished his sentence when a shot rang out and a ball flew past his head, leaving a ringing in his ears.

He pulled Cormac to the ground. Brian and the rest of the men flung themselves down with him, keeping their heads low.

The shot echoed in the hills. After a few minutes of lying prostrate, Brian said, "I can't cower any longer. Let's see if we can uncover the culprit."

They searched every tree, every bush, and every furze and found nothing but a rabbit's burrow. "Whoever it is, is clever," Rory said. "But we have little choice but to plod on."

At Carran, Rory was astonished when Shane appeared out of nowhere, but felt too tired to react. He must have left his company to find them. His hip bones stuck out and a bandage, tied around his left shoulder, covered a wound. He resolved to be civil to him.

Shane endured his father's embrace for a few seconds before pushing him away. The spark in Cormac's eyes quenched and he returned to his sickly state. Shane nodded towards Rory and Brian. "You will travel the rest of the way with us?" Brian enquired. Silently Shane stood to one side.

"We'll rest awhile," Rory suggested.

A low grumbling began among the men. They were anxious to be getting on their way. Brian addressed them. "The O'Hanlon tenant soldiers who so desire can disperse to their homes," he instructed. "God bless ye all." He looked questioningly at Rory and when he nodded assent, he addressed the Maguire contingent in a similar manner. Some of them grunted as they retrieved their few belongings and shuffled away. Many stayed. Shane frowned. Brian looked towards his brother. "Because of Cormac we will be moving slower. They've endured enough."

Shane scowled and strode away from the group.

"I feel shivery," Cormac sounded sad. "We will soon have him at Mulahinsa." Brian gestured towards his father huddled in his mantle. "Old age has thinned his blood," he said in a whisper. "Sleep will restore him. I'll throw this around him." He shrugged himself out of his mantle and wrapped it over the one Cormac was already wearing.

Rory felt sudden tears well in his eyes. Not wanting to display his heartache at Cormac's decline, the men's dispersal, and now Shane's re-appearance, he yearned to be alone. He walked towards a clump of dark woods. It was suddenly very quiet.

In the middle of a grassy patch an old goat lay on her side. From the throes of death her yellow eyes looked at him. She snorted as he approached and tried to rise but failed. Then she put her head down and lay stiff.

Her death reminded him of his own mortality and he felt strangely troubled. He had killed Richard Dolman in a fight. For ten days he had been in prison, had walked the country from one end to the other, seen men die and his countrymen defeated. Yet the demise of an old nanny moved him.

He knew he should take her back with him and skin her but they did not have far to go. After covering her with furze, he walked away, his thoughts filled with death, old age, defeat and Cormac.

Suddenly he stopped and stood still. When he heard uproar from the others, he sensed horror. Smoke from the fire curled through the air. He drew his sword and walked steadily back towards the camp. The trees thinned, the voices became louder and he saw Cormac lying on the ground, Brian's mantle askew around him. A trail of blood drained from his stomach. By his side, on his knees, Brian was trying to staunch the trickle.

Cormac opened his eyes a moment and stared at the sky. Brian stopped what he was doing and sobbed. Then he reached out to his father and gently closed his eyelids.

On the other side of the corpse, two retainers were holding Shane captive.

Brian rocked himself in grief.

What had happened? Rory wondered. Why had Shane a bloody knife clutched in his hand? He stared at him for a long moment doubting first his eyes, then his ears. Shane was speaking.

Dazed he listened to the unfamiliar voice, punctuated by hesitations.

"I didn't mean to kill him. He was my father. Even when he slept with Molly it was her I pitched from the landing bay. Antonio didn't deserve to die, but he was my defence." He looked at Brian and raised his voice, "But you, you should be dead. I thought it was you. Why was he wearing your mantle?"

What he was witnessing was impossible. Rory was immobilised.

Shane began to shudder. In a less violent tone, he said, "Shock did bring my voice back after all." He grimaced as if the effort to talk pained him. "Now people will treat me with respect, not like a simpleton. Everyday, I've imagined this happening." He gripped his throat. "Murrough laughed at me when I tried to touch him. Then he loved Finola. Not for long though. I made sure of that. If I had been *tánaiste* as was my right, he would have loved me." His voice was low and agonised.

Rory looked at him in silence, trying to absorb what he was saying. His expression looked as ferocious as the wolf that had maimed him.

Shane gestured towards Cormac's corpse and said in a parched croak, "He should have stayed with the Law of the *Deirbfhine*. I didn't mean to kill him. Now, I'm glad he's dead."

"The people would have elected me, not Brian. He is the elder son, so he will get everything. Did you hear him order the tenants to go home and my father not even dead?" He pointed at Brian, his eyes glittering with malice. "He is my brother, but I'd choke him to death with my bare hands, even now, to give George his garden."

Vaguely it registered with Rory that Shane was ignorant of George's suicide. Unable to listen to any more, he nodded to the kerne to take Shane away.

Brian's face was contorted in grief as he wrapped Cormac's body in the mantle that had caused his death.

The sun, that had managed to shine feebly for the first time in months, succumbed to inertia behind a cloud. Weak from hunger, Rory and Brian slowly broke branches off the trees, and bending and twisting the boughs, they fastened them into a bier. Their hands bled as they forced the timber to do their bidding. Neither of them spoke.

Next they prised Shane from his keepers and dragged him to where a branch hung low over the path.

Shane did not speak on his way to the gallows and his eyes looked vacant. Like a mad dog, saliva dripped from his mouth. When he reached the tree, he waved his hands as if acknowledging his subjects. "By Brehon law, I should be chief and not Brian," he declared. A churl came and tied his hands behind his back.

The rope appeared, looped and ready. Shane's face lit up with the smile of a fanatic. Brian doubled the rope around the overhanging branch. Then coldly he put it around his brother's neck.

Rory took turns with Brian to draw Shane off the ground. It took about ten minutes for the choking, gurgling sounds to stop and they had throttled the life out of him.

Rory was reminded of Cormac killing Padraic, the servant who gave Matthew the poisoned mead. He had done a deed as dirty.

They both drank deeply from the *aqua vitae*, proffered to them by Art. After the thaw, the earth was moist so the grave was easy to dig. They placed the stones to one side; Rory helped Brian put Shane three feet down; it could have been wheat or corn they were sowing. They threw the muck back into the hole. Then, as the light deserted them, they took the stretcher and carried Cormac the lonely miles home.

Chapter Twelve

Rory helped lower the coffin into the grave and watched Brian shovel clay on top. The Cormac he loved was no more. Finola stood opposite. His eyes held hers. Her tormented expression was a measure of her suffering. He had been too busy reliving the grotesque scenes of the past few days to recognise that she was also mourning the loss of her father and of Shane.

Maeve stood beside her and looked in anguish at the closing grave. Brian had told her that a man, tormented from hunger, had killed Cormac. She believed him; she had seen many such scenes herself; since the ending of the Irish wars, Mountjoy had resumed the plundering and pillage that went on before the Battle of Kinsale. Yet it was hard for her to absorb that a man she had been faithful to for forty years was no longer living. She gazed down at his grave and said in a spiritless whisper, "There is a remedy for all things but death."

Rory felt planted in the ground. He stood again between two corpses on a heath. Thoughts pounded in and out of his mind so fleetingly that he failed to inspect any of them. From the jumble in his head, one thought recurred. Finola had entrusted him with the safekeeping of her father and he had failed her. Closing his eyes, he resolved to keep secret the circumstances of Cormac's demise; he was finding it difficult to believe them himself. Shane's words echoed, "I'd choke him to death with my bare hands, if it would give George his garden." His life could never be as it was. How could he survive the years with his secret?

Cormac's regret at his father's acceptance of English succession laws had nurtured Shane's budding discontent. Though Shane's situation was more complicated, he felt unable to banish an image of himself as a boy of ten, believing mistakenly in his father's infallibility, determined to repossess Glenone. As he thought of Cormac stabbed to death by his son, he wondered if any plot of soil in any country in the world was worth it.

He had no regrets for the execution. The Brehon law, which decreed that a murderer had to compensate the victim's family, would be fully obsolete now that the English were in control. How could Shane have compensated his own family? It would have been a beheading at Tyburn for him and a double tragedy for Maeve and Finola.

Shane had said that Murrough had loved Finola but that he had dealt with the difficulty; he hoped that did not mean he had murdered somebody else.

When he opened his eyes, he saw Finola walking towards him. His palms perspired. She took him by the hand and led him away from the grave. An air of unreality surrounded him as they took a short cut back to the castle.

As she slipped a ring from her finger, compassion and indecision displayed themselves on her face. Then she pulled him into the bawn. "Rather ghostly this," she said. "Reliving the past!"

He thought of it as the scene of his youthful munificence when he had given her his bow and arrow. If the expression on her face were anything to judge by, she remembered it for an occurrence less pleasant.

There were no cattle there, only the lingering smell of cow dung. A wolfhound bitch lay on the ground licking the newborn pups that crawled unsighted over her teats. Her swollen eyes told of her birth pains. Rory, reminded of the dying goat, bent and leaned down towards the litter.

Finola sat on the ground, heedless of the dirt sticking to her mourning gown. She patted the space beside her and moved over to give him room. The tang of manure was appropriate. Dust thou art and into dust thou shalt return. When he sat, she laid her head on his shoulder. For a few minutes there was silence. The new mother cleaned her puppies.

"Something troubles you Rory," she said "and I think it runs deeper than my father's death."

He looked at her but remained silent.

"It's Shane isn't it? Brian acted strange last night when I enquired about him. What has happened?"

He felt as if something were about to split inside him that he must keep whole. A tremor ran through him. She stroked his hair as he had done to her when they met last. "Tell me, Rory, it can't be that bad."

"Bad?" he said, "Oh yes, it is worse than you could imagine."

When he saw her bewildered expression, he knew he was going to tell her. Haltingly, he began ...

She was speechless, as if his words meant nothing. When he told her of Shane's allusion to Murrough, she realised that he was telling of an awful reality

Tired of dissembling, he had to be truthful. In a calm voice, as if it were someone else talking, he told her of the hanging.

When she lifted her head from his shoulder, he reached out and caressed her face. His fingers moved upwards, gently over her eye-lids, feeling her tears. Holding her in his arms, passion mingled with tenderness. He felt her warmth and he longed to crush her to him, to blot out the knowledge they had shared.

Sensing his change of mood, she took his head in her hands and kissed him full on the lips. Her tongue probed and met his desire with her own.

"A chuisle," he whispered. "Are you sure you want to? Do not do it for ..."

"Don't talk," she said. "Help me forget."

He did not protest his love, or compliment her beautiful body, or sensuously explore her flesh. Half clothed they copulated on the dirt. She screamed as she reached her climax; her nails dug into his back.

She had given him her body, but her heart and mind remained her own; she had not forgiven him. He stood up, brushed himself clean and reached down, caught her under the arms and lifted her to her feet beside him.

Avoiding his eyes, she did not see his distress as he prepared to leave.

The gleam of silver as she replaced the ring on her finger failed to draw his attention.

Chapter Thirteen

Queen Elizabeth was dying. Rory tried to imagine her courtiers putting her figure into a dark hole, like they had done with Cormac. But, undoubtedly, the opening would be a tomb with a personal effigy at Westminster abbey. Rumour said that she had gone bald, that she had bitten her nails to the quick. Whatever the truth of this hearsay, he knew one thing was certain. Her Majesty had refused to pardon O'Neill. He was still wandering through his glens, continually pressed by the enemy.

Eventually, in April 1603, Lord Mountjoy accepted his submission at Mellifont. After O'Neill had concluded the treaty, he returned to Ulster. He had put his signature to the document without the knowledge that Queen Elizabeth was dead. Mountjoy deliberately withheld the information that with the virgin queen's death the Tudor line had ended and the Stuart line begun. King James VI of Scotland was now King James I of England.

At twenty, Rory would have been shocked to hear of the English failure to tell O'Neill, before he signed, that Elizabeth was dead. But at thirty-one Rory recognised and even applauded their political skill. For years O'Neill had maintained a correspondence with King James. If he knew of Elizabeth's death before he submitted, he would have held out for better terms on the grounds that his rebellion was not against King James but against Queen Elizabeth.

On the morning he heard the news of Her Majesty's death, Rory had mixed feelings. Queen Elizabeth had arranged his exile in England. It was She who decided when he should return to Ulster and with how much power. Following her orders, Sir Walter Carew reared him in a Protestant household. He was her tool until he went to Kinsale. Now She was dead and he wondered what policies the new king would pursue.

He knew little about King James, especially on the question of religion. Since his mother, Mary Queen of Scots abdicated in 1567, he had been king of Presbyterian Scotland. His accession would please Sir Walter as he would expect him to move the Church of England in the direction of Presbyterianism. Although James had been parted from his mother as a baby and had never seen her again, the Irish hoped he would revert to her

Catholicism. We are a sentimental lot, Rory thought, unable to share their hopes.

His English experience had taught him that religious beliefs took second place to political convenience. King James had no need to change to Catholicism as the Catholics of England were too politically weak to merit such a reversal. Poor Machiavelli was maligned for writing as he did, and yet he reported truly the spirit of the times. However, it was not the religious aspect of the new House of Stuart that troubled Rory. Like Queen Elizabeth before him, King James would be cautious about reinstating an unpopular religion.

When he thought of the change in the strategic geography of Ulster, he was not as confident about the land question. Ulster chiefs had recruited *Gallóglaigh,* who were Scottish mercenaries, for their wars against Queen Elizabeth. She had seen Scottish penetration of Ulster as a threat to English power and had discouraged it.

But King James was now king of Ireland, England and Scotland; he might encourage settlement in Ireland as a way of strengthening his power.

There was overpopulation in his country. War and famine had emptied Ulster. The conquerors could lure people from England and Scotland with the promise of quick wealth. The situation was ideal for another plantation.

The war changed life in Ulster. More English forts were built. English law was dominant. Gaelic customs faded. Most cabins in Ulster had lost a man to the conflict. Families were not surprised when their loved ones did not return from a skirmish. They had prepared for death not defeat. Where once the people had believed that O'Neill was invincible, now they blamed him for Mountjoy destroying their crops, the failure of the harvest, the babies contracting dysentery and dying.

In this hostile atmosphere the northern princes who had started the war were hard pressed. Many felt that the terms of the Treaty of Mellifont were too lenient. Land hungry speculators dogged their footsteps. In line with the *Surrender and re-grant* treaty, if the English proved treason against the chiefs, they would forfeit their lands to the crown.

Rory empathised with O'Neill's discontent under the new

order. It was difficult to go from being an autonomous earl to being merely a landowner.

The English had not decided the fate of Glenone. It profited them to leave Rory as its custodian for a while longer. And the death of Eoin Maguire had taken away the need for any immediate action.

This was the argument Rory used to explain to himself why the English had allowed him to remain in control of Glenone's *uirrithe* despite the fact that he had been disloyal at Kinsale. He preferred to ignore his suspicion that perhaps Sir Walter Carew had again intervened on his behalf. After what he had seen of their maltreatment of the Irish, being beholden to an Englishman was a burden he preferred not to shoulder. He intended to go along with their plans in so far as it suited him.

Many of Eoin's *uirrithe,* who had joined O'Neill's army at the beginning of the war, were dead. Some of those who lived had made separate terms with Mountjoy and now held their lands directly from the crown. This was what Queen Elizabeth had in mind when she first supplied Rory with an army. He thought of his father's desire to retain the lands and decided not to allow Glenone to contract any more. If he did not stop the desertion now, he would be without any power, in control of the mensal lands only.

Turlough Devlin was one such *uirrí*. His father had been independent in the time of Rory's grandfather. But Eoin Maguire had subdued and levied him. Then in 1600 Turlough regained his family's independence by going over to the English side. Now he was battling with the *uirrithe* who had fought on the Gaelic side in the wars. For the first time Rory understood why Cormac had engaged in so many forays. He had been fighting to maintain his authority. The need to do this was unfortunate. It weakened the people even more. But what choice had he?

As he set out on his mission Rory knew that Ireland was a civilisation in decline. The English would prevent the Gaels from taking charge of their own destiny and changing what they needed to change. Kinsale had ended all hope of that.

Turlough Devlin was sitting by a camp fire on the periphery of his demesne.

Rory, followed by his troop of retainers, rode up. He had

chosen his best steed and worn his newest mantle. He placed a magisterial look on his face but inside he felt like the country, defeated and hopeless, fighting a lost cause.

The fear in Devlin's eyes showed there was no need for explanations. Devlin sprang to his feet and motioned to a soldier about to brandish a javelin not to be foolhardy. Rory's men outnumbered them. Smiling, he made obeisance to him.

Rory pretended to believe him then alighted from his horse and gave the reins to Art. Walking over to the kneeling malefactor, he drew back his arm and struck him with a backhand across the face.

Even as he cringed, Devlin mouthed his loyalty. Three months later, he was still paying his rents directly to the crown. Thirteen weeks later, his tenants found him dead among his newly sown corn. Art's father, O'Cathán, had earned his money at last and Rory's intent was clear.

Rory thought of Sir Walter Carew often these days and wondered how he had withstood his son's death. And Anne. Was her 'cousin' the consolation she deserved? Jane and Duncan Erskine - were they happy? And their son Quintin, their only child. Why did he think of him as a child? He calculated. Fifteen. Yes, he would be fifteen now. A young man. He wished he had a descendant himself. Someone who looked like Finola. But ...

Sighing, he walked in from the stables. Although he had many women since then, still none of them equalled her. He thought of the times he was on the brink of contacting her, but lacked the courage. In the past few years whenever he mentioned Finola's name to Brian he became reticent and quickly changed the subject. Brian's reluctance to talk about Finola increased his conviction that she hated him for his part in Shane's hanging. Where would it end? Would it ever end?

The sound of hooves interrupted his thoughts. "Strange," Rory mumbled to himself. "I think of someone and they appear."

As Brian dismounted and walked across the courtyard, his face a thundercloud, Rory sensed that he bore momentous news. "What has happened?"

"They have left!" Brian stared at him.

Was he travelling the same road as Shane? "Who has left? Tell me."

"O'Neill, his sons, nephews, sisters and close friends, all gone. Now the English have the excuse they need to make another plantation."

As Rory pulled Brian down from his mount, he felt light-headed. "Take it calmly. Where did they go?"

"They boarded a ship yesterday at noon to take them to the continent. At nightfall, they set sail from Rathmullen on Lough Swilly. People are already referring to it as the flight of the earls."

"An apt description. What do you think this means?" Deep down, Rory knew the answer. They had discussed it before. He was unable to think of anything else to say.

"It means that the English will find some way to take the land off us, now that the chiefs have left." Brian's tone was bitter. "They will know who was disloyal during the nine years of war. We will be the first they will throw out."

"You always look on the dark side, Brian. Let us wait and see." Rory believed his friend, but preferred not to add to his unease.

Rory was sitting at a trestle table in the dining hall at Mulahinsa, his residence since he had returned from Kinsale. Dinner was over and Brian and Maeve had gone to the parlour, but he had lingered over a wine flagon he had ordered from the kitchen. He refilled his goblet but the wine was not helping as much as he'd hoped. Instead of subduing his anxieties, it had only increased them, goading his imagination into unpleasant possibilities, conjuring up half-forgotten fears and projecting them into a future that suddenly seemed fraught with menace. His antidote was thoughts of Finola.

His mind lingered on the night they had spent under the shelter of a rock while the storm raged around their haven. Safe in his cocoon, he had wished the night would last forever. Then there had been their coupling in the enclosure. He remembered her ravaged face at the graveside of her father. Her concern for him in spite of her own grief. Her passion. All this had kept him waiting. He felt an alcohol induced anger. Waiting. For how long?

He would delay another three months. If there was still silence from her, he would ride to Campbell's fortress and issue an ultimatum. He was not a fool. He couldn't be expected to wait forever for her. Feeling better that, at last, he had decided what to do he left the rest of the wine and went to join Brian and his mother.

Maeve appeared distraught these days. Less resigned to Cormac's death and constantly bemoaning Shane's disappearance. She was continually threatening to leave Mulahinsa, scene of her tormented life. He paused on the stairwell to listen to the enlivened, wine induced, cadence of her tone as she spoke to Brian. "Niall was providential for Finola," she was saying. "They're six years married now and he admires her as much as he did on their wedding day. I know he complains of his health but a creaking trestle never falls." The amusement in her voice changed to solemnity. "I'm glad she has Joan. There is nothing better to help you bear the death of a child than to have another one."

The most influential tidings of his life he had gleaned from overheard snippets of conversation, Rory thought, as he tried to take in Maeve's words. Finola had married Niall from the schoolroom, the one in whose arms her child had breathed his last. Six years ago! She was married to another when she had played nursemaid to him in the bawn. Her diffidence after their union became clear. She was an adulteress ashamed of her infidelity.

When they first made love, she had been married to Campbell. It had not troubled him then. But he could not imagine her going to another's arms after she experienced the joy of his.

He put his hands to his face. It was not solely that. He had always loved her. She had married, knowing how he felt about her. Retracing his steps to the dining hall and shaking his head wearily, he swallowed the rest of the wine without tasting it.

Though his brain felt woozy, he summoned a maidservant, a buxom woman with blue eyes and an unblinking feral stare, to bring him a refill. She leaned close to him as she poured. This must be the licentious servant Brian had mentioned.

His first inclination was to get rid of her, but even as the words of rejection were forming on his tongue, he changed his mind. What better way to banish thoughts of Finola's betrayal than with a nubile female who was willing to fornicate. Tonight of all nights, even the company of this brazen maidservant was preferable to his own.

Smiling at her, he downed another goblet filled to the brim. She welcomed his roving hands and when he massaged her private parts, she sighed. When he felt his manhood inflate, he pushed the chair back from the table to allow her to straddle his knees.

"My beloved is married to another," he said, in a slurred voice he found difficult to recognise as his own.

"You poor dear," she gushed, "'Tis heartbroken you must be."

Without prior warning the import of what he was doing hit him. He was a guest at Mulahinsa. She was a servant not his confidant. His organ shrank as quickly as it had risen. By pinching the tender skin of her breast, he impelled her off his knees.

As he made his unsteady way to his bed-chamber, he realised that his passion for Finola had to be conquered lest he go mad.

PART V

1607-1617

It is dangerous to drive them (the Irish) from the homes of their ancestors, making the desperate seek revenge and even the more moderate think of taking to arms.

- David Rothe, Bishop of Ossory. 1617.

Chapter One

England

Sir Walter sat behind his bureau, massaging his temple, much disquieted. Lifting his goblet of wine, he drank deeply and put it down among the red stain-rings left by the many glasses he had consumed at this desk. He took up a clay pipe in one hand and fumbled in his pockets with the other, searching for tobacco. "Thank God for Raleigh," he thought to himself. He left the contents of his pockets on the bureau in turn, a grimy handkerchief, a piece of string, a short letter in Rory's handwriting and an etching of Anne. Stopping in pursuit of his objective, he stared at his wife's dear face and took another gulp of his drink.

There was a rapping of knuckles on the door. "What do you want?" he said in an irritated tone. "I am busy. Go away." But the door opened anyway. Sir Walter peered up. "Oh it's you. Come to join me have you?" He opened the third drawer and lifted out a second glass which he held at an angle before placing it on top of a pile of manuscripts. It toppled sideways.

A soft white hand reached to retrieve it. "Do not worry. The pile was uneven." Duncan Erskine's tone was patronising as he looked at Sir Walter. As his father-in-law raised his eyes, a wide smile appeared on Duncan's face causing creases to gather each side of his mouth.

Sir Walter poured wine into Duncan Erskine's glass, stopping only when he covered it with his hand.

"Have you thought any more about my suggestion?" Duncan enquired.

If he remained still for a few minutes, Sir Walter thought, the buzzing in his head would stop. The maggots had been appeased. He would not have any more wine. Leaving his half empty glass to one side, he sat back and assessed Duncan.

Duncan stirred in his chair. His sips became gulps.

Sir Walter cleared phlegm from his throat. "You know I hate nepotism. I have gone against my principles for you once already."

"As an officer in the army, George would have qualified for property as a *Servitor*. I would only be taking his place." Duncan

Erskine's expression was tense.

"That is certainly your only hope. You could never fulfil the requirements of an *Undertaker*. You are not a gentleman." Sir Walter enjoyed humiliating Duncan Erskine. "Moreover, *Undertakers* have to settle their estates with Englishmen or Scots. Not Irish. You would be unable to afford to bring tenants from England on what you earn as a tutor. Even the post *I* procured for you does not pay enough to do that. Neither would you know where to recruit any, even if you could afford it."

For Jane's sake, he had already decided to approach the Commission to get Duncan Erskine property in Ulster. He wanted so badly for his daughter to find happiness. If sending Duncan to Ireland would do it, so be it, but he was not going to make it easy for him. "The plantation of Ulster will open doors for little men."

Duncan Erskine's skin became blotchy.

"It is an opportunity for people like you with high ambitions and low incomes, men who enjoy an exalted social position, but who lack the prosperity to keep it." He wagged his finger enjoying playing the tutor. "Do not despair, Duncan. You are in good company. Younger sons of important English and Scottish families, who will not inherit the patrimony in England, belong to this group. Like you, they too are well trained tracker dogs who sniff the prospect of advancement in Ireland." He paused. "You never had a property on which to live, not to mention inherit. Did you Duncan?"

Duncan twirled his glass.

Now that he had started, Sir Walter found it difficult to stop. "Sizable tenants on estates in England and Scotland, landless labourers, fugitives from justice all want to flock to Ulster. The rhetoric about the riches of Ireland impresses them."

He took a script from the middle drawer and read: "Land at four pennies or six pennies an acre; a limitless supply of timber and stone for building; fish and fowl for food. It is more than they can resist."

"I want land in Ireland." Duncan closed his fists. His voice trembled. As if he was willing himself to stay seated, he held his feet firmly on the ground. "Jane is George's sister. He would have wanted her to benefit from his name."

"Ah yes. George. Nothing is sacred, is it Duncan?" Sir Walter felt a vein throb on the side of his forehead. He reached over, drained what he had left of his goblet and poured another. "Leave me. I want to be alone," he said in a tone that brooked no argument.

"I am going to Ireland," Duncan Erskine said again as he unbuttoned his shirt and threw it on the floor. "If I have to swing for it, I will make your father get me land." As he threw his hose in a heap with the rest, Jane turned from the sight of the hairy legs that matched the hairy chest. "It is the opportunity I have waited for all my life. God took his time sending it, but I knew it would come." His pitch rose. "I am not predestined to remain a teacher. Once I had done the unforeseen and married an aristocrat's daughter, thoughts of the ministry flew out of my head." He looked at his wife, his voice full of irony. "How could I have reduced the high and mighty Jane Carew to penury when she grew up with plenty?" Naked, he hopped into bed.

He put his hand on her breast and through her night smock abstractly kneaded her left nipple. Jane bit her lip. His musing continued.

"As a *Servitor*, I will be obliged to take Irish tenants and make them work, something they're not used to. It will be our obligation to control them." He kneaded harder. "They will get the worst land at the highest rent." Hand moved downwards and kneaded again.

Jane lay still, her face ashen.

Duncan Erskine's cheeks puckered. He looked at his thirty-two year old wife, worn out from twice yearly miscarriages, and said, "You were so ardent once you could not wait until we became churched to satisfy your lust. Now you are as stiff as a board."

She shrank from him.

"You only managed to produce one child." He looked sceptical. "Maybe the Ulster air will have a bracing effect on you. Irish peasants have lots of brats. You will soon be too old and I want more sons." He ran his tongue over his top teeth. "Get that martyred look off your face and that rag off your body or it will be the birch for you again." His face took on a self-pitying expression. "Every man is entitled to his marriage rights."

She lay on her back, her discarded gown on the floor. The flickering candle cast shadows on the bony buttocks undulating over her. Soon there was a smell of sweat and semen in the chamber.

"I know we are going to Ireland, Quintin. Duncan has talked of nothing else for a long time," Jane said to her son. He was sitting opposite her in the parlour adjusting the stirrup leathers on his saddle.

"This will be useless there," he said. "The Irish do not use them."

"All you think about is your horse and riding," she said. "This is serious. Do you truly want to go to Ulster?"

He looked around the spacious room and dug his toe impatiently in the leather carpet. "Yes," he said. "I want to go. It will be better than here." As he looked at his mother's drawn face, he said more softly, "There will be farmers there and you know how I love land." He bent and kissed her on the forehead. "Now I should bring this to the stables. I do not want to give father an excuse to berate me."

When her son had left, Jane went over to the secretary, found a quill and ink and then searched for parchment bearing the Carew crest. She sat down and thought for a few moments. Then she wrote:

My darling Rory,

I could not live any longer without breaking the silence between us. I loved you the day you first arrived at Chalk Hall, and have not stopped loving you.

My strength has gone. Since George's death, I feel bereft. I have nobody to talk to, or nobody to listen to me.

I am ignorant of how he died. My father says he was doing his duty as a soldier but I do not believe him. I think he knows another truth about what happened. That may explain his strange behaviour. He drinks alcohol now and pinches young girls on the buttocks. They laugh at the old man who runs after maidens. Can you countenance that Rory? Sir Walter Carew lecherous.

I miss George so much. My mother is happy. Her 'friend' loves her. They are content with each other. I do not like to intrude ...

Quintin is unhappy. He hates his fa ...

She ceased writing. The missive burned quickly when she

367

threw it in the fire. Back at the secretary she took out another parchment. This time, as her pen moved slowly across the paper, her forehead wrinkled in thought.

Dear Rory,

I am still sad about George. You must be, too. You were good friends. I know he died fulfilling his duty, but his death did not enhance my feelings for Ireland. We are going to live there, Duncan, Quintin and I.

Please forgive my presumption on your kindness. I need to know that one friendly person knows of our arrival. If I see you, I will not mention my brother. Let him rest.

Your friend,

Jane Erskine.

Quintin returned and sat on the window seat opposite his mother folding his long legs beneath him. "I left the saddle in the stables," he said. "Who were you writing to?"

"Nobody you would remember," she said her eyes bright. "Nobody you would remember."

Chapter Two

Ireland

Rory stood looking at the castle of Glenone that as a child he had found so forbidding, and marvelled that it had been his home now for nigh on a month. Though it still stood cold and dark, without even a softening cover of ivy, within it fires burned brightly, walls were newly whitewashed and hung with tapestries, and the rushes were sweet smelling. For the first time he had his own household: a chaplain, chief groom, handmaidens, candle bearers, even his own cook and food taster. Eoin Maguire had been scared all his life of being poisoned. Strictly he knew it was not his household but his deceased uncle's, but, after his night in the cups in Mulahinsa, he had resolved to be decisive and move here without delay. To have done so directly after Eoin's death and prior to the war ending would have shown his hand before he was ready. To have moved now was still foolhardy, but he had tired of expediency.

Leaving the immediate environs of the castle, he walked through a stubble field, and let his thoughts wander. The *flight of the earls* had left him dazed and uncertain of the future. Under no illusions about Ulster's weaknesses or the enemy's strength, he and Brian often discussed the price the government would exact from a leaderless province.

During the early part of October, he had tried, several times, to contact Sir Walter Carew who was the only one who could help him gain undisputed possession of Glenone. Though his path had been clear, his heart was not in it. He was an Ulsterman yet his father had fought and died in a civil war he had waged against his brother to uphold English laws of succession. His curse was to have been born to a family such as this. Indoctrination in England had followed. Torn between the two civilisations, the only constant had been that familial loyalty decreed that he regain Glenone.

If, when he returned to Ireland from England, he had been given right of tenure, he would have been content. His aim in life would have been achieved. As he got older, a metamorphosis had occurred. Even before Brian had told him about the northern chiefs' departure, he had begun to wonder if his fulfilment really lay in his acquisition of the land.

With a noisy quacking, a wild duck soared into the air from a nearby field and flew off overhead. Rousing himself from his thoughts, he looked to see what had disturbed the duck.

A small group of men were riding towards him. The corpulent man leading the riders looked vaguely familiar. As he slowly recognised him out of his father Sir Samuel, Rory felt his blood turn to ice. Charles Fenton's expression showed a sense of mission mingled with delight, possibly, Rory thought, at the prospect of gloating over an upstart Irishman such as himself.

Rory feigned indifference as he stood and faced the visitors.

One of the soldiers rode up to him and gestured in Charles's direction. "Lord Deputy Charles Fenton," he said.

Did he expect him to bow? Rory wondered as he absorbed the news that Charles Fenton had been made Lord Deputy under King James. He let the silence lengthen.

Charles with sneering courtesy, said, "I have brought a letter from Sir Walter Carew. He is on the Commission of Inquiry into land distribution in Ulster."

Rory took the paper. His thoughts were swirling. With good reason. The man in front of him must resent taking orders from Sir Walter. Rory remembered his last meeting with Charles's father Sir Samuel in Dundalk. It was he who had ordered Rory's imprisonment. Sir Walter had caused his dismissal as Lord Deputy because of it. Now his son had been reinstated in his stead. Queen Elizabeth was dead. Power had shifted.

It took all his control to hide his panic. He was more fearful than surprised. They were doing what he had expected. Conquerors knew that land was the root of wealth and power and they wanted both.

"They are going to confiscate the land then," Rory said, pretending he was voicing a solicitous solution to a problem.

"Yes, the Papist Irish will lose their lands to Protestant immigrants. Ireland will be Protestant forever."

"By Protestant you mean Calvinist?"

"Presbyterians, followers of Knox and natives of Scotland with some English Puritans. All loyal to the same God and the same King."

"You will get land yourself." Rory knew that he was being reckless, but Charles Fenton, because of his genealogy, was his enemy already. It could only worsen the relationship minimally.

"I hope to get land in Ulster, yes. Perhaps we will be neighbours." Charles crinkled his forehead. "But I'm forgetting. You fought on the side of the rebels. Such an error of judgement for someone who used to be so careful. Breeding will win the day." He shrugged in mock sympathy. Inclining his head in an unspoken order and without waiting for Rory to reply, he led his man back the way they had come.

Rory felt angry. He had always known that Sir Samuel Fenton had been contemptuous of the Irish, but now he had to deal with a similar attitude with the addition of religious bigotry in his son.

For the six months following Charles Fenton's visit, Rory was submissive and congratulatory to the English. They were civilising the barbarians and bringing them to the true faith, his homage was their appropriate due. His return to duplicity brought him a feeling of safety. And he needed to be vigilant with a man like Charles Fenton in a position of power.

And so because he had spent the previous months behaving so diplomatically, Rory felt confident about the prospect of meeting Sir Walter Carew. He took his letter out of his pocket and read it again. It had been brief and to the point,

When I arrive in Ulster, I will call to see you.

"Here I am, as promised," Sir Walter said two weeks later. "I hope my coming has not inconvenienced you unduly."

Rory ignored the remark he was so surprised by Sir Walter's appearance; he was like a tree that had withstood a battering by the wind. It was incredulous he knew, but he suspected him of being inebriated. "You are welcome. It's just I did not expect ..."

"That I would be here without an announcement and without my retinue. I understand." A muscle jumped under Sir Walter's eye. "I will not be discussing George." Softness spread across his face."I was grateful for your presence at his funeral. I will not forget it. Now that is the end of the matter."

"I was reading," Rory was unable to think of anything else to say. He gestured towards the fire blazing in the centre of the room, which threw its shadows on the reading materials lining the walls and on a goblet full of *uisce beatha* on a table. "I was also imbibing. Would you like a repast?"

"I am not hungry."

"Water perhaps?"

Sir Walter bowed his head and jutted his jaw. With a secret smile, he said, "I will have a whis ... *uisce beatha* please. If my memory serves me, I spurned the last one you gave me."

Rory found it hard to believe what he was hearing. "Our trip to England," he said.

Sir Walter nodded.

"I thought that is what you meant but I ..."

"Did not think I remembered or appreciated the young boy who offered me a cure. But I must stop finishing your sentences for you. Now where is that beverage?" As Sir Walter shuffled towards the chair, Rory summoned a servant to bring another goblet.

"This tastes good," Sir Walter said as he swirled his third *uisce beatha* around on his tongue. It is the first time I can say the English are mistaken."

Rory thought he had seen the error of English ways in Ireland at last.

"*Aqua vitae* is more befitting than *aqua mortis* for this beauty," he said holding the glowing liquid against the candlelight.

"I thought you were going to say that you felt plantations were unjust."

"Plantations appear unjust only to those who lose their land." Sir Walter settled himself in his chair. "In my own country I am sure the Picts felt enraged when the Celts took over. In turn the Celts hated when the Romans annexed the land for themselves. Next, you had the Saxons and then the Danes. Each new people got rid of the other."

"You never lost the ability to hold forth," Rory said with false levity.

Sir Walter laughed, "I will finish with the Normans who ousted all the rest."

"Do not forget the Yorkists, the Tudors and now the Stuarts."

"Yes, but then Ireland has the same story." Sir Walter looked pensive. "How does it go? Romans? No, their armies did not go past Pembrokeshire. The Danes? Yes. They conquered around the coast. The Normans, they were a bit more aggressive and ..."

"Their Tudor successors completed the conquest. Well, almost." Rory felt his face redden. "King James will finish the task."

"I am sure you have the blood of an invader in you somewhere Rory." Sir Walter plucked at his sleeve and contemplated a private thought. "No," he said, "wars will always happen. We are avaricious by nature. Even Quintin, Jane's son. As a baby he fought for playthings he didn't own."

"So you are going to annex all of Ulster?"

Sir Walter's expression became pious. "We are doing nothing wrong."

"Yes. It is legal. England likes to keep the law on its side." Rory felt braver now that Sir Walter was a bit intoxicated. "Let me think. How did you do it? At the end of 1607, juries at Lifford and Strabane found O'Neill and O'Donnell guilty of treason. That meant you could confiscate Tyrone and Tyrconnell." He knew his tone had become acerbic. "Yet, although the O'Hanlons, a different branch of the family to my fosterers thankfully, did not rule all of Armagh, you attainted them and confiscated the whole county."

Sir Walter looked at his drink. "In 1608 we punished O'Doherty of Inisowen for rebellion. We condemned Niall Garbh O'Donnell and Domhnaill O'Cathain to die in the Tower for helping him." He appraised Rory. "You cannot say but that our acquisition of the Derry lands was legal." He drank deeply. "When we have passed final legislation under the heading *Acts of Attainder and Ulster Plantation* in Chichester's parliament, arranged for 1615, it will be completed."

"So you intend to annex, Rory counted them out on six of his fingers, Armagh, Coleraine, Cavan, Tyrconnell, Fermanagh and Tyrone and clear the land of the Irish"

"Except the loyal ones. I hear *you* are cultivating the right people."

"When someone like Duncan Erskine qualified for land, I decided that having influential contacts would be helpful."

Sir Walter stirred in his chair, his cheeks mottled, his voice trembling. "For Janie. I am making Duncan Erskine a man of property for her, and her son's sake." His face now looked crimson in the firelight. "I want you to watch out for them, Rory. She trusts you."

The flames of the fire had died and they were warm with *uisce beatha* when they went unsteadily to their different

373

destinations, Rory to his bed and Sir Walter to Newry with Art O'Cathán.

It was early morning when Rory found himself on the road that led to the docks at Dundalk. Nobody was more surprised than he at his decision to come to meet the Erskine family. It was not for love of Duncan Erskine he had made the journey, but because a year previously Sir Walter had asked him to look out for Jane and Quintin. Perhaps he felt guilty for the way he had treated Jane when she was only sixteen. It was strange to have heard from her after such a long silence.

He thought of George. It was his duty too to help George's sister if he could. From behind a curtain of the past, he remembered a lonely young boy who had arrived in Kent, friendless. George in his velvet dressing gown had come to his room to encourage him. He wanted to show George's nephew that there were some natives who were friendly. But underlying these purer motives, there was a tactical one. He wanted to keep his lands.

Hawkers around the dock area looked disappointed when he did not show an interest in their wares. Unkempt women crept out of the ale houses and began plying their trade for a shilling. When he shook his head, they scurried away. A sailor, looking with doe eyes after a trollop, reminded Rory of his own liaisons with loose women and the debacle at Mulahinsa the night he discovered Finola had remarried. Thinking of his thirty-eight years, he realised he was getting old.

The Irish Sea was rough. High waves must have buffeted the ship on which the Erskines had travelled. He hoped they did not have an uncomfortable journey, especially Jane and Quintin. A battering would not have done Duncan any harm. He looked towards the prow of the ship.

"Unload those crates and bundles." Rory heard Duncan Erskine order a seaman who was lounging against a rope.

"Practising giving orders," Rory muttered. "He will expect the Irish to be his slaves." When he raised his hand, he caught Duncan's attention.

Duncan Erskine looked down at him still scowling. His angular, hungry look took Rory by surprise. He did not know whether he liked him fat or thin but in the end he concluded that he disliked him both ways.

"Rory. Fortunate. You can help us to disembark. These louts are not able to do anything. Some of the crew are Irish. We are lucky to be here."

When he looked over Duncan's shoulder, he saw a myriad of emotions on the face of the woman behind him. He said in a loud voice, "I have been requested by Sir Walter to welcome you to Ulster."

Duncan's thin fingers took Jane by the elbow and propelled her towards the gangway. Quintin followed behind.

As Rory went to meet them, a line of carts and wheelbarrows loaded with boxes and bundles from the ship blocked his way. A sailor, balancing goods on each shoulder, elbowed Jane aside so that she had fallen against the rope half-way down the ramp. When she reached the bottom, she looked ready to swoon.

"I have our belongings to look after," Duncan said, retracing his steps.

Now that he was alone Rory was unsure what to do with this gentlewoman and her son. Better take them somewhere warm. Jane looked cold and he only knew one tavern acceptable to a woman.

A smell of stew greeted them at the door of *The Rabbit Inn*. The room was filled with long tables with rows of men lounging and drinking noisily. Spaniards, smelling of sweat and stale fish, bargained with Planters who were gathered in a corner. The men from Spain were determined to rid themselves of their leftover cargo of wines, spices, glass, iron and silk. Planters' wives were a new market.

A sleepy-eyed sailor pushed in on a form and allowed the trio to sit. As she unfolded her legs under the table, Jane surreptitiously loosened her stays for more comfort. Finola's short legs would have fitted comfortably in the close space. Rory scolded himself. She was not Finola. He was being unfair.

She looked beaten down and though she was younger than he, she looked ten years older. And silent Quintin. Sweat and grime smudged his face and his carroty hair looked dark with dirt. He had gulped the whey a maid servant brought him while Jane was sipping hers.

"I could not believe you came to meet us," she said. "After that terrible journey it was like a miracle."

"I was afraid it would be rough," Rory's tone was sympathetic.

"Rough. I thought I would die." Like a small child, she rubbed her knuckles against her eyes. "I have never been on the water before. The motion of the ship made me sick. Then the wind began to rise. I will never forget the way it tore at the rigging. I thought the sails would rip to shreds."

"You are safe now. You will soon forget it," Rory said.

"Safe! Here!" Jane plucked at the neck of her gown as if she were in danger of choking. "I didn't want to come. That was why I wrote. Was it not that I knew I would see you, I would have gone mad. I hated ..." She stopped. Confusion and determination fought on her face. She looked towards the door. "There is Duncan. I must leave." With an abashed Quintin by the arm, she scurried away.

Rory felt the weight of Duncan's beady eyes upon him.

Concern for Jane assailed him. Jane's husband would have some idea of the frontier type conditions in Ulster. Jane, unless she had changed her reading matter, would have only read the announcements made to attract settlers. She would have heard of the fertile land and the riches to be had here. Nobody would have prepared her for the stretches of bog and sluggish streams so different from Kent. Neither would she know of the poverty, the squalor, the rude huts and a countryside torn asunder by O'Neill's wars.

He thought of her blurted words, but did not dwell on them. The loneliness of life at Glenone, the uncertainty of his land tenure, the hypocrisy of being polite to the conquerors, writing letters to his contacts in the castle - his former prison, paying calls to the 'Irish of good merit ' who had retained their lands like him, were troubles aplenty for any man. The added burden of Jane he felt unable to shoulder. She had her husband and her father to take care of her.

Sir Walter Carew and his assistant were sitting in his office in Newry and sifting through lists of people whose lands were being considered for confiscation. Sir Walter's eyebrow lifted as he looked at the red lettering across the centre of the one of the pages.

Rory Maguire, former ward of Sir Walter Carew. Exemption? Refer to Sir Walter

He left it aside.

Then he remembered Rory's Irish fosterers, so recently mentioned by him."Check and see who inherited the Mulahinsa branch of the O'Hanlon lands, would you?" he ordered his clerk.

As he went to do his bidding, Sir Walter took out a book and opened it to reveal pages yellowed by age. He read the date and location before he came to the name. Written in his own hand, in bold letters was:

Brian O'Hanlon ... renegade.

When the man returned, Sir Walter was still clutching the book.

"Brian O'Hanlon, Sir. Cormac O'Hanlon died."

Memories of his humiliation in front of Sir Samuel Fenton, when he had interceded for Brian during the Munster rebellions, raced through his mind. Time to even old scores. He put information regarding the Mulahinsa demesne among the stack of papers marked *Land to confiscate.*

The seasons turned. Planters spun, measured and cut the thread of Ulster men's lives. They came with sombre faces and mirthless laughs to take the land and preach allegiance to the true God and the true King. In spite of their censures against idolatry and heathens, their eyes lighted greedily on Ulster's fertile soil. Their minds dwelt on the profits the land could yield.

As he read the lines penned by Miles McGrath, Rory remembered the poem Mile's grandfather Ultan had written for himself and Matthew before they set out for the fatal feast. Twenty-nine years later, another McGrath had the same gift.

Blessed opportunists occupy all our dwelling; they burst with men of God and greed.

Not yet. He still had possession of his lands. It was not a legal possession, of course but then it had never been, even when The Queen was alive. He preferred not to acknowledge the debt for his continued proprietorship. Sir Samuel Fenton had said, before he consigned him to the dungeons of Dublin Castle, that as a *protégée* of Queen Elizabeth and reared in civility, the English would afford him every opportunity to show his loyalty.

Earlier that day Brian had come to visit him. Both dispirited they had sat in the shadowed gloom. "The fire is almost out, Brian. Shall I fetch a servant to stoke it?"

"No do not trouble yourself but you can get me another goblet of wine." Brian had gazed into the dying fire and put his musing into words. "Some friend of the Irish King James has turned out to be." His eyes had been as remote as the Mull of Kintyre as he told Rory of the sheriff presenting him with a writ from the king. "He had a man with him, a puny weed with grasping hands who looked at the castle with owner's eyes. He was picturing himself and his brood sitting in our parlour, eating in our hall and sleeping in our rooms. I hope God blasts his Scottish backside before he uses the privy it took me so long to build. I wish I had someone like Sir Walter Carew to support me.

As he looked at Rory's discomfort, he added, "I'm envious. If I had someone to grovel to, to retain my land for me, I would grovel also."

"What will you do, Brian?"

"Burn Mulahinsa. When it goes up in flames, I'll retreat to the woods and hide myself among the leaves." A light had crept into his eyes. "When I sneak out of my hibernation, foreigners beware!"

The change in his demeanour had occurred so quickly Rory now wondered if he had imagined the mad glint in his friend's eyes.

Chapter Three

On a Saturday morning, months after Brian's visit, Rory was still conscious that Maeve was unaware that Mulahinsa was being appropriated by the crown. He also knew from his conversation with Brian then that *he* had no intention of informing her. She had, after all, deserted her home without any justifiable cause. It was because of the love he bore her family he felt an obligation to find Maeve and inform her. So he mounted his gelding and rode north towards the little settlement of Ballincro. An additional benefit to the journey was that he would see the new towns about which he had heard so much.

The landscape was very different from when he had passed this way en route to Kinsale. Planters had cleared the scrub away from the fields and the sickly smell of the burnings was long gone. Surveyors travelled the province choosing sites for new towns. Carpenters cut wood and erected scaffolding. Masons scurried with hods of bricks. It was hard to believe that as recently as 1603 Carrickfergus and Newry had been the only true towns in the province.

Around the forts used by the English during the nine years of war, towns were being built with names like Cavan, Enniskillen and Omagh. While they waited for the masons to build Dungannon and Armagh, settlers lived in castles and castle ruins and in remains of monasteries. "The new towns will be in the English style," Brian had remarked bitterly to Rory when he had last talked to him.

He discovered that what Brian had said was true when he passed through Ballinskollin and saw the wide cobbled streets, town hall, courthouse, and jail that surrounded a central square. The inevitable Presbyterian church was half built. Each worker whether they were cutting wood or quarrying stone had a musket close at hand. Though trying to ignore their suspicious glances and impudent looks, he felt anxious. Presbyterians like Duncan Erskine and his companions from Scotland were now the ruling class.

Life had its ironies. He had spent nine years in a Calvinist household in the heart of Kent. Now Presbyterians had come to Ulster. He was destined for evangelisation, he thought, as he passed a minister speaking to *the elect* beside where they were building their chapel. The gesticulating orator mouthed a tirade against the ignorant people *The Almighty* had sent him to save. Scriptural references and words like *dirty papists*, and *idolatrous ways* spewed from his Christian mouth. Such was the planter's contempt for *Romish infidels* and *traitors to the king* that Rory could envisage them putting walls of stone or earthen ramparts around the town to protect them from contamination.

These new towns were different from the older Irish towns that had developed at random over the centuries. He never imagined, when he visited the great city of London with Sir Walter, that there were merchants living there who would profit from planting Ulster or that when the ruined city of Derry was rebuilt it would be renamed Londonderry. He thought of the exiled O'Neill and his native Tyrone, part of which was now being joined to the county of Coleraine and called County Londonderry.

As he nudged his horse into a trot, he knew that it would always be Derry to him. The settlers could proclaim an English allegiance if they wanted, but the Irish would not. What was in store for an Ulster, he wondered, where, to prove their dominance, the conqueror felt it necessary to change its place names.

He turned the corner into the pass, crossed the road opposite the castle and rode down the scut to a whitewashed cabin. From the beginning he knew that Maeve, unmistakable in her brightly collared frock and red head linen, had spotted him.

When he dismounted, he let the horse champ the grass. "You have not changed Maeve." As he got down from his horse, he had caught the glance of dismay that flooded her face and noticed how her complexion had reddened like a radish.

Putting down her head again, she continued to clean hen's droppings from the doorstep with water and a brush. Steam rose from the bucket and dampened the hem of her apron.

She stopped at last. Without looking at him, she said, "Come inside." Her weight rested against the side of the door as she waited for him to follow her.

The cabin was no better than the ones around her dwelling at Mulahinsa, except no chickens squawked under the table and there was no smell of pig. The trestle bore evidence of the stringent cleaning he had seen outside. Two hand sewn cushions lay on the stools. There was an unfinished one lying in a heap on the table, its frieze grimy from smuts from the fire. He smelled peat. Why had she left the castle to live like a churl on the charity of a distant kin? What demons had driven her from Mulahinsa?

"Tell Cormac I'm not coming back," she said as she poured milk out of a vessel and counted out two biscuits. "Cormac said he would leave the women of my house alone, that he wouldn't seduce Molly, but he did. Brigid always loved him. She was not the one who told me about Molly. I just knew." She crossed herself with a dramatic flourish.

Rory was perplexed. Maeve had obviously become unhinged from the weight of her tragedies. Cormac had been a philanderer but he knew that Cormac had loved his wife. Fidelity was a marriage vow for women. From Maeve's acceptance of his roving, he had assumed that it did not distress her. Cognisant of her gaze, he realised she expected him to say something. He tried to summon sympathy for her but to no avail. He'd come here out of love for Finola, and Brian and because he thought she should know what was happening to her beloved Mulahinsa.

At a loss what to say, he just blurted out, "The sheriff served Brian with a warning. The English will dispossess him of Mulahinsa without delay. Undertakers have got it.

"Curses are like chickens; they come home to roost," Maeve said. "Murrough would know what I mean. *Sioga*! Little people didn't kill Murrough. My own flesh and blood did. Now he is gone with the fairies himself." Maeve's tone held a note of appeal. "Where else could he be except in the land of *na sioga* with *Aebhinn*? She is the only one who could woo Shane away from a mother who adored him." She pirouetted like a young girl and raised her worn eyes to his. "Do you think she's nicer than me Rory?"

The sight tore at his heart. "I don't know who *Aebhinn* is Maeve?" He knew his puzzlement must show on his face.

"The queen of the fairies in north Munster. Beautiful she was called. I always loved her name. Better than I loved our own northern ones. Do you think Shane will like her better than me and stay in Kinsale? I talked to him last night. He said he'd be back next week. Do you think he will Rory?"

As she stared at him with a burning intensity, Rory felt riven by guilt at Shane's murder. He saw her composure disappear. Tears rained unheeded down her face, as he held her heaving body and felt her arms around him for the first time ever. "There is a measure in all things," she muttered.

Chapter Four

Finola had returned to Mulahinsa for the last time. She had come back to help with clearing the castle of their belongings before those 'land-stealers,' as she called them, took it over. Each day had seen more furniture pile up in the castle at Glenone, the nearest storage space that could provide safety for it. Prosperity and power derived from land, Finola thought. When the English took it from Irish Catholics and gave it to Scottish and English Protestants, they were diluting opposition to English rule. A Protestant colony, large and powerful enough to keep the natives segregated and inferior, had come into being. The old scourge of *Surrender and re-grant* had been the excuse to confiscate part of the planted lands. If the government had not the excuse of the chiefs' treason ...

The settlers were acting as if the natives should be grateful to be left on their own land to slave for them.

Many like Brian had joined the Woodkerne and preyed on the newcomers from the woods and the mountains.

She knew that Niall felt as helpless as she. The impending confiscation of Mulahinsa added to this feeling. He berated himself that his lumber business entailed working with the conquerors. His anguish about *Oileán na Stoirme* had returned too. Each night when he woke calling Andrew Óg's name through the darkness, she cradled him in her arms and lulled him back to sleep. Despite the number of times it happened, it unnerved her. It was a relief to get away from him and leave him in charge of their daughter Joan while she went to Mulahinsa.

Each day when she arose, she thanked God for the snow and icy breeze. Each day of bad weather postponed the time when they left their *uirrithe* under the domination of the Scottish settlers.

Her pack bulged with jewellery, worn chess pieces, dog-eared playing cards, a large chestnut, a knife blunted from carving on tree-trunks, and other treasures of childhood. The tapestries woven by Maeve were last to go. Thoughts of her mother had come back to her when she watched Brian load the wagon with the last of the stuff to transport. Her mother had been so proud when she had finished those pieces. She remembered her with her face smudged red and green, her slender arms deep in a vat of dye. It was all so long ago.

The last hour she had wasted searching for her old woollen doll, wanting to give it to Joan as a memento of her own childhood. She understood how a doll could have got lost in the chaos of packing, but she was perplexed by the loss of the arrow Rory had given her as a child. The bow was still safe in the old trunk but without an arrow, and she was certain she had left the two together.

She was reminded of Murrough's death at the horns of that tame cow. "'Twas *na síoga* who put it there. 'Twas them that stuck that arrow in his ear. Little folk gone mad 'twas." Who had said that? Could Shane have been responsible for Murrough's death? She had suspected it when the 'accident' had happened but it was easier to evade the truth that your brother could have killed a second time ...

As she reached the bottom of the winding stairs, she felt the whole of the ground floor fade from under her. Sinking to her knees, she laid her head against the coldness of the last step. For years her life had been full of turmoil. Her marriage to Niall was challenging. Planters had possessed Campbell's fortress and now they were seizing her only real home. Thank God for her daughter! Joan would sustain her.

Then she heard the sound of horses' hooves outside and an English sounding voice cried, "Dismount!" As she stuffed her valuables into her shoes for safety, she wished Brian and Rory would come back from Glenone with the wagon. Rising to her feet, she filled her lungs with the cold air and decided she had come through worse than this and would again. She felt her colour deepen as she walked to the door to confront the enemy.

"Do you think we tied the tapestries securely enough?" Brian asked. "They are important to Finola. Must be because mother spent so much time weaving them."

Rory did not feel like answering Brian's chatter. Quietness was what he desired. The rattling of the wheels as they made their way along the frozen track was noise enough. Maeve would not be much in their lives now, anyway. She was an old woman and would not last long in her cottage where only fantasies sustained her.

Brian looked as if he didn't expect an answer so he went back to his thoughts. He wanted to think about Finola and his reaction to her presence at Mulahinsa. Though he had disciplined himself to hide his feelings, he had been unable to control the tremor in his voice any time Niall's name had come into the conversation.

At one point he had been on the verge of declaring his love for her. He wanted to ask her to divorce Niall as he once asked her to divorce Andrew Campbell. It was that thought that stopped him. She had felt loyalty to her first husband then. What must she feel towards Niall, who had held her dying son in his arms, who fathered her beloved daughter? He was glad he had not risked another refusal. For his own sanity he must banish any thoughts of a life with Finola. Niall could live longer than both of them.

"Sorry about this lady," the commander spoke politely to Finola. "Just obeying orders. You should have left when we asked you like the rest of them."

The sound of rough men stomping through the hall stripped the crust of unreality from Finola. She knew that the common soldiers would be as less polite than this man. Her heart beat rapidly as she recalled Rory telling her about his difficulty recruiting decent men to enlist for the mission to Ireland.

One of the newcomers picked up one of Maeve's mousetraps from the kitchen and unaware that dead rodents had lain on it, began to fiddle with its spring. The sight of it brought back memories of Murrough's quick thinking the day the baby's fingers had been injured. That she now suspected Shane's involvement in his death made the memory doubly painful. Would that it would mutilate the stranger's fingers in the same way. She lowered her eyes lest he sense her loathing.

A puny man took his knife from his pocket and waved it around at nothing, the swish cutting the air. "Aye, we can reckon your brother has flown the coop, canna we little lady? On his way ta Glenone he should be. Thief that he is. 'Ere isn't nary a soul here what wouldna agree wit' me."

She felt his breath on her neck as his hot eyes combed her bosom. "Never ha' a bit of aristo'ratic tit," he said with a drool.

Imagining his sweaty hands mauling her, she felt weak again.

"Stop waving that about," his commander shouted. "And I

want less of that kind of talk." He shook his finger at the offender. "There is nothing more for us to do here. Orders were no force."

"These must have powerful connections to be allowed hold out this long. It's a wonder they evicted them at all." The man holding the mousetrap was bitter.

The little man said, "Aye, we can reckon this package seduced one o' our captains." He tweaked Finola under the chin. "Must ha' been goo'."

The taunt rankled, but she could not bring herself to answer it. Her attention was concentrated on keeping her legs from crumbling. The pendants and necklaces were digging into her feet. As if it were yesterday, she heard her boast to Rory when he wanted to carry the jar of *dearógs* for her. "My back bone is short not weak." She had lasted this long with the discomfort; she could endure another while. Brian must have articles of value to rebuild with when the planters annexed his property.

A slow blush stained the benevolent commander's face, "Tell your family they have to be out of here by tomorrow or else."

The knife man looked at her with lecherous eyes. "'Tis a pity it be tha' we have ta leave. A rank poor pity."

The sound of their retreat brought little relief. Brian wanted to do more than deprive the new owners of their *rightful belongings*. He was still insisting that he would burn the place. Peeling off her shoes, she sat to wait for Brian and Rory's return.

Chapter Five

The English settlers were usually not as successful as their Scottish counterparts. For one thing, they gave in to a fear of the Woodkerne. Rory had heard of many who exchanged or sold their lands to the Scots rather than risk an attack on their families. Neither were they as prepared to go out themselves and till the land. The Scots, however, took the plough by the handles and made furrows that excelled any mere tenant of Ulster origin. They worked long hours, fatigue their only companion, as they coerced the land to yield its full capacity. Rory's theory on this was that Puritans and Presbyterians felt uncomfortable with failure. As their success and riches was a sign of God's election, ill fortune was an indication of His disfavour.

Although Duncan Erskine was English, the Scottish settlers respected him because he shared their religious beliefs, their wiliness and their work ethic. Neither was he ashamed to ask for help on farming matters. He knew the day would come when he would know enough to lord it over his advisors, so meantime he garnered the grains of their knowledge.

Thoughts of Duncan Erskine reminded Rory of the summons he had received from Jane the previous week. A budding merchant had brought it to him. "Gave me a penny to bring it she did, Sir. Said I was to give it to nobody but you." That the boy thought Rory was a settler was obvious from his deferential manner but his mistake *was* understandable; he was still in possession of Glenone.

The tone of Jane's note had been a mixture of plea and command. Although he knew it was difficult for her to lose the inflection of mastery she used with servants in England, he resented being treated like a hired hand. He had come because her words, too restrained and over disciplined, obviously cloaked her agony.

When he had seen Finola's sorrow as she left Mulahinsa in the certain knowledge that she would never enter it again, he had felt her pain as his own. Now Jane was in trouble and all he felt was irritation.

As he dismounted, his thoughts were in disarray. He let his horse chomp on the grass and wait. The Erskine house, a native style makeshift abode of clay and wattle, was unlike the other planters' timber framed houses, which stood on well chosen sites and were laid out with fortifications.

Jane answered his knock and as she beckoned him in, a slow flush warmed her face. "Quintin is out with Duncan. Duncan wants to show him how hard you must work to be a success." She pushed a strand of hair behind her ear and gestured to the small room behind her. "This is just until we build," she said, "the new house will be completed soon." As she spoke, she fiddled nervously with the tassels of her gown.

Rory eyed the few pots and bits of china resting on the pallets that stuck out from behind the door of their bed-chamber.

"The storm damaged some of our belongings on the crossing. We don't have the time to replace them. Duncan is so busy with the land." Her voice trailed off and her neck grew as pink as her face. Then, squaring her thin shoulders, she looked directly at Rory. Her eyes glistened with desperation. "I am with child again." After the utterance, she lowered her eyes and wrung her apron tightly in her small fists.

Rory felt as if she had punched him in the stomach; his breath came in short gasps. He knew vaguely that he felt deeply shocked that she had made such an intimate disclosure to him. His vicarious experiences from literature had not prepared him for such an announcement. Childbirth was not something with which he was familiar. Although he was in Chalk Hall when Jane carried Quintin, he had never mentioned it to her; that was a subject not meant for men. Husbands did not discuss it with their wives. They merely planted their seed and then drank *uisce beatha* when the child was born, and more if it were male.

Sensing his discomfiture she tried to make him understand her desperation. "Duncan does not know. I did not tell him yet. I do not want a child by him. I hate him."

"You love Quintin."

She answered softly, almost to herself, "Quintin is different." In a tired voice, she continued, "Duncan strikes Quintin and me. Now that Quintin is old enough to fight back, I am afraid of what will happen. Last night he hit me with his fists. The marks of his knuckles are still there. I would endure, were not that I am so afraid for my son. Rory, what will become of us? He is worse since he came to Ulster. You are my only friend."

"What about your father?" Rory did not know what else to say.

Her face darkened. "My father!" Her tone held a mixture of anger, frustration and contempt. Then, she said in a normal tone, almost with a laugh. "You looked disturbed enough by what I said. Can you imagine how Sir Walter would react if I said the same to him?"

The feeling that he did not want to be implicated in all of this came upon him suddenly. He had to get out of the little house; he needed air. Nor did he want her to sense his unwillingness as he knew it would humiliate her. Had he lost his ability to dissemble or was he developing a conscience?

"I must go." He headed towards the door but unfortunately looked back. Her helplessness reminded him of an ensnared animal. Without knowing how it happened, he found her in his arms, clinging to him. He wanted to get away; he loved Finola with a passion that left room for no other, but when he saw Jane so faded, tears running down her cheeks, he could not hurt her by ending the embrace too quickly.

It was while they stood like that, she drawing strength from him, that they heard footsteps outside. They drew apart when the door, slightly ajar, burst open to admit Duncan Erskine.

"I was leaving," Rory said. "I will come back to see you both soon." The lie caught in his throat. He inhaled deeply and only breathed normally when he had put a mile between him and the Erskines.

Rory moved over the grass at an easy trot, the damp leaves muffling the sound of his horse's hooves. He was near Mulahinsa he knew and becoming nostalgic, he decided to ride around by his old home. The longer route would help to clear his mind.

The new owners would be there. He wondered how he would feel. Would Sir Walter's ideas about the inevitability of colonisation lessen his distress when he saw strangers where he and Matthew had spent their childhood?

As he approached the outlying lands, he smelled smoke on the breeze and when he rode nearer, it grew more stringent.

Hot currents of air assaulted his face and a confusion of sounds came from the centre of Mulahinsa. He heard yells and frenzied screams and a child's voice crying out the name

Elizabeth. A boom split the air. A new blaze reddened the sky.

Then it dawned on him. Brian had carried out his threat and used that saltpetre substance he was always experimenting with to blast the castle. He hoped he had done it this morning. Burning children in their sleep would not have been anathema to the Brian he knew.

As he encouraged his horse away from the glare of light, he tightened the reins.

The house was ablaze. There would only be the planter family and the servants to extinguish it. He could still hear the childish babble about Elizabeth. Probably the child's sister was caught in the flames. She could die there. It had nothing to do with him. Elizabeth! The name did not encourage him to stop and help.

As a native he understood the need for the revenge that had prompted the fire. He had tried to dissuade Brian from destroying Mulahinsa only because he knew the English would pursue him relentlessly, not because of any morality. The qualms he now felt about the results of that revenge surprised him.

The reins again loose in his hands he sat motionless. The memory of Finola's son and the death he endured on *Oileán Na Stoirme* crowded his mind. He could not ape the barbarism of the *civilised* Dolman. Conscious of the livid sky behind him, he turned the horse and retraced his steps.

The flames climbed over the roof of the castle and bloated into a red blot before Rory's eyes. It looked as if the fire were spreading. The sky provided a canvas for the twirls of smoke clouds above the blaze. The glare had a celestial aura, with its associated imagery - tongues of fire, the fire of God's love, Jesus ascending into heaven in a blaze of light. As he watched it burn, he knew why fire was also of the devil - the everlasting flames of hell, the most fearsome image man could devise. The strident religion in the province must be affecting him.

He was now near enough to feel the fire's breath on his face. Men with scorched hair and grimy faces shouted to keep back lest they be hit by flying sparks. Puzzled, Rory obeyed. The house was burning yet there were no tears or wrath discernible in any of the faces encircling the inferno. The castle held no memories for them. Their sombre faces showed that it was what they had expected when they came to this wilderness.

Feeling conspicuous among planters who were now his neighbours, he took one last look at the blackened stone. A little hand pulled at his trews. When he looked down, he was staring into the face of a child clutching a woollen doll.

"Elizabeth nearly got burned. My uncle saved her." The child pointed to a man who squirmed under Rory's scrutiny and his niece's adoration.

The Scottish burr continued, "She was waiting in the house for me when I came. Isn't she bonny?"

"Bonny," Rory answered feeling choked. The doll's neatly plaited hair had reminded him of Finola, its previous owner.

Chapter Six

Finola had become quite worried about her husband Niall. After the slaughter on *Oileán Na Stoirme*, he had the same cowed look now visible in many faces since the Battle of Kinsale. O'Neill's defection had worsened it. Due to poor health Niall had not taken part in the war, and this too had exacted its own cost.

Each night when he came home wearied after his day of trading in timber with the conqueror, the cabin where they lived became his haven. When he was at home, he pored over cures and herbs looking for one that would change his life.

Were it not for Edward, Andrew's brother, they would have starved when the English confiscated Andrew's lands. Immediately after their eviction from the Campbell fortress, Edward had rallied his Scottish clan to help her and Niall. It was her in-laws who had first seen the potential for importing timber.

They knew that the settlers were ignorant of the country and would want to find an easy way to renovate and rebuild. Not all of the settlers brought building materials with them as they had contracted to do. Like the *Undertakers* who had broken their pledge and employed Irish tenants, the *Servitors* were lax in fulfilling their requirements also. Hence they needed more timber than they had brought. Finola and Niall provided a service that enabled them to restructure with a minimum of aggravation.

The beginning of new towns had added to their lucrative trade. In calm weather her in-laws rowed across from the Ards Peninsula and returned the same evening loaded with merchandise.

However, Finola knew that, although up to a year ago she and Niall had been vital to the planters, they had now outlived their usefulness to them; they were no longer the only ones who saw an opportunity to make money out of lumber. They still had some customers for the building materials they imported from Stranraer, but the Scots had begun to resent their prices and the planters were now organising the trade for themselves. Opportunists too had usurped them by selling poor grade lumber for the price of good wood.

As she felt Niall, restless, beside her, Finola acknowledged that this was only part of his problem. Niall was behaving strangely and she suspected that it was more than his worry over the business or his preoccupation with his health.

So that was the reason she had pretended to be asleep and had not interfered when, earlier on, without warning, he had jumped out of bed, his demeanour a mixture of excitement and fear, pulled on his clothes and left the bed-chamber.

She identified with his frustration with the new settlers as she also felt sorely the change in her native province and in their way of life. If their survival did not require it, association with the planters would not have been their choice. The gap between the settlers and the natives was so big, she wondered if anybody would ever bridge it. When, for example, she had first discovered that the authorities forbade Catholics to live inside Derry, and forced them to assemble shelters on the bog side of the walls, she had found it tough to accept. She dreaded what might happen next in Ulster and also in her own life. On that thought she slept. In the budding hours of the morning when Niall came back to bed, she kept her eyes closed.

Next day Niall left the house again early, mounted on his mare. Once more Finola did not wish to ask him where he was going. From his tired face and his downcast eyes, she knew that he would be loath to discuss it.

To distract her from her ominous thoughts she took to cleaning the house. The shelves were filled with various preparations, herbs, potions, powders and liniments. She must persuade Niall to select what he wanted to keep, and destroy the rest. Many vessels had only one spoonful taken from them. Niall knew his ailments so well that after one dose he could say, "It's not what I want. That's for my back. My neck pains me today."

Some bottles looked murky and suspect to her. She had distrusted the old man with whom Niall had bartered to get them. Niall's willingness to try every new remedy had increased since the English had planted the province and he was not as careful about their origin.

Later Joan took her head out of a script she was reading and asked, "Where did father go? He is away a long time. Do you think so Mother?"

"No, I don't know where Niall went. No, I don't know when he'll be back." She wished he'd return; she was tired of pottering around the house trying to find work to do.

"I think I hear his horse," Joan said.

She could hear nothing. A thirteen-year old daughter could be a nuisance sometimes. From then on every sound, every bird call, every squirrel's chatter made her jump. Continuing to clean the house, she scoured every niche. As she dusted the tablecloth with a feather for the fifth time, Joan pointing to the duster joked, "You must have hated the hen that came off."

She was glad that she and Joan were smiling when Niall came in at twelve noon, his glib in his eyes. He must have lost his headband, she thought. His next complaint will be sore eyes.

Niall's expression was grim, but satisfied.

Although she was curious, she refused to pry; he would tell her when he was ready. She doled up his stew; he always relished his food. If only he'd eat slowly. When he ate too fast, he broke wind and complained of stomach cramps. She felt guilty again. He was the best husband alive, had always given her solace. Her loss of Andrew Óg in the massacre of *Oileán Na Stoirme* had taken precedence over his ordeal there. When the English confiscated Mulahinsa, his sympathy was for her alone. Nobody considered that he had spent many years there, and must cringe at the thought of newcomers living within its walls as much as she and Brian ... and Rory.

The last time she had seen Rory was when they vacated the castle. Memories of him had sustained her since. He still loved her, she felt sure; she had seen it in his tender secret glances, in his inability to refer to Niall without stuttering. Her promise not to couple with Rory following the death of her son that she had broken in the bawn was less important now. Knowing that even if she had crossed to the island immediately the storm abated, she would have been unable to change anything that happened had made her weakness easier to accept.

While they were packing to leave Mulahinsa, she had ached to hear him voice his feelings. There had been a yearning within her to say something that would prompt him to admit his feelings for her. One sigh from her of love or desire, one unguarded glance that pleaded for his embrace, and he would come to her. But Niall would have suffered and she refused to allow that to happen.

Brian, like many other dispossessed landowners who refused to reduce themselves to the level of tenants, had become an active participant among the Woodkerne. He had been joined there by soldiers who once were the mainstay of their clan but whose leaders had lost their authority. The Irish wars had destroyed their civilisation. Their common bond was that they hoped to get revenge for injustices the settlers had perpetrated on them.

Brian used to visit Finola and Niall at unexpected times. He changed his 'bed' every night and was always wary of being captured. Finola always kept a batch of crisp biscuits baked lest he come. The cow, tethered to a post at the rear of the cabin, made sure there was always fresh milk. This evening, as she sat opposite him at the trestle and watched him eat, she felt at peace for the first time in days. Niall and Joan were asleep. Everything felt right.

"I felt a failure for not setting the castle on fire," Brian was telling her, munching his first biscuit. "I'm loath to tell you this, but it's gone up in smoke anyway."

Finola's new found serenity deserted her.

"Oh, I did attempt it, I admit," Brian went on. "I told Rory I'd resist, but I felt a need to put it to the torch." He looked pensive. "There were soldiers guarding it as if they expected an attempt to fire it; they would have gunned down anybody they caught. It was too risky. I turned back feeling lucky to escape"

She looked at him for a hint of a smile, but there was none.

"Now their tenants are armed and are ready to defend. I'd hate to be the poor soul who did the job I failed to do. He was not a Woodkerne so he will be without protection."

The nauseated feeling beginning in Finola's stomach revealed the truth her mind refused to acknowledge. But she decided to remain silent about her suspicions. Brian had enough to grieve him.

Chapter Seven

The countryside had a windswept, chastened look as though the winter snows and frosts had tested its endurance to the limit. The braver oaks sprouted new leaves and a ribbon of bluebells ran down by the river's edge adding much needed colour to the landscape. But the fresh breath of spring did nothing to soothe Rory's ragged nerves. Sir Walter's horse-boy set a quicker pace than Rory would have if he were on his own. He would be there soon enough. From what he had read in the missive, Jane was having a difficult birthing.

The missive itself had not given many details. "Who penned the note?" he asked of the horse-boy after he had spent ten minutes deciphering what the unqualified hand had written.

"'Tis from the midwife m'lord."

The substance of the scrawled words was that Jane was about to give birth and wanted to see him. There was mention of a letter which he found confusing and promptly ignored, resenting Jane's demands on him.

The horse-boy had told him that Duncan was not at home, but that on the previous night Sir Walter Carew had come from Newry.

In spite of himself, the loveliness of the day had a calming effect. The miracle of another spring was unfolding. The last time he had ridden this way, it had been the dead of winter. No matter how bleak life looked, it got better. The thought lessened his apprehension.

The door of the Erskine house was open. Rory saw a strange dread in Sir Walter's eyes as he entered. "How does she," he asked.

Sir Walter shook his head. "No change. Twenty-one hours it's been."

"Is that unusually long?" Rory asked.

"Not if the pains are light, weak. But the midwife, two midwives, Grania, the native Duncan has procured," he grimaced as he said the name, "and Clara a planter's wife, who accompanied me from Londonderry, says that Jane's pains are sharp and coming close together. She has had no respite since they began. No rest all night. When the birth is long drawn out, a lot can go wrong."

Rory could discern that Sir Walter was in one of his expounding moods so he let him ramble on. He might even learn something.

"A babe can sometimes lie in the wrong position in the womb. If that happens the midwife will have to reach in and try to correct it. If she fails, both mother and child are likely to die." Sir Walter took a breath. "Or the babe can be too big. Or the pains can go on so long that the woman weakens. Then there's always the danger of sudden bleeding. And afterwards that she'll not be capable of expelling the afterbirth."

Rory's lack of knowledge must have shown on his face because Sir Walter said impatiently, "The afterbirth is the skin that cushions the babe when it is in the womb. If it does not come out of its own volition and the midwives cannot drag it out, the woman will sicken and die. And even if she gives birth safely and then expels it, there is still the menace of milk fever. They say many women die from that."

Rory already had a bellyful of childbirth information. "How do you know so much about it?"

"I ordered Clara to inform me en route." Sir Walter stared into the fire. "I was like you when George and Jane were born. Had no interest. Even when Anne bore a man child, I was absent. I thought fathers who waited long hours outside the birthing chamber were foolish." After a long silence he said, "I wanted to know about it for Janie's sake. She is all I have left."

Clara appeared in the doorway of the birthing chamber, the only other chamber apart from the one in which they were sitting. Her hair was dishevelled, her gown spattered with blood. "The baby will not come Sir Walter. We are at a loss."

"For God sake there must be something you can do woman!"

The planter's wife was clear and unambiguous in her reply. "We have tried everything sir. Hours ago, when accepted methods failed, we massaged her belly with hot thyme, persuaded her to eat fruit from the *cassia fistula,* and even tried pepper to make her sneeze. All age old remedies." Tears of frustration brimmed in her eyes. "The pains are still coming quick and severe, but the babe is no nearer to delivery. Sir Walter she cannot go on like this much longer. Her strength is all but gone and she has begun to bleed."

At the stricken look on their faces she said quickly, "No my lord bleeding need not be fatal, but if she loses the will to continue, she and the babe will die ..." She wrung her hands. "Does she want the mite to be born at all?"

When the midwife went back to her work, Sir Walter rapped his knuckles on the table. Each beat burned into Rory's brain until he wanted to scream at him to stop, but he looked so vulnerable it would have been like beating a man with his hands tied. Appearing immune to the tune he beat, Sir Walter's eyes focused inward on a sorrow he was unwilling to share; he clapped his hands, the sudden sound as loud as the drumming had been. The change from learned concerned father to this distracted pitiful mess astonished Rory. Sir Walter was always so contained ...

A moaning came from the room ... Then silence.

Sir Walter got up from his seat and went to a leather case, left beside the table, a secretive glint in his eyes. Taking a small key from his pocket, he inserted it in the lock. Then reaching inside the soft leather he took out a container of whiskey.

His pallor took on a more lifelike tinge as he took off the stopper. A lover's touch was in his fingers as he ran them down the side of the vessel. The liquid, caught in a random beam of light, winked back. Putting the decanter to his lips, he drank quickly, nervously, as if there were a danger that someone would snatch it from him. Many gulps later, he shook the vessel around and finished the drop left at the bottom. Then he returned it to the case, took out another one and started again.

The silence was broken, this time by Jane's voice. The tone was her usual one, but the words sounded ribald and slurred, as if she were the one intoxicated not her father.

Rory tried to blot out the mixture of groans and screams from the birthing room but failed. His conscience began to smote as a picture of the women he had bedded since puberty flashed through his mind. For the first time in his adult life, he considered what may have been the result of his nights of pleasure. How many babies could he have sired without his knowledge? It was perhaps a sign of his advancing age that the responsibility had at last dawned on him. When he had abstained from fornication, it was because of his attachment to Finola. He felt every day of his forty-three years as in Sir Walter he imagined he saw a mirror of his own shame.

At one o'clock, Duncan Erskine returned. When they told him about Jane's confinement his eyes became shifty. He said, "She always chooses absurd times to try to produce. I'm starving."

He grabbed a pitcher of milk and drained it.

Rory stared at him.

With equal vehemence, Duncan Erskine returned the gaze. "Sir Walter is here I see," he said and left.

Three hours later Grania emerged, walked towards Rory and ignored Sir Walter slumped on his chair. "'Tis not into the lying in chamber you should be allowed Sir, but the poor girl is pleading for you for nigh on two hours now. "Tis not welcome you'll be. Mabel is fierce against you entering."

Grania opened the door just wide enough for Rory to slip through. He stood motionless for a moment, staring at Jane. She was clad only in a shift which, though not a clinging material, was stuck to her body with perspiration like a second skin. The tight corded muscles in her throat told Rory more of her pain than any of her screams had done.

He went over to her bedside and knelt. When he murmured her name, she turned her head towards him. Sweat was running down her face. Now he was close enough to see that her frock was soiled with mucous and urine and blood. But what appalled him most was the expression in her eyes, the hopeless, despairing look of someone who thought there were worse things than dying.

"Rory ..." He'd never before heard his name called upon as a prayer and he felt his insides dissolve. When he took her hand, she gripped it tightly, clung desperately. No longer able to detach himself from her anguish he blinked back tears. As he watched the blood spread over her skirt, he felt a sense of utter impotence.

"Rory, have to tell you about a letter ..."

"Hush Jane, my precious, save your strength."

When she smiled weakly, he knew she had heard the endearment.

The midwives, still not reconciled to his male presence in a female domain, temporarily forgot their angst and turned all their attention to Jane as her pain began anew.

Grania stripped off Jane's garment and kneaded her abdomen.

Kneeling, she poured oil on her hands, and prodded the neck of the womb. "'Tis to break the waters I must." She took what to Rory looked like a goose quill from Mabel and leaned forward.

Jane writhed, groaned and took deep gasping breaths, so intent on her torture she no longer seemed aware of Rory as she dug her nails into his wrists.

Suddenly there was liquid gushing from her on to the bed, the floor rushes and even splashing over his trews. He could tell that Jane's discomfort had lessened a little. But then the contractions increased in frequency and intensity.

"I can see the crown," Clara said.

Her body convulsed again, but the baby was immobile. Nobody moved. Grania tried to prise the infant out with her fingers; the two midwives took turns. Jane moaned, squeezed and bit Rory's hand.

It happened so quickly in the end that he was shocked when the baby slid between her thighs into the hands of Clara. He felt a sick horror that Jane should have suffered so, only to give birth to a dead child. The planter's wife left the dark shape, splotched and smeared with blood, down on the rushes.

Oblivious to all, Jane jerked spasmodically, blood spurting down her thighs. Rory remembered what Sir Walter had said about the afterbirth. That if she couldn't expel it herself or the midwife was unable to pull it out, she would weaken and die.

Clara inserted her hand into Jane's womb but withdrew it in seconds and beckoned the other midwife aside. When Grania continued to shake her head, the planter's wife turned away from her and said abruptly to Rory, "She does not know we are here. You are more use to the living. Will you impart the news to her father?"

Jane's breathing was rapid and shallow as he left the room. Two hours later she died.

Back at Glenone, Rory gazed at the manuscript in his hand, the words swimming in front of him. The figure of Jane when he had seen her, prior to her lying in, reappeared. She had looked like a skeleton with a bundle under her gown. Her feet had dragged and she had looked as if she were trying to make herself invisible. Her words returned so clearly they made a parody of her death. "Duncan thinks it is your child, Rory. He whipped me to make me admit it. He saw us clasp each other that evening and was mad with rage."

"But, but ...," Rory remembered sputtering, "The child was already started then."

Again her voice soft and tremulous, "I know. I told him but he refused to listen. I will go back to England when the baby is born. Much as I hate having to do it, I'm prepared to live on my father's charity."

Jane's lack of emotion had frightened him. Her resignation even then had been unnatural.

Abandoning the script on a bureau he gave up the pretence of reading. Since Jane's demise, he could not get Quintin out of his mind. Believing that Duncan Erskine was not the right man to have authority over a son, he was on the brink of telling Sir Walter so.

When they had finished with the rituals of death, he planned to offer to take the boy to Glenone. Duncan would acquiesce if he used the right kind of persuasion. It was amazing what the muzzle of a gun could do. Jane had told him that Duncan used to strike his son. Quintin's haunted and withdrawn appearance was testimony to that.

He did not know why he felt responsible for the lad; he had rarely thought of him when Quintin still lived in England. It was only when he had seen him at the docks, striding beside his mother that he had remembered the gurgling baby he had left in Chalk Hall.

It could be lonely by himself at Glenone. There would be no children of his own, he knew. And Art was now an apprentice blacksmith and no longer lived with him. He would offer Jane's son a secure home away from the threat of his father.

Two days later Quintin came to see him; it was prior to his trip to England with Sir Walter to inter his mother and infant brother. His clothes were wrinkled and dusty and had a general air of neglect. Gruelling work had hardened his hands and Rory had to force himself to stop staring. Unconsciously he was trying to build a pen picture of Quintin who was born in 1592, the year he had returned to Ireland. For a man of twenty-three, Rory thought him unsure and awkward.

As he handed him a letter, he said, "Rory, two days before she died, mother gave me this for you."

Rory recalled the midwife Grania's note, and Jane's mention of a letter. "Do you know what is in here Quintin?"

"No, well a little. Mother said she was following an old Irish tradition. She thought that was funny. She laughed for a long time, but I was not sure whether she was happy or sad. When she stopped, tears were running down her cheeks."

Later when Quintin had returned to Dundalk, Rory sat to write the diary he had persevered with since his journey to Kinsale. Writing of events still helped clarify them for him but, in truth, he was trying to defer opening the letter. He would have to do it sometime. Closing his diary, he unfolded it and read:

Dearest Rory,

When you receive this, I will have found peace, and I pray God so will my baby.

I want you to take Quintin under your protection. His efforts for the last ten years to protect me from Duncan have retarded his development. Do not judge me harshly. When he was eighteen, I tried to launch him in a career at court, and in the military. He failed as a diplomat and a soldier. Neither has he regard for trade. His interest is in the land.

There is no easy way to say this. I cannot wait to make the traditional deathbed announcement. I may be too weak or there may be nobody to listen.

I have always loved you. Look out for our son.

Signed the thirteenth day of March, 1615 Jane Erskine.

Rory ran his fingers through his hair. Beneath where two churls had made their marks as witnesses, there was a postscript, an almost illegible scrawl written by a shaking hand. In a trance, he continued to read.

All those years ago, I would have told you about my baby. I am a selfish person. I used Duncan shamefully to attract your attention. If I could, I would have forced you to marry me, but I knew my father would not allow it. In father's diary, I discovered ... ask him about it yourself, if you so wish. I married Duncan and bewailed it each day.

My father has atoned for his sins. He is a kinder man than when you lived with us. George's death, Mama's desertion and my own situation softened him.

Be kind to him, Rory. Let him die of old age, not excess of alcohol or fornication.

I will wait for you.

With a portion of his mind Rory read the last words, *I will wait for you.* Wait for him. Where? Dimly, he was aware that Jane must have written the first part of the letter sometime before the last piece. There were no unfinished thoughts in the first portion, no hint of emotional or physical fatigue.

She said Quintin was his son. Flesh of his flesh. Not Duncan's, not anybody's but his. What a fool he had been! That was why she appeared to have gained weight when he returned from his court appearance in London. Why she wooed Duncan.

A mental censor reminded him not to get wistful about the past. He had been delighted when Jane had changed her affection to Duncan. Even if he had known the truth about the child he would have deserted her without a qualm.

He wondered whether he had changed much. That selfish youth inside the forty-three-year old man still enabled him to keep his lands when the English were dispossessing all those about him. Was loyalty to his *uirrithe* the true reason he was bowing to the English? Holding onto his inheritance at any cost was unjustified. The habit of dissembling always ruled his actions.

Getting up, he moved out into the yard. Children were feeding chickens, women giving slops to the pigs. The tenants were going about their work. It surprised him that life though changed to a dreamlike state for him, was still commonplace for every one else. He was a father.

Chapter Eight

Finola left Joan in the cottage in the care of Niall and walked along by the river. When she looked at the flow of smooth water, she felt a measure of ease she had not experienced for a while. Since Brian told her of the burning of Mulahinsa, Niall's night escapade followed by his early morning ride had haunted her. Closing her eyes, she unclenched her fists. "What a mess," she muttered. She was unsure whether to reveal to Niall that she guessed it was he who had set Mulahinsa afire. It was because of her he had done such a dastardly act. By nature he was not a destructive or a violent man. How mistaken he had been if he had expected that destroying the home of her childhood would ease her pain.

Whatever Niall had done he would have her loyalty. She had betrayed him with Rory in the *bawn* at Mulahinsa after Cormac's funeral, but never would again. She owed him too much.

The sound of voices interrupted her thoughts. On the other side of the river a number of horsemen were traversing the ravine. Their voices carried towards her as she crouched among the bushes, her green mantle merging with leaves.

"We will have to make an example of the fellow," one was saying. "Cannot let the torching of a planter's house go unpunished. It could start a wave of burnings."

"Let us do it now," another voice said. "We know where he lives. We know he ha' reason to do it." At the prospect, the voice throbbed with excitement. "His woman is the uppity whore who was there the day we went ta the house." There was a pause. A note of doubt crept into the opinion. "We ha' better do it quickly. Maguire's patron might come off the alco'ol long enough to intercede for him."

Recognising the voice this time, she peeped from behind the bush and saw, as she knew she would, the pinched face of her 'knife man'.

"No, let us bide our time," the first voice continued. "The captain says he found irrefutable evidence. An article that had the bastard's initials stitched on it. We do not want natives saying it was a vendetta to prevent him from trading with the planters. Nor do we want any more joining these Woodkerne. We will get him when it is more propitious".

Shaken from the import of her eavesdropping, Finola rushed back to the house, her skirts dragging on the moorland. The river had lost its magic for her. The bird's song became a lament. Moisture soaked from her arm-pits onto the wool of her dress. She must slacken her pace or Niall and Joan would know something had gone awry with her stroll. She forced herself to walk normally and thought about what she heard. They had proof. The soldiers said the culprit had left evidence at the scene.

There had been something unusual about Niall when he returned the morning of his mysterious disappearance, an article of clothing missing from his person.

If her suspicions were correct their life as building suppliers was over. Whether convicted of arson or not, the planters would cease trading with them altogether now. They had already begun to buy from their own. Now they had the justification they needed to get rid of them entirely.

She walked in silence. Calmer now she noticed the growth of spring and felt the sap rise. Through her many trials she had always felt that somehow she would pull through. This belief in her own survival resurfaced, gave her sustenance and awakened her courage. As she picked her way through the bracken, she determined to have a long talk with her husband.

Like patience on a pedestal, she bided her time until Joan was out of the house. Clearly, from the way Niall was avoiding being on his own with her, he knew of her suspicions.

"I wish to talk to you. Niall, please stay." When she saw him tremble, she knew she was approaching this in the wrong way. Though not the man she loved, he was her protector and her friend. The lacking was in her. She would have to do this in a more composed manner if she were to succeed. Rising from the chair, she went and knelt beside him and pressed her head to his chest. The physical closeness defrayed the tension.

He played with her hair. "You're beginning to turn gray," he said. Then he held her in front of him and looked at her. "I'll soon have an old crone on my hands."

A premonition that they would not see old age together struck her. Before she could stop herself, she said, "With all the worrying I'm doing about you, is it any wonder?"

His expression shadowed. Without speaking he stroked her face. She waited, giving him the chance to unburden himself if he wished. But silence swelled between them, the only sound the persistent rhythm of his heart next to hers. As tenderness overtook her, she wrapped her arms about him. His face was buried in her neck when they heard their daughter calling to them of horsemen approaching.

"They're coming for you," she said. "You must hide. They know it was you who burned Mulahinsa."

He looked at her strangely, not understanding. His voice was emphatic when he said, "It was my intention, but when I went to do it, soldiers were all over, guarding it. Then I saw the silliness of the idea. I reckoned that, as it was lost to you anyway, it was unimportant who had it."

"The same happened to Brian," she told him. She felt relieved. It would be easy to put the misunderstanding to rest.

The commander, whom she had met at Mulahinsa, entered his manner more brusque than at their last meeting. He was brandishing a headband.

Finola's memory alerted. Of course! That was missing the morning Niall returned to the house, disheveled after his morning ride. His band, the one she had woven with his initials, was what was going to hang him.

"We are arresting you for the burning of one castle known locally as Mulahinsa," the commander said. "A royal court will try you on the fourteenth day of May. Meantime you will remain incarcerated in the military prison at Bearnarua."

"I'm innocent," Niall said, "This is a mistake."

"There was a mistake," the commander said, giving him a shove. "You made it. Get your belongings. We have wasted half a day already."

Niall got a few items ready. Before he left with the soldiers he turned to Finola and said, "You can throw away what you choose from my medicines. I know you're longing to get rid of them. By the time I return there will be new cures."

Finola watched, dazed, as they marched him out the door.

Joan ran after him, attempting to clutch at his legs. But her scream of, "Don't take him," sounded far away.

This time Finola knew she was incapable of keeping weakness at bay.

Chapter Nine

Finola had arranged to meet Brian at an agreed location some miles from her home. The air was cool and crisp. A flotilla of rain-swollen clouds drifted across the sun, casting unexpected shadows upon the ferns. She shivered and pulled her mantle closer. When the sun broke through again, reviving all the grandeur of a spring afternoon, the rebirth of warmth and light took her by surprise. It was almost, she admitted, as if she desired grey skies and cooler winds, wanted a world that reflected her continuing disillusionment with life in Ulster ...

The Scottish and English still wielded the power. They were the possessors of the land and loyal to a crown that supported them. English soldiers still garrisoned Ulster and lorded it over the natives. The most Gaelic province in Ireland was under English administration.

Brehon law was extinct. The sheriffs summoned civil courts and anyone arrested was at its mercy. If, for example, one merely sympathised with the cause of the Woodkerne one could be imprisoned. The settlers wanted every member of the Woodkerne hunted down and captured.

The worst of the settlers were adventurers and opportunists who had come from England and Scotland to chance their luck in Ulster. The better class planters, however, farmed 'their land' and adored 'their God' without intruding too much on the natives.

The sound of hoof beats alerted her that Brian was approaching. When he dismounted quickly, it was clear that he was harried, with little time to waste on trivial conversation. "Where did they take Niall?" he asked.

"I don't know," she answered.

"What is the date of this supposed court?"

"The fourteenth of May."

"We'll have time to organise."

"Niall's innocent, Brian. Even the English wouldn't condemn an innocent man."

"Don't worry Fin. He won't be condemned because he won't be tried. Trust me."

"Even if I were never to see him again it would be better that he be alive."

Brian looked at her speculatively before mounting his horse again. "I'm feared events may test how much you mean that," he said.

Andrew Campbell's brother Edward came to Finola's rescue as he had done once before when he had helped her and Niall set up the lumber business following the annexation of Andrew's lands. Now he helped her to it sell it off to a Scottish rival, making enough money to support herself and Joan. He had refused to accept any payment for his trouble. There was enough money from his black-renting days to last him many years, he'd said.

Her life became like the widow of a landless labourer. She had no husband to support her and live with her. Edward visited her often but that was different. Even suspect! She could hear again the gossiping of the thin-lipped planters' wives. Why was someone she purported to be her first husband's brother so good to her? Could he be getting sexual favours? Her husband was a Woodkerne. A murdering firebrand. In prison for arson.

She remembered the idle talk she had heard about Rory's visit to Jane Erskine, a planter's wife, and daughter of the house where he lived in Kent. She recalled Rory's denial that he had been in love with Jane and tried to put aside her pangs of jealousy.

Time passed slowly until the day of the ordeal arrived. They were trying Niall for a crime he denied with little hope of justice. Finola had heard nothing from Brian since their brief encounter that day. He had said then to trust him.

When she walked through the garden unable to be still, the dry grass caressed her feet. Joan was playing with their small cat, a descendent of Lizzie.

Her heart jumped at the sound of horsemen. As she peered through the trees, she thought at first she must be hallucinating when she saw Niall and Brian come towards her. Niall was wearing his grey tunic and one of Brian's trews, loose for his slight frame. She ran to greet them and whispered, "You are safe, thank God."

For some moments he held her tight before raising her face to his.

She held her breath when she saw that his expression was full of loneliness and pain and a strange kind of determination.

He let her go and turned away.

Something was wrong. They had acquitted him. Hadn't they? She remembered Brian's words, "They won't condemn him because they won't try him."

"You escaped," she said then, realising. "They will be hunting for you."

"Yes. On the way to the assize. A band of men with muskets took my escort by surprise and rescued me. It happened in a flicker. I don't know myself how they did it. All I know is that I'm free. And yet not free."

"Tell me. What do you want me to do? We will make ready to leave immediately." She called out to Joan.

"Don't Finola, leave her," Niall said. "It's better if she doesn't see me. One parting was enough."

"Parting? Oh! You mean you'll have to leave again for awhile until this dies down! Yes, perhaps it would be better if we kept it from her."

"Finola I ..."

"What Niall is trying to tell you," Brian interjected, "is that he is leaving Ulster never to return. If he does, he is a dead man."

Finola's face was ashen. "Where ..."

"Jesuits have an Irish College in Salamanca. Niall is proficient in Spanish. They will give him a tutoring post." Brian's voice held a note of tenderness as he spoke the harsh words. Nevertheless the need for speed was clear.

"I have to leave immediately. Many men risked their lives to save mine. There is only space left on the ship for one. I'll send for you." Niall crushed her in his arms and continued, "If I stay, I will put you in danger."

As she bit her lip to stop the howl she felt in her throat, Niall galloped with Brian through the copse. He turned once to gaze back at her. Joan, oblivious to the heartbreak around her, was still sitting caressing the cat. Again the dry grass touched Finola's ankles, this time causing her to shiver despite the sultriness of the day.

Chapter Ten

It was cold in the tavern and half-dark. The raw whiskey burned Rory's throat. He was celebrating that he had a newfound son. But he was masking his distress at the same time. Finola's husband, Niall, had fled the country. The worst possible outcome for him. She would not divorce him now but would live a widow's life until she went to Salamanca. Either way he had lost her.

Somewhere in his mind other problems, not reasons for celebration either, niggled him. The drink would help him forget. Standing in the middle of the floor, Rory was careful to keep his head bowed; he had bumped it on the low ceiling too many times already tonight. The candles, their wicks burned close, did little to light up the rickety tables or the rugged faces circling them. There was little chance that this landlord would supply new candles for the comfort of his drink-sodden customers.

Rory narrowed his eyes in concentration as he tried to identify the man who was swaying towards him. "It *is* you," he slurred, when the man came nearer. "I recognise you. Tadhg, isn't it? Don't try to sell me anything cause I'm not buying. I know it's hard for a gray merchant to stop selling, but I'll say it again, I'm not buying."

"Who the hell is asking you?" Tadhg retorted.

At the sound of the voice Rory visualised a wood, a boy, a wolf and an arrow and was certain he was right. "I can't believe I have met you again." He staggered. "The first time I saw you, I was afraid of you. You ... You haunted my dreams for years." As they measured each other afresh, Rory laughed.

"Well!" said Tadhg. "'tis behind us now that is." He stumbled towards Rory and together they tottered to the nearest table.

Rory clasped a pewter jug. Droplets ran down the side of his goblet as he poured *uisce beatha* into it.

"'Tis wastin' good *uisce beatha* you are. Here, give it to me and I'll do it." Tadhg snapped the jug from him and filled a generous portion for himself.

Rory took it back from him and refilled his own.

"Fate's a curse," he said as he downed another slug.

As he looked at Tadhg across the table, he felt surprised again at their meeting. He had not expected to come across anybody he knew in this place. Many people were afraid to come into a tavern especially on a day the Presbyterians called 'The Sabbath.' The tavern owner had better be careful. He should not be selling them drink. If the authorities caught him, they would close him instantly. Presbyterians dictated the law of the province. "To the divil with them," Rory said out loud, the sound of his own voice surprising him.

Getting drunk was not his way. There were layers beneath his exterior that he did not want stripped. Finola was the only one in whom he could confide and she was gone for ever. He must not think of that; he had a son; he had his land; he was happy. No gloomy thoughts. Life was good!

"Sure the world is a wonderful place," he said, this time raising his goblet. "Haven't I a son, a man as tall as myself?" He put the goblet to his mouth.

Tadhg drank to his son and his health. Tadhg was his friend. He could talk to him all night.

By the time they got to the subject of the Maguires it was early morning. They leaned their heads together across the table, the world's closest allies.

"Rory. Do you know that 'twas to know your grandmother I did?"

"How would I know? I was ten when I met you before."

"She was mine once. Catherine Reilley was mine. Then, your grandfather came and stole her from me."

"I scarcely remember him. I was too small. When I was in England, I read about Con Maguire in a book. The English called him, wait until I remember, oh! yes! 'an indepe'ndent Ulster dog.' It was a compliment, I thought."

With a drunken stare, Tadhg leaned closer. "What age are you? Forty, forty-five? You still believe that, do you? That 'tis Con Maguire's grandson you are."

Rory, through the haze, felt the stirring of an old doubt. "What are you talking about?"

"An English soldier it was who sired your father. When Phelim was a baby, a rat bit him on the chin. 'Twas your grandfather that pulled the bugger off. He didn't like it that a rat had bitten his son. Took him four years to persuade Catherine to give up the baby, and 'name' Con Maguire as the baby's father. Con

Maguire bedded many women; he must have bedded Catherine, too." He drank a mouthful. "A beaut'iful woman, she was." He smacked his lips.

Like Helen of Troy, Rory thought. Who had said that to him? He tried to remember. Spittle dripped from Tadhg's mouth onto Rory's sleeve but he was too interested in what he was saying to move.

"Trapped Con Maguire nicely they did," Tadgh continued. "At five years of age, Phelim acquired a power'ful chieftain as a father. Wasn't it scornful of the gullible Irish your real grandfather must have been."

Tadhg leaned even closer towards Rory, almost kissing him. "It worked out for you, didn't it? Still have Eoin's lands, you have. How did you keep them? 'Tis the English blood that's helping you, I'm thinkin'. "He pulled at Rory's sleeve. "I always liked you although I knew your secret. I didn't tell anyone. Deserve some reward."

For an instant Rory felt his muscles tense for violence and then slacken. He was a father now and must act responsibly. He poured more *uisce beatha* into Tadhg's goblet.

In the early light he hiccupped his way home, Tadhg's story echoing and re-echoing in his brain until he found refuge in a drunken sleep.

When he woke, all he remembered of the previous night was that he had met an old friend and they had imbibed too much. They had had a wonderful time. But if it were so pleasant an evening, he thought, why was there an uncomfortable feeling at the back of his mind? As if he had learned something he would have been better not knowing.

Finola knew that Edward Campbell had always seen her despondency at his brother Andrew's obsession with his deceased wife. Now, again, he was behaving as if he knew the reason for her unhappiness. She could have stood his solicitude if her restlessness was due to pining for Niall. But her husband had been gone just over a month, and already she was back to thinking of Rory.

During the first few weeks of their separation she had worried constantly about Niall's whereabouts and his safety. Now, although she had heard nothing to confirm it, she was sure he

412

must have reached his destination. It was only then, when she was able to find some ease, her mind strayed to Rory.

If she could sleep without dreaming, she might recover her spirits. Every night the dreams were the same. Niall walking towards her on water. She running away with Rory on land. While the wind howled, she spent the rest of the night in ecstasy with her lover. In the morning she would wake, the bedclothes in disarray and she bathed in sweat. Always it was Rory's image in her mind, Rory's voice in her ears, his touch on her skin.

She began to dread the nights. Instead of sleeping, she would sit and look at the stars through the open door and agonise on the confusion of loving two people. As children she and Rory sometimes shared the same dreams. Did he ever suffer like this over her? she wondered

Other times she buried her face in her hands and thought about them both. They were so different. When she thought of Niall, it was his kindness she remembered. He had spent his life teaching. Then she had distracted him with marriage. If there had not been Joan and her to maintain, he would never have become a merchant, selling timber to planters. A truly civilised man, he would have been incapable of the punishment Rory meted out to Shane when he had helped Brian hang him from a tree. Rory had been born with the curse of a divided identity. He was a mixture of scholar, dreamer, and man of action. A rebel and a follower of tradition. A sage and a child. She loved him as she had loved no other. God forgive her.

Finola sat by the flickering blaze, her eyes tracing the shades of yellow and purple in the peat flames. The day was warm and she had lit the fire for comfort rather than heat. Joan was sitting opposite her reading. A teacher's daughter, she thought, a glow warming her heart. It was the first time for weeks they had sat thus, absorbed in separate activities, but with a close united feeling between them.

A knock at the door startled them both out of their composure. She felt irritated at the disturbance this late in the evening. But when she went to the door and saw Brian, her expression changed. Joan jumped up to greet him; she was always glad to see her uncle. He merely gave her a glance, however. As a member of the Woodkerne, he had to be careful when he visited the house of an arsonist on the run, so he was usually tense when he called.

"I suppose you don't know anything about the raid at The Grange." Finola thought her levity would break the tension that surrounded him. "They say they swept the estate clean."

He smiled without enjoyment and nodded towards Joan.

Finola sensed his urgency. "Joan why don't you finish your reading in the bed-chamber?" She kept her tone level. "Your uncle and I have something to talk about."

"Is it about Father? Are we going to join him soon? Why can't I stay?" Joan's tone was full of longing

Finola noticed a flicker on Brian's face and her heart fluttered. It *was* about Niall. Brian was reluctant to disturb Joan with details. She agreed it was better not to know the hardships in front of you before you undertook a journey. Her previous trip to Spain had taught her what to expect. Although she was not looking forward to another sea voyage, she would be glad to leave. Preparations would occupy her so she would feel too tired to fantasise about Rory. She had decided not to tell him she was leaving. It was easier to escape from unkindled emotions. If she saw him again, she knew she would burrow into the circle of his arms and cry out her desire to stay.

She said without anger. "Do as I tell you Joan."

Without a backward glance, Joan ran towards the other room, her script clutched in her hand. "Don't worry uncle. I won't listen," she teased as she blew a kiss in his direction.

Poor Brian, Finola thought. He found it hard to unbend with women even close relations. A girl like Joan could be a trial to him.

He touched her on the arm. His set face alerted her to bad news. She had been so full of her own thoughts that she had failed to contemplate anything untoward happening to Niall.

"Tell me Brian. Is it about Niall? Has he settled in Salamanca? Can he not send for us yet?" She tried hard to dismiss a sense of doom; she was unable to stop talking. The foreboding she felt on the day he left had returned.

"Finola. Finola, listen to me. I haven't heard from Niall, but I know about him." Brian sat beside her and heaved a deep sigh, reached into his pocket and took out a letter. "I have to tell you that ..." He paused.

414

Guessing what he was about to say, she was reluctant to hear. She wanted to remember Niall in happier times, mending the wing of a bird, getting a gift of pressed flowers from Joan, laughing with her as she tumbled down the hill into his arms, comforting her, spoiling her. As she sat and waited, Brian took her cold hand in his. He handed her the letter. "Here, read it yourself."

The letter was from a ship's captain at Corunna, dictated to an English speaking passenger. As soon as his anchor was down, he 'wrote' explaining what happened to Niall. Her voice trembling, she read aloud:

I find it hard to understand why this misfortune should have struck my ship. The Spaniards and the Portuguese are familiar with provisioning for lengthy voyages. They ordered and loaded the supplies under the usual circumstances. I had not a chance, even if I thought it necessary, to unload them all again.

That some food began to rot towards the end of the return journey is the only explanation. Your friend, unfortunately, was one who ate vittles stored in a particular group of barrels.

He and others lay around the deck with stomach cramps, symptoms of food poisoning. He was the only one who did not recover.

I am sorry about his death. I will arrange to send his belongings home. I understand that because he left in a hurry there is not much. A lock of ebony hair and some dried flowers.

The chaplain blessed his body and we 'buried' it at sea.

I wish to tell you again of my regret that this should have happened aboard my vessel.

Arthur Englefield for Captain Cesareo Alonzo Duro.

Finola lay the letter aside. Her mind was a conundrum of emotions. She wondered whether he suffered. Whether he knew that she had always cherished him. That Joan loved him so. A yearning for him, a need for his arms and soothing words overtook her. Now that he was gone, she would be unable to endure without him. Where would she live or what would become of her and their daughter? On the periphery of these feelings was a blob of guilt. Rory must not be told. She looked to Brian for a suggestion that would shake her out of her stupor.

"We'll tell Joan. She should know immediately," he said.

"I'll tell her." Finola dragged herself from the chair.

"There's no need. I listened." Joan's voice was toneless.

Chapter Eleven

Rory received two pieces of equally startling news from Brian. The first was that one private Francis Seymour ex felon and knife thrower from the city of London had boasted in the wrong ears about the castle he had blown up with the king's own equipment. He had just concluded telling the story when one of his listeners stuck his favourite plaything in his ribs.

Brian also told him of Duncan Erskine's departure. "The Woodkerne would not have harassed him so soon was it not for me," he admitted. "But when you told me about Duncan's maltreatment of Jane and Quintin and about his behaviour the day of Jane's death, I felt he deserved priority." There was a venomous tone in Brian's voice. "I'd always thought that men like him were lily-livered. I'd had complaints also about how he treated his tenants. It was time he went back to England."

His expression grim, Brian had reminded Rory that he was familiar with the tactics employed by the dispossessed during the Munster Plantation to frighten off would be settlers. First he had slit the throat of Duncan Erskine's favourite wolfhound. Next he had poisoned his most copious milker. He cut his scarecrow's clothes to ribbons. On top of the remains of the scarecrow's cap, he had left the words, *you will be next.*

But, he told him, "It was the musket shot that darted past Duncan Erskine's ear on his way from a service in the new Presbyterian church that finally frightened him. He immediately put his lands in the hands of an agent to sell to the highest bidder."

Rory thought of Quintin who was his concern now. During the past nine months he had gotten to know his son. He would not be disappointed by the desertion of the man he considered his father. What would distress him, though, was that Duncan was selling his property. Any hope he had of owning land would have disappeared.

The only time Quintin was at peace was when he was working on the soil. Quintin knew more about the working schedule of Glenone than he did himself. Rory seldom interfered with the decisions of his *uirrithe*. As long as Glenone yielded a profit he was uninterested. But, in his son he saw a genuine love for the land that he never had. Rory's desire to retrieve his inheritance did not stem from a longing to be close to the soil, to watch crops grow, to experiment with new methods, to cherish every inch of dirt under his care. He had wanted to get back what his family lost. Since the day Matthew had died, it was a love of repossessing that had enveloped him, not a love for the repossessed.

What had given him most pleasure and preserved his sanity during his entombment in Sir Walter's house was the library. Even then he had delved into a variety of subjects, but never husbandry. He dreamed of becoming a politician, writing his own speeches, but not of changing primitive farming methods. That dream was now a delusion. But, since its germination, the one love consistent in his life was his love of literature.

A few days after hearing of Duncan's departure, Rory was in his study writing in his diary. After he had written his thoughts, he left down his pen and gazed through the window. Outside the first buttercups were beginning to show, the sky was a clear blue. The freshness of it all brought back the old longing in him. He often wondered was it idiotic for a man of his age to be forever dreaming of a future that constantly eluded him. Should he abandon his passion for Finola and marry a woman who would bear him children. He thought of the girl, about whom he had once had romantic notions soon after he had heard of Finola's marriage. She was now a divorced woman and living in Carrickfergus. He would pay her a call, he decided.

He hated it when his mind took this type of turn. Sighing, he took refuge as he usually did in a book, one he always went back to when the longing within him needed assuagement. Petrarch's love for Laura mirrored his desire for Finola.

Engrossed in his reading he barely heard Quintin call, "Rory you in there? Someone to see you." He came out to the hallway to see a young woman and a man standing there.

The nymph tossed her head and pulled off the bonnet that had framed and partially hid her face. Rory's stomach lurched. Before him stood the young Finola, taller but unmistakable in her dark hair and foreign looks. Conscious of his overlong scrutiny, Rory took her by the hand and drew her into the parlour, beckoning to her companion to come in, too. Now that he was not squinting in the sunlight anymore, he saw that the man was pleasant looking and of an unreadable age, and with a deceiving appearance of naivety.

"Finola O'Hanlon's daughter," Rory stated. He had not allowed himself to dwell on Finola for months, not since he had discovered that she was without Niall. Now, he had just been thinking of her. Any surprise that registered on his face he did his optimum to conceal. She was pretty enough to gladden his ageing heart, and transport him back to happier times. Her red satin dress displayed the slender lines of her tall figure, the carefully moulded basque covered breasts in their infancy.

For all the demureness of her stance, and the nervousness of her white hands as they plucked at her sleeve, he guessed that she still had all the lust for life her mother had described.

"We won't have to introduce ourselves?" The girl said this with such relief, Rory smiled. The anxiety lessened in her eyes leaving only the determination.

"You look like your mother." Rory's voice was soft. "What brings you to this part of the county?"

"I'm Edward Campbell," the man by her side said by way of reply. "Joan has something to say to you. I'm merely her escort not her confidant." He paused. "As I was riding in, I noticed carpenters at work. Stables is it? I'll take a walk outside to see them. Building is an interest of mine." He did not wait for a reply.

"You'll have something to wet your lips," Rory said to ease the unexpected tension. When he rang the bell for service, Joan looked on in wonder. He understood. Her manner of living would have been frugal since the English confiscated their lands.

"Nothing," she said.

"I will have nothing either." Rory waved a hand in dismissal. Surprised by his own calmness, he prepared to listen. When she told him of her father's death, his mood changed. He had respected Niall and was sorry he had died but he failed to stifle the hope that rose again at the back of his mind.

She told him of her mother's malady, that Finola was wasting away and constantly brooding. "It's as if she has lost the will to live."

Rory felt surprised by the fluency of her speech and the practical way she expressed herself.

"I know she misses my father. We all do. But she used to be so buoyant. My only consolation is that she has borne worse than this and came through."

He did not want to get into a conversation about the tragedies of the past. So as gently as he knew how, he asked, "What do you think I can do to help? I have not seen your mother since she reclaimed the contents of Mulahinsa from Glenone. Does she know that you have come to see me?"

"My mother is ignorant of my visit and I won't enlighten her." Hesitantly and colouring a little, she added, "I'd try anything to get her back like she used to be. She talks in her sleep and mentions your name." Her voice faltered and she looked away. "She says my father's name, too, sometimes."

It did not take the tremor in Joan's voice to show Rory what an ordeal this was for her. He could see it in the way she had clasped her hands so tight, the knuckles had gone white.

His confidence had strengthened since the conversation began. He had made strenuous efforts to forget Finola since their last meeting. To resign himself to a life without her. If what he now heard were true, perhaps there was a chance of happiness for them after all.

A morning sun peeped through the window slits in the dining hall and stalked shadows across the fresh rushes. Rory was trying to eat a breakfast but his excitement had taken his appetite. He had told Joan he would call to see her mother someday this week but he lacked a clear plan. All he knew was that he was going to see the woman who haunted him; this time there were no obstacles to their union. He would tell her of his love; together they would chase their phantoms away.

As he picked at his cheese, a parade of apparitions marched through his mind. There was the parchment, yellow with age, outlining *Surrender and re-grant*, his sojourn in England responsible for shaping his past, his father, Matthew, Dolman with his strut and raucous laugh, Cormac lying dead, Shane hanging from a tree, Mulahinsa in flames. How England and people English had blighted his life!

The chafing that bothered him since his drunken spree returned. Snippets of the conversation with someone from the past came back to him. He had a feeling similar to the one he experienced before Joan came ... that England or people English had not done their worst.

The Lord Deputy was rechecking the background of natives who still retained land. He possessed Eoin Maguire's estates. Charles Fenton would examine such an aberration rigorously. An unexpected feeling of exhaustion dogged him. He was forty-eight years of age and now had an opportunity to claim the woman he had always wanted and yet he was not completely happy. It was the land. He did not have security of tenure. But was that the true reason? Even if the English were to confirm his stewardship, he was not sure he would be satisfied.

Better banish these notions from his mind and don his armour. No point in claiming his princess with a middle-aged gait and the uneasiness that had tracked him all his life.

PART VI

1617-1620

If a man will begin with certainties, he shall end in doubts, but if he will be content to begin with doubts, he shall end in certainties.

- Francis Bacon, Ist Baron Verulam, 1561-1626.

Chapter One

On the night she heard of Niall's death, dreams of Rory had returned to Finola and remained with her. Her remorse over this gave her a fear of sleep. To make up for her night-time fantasies, she forced herself to grieve for Niall during her waking hours. He was such a kind man. He had nurtured both her and Joan until she had forgotten her bitterness over the two Andrews' deaths. How could she become accustomed to his being gone? She thought she had infinite time to learn to love him. Now it was too late. Indebted to him as she felt, it was imperative that she mourn him.

Loneliness was a merciless foe, one she had come to know well since Niall's death. The hours of each day seemed never-ending. Since she had married Campbell hers had been a life of continuous activity and unremitting responsibilities. She ensured candles were dipped, bread baked, meat salted for winter and linen woven; she also took care of the tenants' ills and, of course, her darling Andrew Óg.

Her months spent in Spain on a diplomatic mission had been partially responsible for Philip III's sending an expedition to Ireland. She'd married Niall and her life still retained its busyness. Then she had Joan to love. Even after the dispossession, she had been occupied helping with the lumber business.

She wandered about the chamber until, at last, she settled down at a table. Yesterday, when Joan had gone with Edward to visit his kin, she had closed her eyes and imagined she was back in the lulling stillness of Mulahinsa. She forgot that her restlessness, her tragic affair with Murrough, her marriage to Andrew, all had their origin in that castle and recalled instead the evenings of card playing, the harper accompanying the *reacaire* in his praise poems, the booley. Good times gone, it seemed to her, for ever.

Finola stiffened as she heard footsteps on the limestone flagstones outside the open front-door. Her breathing quickened. These past months had honed her nerves to breaking-point. Someone was coming up the path. Perhaps it was just a workman expecting to find Edward here. At least she would have someone to divert her, even for a short time, from the past and memories, always memories.

She took a cursory look out. The figure approaching the house was no workman but a familiar figure whom she couldn't but recognise. Her jaw muscles tensed. She wished she had complied with Joan's request to wear something different than her old beige frieze today.

Joan had been acting strangely before she left this morning, as if she were anxious about something. Her kiss had been as warm as usual, but she had evaded Finola's eyes. Now she began to understand why.

Rory was looking towards the house as if he were summoning the courage to take the final step.

When he entered, she uttered his name, her voice trembling.

He put his hand on his heart and bowed, playing the mock gallant. "At your service as always."

His revival of their childhood game, he the great chieftain and she his lady, made her smile. He took her hand and squeezed it. "How wonderful it is to see you again," he said.

Rory did not hide that Joan had been to Glenone to see him. Instead he recounted the details of their meeting. He praised Joan for her initiative and her clarity. In return Finola questioned him about Glenone and enquired about Art. It was obvious from the strained atmosphere that neither was saying what they wanted to say.

Rory was the first to end the subterfuge. "What is the matter Finola?" He looked at her with seriousness and respect. "Is this why Joan made the journey to Glenone? So that we might mouth polite noises. We owe her more than that."

This was a different Rory to the one whom England had fashioned. There was no sign of the fawning she feared had become a part of him.

"I refuse to play the diplomatic game. That was not my intent in coming. I am not sure why I am here, but I know I feel differently to what I expected." He hesitated, took a sharp breath and plunged on. "This may be insignificant, but usually when I am with you, I allow myself to be swamped by desire. Today I think it's more important that you tell me what is troubling you. Passion will have to be denied – for now." He paused. "It is more than Niall dying. Are you ill?"

"I feel my life has come to naught." She felt tears hovering on her eyelashes.

Rory touched her face with the palm of his hand.

The words tumbled from her. She retraced her steps back to Murrough, and related honestly and for the first time the saga of her life that had culminated in Niall's death. "I married first to escape Mulahinsa. Then, I married because I wanted another child. She ended by saying, "I want to do something meaningful. I want to start a hospital."

When she had finished, she felt she had emptied her mind of all its troubles, had spent herself. It was now Rory's turn to talk and she felt ready to listen

He told her of his imprisonment, his fears for her when she was in Spain, his pain when she had talked about Niall at Mulahinsa, the emptiness that had never left him. Hesitating, as if about to tell her something of greater consequence, he seemed to change his mind and talked instead about Jane's death in childbirth, about her husband leaving the country, about Sir Walter's fondness for alcohol. Then he paused again. The words stumbled out first, then renewing his courage, he said clearly, "When I was nineteen, I fathered a son ..."

He described the nature of his liaison with Jane and the circumstances of Quintin's birth. Later the focus shifted naturally to his land and the danger of its being lost to his family.

"Don't let the English annex it. They've taken enough. You've sacrificed too much to let it go now," Finola counselled.

Rory nodded slowly. "My life has revolved around retrieving the land in memory of my father and brother. The natives have either lost their original holdings or transferred to poorer land, but I am still in possession. My existence is centred on remaining in possession. The planters have replaced Eoin as the foe."

"You need something else for your fulfilment."

"Yes, you are right. But I do not know how to say it. It is a feeling I have had for a long time ... That I, too, have wasted my life. That I should not be a landowner. That I have no right to the land."

This, also, was a Rory she had never seen. Taking her time, she measured her words. "What do you desire?" she asked. She knew the impracticality of the question. For the first time Rory was being open with her. To say the wrong word now would put him back into his shell. She felt excited. It was a day for beginnings.

When he did not reply, she sought to enlighten him as to her own view. "You like reading. You must have read an enormous amount since you first went to England," she said. "Like me, you hate the way English writers depict us. You would like to make changes in Ireland. Did you ever yearn to write? Perhaps, give a Gaelic view of Ireland."

When he answered, he sounded uncertain, as if he were afraid of being ridiculed. "You have uncovered an ambition dormant in me since my time in Sir Walter's library in England. Writing was what I often thought about and discarded in the years leading up to the war." He faltered. "On the march to Kinsale I started a diary. It is now a thick volume."

He jumped to his feet. "I cannot believe you said that. No one else ever has. It is something I have always wanted to do." His eyes glistened. "This is one of the most exciting things that has happened to me." He sat down heavily again. "Sorry, I'm behaving like a child," he said. Then from under his thick eyebrows he looked at her. "It is the first time somebody guessed my deepest longing and it feels wonderful." Up he jumped again. "To hell with age."

Lifting her lithe frame from the stool, he twirled her around. She felt a kinship with him. He wanted to write. Anticipation stirred in her. It was as if the ambition were hers.

Neither of them was able to eat the bread and cheese she had prepared prior to his leaving. They were both too excited. When they said farewell, they had been together for four hours. Though they had remained chaste physically, emotionally they were closer than at any other time in their lives.

Chapter Two

The delight Rory felt after his visit with Finola had no limits. The world appeared different to his eyes. He had visited three more times since that first meeting and knew that she was the essence of his existence.

But he realised that for something to have an essence it must first have substance. His life had none. Finola was everything he wanted in a woman, and it was her understanding that gave him the courage to seek to achieve all of his ambitions. He became gripped by a need to abandon the past, to throw away the fawning smiles and the knee bending, to forge his own way.

Eight years he had spent in England after a childhood lived in the atmosphere of a civil war, in killing and counter killing. In Kent, he had experienced an ordered world and had learned from it. In London he had begun to understand the nature of power and added these lessons to those already gleaned from his own race. These influences had formed his character and ordained his life. Now for the first time he had the confidence to face his dilemma. He wanted to throw off the shackles of an obligation placed on his shoulders at the age of ten while still retaining his honour.

Rory was to meet Lord Deputy Charles Fenton, in his headquarters in Newry. He knew that, in Charles's opinion, he was the worst kind of menace. His upbringing in England had given him the veneer of gentility yet he was as loathsome as his fellow countrymen.

Charles Fenton had nothing but contempt, inherited from his father, for the Irish. But this attitude did not extend to their land, obviously. Rory smiled a weak smile. He was one of the people who gained much property out of the 1609 confiscations.

The Lord Deputy found the Gaelic religious practices uncomfortably close to paganism and regarded their superstitious natures as an insult to civilised man. He considered the tenants, on his estates, unlearned and unclean; they belonged to a wild and worthless breed. He avoided fraternising with them except where necessary. Rory's summons meant such a necessity had arisen.

As he rode to his interrogation, he swore into the unexpected wind that whipped in icy gusts under his mantle. He mourned the fire he had left at Finola's house and the unfinished chess game he had abandoned to Joan.

When he got to Charles's headquarters, an English groom took his steed from him. His footsteps made no sound as he walked from the stables on the thick muck quilting the ground. The archway at the residential entrance gave shelter from the wind and he paused here a moment to calm himself. It would be foolish to show his anger whatever the provocation.

He climbed the stairs to the upper floor and opened a green door. It revealed a long hallway, which led to another more imposing entrance.

His legs would be unable to carry him to the end of the passageway, he thought. It was only now that magnitude of the ordeal looming ahead struck him. Happy with Finola, he had not dwelt on the summons.

When he opened the end door, an official, a youthful man, glanced up and signalled him through, stiffly muttering, "They are expecting you".

The next chamber was spacious and ornate. At its end was a wide desk, behind which sat the large frame of Charles Fenton. An over filled spittoon was perched on the edge of the desk. The tobacco blobs beside it told Rory that he did not always hit his mark. Behind him, at a smaller bureau, sat a clerk.

Charles continued to read a dispatch in front of him so that Rory was looking at the hairless patch, speckled like a bird's egg, on the top of his head. As he got nearer, Rory recoiled from the garlic fumes wafting towards him from the corpulent figure.

His attention still on the report, Charles made a movement with his arm. The clerk stirred into action and leafed through listings until he found an imposing looking script. Then he began to read in a droning voice. "*It is hereby decreed that one Rory Maguire, presently of Glenone, will take the Oath of Supremacy thus swearing that he accepts King James as head of the church or forfeit his lands.*"

Rory swallowed hard. So this was their plan.

"When did you change the law?" he asked. "Until now a native did not have to take the oath.

For the first time Charles Fenton looked up. But he stared ahead, past Rory.

"No native has kept his original land," he said.

Rory realised he needed more time to work out a plan. So to placate Charles, he said, "I will take the oath, but not tonight."

The clerk blinked his pale eyes and said to the back of Charles's head. "He will take the oath, but not now."

"I heard." Charles scratched the folds of flesh behind his ear. "I should have known these savages would have no principles."

Rory looked at these two invaders of his country. Suddenly he felt tired of play acting. He thought of a Duncan Erskine of nigh on thirty years ago and how he had degraded him in the school room. The abuse of the weak by the strong was perennial. He was not a young boy now. He was a middle-aged man with a son.

Forcing the Lord Deputy to meet his eye, Rory watched him coldly. Then slowly he reached inside his jerkin and took the hand gun from his tunic pocket.

If it were a less serious situation, he would have laughed at the effect of the gun's production on the two. The body of the Lord Deputy floundered like a sinking ship on the desk. The clerk's eyes disappeared into his head. A fly buzzed somewhere in the room magnifying the silence.

Rory fiddled with the trigger.

Charles's breath came in little gasps. "Do not do anything foolhardy," he wheedled. "It is a mistake. We will forget the oath. You may maintain your land."

The room faded. There was nothing but a voice in Rory's head that said, "Kill them." He primed the trigger; his expression hardened.

The clerk turned white and stood like some grotesque, alabaster statue. A nervous ripple ran through the layers of fat on the Lord Deputy's belly; a belch erupted from his cooing mouth.

The humanity of the sound awakened Rory's compassion. He ungritted his teeth and relaxed his finger on the trigger. His tone deliberate, he said, "The balls in here could be in there." He pointed to Charles's chest. "Remember that the next time you treat somebody like offal." He had reached the door when he heard it.

"Barbarians. We will never tame them." Charles had turned his head to mouth to his clerk.

Noises thundered in Rory's head. In seconds, he was across

the floor. Unwavering, he held the gun in front of Charles's face again.

The pudgy countenance collapsed in renewed shock. "Please I did not say it. It was him." He pointed a finger towards the hapless clerk. "Kill *him*."

Rory felt revulsion at the deceit and treachery of the man who was begging for his life. Charles Fenton was not worth killing. He walked away from the so called conqueror who was willing to let his servant die in his stead.

As he strode down the passage way, he felt satisfied that although he would suffer for this, it was worth it. Nobody challenged him as, his head held high, he walked through the outer door.

However, when he breathed in the fresh air, the triumph disappeared. Charles Fenton would be loath to forgive a humiliation such as he had endured. For a few minutes of glory, he had thrown away the advantages built up over a lifetime of fawning. Charles Fenton would dispossess him now whether he took the oath or not. They would bestow Glenone on Fenton kin, newly arrived from England. He had let them achieve his downfall.

The Dublin government postponed a confiscation of Rory's property. They lacked the spur of personal hatred that ate at the heart of the Lord Deputy. They did not have truths about their own cowardice with which to live. It was not their brother who wanted the Maguire demesne.

Many of its members had worked with Sir Walter Carew in the past. They knew he was still a powerful figure, though he was an old man. He had an interest in this Rory Maguire. They advised Charles Fenton to compromise with Rory for the surrender of part of Glenone.

Charles, as wild as any Irishman, tore up the letter and rushed to Dublin to challenge their advice. For five weeks he beseeched the Council to let him confiscate. Wearied, the council relented and asked the sheriff to serve Rory with an eviction order. The sheriff shirked the task.

"I will wait until his protector dies," the Lord Deputy said. "Like Sir Samuel Fenton, my esteemed father, I am a patient man. I can adjourn the confiscation. That is all it will be - an adjournment."

Chapter Three

Finola found that getting to know Rory in all his facets was an unearthing. His intelligence and his knowledge of literature impressed her; his wit kept her amused; his patience with Joan touched her. He dropped his impenetrable pose and told her in detail of his misfortune with Charles Fenton. She knew it troubled him. The land question had always concerned Rory. Until he settled it for good or ill, she knew he would be discontent.

She, too, seeking to fulfil her ambition to set up a hospital had begun to petition aid. Her experience of dealing with planters when they had first moved to Ulster and were looking for lumber, helped when she asked for their assistance. And she had Rory's total support. She watched now as he finished wading through a list of Scottish and English names of would be subscribers.

Sensing her scrutiny he turned his head, left the listing on the table and stood up. "I have placed the names of those with the most land at the top, intending that you ask them for money first." Smiling he added, "As Maeve would have said, a job begun is half done."

He ran his hand down the length of her hair. "It's noon. Time I left for Glenone. I will return on Thursday." Bending, he whispered in her ear, "I will always be back."

When the door closed behind him, she realised that he had left two hours earlier than he had intended. Her impulsive Rory from childhood had not completely disappeared.

With an impatient gait, Rory paced the flagged floor of the parlour at Glenone. His shoulders drooped; he wondered why he had rushed off from Finola without any explanation. She was the only authentic love he ever had. His years of romantic dallying, albeit with her image, were tinsel compared to her. He longed for the day when she would give herself to him permanently and completely.

Thoughts of his past loves put him in mind of Jane and he got a sudden urge to study her letter. He went over to the bureau, took it from the drawer and sat down to read.

There were references to Sir Walter and his diary. This time he did not just glance over the contents, but devoured each word. He agreed with Jane that Sir Walter had mellowed over the years, had acted less self righteously.

Other feelings came back to him. The suspicion that he had voiced for the first time to Finola, that he had no entitlement to the land of Glenone. He was puzzled too at the regard Sir Walter had for his father, Phelim, and his support for him in the war against Eoin. Sir Walter's affection for Rory that rivalled what he felt for his son George was also a mystery. The portrait in Sir Walter's art gallery in London which had looked so like Rory's father came back to him now. Then, as if somebody were tearing a curtain from his mind, he saw and heard Tadhg in the tavern. "It was an English soldier sired your father."

He examined the facts as he would the dues of an *uirrí*, calculating ages and locations. They led him to the one conclusion. Slowly he got up from the chair, the letter clenched in his fist, his eyes blazing. When Catherine Reilley *named* Con Maguire as the father of her son, Phelim, the lives of her descendants were based on deceit.

Rory's father Phelim had not been the son of a wheelwright as asserted by Eoin. But neither was he Con Maguire's son nor Eoin's brother.

Rarely had Finola felt so tense. She had spread a length of material upon a trestle table and started to cut out a frock for Joan who was away, staying at Edward's manor. It was to be a surprise for her return on the morrow. But she could not keep her mind on the task at hand, could not keep her eyes away from the door. It was Thursday and two hours past noon, yet Rory had not returned.

She laid her scissors aside when at last the door opened and Rory entered. The atmosphere of the room changed. It was as if he were a different person to the one who had left three days previously.

"Rory."

He was the picture of uncertainty. His lips parted but he did not speak.

"Rory," she said again in a louder tone. Something grave had happened since their last meeting. His eyes had dimmed. The broad shoulders she loved had slumped. He was behaving more like a gauche boy than a man in his forties.

There was a tight feeling in her throat. She swallowed noisily. "What is it my love?"

He came towards her; she put out her hand to touch him.

He kissed her palm. His voice shook. "Sir Walter Carew is my grandfather. I am part English."

Hesitating she chose her words, "You are still the Rory I've loved all my life." She traced a line down the side of his jaw. Her calm was rewarded as she felt his confidence return.

He took her to him and kissed her deeply. She basked in his tenderness and his passion as he whispered how much he loved her, wanted her.

Desires and yearnings she had submerged for years swam to the surface. He transferred his mouth to her eyes, then to the hollow of her neck. He kissed her shoulders and her breasts. His hands slid over her skin, and touched each part of her. A burning sensation flooded her. Her body inclined towards him.

"Mo leath eile," he whispered in an awed tone.

In the comfort of the pallet, her hands massaged his manhood until he moaned in ecstasy. She relished his delight and revelled in her own pleasure. As he stroked her most intimate parts, she trembled. When she felt him inside her, she thought, this is how it was meant to be. There would be no more partings, no more secrets.

Next morning, at breakfast, 'mid their laughter and teasing, Rory's face filled with a sudden anxiety. "I am meeting Sir Walter tomorrow."

Chapter Four

Nowadays, Sir Walter felt as if cobwebs hung over his eyes; the veil forced him to walk slowly to avoid bumping into furniture. He wanted to steer clear of accidents, especially this morning. It was cold so the pains in his joints had worsened. His delicate state of health reminded him of his mortality. He was an aged man; the bodies of many of his peers were lying in the clay. Anne had left him. George and Jane were dead. Rory had fought against England in the last battle of the war. There was nobody who cared for him.

Quintin visited him out of duty but they had little in common. Jane's son was interested only in land not politics or the army. If he were honest with himself, he would admit that he regarded Quintin as backward. Of course, that was because of Erskine blood. What could be expected from descendants of a tailor from Shropshire. He was returning to Chalk Hall permanently at the end of the week, yet he felt only relief at the prospect of leaving *this* grandson behind him.

He searched through the papers on his night table. When he found the manuscript he was looking for, he left it on top of the other correspondence in a neat bundle; he must remember to bring it to Glenone on Saturday. Although he was looking forward to seeing Rory Maguire, he suspected that Rory's affection for him was expedient, that he endured listening to his wisdom, but kept his own counsel. Sir Walter felt excluded by him.

Rory was like Phelim, whom he had so loved. Phelim had been very like his mother, Catherine Reilley, Rory's grandmother. She had been a harlot, yet sixty-two years later, he could still hear her voice, feel her touch, and regret that he had deserted her.

As he got older, he had found himself looking for resemblances to Catherine Reilley when he met Rory. In the tilt of Rory's head or the way his eyes crinkled at the corners, he saw a likeness to his beloved. How different his life would have been if he had done as his heart dictated and married her.

Phelim was a year old when he had stopped fornicating with Catherine. Though he had spent four years persuading her to part with the child, he had resisted the lure of her beautiful body. Apart from that one liaison he had lived an upright life, was worthy of a place in the *elect*.

But since Anne's desertion he had begun to doubt his faith. He now believed that he had fought temptation, greed and pride all for nothing. There was no hell in the hereafter. Hell was this world.

Sir Walter had met Phelim Maguire again when Phelim had grown to be a young man. From the beginning they had liked each other, the successor to the Maguire chieftainship and the English general. Not caring if people remarked on the strange friendship, he was content. In Phelim he saw Catherine Reilley's smile, heard her laughter. He felt as if God had forgiven him his wrongdoing. When his own clansmen killed Phelim in the civil war, Sir Walter wished they had killed him instead.

Then came the missive from Queen Elizabeth and Rory had entered his life. From the moment they journeyed on the ship to England, he had loved him. When he returned to Chalk Hall after his tours of duty, it was Rory he looked forward to seeing most. It was with Rory he had discussed Ireland and the Irish. He had regarded him as more of a son than George.

George punished him for this love with his suicide. Anne punished him for his love of Catherine Reilley with her desertion. Jane punished him for forcing her to marry Duncan Erskine by dying. He had punished himself by living an arid and rigid life. Not anymore. He had Eimear O'Cathán. Eimear was beautiful. It was like reliving the past.

A little libation was what he needed before she came. Could not have the maggots attacking when he entertained an attractive woman. He took a flagon from the table and put it to his lips. As the liquid trickled down, his morose thoughts faded. When he had drunk that to the dregs a sly smile touched his lips. He had more; had even hired a carpenter to make a box in which to store it. Yes, there was always a plentiful amount of alcohol available; many wished to supply Sir Walter Carew either for money or payment in kind.

That was what Eimear O'Cathán aimed to get from him, payment in kind. She wanted security of land tenure for her virile husband MacRiocard. She would earn it, by God. He would have a last hurrah before he went down in the dirt.

434

He scarcely heard the soft knock on the door. When he did, he smiled to himself. That would be Eimear. She had never been to his room before and she would be apprehensive. He had instructed her to tell his aide that she was delivering a dispatch from her husband.

When he opened the door, the displeasure on her face at his appearance angered him. He fingered the spot on his face, where her gaze had landed. For the past few days, he had experienced a burning sensation on the side of his jaw. Yesterday, cursed blisters had appeared. Another one had burst today. He usually took great care with his appearance just for her, wearing ruff shirts and velvet jackets. It was not his fault that tonight his robe did not quite close over his paunch, or that his sleeve had a stain of sherry on it.

She thought he was an ugly old fool. Merely because she was the widow of the powerful Gaelic chieftain Eoin Maguire and was beautiful, she felt she had the right to be contemptuous of him, Sir Walter Carew, peer of the realm. He raised the flagon to his mouth.

Her bosom brushed against him as she came into the room and he wished he could see her voluptuous figure more clearly.

She giggled, "I can't stay long." She pointed to his glass. "I'll have one of those."

He gave her a port and refilled his own glass.

She said, "MacRiocard didn't get the deeds yet."

He lifted his eyebrows; he knew what she was talking about but he did not want to get into a discussion about that just yet. The government had rewarded her husband with five hundred acres of land for services to the crown. However, the authorities had not ratified MacRiocard's deed of ownership. An official could throw him out on a whim. Eimear knew that Sir Walter Carew had the power to get the deeds for him.

MacRiocard was a young virile man, Sir Walter thought. That was why Eimear married him when Eoin Maguire was scarcely cold in the grave. "If you care so much about your husband, I am at a loss to know what you are doing here." He moved restlessly.

She made a valiant effort to be coquettish. "Now, now Sir Walter," tisn't attacking a sweet little girl like me, you are. Is it?"

The cocky face of MacRiocard with his strapping body, clear vision, and flawless skin, rose in front of him. Flushed and breathing thickly, he felt the need to be in command. He patted the place beside him. "Sit here," he said

"'Tis to stand I will Sir Walter," she replied.

"Sit." He was not in the humour for playing games.

Hesitating, she looked at him, weighing what his reaction would be if she refused. She sat at the bottom of the bed, her face pale, her limbs trembling like a fawn sensing danger.

He slid down the space towards her but she inclined away from him. Pretending not to notice her withdrawal, he reached out and touched the garish ornament adorning her neck.

"You like the necklace I gave you?" He sought to keep the dislike he felt for such ostentation from of his voice. It was difficult to change the belief of a lifetime. The trinket made Eimear appear even more debauched but it had been cheap and it pleased her.

"Oh yes. It's lovely."

"I can buy you more jewellery like that."

He could get a scent of lemon from her skin. Her slim ankles peeped out from under her dress. The fire, he had set himself, was beginning to heat the room. Perfect. It would be warm enough for her to take off her gown. It was so long since he had seen Catherine Reilley without her clothes.

He had respected Anne too much to suggest that she undress. But he had disciplined himself to one night of sex a week and as a result she had taken a lover. Probably stripped for him every night.

His breathing was heavy. The woman beside him became more of a blur. She was a combination of Catherine Reilley's sensuousness and Anne's guile. Catherine Reilley with her beauty had led him into temptation. Anne had betrayed him. His heart thumped, a knot of fury untied in his brain.

Seconds later he was gripped by agony. It felt as if his head were splintering. He removed his hands from the vicinity of Eimear's neck and clasped them to his skull. "Dirty lecherous old man," were the last words he heard before he sank into unconsciousness.

He did not see her refill her goblet and have another drink before she left, nor her look of distaste for his spartan quarters, and his prone figure splayed on the bed. Nor did he hear her curse through gritted teeth, "To the divil with the English. No principles that's their trouble. That 'tis."

Chapter Five

Day after day spring wooed the earth persuading it to deck itself in myriad shades of green. The freshness of a beginning was in the air. Back from an odyssey with his *uirrithe,* Rory was waiting for Sir Walter and Quintin to visit. Sir Walter planned to return to England at the end of the week - never to return, Rory suspected. The thought gave him a feeling of both sadness and bitterness, and other feelings, too, that he still had to analyse.

Standing in the parlour, he waited for his family to appear. An hour later, he stood in front of the castle his eyes on the road. Soon afterwards, it began to mist. Droplets wormed their way beneath his jerkin and inside his boots as he walked back to the castle. He sat reading, still waiting. An hour later he ended his vigil. Sir Walter and Quintin were not coming.

His head throbbed, not only from lack of sleep, but from the recollections that had beset him through the previous night. He had English blood in him. His father Phelim was Sir Walter's son. The uncertainties he felt all his life made a confused sense. Why had Sir Walter failed to appear? He was not aware of Rory's new found knowledge.

Later a servant brought him a letter from Quintin Erskine. The communication was brief. Quintin had said that Sir Walter had collapsed in his chamber and was gravely ill.

Rory shook his head in weary exasperation. He had spent the night agonising about how to challenge Sir Walter with the truth of their relationship. If he were well, he would have done it some way. Now ...

Sir Walter had had a seizure, like the previous one, only this time there was the additional weakness of old age. The army physician, a clean-cut man looked at the blue tinge of Sir Walter's skin and nodded sagely, "There is not much I can do. I would bleed him, but it would be to no avail."

"What will happen?" Quintin stammered. Among the sombre military faces of the others present, his was the only one reflecting genuine grief.

The physician looked directly at Quintin, "He will get progressively worse and die." He put his arm around the younger man's shoulders belying the harshness of his words.

"He has had a long life. Longer than most," he said.

When Rory entered the room, the only sound was of the uneven breathing of the figure on the bed. His eyes swept over Sir Walter's face, shrivelled looking in the cold light. He realised that there was more wrong with his grandfather than overindulgence in alcohol. His heart sank as he recognised the tell-tale signs of death.

The air in the room was warm. The whitewashed walls that ended in a lofty ceiling were without embellishment; the boards underfoot were bare. Grey ashes filled the recently installed wall fireplace. A heap of manuscripts lay on an ebony night stand beside the narrow bed. Decanters filled with port and whisky were perched haphazardly atop a makeshift box. The goblets beside them glimmered in the morning light. A portrait of Queen Elizabeth hung above the fireplace.

Sir Walter had arranged his scant personal articles tidily. The soap, facecloth and towel on the washstand and the writing materials on the desk were arranged so orderly, they looked as if they expected Sir Walter to rise from his bed to scrutinise them.

"I am glad you have come," Quintin said, emerging from the corner shadows and rubbing his face with his hands. His shoulders were hunched in an aspect of resignation. "Grandfather has been asking for somebody called Phelim." He looked perplexed. "I think he is rambling."

Rory sat on the stool next to the bed and, when he leaned over, he smelled stale tobacco and port. As he looked into Sir Walter's eyes, Rory sensed them come alive under his gaze.

Sir Walter tried to speak. His lips writhed. Saliva dripped on the sour smelling covers as he grimaced. Bubbles of sweat stood beside the swellings on his skin. His lips appeared blue against the redness of his nose.

Rory felt a hard lump at the base of his throat, and turned away from the spasmodic movements. He forced himself to turn back.

There was a gleam of triumph in Sir Walter's eye, as he mumbled, "It is you Ph ... Ph ..." Exhausted by his attempt to frame the words, he ceased to talk but kept his eyes fastened on Rory.

When Rory placed his hands over Sir Walter's, to still his

restless pulling of the tassels on the bed cover, he felt an answering response to his touch. Time after fruitless time, Sir Walter tried to pronounce the name Phelim.

Quintin coughed tearfully and left the room.

All was still. Only the rustle of the cassock of the Presbyterian minister, as he entered and read Scripture, broke the silence.

At three o'clock, Rory felt Sir Walter's fingers go limp. The droning voice of the minister stopped.

Rory leaned over and closed the lids on the staring eyes. As he did so he noticed two sealed parchments atop some manuscripts on the night table beside the bed. The words, *To remain unopened until after my death* caught his attention. What looked like a large R piqued his curiosity. He took the missives and pulled in his breath. His name was on each of them.

As he walked down the spiral stairs, away from Sir Walter's death place, he felt many emotions. By the time he reached the stables the air had dried the tears on his cheeks. Curiosity filled him, but he did not break the seals on the parchments.

The military buried Sir Walter Carew with full honours in the chalky soil of Kent. He is the first Carew of his generation to lie there. His daughter Jane had been laid to rest before him, second generation first. George lies in Ireland. Anne was not present at the internment. Quintin Erskine was the principal mourner.

In the candlelight Rory's face looked pale and sad. By writing of the past week's events in his diary, he had made them more real. He had not opened the missives from Sir Walter yet; he had wanted to follow the ritual of death in all its full ceremony.

Finola knocked on the door.

"Yes. I have finished. Come in."

He felt relief at the prospect of her company. Since his return from Sir Walter's funeral in England, he knew that she had been treading cautiously around him so he smiled to allay her anxiety. She was the most important person in the world to him; he wanted her to be with him when he read what Sir Walter had written.

In one hand she held a goblet of red wine and one of *uisce beatha* in the other.

"I thought this would be welcome." She left the *uisce beatha* on the table and sat on the ground by his feet, her head resting against his legs.

"I'll read them now." It was not necessary for him to expand on what he meant.

"It is time."

He undid the seal, unrolled a parchment and read aloud through a blur of tears trying to absorb its clear and concise substance.

Rory, - I commend me unto you; Charles Fenton was not satisfied to forget your 'attack on a servant of the crown,' but would compel you to prostrate yourself for mercy.

His Majesty King James would rather collect monies than seek retribution for Charles Fenton's humiliation.

At my death, in recompense for your defiance, the estate of Chalk Hall will pass to the crown.

Presume not on your pardon. Your destruction will follow if you repeat such undisciplined behaviour. His Majesty will not grant clemency a second time.

From Newry this 17th of May 1620.

Yours, Sir Walter Carew.

"I have got a royal pardon," Rory said. "I should open the other one while I am still able to read."

Finola smiled her encouragement.

He perused the brief lines and looked up. "This is a writ of ownership to the demesne of Glenone," he said in disbelief.

Finola gasped.

As if he had drunk his *uisce beatha* already, a glow spread through him. He thought of Sir Walter with respect, forgiveness, grief but most of all gratitude. Thank you for a second chance, he thought.

Finola looked at him with a mixture of uncertainty and relief. He stood up. He felt at the start of a new adventure, just like he had at nineteen on the eve of his return to Ireland. For the first time in years he did not feel the responsibility for the land with which he was reared.

He took the wine from Finola, left it on the table and lifted her to her feet.

"I will not accept it," he said. He held her face in his hands. "Do you see Finola? I can have it all. Planters will be unable to take over Glenone. Ulster Irish will work on the land as they have done for centuries." He paused. "With a Maguire at the helm."

"You?" Her voice rose.

"No."

"Tell me, Rory, who then?"

"Quintin Erskine Maguire."

"It's a reversal of *Surrender and re-grant,*" Finola said.

"In a way, it is." He added, "The mix of English and Irish blood will help to heal the breach between settler and native."

"Don't get sombre on me, Rory Maguire. This is momentous."

"Wait. Does the prospect of marrying a writer daunt you?"

Her tone was tantalising, "No, but I'd like to see some of his work first."

With a shy sideways glance he produced a manuscript and gave it to her.

She read:

In 1601 Ulstermen marched from their native province to Kinsale in the south. In one last battle they tried to stem an English conquest of Ireland but failed ...

The English made The Ulster Plantation at a time of peace, when we were defenceless. They ...

It will take a long time to rid ourselves of bitterness. However, with generous minds we will succeed. Ulster will prevail.

GLOSSARY

Abú - victory

Bá na Stoirme - bay of storms

Bawn - stone walled enclosure where cattle and horses were kept at night to protect them from raids of neighbouring lords or from wolves

Bir - spit

Crommeal - long drooping moustache

Cac bó - cow-dung

Cuid oidhche - a night's food and lodgings supplied by *uirrithe* (sub-chiefs) for their chiefs

Dearógs - minnows

Duanaire - poem books in which noble families collected poems that had been written in their honour

File - poet

Garsún - young boy

Girseach - young girl

Gallóglach - (pl Gallóglaigh)-Gallowglass - Scottish mercenary

Mná caointe - keening women

Oileán na Stoirme - Isle of Storms

Oireach - rash caused by dampness

Reacaire - orator

Scaltán - fledgeling

Sióga - fairies

Snas - polish

Tánaiste - next in line to be chief

Uirrí (pl. *uirrithe*) - sub-chiefs

Uisce beatha - whiskey

Lightning Source UK Ltd.
Milton Keynes UK
UKOW03f2143300514

232615UK00001B/1/P